Captain Hale's Covenant

CAPTAIN HALE'S COVENANT

The Saga of an American Merchant Prince

THOMAS E. CROCKER

McBooks
Press

Guilford, Connecticut

McBooks Press

An imprint of Globe Pequot, the trade division of
The Rowman & Littlefield Publishing Group, Inc.
4501 Forbes Blvd., Ste. 200
Lanham, MD 20706
www.rowman.com

Distributed by NATIONAL BOOK NETWORK

British Library Cataloguing in Publication Information available

Library of Congress Cataloging-in-Publication Data
Names: Crocker, Thomas E., author.
Title: Captain Hale's covenant : the saga of an American merchant prince /
    by Thomas E. Crocker.
Description: Guilford, Connecticut : McBooks, [2022]
Identifiers: LCCN 2021049017 (print) | LCCN 2021049018 (ebook) | ISBN
    9781493066216 (cloth ; alk. paper) | ISBN 9781493066612 (epub)
Subjects: LCSH: United States--History--1783-1865--Fiction. | LCGFT:
    Historical fiction. | Sea fiction. | Novels.
Classification: LCC PS3603.R63527 C37 2022 (print) | LCC PS3603.R63527
    (ebook) | DDC 813/.6--dc23/eng/20220107
LC record available at https://lccn.loc.gov/2021049017
LC ebook record available at https://lccn.loc.gov/2021049018

**In memory of LVC (1868–1970) and
AGC (1871–1971) of Portland, Maine**

With profound respect and gratitude for having known you

"Now the finish comes, and we know only in all that we have seen and done, Bewildering mystery."

SOPHOCLES, *OEDIPUS AT COLONUS*

Contents

1

The King's Broad Arrow

1783

CAPTAIN ADAM HALE OF BARNSTABLE BURIED HIS HANDS INTO THE pockets of his woolen greatcoat as he bent against the wind. He walked a purposeful line to the top of the hill. The wind off the harbor scudded the last of October's leaves along the rain-sodden Old King's Highway which ran like a spine up the narrow Cape. Captain Hale knew that in Old England this night was known as All Hallows' Eve: a time for bonfires and superstition. In the cradle of democracy it was autumn's first night of dirty weather. It was a night when, as Captain Hale also well knew, no sensible man ventured out.

But the Captain was in a celebratory mood.

Despite the foulness of the night, the lights gleamed in Roger Bodfish's tavern that stood hard by the highway west of Barnstable. As Captain Hale grew near, the tavern's signboard creaked against its hinges in the nor'east gale. Its fine portrait of Cincinnatus at the plow strained skyward and waved toward the harbor and out to sea before a gust slammed the board back against the tavern's wall with a crack.

Adam Hale reminded himself that the "Cincinnatus," as the public house was now known, had not five years previously been the "Royal George." The name had been a point of indifferent neglect in the view of most patriots who habituated the tavern, until a visiting parson from Boston with the benefit of a classical education had pointed out that the

"Royal George" would no longer serve. The "Cincinnatus's" clientele was solidly patriotic, a reflection of the sentiment on this part of the Cape. Long gone were the few Loyalists who had lived in Barnstable.

Captain Hale eased open the door—just enough to allow entry—and slipped in. He stood in the vestibule of the tavern for an instant, taking the weather gauge of the room. A few eyes glanced up from the hubbub of the drinking tables and just as quickly moved on.

Calculation was second nature for the Captain, a professional habit developed through his early years in the coastal trade that secured his reputation as a young Captain worthy of the Cape Cod seafaring tradition. His exactitude, born of a professional eye, was habit only now. Captain Adam Hale had long since folded away into his sea chest his blue and buff and gold buttons. Attired in a subfusc gray coat, nankeen britches, and cotton stockings, almost the proper Puritan, he stood, merely stood, at the entrance to the local tavern, no longer vested with the privilege of pacing the quarterdeck in solitary grandeur. No powdered wig for Adam Hale. He wore his thinning sandy hair clubbed with a plain black silk ribbon.

The Captain still looked the seadog, however. At thirty-four, he maintained a generous frame with a barrel chest and the strong rope-worn hands of a working Captain. Some might have taken him to be one of those rare able-bodied seamen who had risen from the ranks—were it not for the overwhelming intelligence of his aspect, his sharp blue eyes, and Roman nose. His face, though flushed and weather-beaten from his early years at sea, bespoke the authority of born command. However, command, like the blue and the buff, was a memory for Captain Adam Hale.

Captain Hale once again scanned the room, hoping to find a friendly face.

"Evening, Cap'n," Eaneas Loring, who stood across the room, piped up. A half-dozen nods from about the room followed his lead and confirmed the greeting. But Adam Hale, ever quick to judge the weather, knew in an instant that he was not to be the center of attention this evening, for greater things were afoot. News of the Treaty of Paris had just reached American shores. Captain Hale silently slipped his great frame toward the mooring of a free corner at the far end of the room and ordered a tankard of ale.

On this wretched night the patriots had tarried long by the roaring fire in the taproom's double fireplace. They were in a celebratory mood, and by this late hour on a Friday night the room was a clutter of broken pipe stems, ale-soaked cheer, and bright red faces.

"To the Republic!" proclaimed the crook-nosed barber-surgeon Caleb Nye for what must have been the tenth time as he hoisted his tankard. A chorus of agreement greeted his toast led by the farmer Asahel Hinckley and his table of West Barnstable neighbors, rough-hewn, large-fisted, and still wearing smocks and leather aprons from the afternoon's chores.

"Goodman Bodfish!" farmer Hinckley shouted. Barnstable, though a shire town, was a quiet place of small farmers and fishermen, where wealth was still measured in oxen and the old forms of address lingered. "Goodman Bodfish, I pray thee set up another round for the barber and the Selectmen."

One of the Selectmen, splendid in a yellow waistcoat and mane of white hair, rose ponderously to his feet.

"Thankee, good neighbor!" the Selectman acknowledged as he assumed the gravity appropriate to his estimation of the occasion. With an obligatory clearing of his throat the Selectman commanded the attention of the room. Adam Hale, ensconced in the corner with his tankard of ale in hand, snorted and thought irreverently to himself, "Which of those present would not want to hear, nay, *marvel* at the prodigious remarks that the Selectman has reserved for us . . .?"

The Selectman began his oration.

"Today is a day we shall long remember in Barnstable." He paused to survey the room to confirm that all were listening. Reassured, he continued, "For today word reached us by swift packet of the treaty of peace signed in Paris of late. Our struggle, the cause of democracy, has triumphed over tyranny. And now, as a free and sovereign people, we are born anew. Born anew to—"

A sudden gust of cold seaborne air assaulted and chilled the room as the heavy wooden door swung open. The Selectman looked up, abruptly aware that all eyes had deserted him for the entrance to the tavern.

"Pity the poor wayfaring stranger!"

The statement coming from the door was not a plea but a demand, delivered with an urgent, peremptory edge like the rasp of a hard file.

Before the assembled citizens of Barnstable stood a specter enveloped in a blue woolen cloak, its folds still billowing in the wind that howled through the door.

"Pity the poor wayfaring stranger!" the intruder demanded again as the citizenry studied the visitor.

The accent was not right to gain admittance, Captain Hale thought. British certainly, but outlying, more of a brogue. And the aspect!—from the rain-soaked cocked hat to the full, if bedraggled, black wig, to the tattered jabot that peeked through the collar of the great cape. The Captain made him out to be not more than thirty. And prepossessing he was not, his stature short and his visage marked by a long equine quality that would have been his dominant feature were it not arrested by the wart that blemished his right nostril. The intruder did not encourage admittance.

The stranger's alert, cunning, gray-green eyes—eyes from another realm, thought Captain Hale—danced to gauge the reaction of the assembled Americans. Concluding that he met no physical challenge, with a barely perceptible click of self-assurance his mien changed to one of casual elegance as with a swift sweep of his right hand, executed almost out of habit, he unhooked and let fall his cloak in a swirl of folds at his feet.

Before the Americans stood the unexpected sight of a dark blue dress uniform of an officer of the Royal Navy. Adam Hale put down his tankard.

The intruder stepped further into the room.

Not an American moved. All eyes on the stranger, the room sat silent save for the crackling of the fire.

"I guess we have no manners," the intruder at length observed.

The stranger's cunning eyes surveyed the stares of each and every citizen.

Goodman Bodfish broke the silence. "What?"

"'What?' 'What?' In England, one says 'pardon.'"

"And 'what' cove is it that enters our ordinary and instructs us so?" retorted the Selectman.

The intruder delivered a sweeping bow.

"Lieutenant Sir Ponsonby Spicer, Baronet, Royal Navy. At your service."

Spying the empty scabbard loop that dangled at his left side, the Selectman decided to parry.

"And 'what' ship does Lieutenant Sir Ponsonby Spicer, Baronet, command now, might I ask?"

"We are late of HMS *Helot*."

"The *Helot*! Now that was a pretty piece of work! A twenty-six-gun sixth rate! Cut out not two years ago by Captain Spruill of Portsmouth, one of our Yankee privateers! A handsome prize too. Captain Spruill has built a brick mansion on Strawberry Bank," the Selectman chortled.

"Indeed, sir. In consequence of which I took up residence for eighteen months in one of your hulks off Newport. That is, until a kindly warder gained the officers better accommodation, upon our parole, in a boarding house in Newport town."

Captain Adam Hale drew his chair closer.

"And so, Lieutenant Spicer, you lost your sword to Captain Spruill?"

"I relinquished my sword according to the Articles of War," replied the irked Lieutenant Spicer. "Honorably. That is, honorably were it not for being taken by a Yankee pirate, the deceiving creature. In the end I merely chose not to fight. Had I elected otherwise, the contest would not have been close. I can assure you, sir, that I am deadly efficient with the épée. *J'ai etudé sous le Maître Bâtarde de l'Academie d'Armes à Paris.*"

Goodman Bodfish, who understood not a word, joined the probe.

"What kind of Englishman are you? Your accent don't signify."

"If by 'don't signify' you refer to my manner of speech, it is because I was born in Ireland. My grandfather removed there from Wiltshire at the time of the Boyne. My family has property in County Cork, Youghal the vicinity, Plaisland of Coolelough the seat. As I said, I am an Englishman, a subject of His Majesty the King. Unlike rebels like you."

The intruding Baronet slowly edged closer to the fireplace. He rubbed his hands to chase off the cold.

Goodman Bodfish had still not decided whether he should admit Spicer to the company of the men of Barnstable.

"Well, Lieutenant Sir Ponsonby Spicer, if that be so, then what brings ye to Barnstable on this cold and wicked night?"

"A mistaken turn, I fear. I had followed the Post Road for Boston when my American nag, out of fatigue or stupidity, I'm not sure which, turned right onto the Cape when she should have led on to Boston, where I seek passage on a ship bound for home. Whether it was the rain or the dark or my own state of drowsiness that allowed her to do so I cannot say. In the event, it is late, I am cold and there is little point in continuing til the morrow."

Goodman Bodfish nodded his head.

"What say ye, neighbors? Shall we admit this stranger to our company for the evening?"

The Selectman cleared his throat in a fit of coughing.

"But our late enemy? Here in our midst? And one so unrepentant as this?"

"We must be magnanimous in victory," the barber-surgeon Nye admonished. "Besides, no Irishman is a lobsterback at heart, damnation on him though he say otherwise."

Lieutenant Sir Ponsonby Spicer, Baronet, looked up from the fire to reveal a faint smirk.

The men about the room grumbled, some wanting to bar the stranger and others taking a broader view.

Captain Adam Hale spoke up from his corner.

"Goodman Bodfish, I think we should welcome our wandering stranger. There is a place in the empty chair beside me. Pour him a glass of warm grog, and place it on my account."

The intruder nodded, ever so imperceptibly, toward the Captain. When he sat in the corner by the Captain, with his grog in cupped hands, Adam Hale could see the tears welling at his eyes from the cold and the abrasion of exposure on his cheeks.

He inhaled the grog with reverence. He spoke only after a second glass, which Captain Hale ordered up and proffered.

"So you were a prisoner of war?" Adam asked.

6

"Yes, if you could dignify my incarceration on a hulk with such a term. It was almost a sentence of death."

"I know. I also was an unwilling guest—in my case of King George at the Mill."

Adam had sat out, shore-bound, the prime of his life during the seven years that turned the world upside down. It had not started out that way. For a brief season at the start of the war he earned the adulation of his peers—and a tincture of profit—as a blockade runner who defied the Royal Navy to relieve the Patriot-held towns of the North Shore outside Boston. But how quickly fortune had changed! His season of glory was brief, for he suffered the ignominy of capture after six short months and the loss of his sloop and all its cargo.

Then the detested memory flashed through his mind: he and seventy other Americans shackled to bilboes in a warship's hold for fifty days in passage to England. Their floating prison measured twelve feet wide by twenty feet long by three feet high, three decks under water, without light or fresh air. Upon their arrival at Plymouth, they could not stand. The daylight at first blinded them. They were forced to crawl on all fours straight into the Mill Prison, which stood not a mile from the Pilgrim Steps from which Captain Hale's ancestors bade farewell to England.

Spicer's gray-green eyes from another realm signaled disinterest.

"There were no blankets," Adam resumed. "For three and a half years the snow swept through the open windows. My fellow Americans died from exposure and smallpox. The bread was full of straw ends. We picked up old bones that had laid in the dirt and weeds and pounded them to pieces and sucked them. We dug for snails in holes in the prison walls and boiled and ate them and drank the broth. Snails."

No reaction from Spicer.

"At length, we were paroled as part of an exchange of prisoners. Do you know what we did? As we departed, we pinned to our chests cockades we had fashioned of paper, painted with the thirteen stars and stripes of the Union and inscribed at the top 'Independence' and at the bottom 'Liberty or Death.' On boarding the ship, we cheered thirteen times in unison."

Adam knew it was like a pennant hoisted atop the main mast, a gesture, and he had simply gone along.

Still no reaction from Spicer.

What Adam did not say was that while most of his fellow prisoners never looked back, not so Captain Adam Hale. He harbored an abiding antipathy to Britain's abuse of authority which burned like a flickering ember in his heart. In his more objective moments, he knew this antipathy consumed and diminished him long after his ordeal had ended. The more difficult question for Captain Adam Hale was what concept of citizenship he believed in to replace his antipathy. He knew what he was against; he did not yet know what he was for.

Upon his release and for the last four years of the war Adam Hale had holed up ashore in his hometown of Barnstable. It provided a sanctuary from the chaos of a blood-stained America at war. Consistent with his parole, he did nothing to serve the cause. He regained his health, and the interlude of trying his hand at farming and harvesting reeds from the Great Marsh at Barnstable had been pleasant and indeed profitable. He had enjoyed the company of a few of his fellow townsmen many a late evening at Goodman Bodfish's tavern where he and other patriots had played tankard board generals, retracing the movements of Washington, Howe, and Burgoyne at New York, Trenton, and Saratoga and guessing at the movements of Washington, Rochambeau, and Cornwallis at Yorktown. His seasons ashore had been a time for intellectual growth as well. Repelled by the mindless monotony of prison life, he determined that he should never again sink so low, and during the long winter months he had added Greek and rudimentary Hebrew to his self-taught Latin. Now that the four Gospels in their original tongues took their place beside the well-thumbed and sea-soaked polished pagan Virgil on his shelf, Adam Hale judged himself, at long last, to be an educated man if nothing else.

Snapping from his introspection, Adam closed his line of thought. "Not only was my freedom forfeit, and I wasn't even a combatant—bad enough and an affront to my God-given rights even though lost through the vicissitudes of war. It was a hard time. Your government wanted us to starve . . ."

"One does what one must to—" the Baronet finally said, with knowledge.

"Survive?"

"Yes, to survive."

For the briefest moment Adam felt that a tenuous bond of experience and convenience linked him to the intruder, but he dismissed it and guarded his silence on this point.

"To wit," Lieutenant Spicer continued, "I am but a penniless stranger and at your mercy. I seek only my passage home, back to my native land and away from these shores where fortune has cast me up. I know not even how I shall pay my passage once I raise Boston."

He reached in his breast pocket and withdrew a packet of papers wrapped in oilcloth.

"See, here, I hold in my hand my only hope of purchasing my passage home."

"And what might these be?" asked Captain Hale. "Might I see them?"

Lieutenant Spicer tightened his grip on the papers with spindly fingers.

"I'll give them back to you, not to worry," Adam reassured him.

The Lieutenant looked Adam in the eye, assessing whether he should trust him. At length, warmed by the grog, he slowly proffered the papers.

Adam Hale untied the knot that held the oilcloth wrapper. Five maps and an inventory lay within. Adam picked up the candlestick and drew it nearer. He held up each map in turn before the flame as he tried to decipher it.

"I see the coast of Maine, the Kennebec if I'm not mistaken. And places inland, well into the mountains."

"You are not mistaken."

"And I see the maps marked in numerous locations with the King's Broad Arrow," he said pointing with his index finger at one of the numerous three-stroked arrow designations for property of the Royal Navy that cluttered the map.

"Yes. They are the complete survey of His Majesty's forests in the District of Maine, showing the locations of the largest timbers fit for harvesting for masts and spars to supply the Royal Navy. Surely that will fetch the price of a ship's passage."

Dropping the papers, it was Adam's turn to look Lieutenant Spicer straight in the eye.

"But where did you steal—"

"I didn't steal them."

"Very well. How did you manage to . . . come by such documents?"

"They were willed to me fair and square by His Majesty the King's late deputy mast agent with whom I shared a berth in the hulk off Newport in less happy times. Poor soul! Three years in the hulk, and he died of the scurvy, never to set foot ashore again. Buried at sea he was, right in the harbor, wrapped in a sheet and weighted with shot. Such an end as was unbecoming a right and true gentleman!"

"I see. Or so say you," Adam demurred.

"Bah! What use would we have of such a passel of papers!" grumped the Selectman as he looked about the room of farmers and fishermen who had been craning to overhear the conversation in the corner. "Probably the work of the forger's art in any case!"

The yeomen, good and true, nodded in agreement.

But Captain Hale determined to engage on a cutting-out expedition of his own. The Captain had known such men as the Baronet before, a person of thoroughly awful character but no doubt competent: the type of man on which the British Empire was built. However, in the case of this latecomer to adventure the tide of empire had run out, suddenly and irretrievably, and had left him grounded. More to the point, Captain Adam Hale, unlike his farming and fishing neighbors in Barnstable, had sailed the coast of Maine and knew the immense, indeed pivotal, importance of tall timbers to empire. And he had the money to purchase the maps.

"So you want the price of a passage home? You are quite the tempter. Sit closer and talk to me," the American Captain commanded the Irish Baronet. Without awaiting a response Adam slid forward his Windsor chair and settled his massive frame so that he had Lieutenant Sir Ponsonby Spicer, Baronet, at once cornered and shielded from the prying eyes and ears of his neighbors.

"I came tonight to celebrate, so I am incommoded, but what needs have you that I may help?" Adam asked, and then added with a thoughtless wisp of patronage, "Talk with me, my cully."

"Your fool then, am I?"

"No, 'twere the other way around. Only on this night, what choice have-'e?"

Captain Adam Hale, who had entered the tavern merely to celebrate, knew that his life was about to take a turn the consequences of which he could only conjecture.

* * *

Five, maybe six, hours later Captain Hale found himself in the courtyard of a European manor house paved with square-cut granite cobbles. Its surface ran wet and slick in the autumn rain. The Captain reminded himself that he could turn an ankle as he drew his Navy greatcoat tighter about his hunkered body and walked faster. The rain still soaked through his collar to his neck.

The Captain directed his eyes straight ahead with purpose. Beyond the great house, the courtyard and its entrance arch of limestone stretched an *allée* paved with scallop shells and bounded by parallel rows of privet as high as his head. To the Captain's eye, it was a veritable strait. He picked up his pace, pressing himself, and passed under the arch to the *allée*. He was in a hurry. His feet crunched on the shells.

Minutes later the clatter of horse hooves sounded on the pavement in the distance behind him. Captain Hale allowed himself a glance over his shoulder. In the gloom a coach and six horses moved smartly out of the courtyard and under the arch. The Captain reverted his attention to the road ahead.

The noise grew. The Captain now discerned the jingle of the harnesses mixed with the pounding of the mighty hooves on the scallop shells. The alarming intimacy of the vehicle's noise caused the Captain to look back again. This time he made out the rapidly approaching coach to be a massive hackney worthy of a lord. It was all black except for the gold chasing that highlighted its metal hardware. Six black stallions veered and snorted at its head in a reckless gallop.

The Captain picked up his pace.

The rumble of the vehicle and the pounding of the steeds grew louder. The Captain darted a further glance over his shoulder. The driver lashed the horses left and right with his whip. On the coach box at the driver's side sat erect a black and white Dalmation. Two footmen stood at the rear of the coach like long-faced sentinels in their lacquered black stocks and beaver hats. Black ostrich feather plumes, as upright as the footmen, were arrayed in sprays atop the horses' harnesses.

The Captain realized that in a few moments the coach would overtake him. But the *allée* was narrow. There was no place to hide.

He broke into a run. The rain and his water-logged overcoat no longer mattered. He ran so hard that his lungs burned.

The Captain now felt the presence of the lead pair of horses behind him. He looked back again. Steam rose from the horses' flaring nostrils not a yard from him. Dirt and fragments of scallop shell flew from their feet. Harness leather creaked with the strain, and tack rattled, almost drowned by the roar of the wheels and the mad pounding of the hooves.

He ran now with abandon. His arms pumped. His coattails flew. When would his time run out and the steeds and barreling hackney crush him beneath hooves and wheels?

Earlier that night he had seized an opportunity or succumbed to temptation, depending on one's optic, but surely for the noble motive of preserving, prospering, and passing on his wealth. The problem was that he could not predict the consequences of his bargain: whether the pact he had made would unleash some unforeseen retribution that would run him down and trample him in ways most evil or whether death itself would overtake him before he achieved his ambition to become a merchant prince. After all, could he outrun the inexorable?

He ran, and he ran. But the vehicle remained just behind him.

Adam Hale bolted up. His throat was dry, and his heart raced. Panic and disorientation gripped him.

"My God!" he cried. "What have I done? Where am I?"

And then he sank back into his bed.

All was calm and dark. The Captain perceived the soft curves of his wife Abigail at his side. He heard a gentle rustle of the bed covers.

"Adam, what is it?"

"Just a dream, Nabby. Just a dream."

2

Down East

1784—Part I

"By the mark ten. By the deep nine; and a half seven," the humpbacked dwarf croaked as he perched in the chains and cast his sounding lead portside into the depth of the channel of Casco Bay.

Captain Adam Hale heard the plop of the lead as it struck the chill North Atlantic, but he saw nothing: not the misshapen leadsman who clung to the chain shrouds not ten yards from him, not the line, not the wax-armed lead, not the telltale mud it plucked from the bottom. An early spring fog—it was only March—smothered the *Blind Bartimaeus* as she groped her way through the channel to Falmouth.

Captain Hale knew these Down East fogs. They were thick, all-enveloping murks that hugged the coast, infused with cold air and gloom. He had encountered his first such fog almost twenty years before, while still a midshipman scudding down the coast toward Penobscot Bay. In those days the shores were still populated by Abenaki, who burned off the undergrowth in hundreds of brush fires to facilitate hunting. The smudge and aroma of the shore fires mixed with the fogs that hugged the coast to produce an intoxicating brew that even then had perversely lured Adam Hale to the District of Maine.

Captain Hale also knew this channel from many years before. There was scant forgiveness in the strait passage bounded on either side by glacier-scrubbed granite sheets that rudely jutted into the cold water.

Passage of the channel was old stuff, to be sure, a trick of the trade he had long since mastered. Today, however, the responsibility was not his. The Captain stood amidships as a mere passenger.

The signal cannon high atop Munjoy Hill, not more than a few miles distant but an eternity away, began to fire its salvo, as it would every three minutes until the fog lifted. Five retorts blasted forth from various unseen ships plying the channel, including one from the *Blind Bartimaeus's* own bow-chaser. Adam Hale allowed himself to wonder if the salvo caused the windows at the First Church in Falmouth, known as Old Jerusalem, to shake and the dead to arise from their graves in Eastern Cemetery at the saddle of Munjoy Hill.

But then the humpbacked leadsman snatched his speculation from him as he croaked in a voice tinged with anxiety, "By the mark six! By the mark six!"

The laden ship creaked forward, listing toward the granite shelf.

"Bastard!" Captain Hale muttered under his breath. And then he thought better of his language. "Negligent cove!" he corrected himself as his fingers drummed a ratline with just a hint of impatience. The ship's sudden heave leeward, far too leeward in the fog-enshrouded, rock-bound Falmouth channel, was open to criticism. Indeed, there was much for Captain Hale to criticize in the bum coastal skipper of the *Blind Bartimaeus.*

But the Captain stopped to remind himself that his exactitude was born of force of habit rather than right of command, a distinction that he was now determined to eliminate.

"Fid! Fid!"

"Seth?"

"Fid, do you have the papers?"

Adam turned to see his oldest son at his side looking up to him. A thin and finer version of himself, with blue eyes and sandy hair, his face was flush and his eyes agitated. Years ago, when only two, Seth had coined the name "Fid" when trying to say "Father," and it stuck within the family. The name pleased Adam because it denoted both a basic sailor's tool and the Latin root for "loyal." Now, at fifteen, Seth already knew the burden of responsibility. A commendable quality in a seaman, thought Adam. Good judgment and the rest would come with time and instruction. And yet Adam suspected that his son was innately a better man than he, for he had a measure of his mother's goodness, a righteousness even, that he himself lacked. Adam knew he might achieve such character but to do so he would have to be a man bent against himself, a saint or a stoic depending on one's optic, the stuff of a life's journey. All in all, Adam judged Seth to possess a felicitous combination of attributes, in time a veritable sternpost on which some day he might lean.

"Fid! The papers! Mama looked in the chest, and they was gone!"

"Easy, son," Adam reassured him as he patted the breast pocket of his coat. "They're in good hands. Where safer could they be? Look starboard if you can, son, through the fog. We are about to arrive!"

The boy, visibly relieved, exhaled and released the tension that bent his thin frame, although he could see nothing through the fog.

By then the rest of Adam's family had joined him on deck. Jezreel, two years Seth's junior, and named for the valley of invasion in the land of the Israelites, the site of Armageddon, paced the deck in anticipation, unable to contain his coiled energy at the prospect of the impending landfall and new life at Falmouth. With dark eyes, coal black hair from heaven knew where, and an impetuous disposition, he was his older brother's opposite in so many ways.

"Fid, does this captain know his seamanship? I could steer better than he does," Jezreel protested.

"I don't doubt it, son," Adam replied.

Guileless and with dartlike truth always at the tip of his tongue, Jezreel was also sentimental. In his left arm he cradled his most prized possession from home, a battered Bergonzi violin and bow that Adam had purchased for him thirdhand in a Boston music shop years before. Adam winced to see him expose the fine instrument to the moisture of the fog, but it was his constant companion. He had mastered it, as well as the rudiments of seamanship.

Next to him, with her hand now placed on Adam's shoulder and assessing the narrow fog-bound passage with a worried eye, stood Abigail—"Nabby" to Adam—and all Adam could want in a wife. Nabby was lithe and fine, a complement to her husband's robust vitality. She bore herself with a quiet, straight-backed dignity and needed no Parisian *maquillage* to detract from her beauty. Even as he looked at her now, she brought joy to Adam's heart and made his soul, deep within, leap. In Nabby, born into the Bacon family of good Chatham stock, Adam had married up. Nabby was herself the daughter of a captain, and she knew the ways of the sea.

"Are you sure of this, Adam?" she whispered in an edgy voice as her gaze held steady on the rock ledges. "I fear you've gotten us into something we know not."

Adam winced, for she spoke the truth. The captain of the *Blind Bartimaeus* was courting disaster. But her question reached a deeper level, for uncertainty abounded in their destination of Falmouth and of what their new life might bring. The District of Maine for years had been little more than a wilderness with a sparse population of fishermen, seafarers, and rocky soil farmers settled under Royalist proprietors. In a burst of hubris in the wake of the Calvinist victory in the English Civil War, Massachusetts Bay Colony annexed it as booty and had disdained it ever since.

"It will be all right, Nabby. We are close to arrival."

"I do hope so," she replied and then, thinking the better of it, added gamely with a wink, "I am certain it will be so."

Just then the signal gun atop Munjoy Hill sounded again. The ghost ships plying the channel obliged with their answers. Nabby shuddered at each discharge. Adam placed his arm about Nabby's shoulders and drew her closer to reassure her.

The ship yawed suddenly to the portside. Her keel scraped bottom with a grinding lurch that sent almost all the passengers on deck in a scramble to grab the nearest railing to steady themselves, many of them gasping and screaming. Not so Adam, who stood firm. Or Nabby, who reached instinctively for her two smaller children who stood by her side.

Next to Nabby, but barely able to see over the fife rail and clutching a doll, stood wide-eyed, eight-year-old Thankful, who until that moment had looked forward with excitement to a new home in which she would grow into womanhood and to new adventures in which she was certain she would meet a dashing suitor and be swept off her feet.

"Mama!" she shouted when the ship scraped the bottom, and she dropped the doll to seek her mother's embrace. Nabby bent down to enfold her.

No sooner had Thankful sought the reassurance of her mother's arms than four-year-old Juvenal wriggled from her embrace to join his father, exclaiming, "Fid! What was that? I know! It is a whale under the ship! There must be a whale right there under the water! It's the same whale that swallowed Jonah!"

"There's no whale—" Adam started to correct him before stopping himself and breaking into an indulgent smile. After all, the child had just had his first brush with the abyss, where all was cold and dark and human flesh was eaten by nibbling predators ugly beyond contemplation: the realm into which no sentient person would want to fall. No, reassurance rather than reprimand was in order.

"It's alright, son," Adam stated with authority as he placed his hand on Juvenal's shoulder. "The ship just scraped a ledge. See, she's already steadied herself."

Juvenal's arrival in life was a surprise and an afterthought to his parents. His name, an aberration to be sure, was Adam's inspiration, derived from his reading of the classics. He was a bright child with an early command of words. He has already taught himself to read, although at home he struggled with the mastery of "please" and "thank you" to ensure the gratification of his passing whims. Being much the youngest of the children, he often had a dreamy quality about him and played by himself. He had imaginary friends.

The ship edged further into the channel. Adam stood upright, while the rest of his family, with their jumble of anticipations and fears, put on a brave mask: Seth and Jezreel his outliers and the rest of his brood comforted in his and Nabby's embrace and uplifted countenance. The ship groped her way toward their new home.

Not ten minutes later Adam erupted in excitement.

"Look, family! The fog is lifting! There's Falmouth!" Adam shouted as he pointed to starboard. All eyes in the family looked up. Ahead of them, gilded by a sudden shaft of sunlight, shone the rising hulk of the promontory known simply as "the Neck." It jutted into Casco Bay, protected by its triple line of islands, as fine a deepwater port as existed on the North American coast. Adam's heart pounded.

"Seth, there is much good work to be done here," Adam declared as he turned to his eldest son and weighed the treasure of a second chance in life. "Why, think of Falmouth not as a town bound by the land, but as an opening looking forth and connected by the unbroken ribbon of the sea to such lands as Europe, the Indies, and China. To reach those exotic climes and their riches, all you need do is sail forth. They are ours! They are connected to us!"

Adam permitted himself to dream for a moment of his imagery, well put, he thought, for a sea captain. However, the romance of being one of the elect whose eyes might gaze on Cathay was shared by Seth only with qualification.

"Fid, is it moral to make a profit from another man's misfortune?" Seth asked as the *Blind Bartimaeus* creaked forward into the harbor channel. He knew well the fact of his father's purchase of the survey from the Irish Lieutenant.

"Some might call it Yankee ingenuity, if I smoke your question. Besides, Lieutenant Spicer's very presence in America was to take advantage of our misfortunes. So what's fair is fair about. If he committed treason by selling the King's survey, it's no worse than the treason we Americans committed against the King."

"But Lieutenant Spicer still purports to be a subject of the King and to live under his flag, while we do not."

"Quite so. And I'd grant you he'd no doubt prefer me dead so that I could not tell of his treason—but the oceans are vast and the chances of our ever meeting are slim. Other than that, it is a matter for his conscience alone and no concern of ours."

"I would like to think that were the case. But I don't know where conscience might lead."

Adam looked hard at his oldest son and marveled mightily.

"In any event," Adam said, "our profit is far from certain. Much will depend on timing. The bankers in Boston have commissioned us to procure a ship—no easy thing—outfit her, sail her to the Kennebec and thence to France, all without a moment to spare, while they sort out questions of title. Divine Providence will play a role out of all proportion."

Adam had known from the start the risks that the venture entailed but until now had not been prepared to confide in his son. Before the recent hostilities, the British Admiralty had paid over a hundred pounds for a great mast, thirty-six inches at the butt. That was the price of a fair home in Boston. And bowsprits and spars, great sticks in their own right, brought sums close behind. The size of these New England masts made a prodigious impression on the shipwrights of England. And so they should on those of France—unless someone beat him there or unless they looked elsewhere. Adam's mission was to ensure that no one did beat him there, and, as to the latter, Adam reassured himself that there were but two sources in the world for the great timbers needed to outfit a ship of the line—America and the Baltic. America's great timbers were the choice of the two.

However, Seth would not let his line of inquiry drop.

"But if title to the trees were in the Crown, what right have we to take the timber?"

"By the right of succession, if nothing else, I suppose," Adam responded, growing weary of his son's questioning. "One thing for certain, at least as far as I'm concerned, is that title is no longer with the King. I'll leave such niceties to lawyers and other indolent arguers. It should be years before the claims are settled out. In the meantime, I know, and the Boston bankers are willing to wager, that the first American ship to reach the Kennebec and pay Maria Theresa dollars in silver for the great timbers—the first money the mast loggers have seen in eight years!—will take the cream of the harvest and have a ready market for their sale to France. Now, son, what do you think a cargo of prime masts and spars will fetch from King Louis, who has been starved of mast timbers all these years?" Adam asked as he tried to warm Seth to the venture.

"Enough to be worth our while?" Seth replied timidly.

"Hah! Enough to buy out our venturers back in Boston and be done with debt and reliance on any man! Enough to sail our ship under our own flag! Enough to be—" Adam checked himself lest such talk approach the sin of avarice—"enough to be *free.*"

"Beggars can't be choosers," Asa Penwistle admonished Adam and Seth as they stood at the head of his shipyard. "Been no launches in these waters since the year '76. Expect most of the yards will be starting up again once demand takes hold. But not for delivery today. Nope. If you want a ship to sail now, you'll have to go with what's available. Ain't a lot of that either. You say it's a timber ship you want?"

Adam and Seth both nodded.

"Follow me," Penwistle ordered.

To Adam's mind, Penwistle was a small and dark man, full of dark humors and surprises. If asked, Penwistle would acknowledge, indeed almost volunteer, that both were attributable to his Cornish blood. What he would not volunteer, but what was known up and down the coast of Maine from York to the Penobscot, was that he ran one of the best ship-yards Down East. Of the scores, if not hundreds, of yards that dotted the coast wherever a freshwater stream spilled into the Atlantic, including even the big yards on the Piscataqua, Sheepscot, and Damariscotta, his yard at Smelt Hill on Casco Bay, near the falls of the Presumscot, had led the trade in quality in the years before the war.

Penwistle guided them past hermaphrodite brigs, jackass brigs, snows, and pinks in various states of construction.

"Now, why would you be wanting a timber ship?" he pried as they walked.

"Oh, 'tis only a matter of price, Mr. Penwistle," Adam found himself dissembling despite himself. "What with the mast trade dead, my bank-ers figure there's little demand for such a ship and she can be had at a relative bargain and fitted for other uses."

Penwistle cast a skeptical glance but did not respond. He led them to a slip at the far side of the yard.

"The Brig *Freckled Whelp* was built as a timber ship not five years before the war, a fine ship, broad in the beam, a solid deep-sea sailor," he explained.

Before them loomed a large brig. Adam guessed her to reach upward of three hundred tons burden. She was full rigged, with both main and

fore masts sporting three spars each, all square-rigged save for a standing
gaff on the main mast to support a fore-and-aft spanker. Adam recognized her immediately as a classic Down East brig of generous proportions, her grace accentuated by a most unusual stepping of her bowsprit
directly into the sheer of the fore curve of her deck.

"Ain't she pretty?" the salesman Penwistle mused to himself, just in
earshot of his two customers.

However, her hull was draped in canvas and barred closer inspection.
Adam therefore allowed his inspection to continue of the outward and
visible.

"Her masts have been stepped with a rake most uncommon for a
timber brig," he observed. "A picture as pretty as ever I've seen. But one
to serve a function, no doubt."

"She has been undergoing alterations," Penwistle responded without
further explanation.

Adam studied her pine log masts, each constructed of a single timber
and banded with six iron hoops painted black. She could press canvas out
of all logic to her purpose. Judging by her yards, she could boast three
skysails and crossed double topgallant yards, with studding sails to boot.
To Adam this spelled speed, a most uncommon speed for a timber ship.
To a landsman she would be a mare turned racehorse.

Adam and Seth followed Penwistle in clambering aboard for a closer
inspection. Indeed, she was a commodious vessel. On deck stood a whitewashed quarterdeck house containing the captain's cabin, complete with
a small dining saloon and chartroom.

"The captain's quarters are a departure from the customary," observed
Adam, who out of habit had expected to find the captain's accommodations not atop the quarterdeck but below on the main deck aft, with
perhaps a pretty transom through which to study the sunsets.

"Aye, Captain Hale," Penwistle responded. "But then you'll be
remembering that she's a timber brig. The timber ports, Captain, the
timber ports."

"Just so, Mr. Penwistle. I had forgotten."

To his chagrin, his years ashore had caused the Captain to forget
that a timber ship's stern below decks was pierced with broad ports to

facilitate the lading of the mast timbers. It was a design shared by no other ship.

Further aft stood the wheelhouse with the ship's wheel and prodigious rudder. Off the aft, suspended from twin davits, hung the ship's dark green jolly boat.

The Captain allowed his gaze to sweep to the fore. There, just aft of her most uncommon bowsprit, stood the whitewashed house with the crew's quarters, carpenter's shop, and galley. Long boats rested atop the house, lashed to their skids.

"Come below," gestured Penwistle as he lit a lantern and opened the forward hatch. "Mind your step."

They descended straightway to the bottom-most deck, the orlop, which constituted the ship's hold well beneath the waterline. Bowing lest he crack his head against the ceiling timbers and gasping at the unwelcome damp closeness of a ship's hold, Adam adjusted his eyes to the darkness.

"The keel and keelsons are pitch pine from the Kennebec, well scarphed, and the ballast cobble from Purpooduck," explained Penwistle.

"I must take your word for that," mused Captain Hale. The prime timbers and ballast were invisible beneath even this lowest deck. "However, I see that she has little dead rise, like most good Down Easters," he observed as he tried to estimate the angle at which the bottom rose from the keel. "She has a flat floor and good capacity for cargo. Stable, too, I'd wager."

Captain Hale ran his finger along the white oak ribs and planking and ceiling of pitch pine. He judged the hull to be stout at a full sixteen inches thick.

"Look," said Penwistle, as he held up the lantern and pointed his finger in appreciation, "Copper bolts below the waterline and iron above. Best construction."

Captain Hale poked his head into various compartments separated by bulkheads for the storage of provisions. Returning quickly to his inspection of her structural integrity, he studied the camber of the deck, pausing only to note the placement of the ship's well in the darkened and close quarters.

Penwistle opened the hatch to the well. "Coles and Bentinck chain pump," he announced as the Captain assessed with an appreciative eye a pumping system worthy of a frigate or even ship of the line.

"Are we ready to ascend to the main deck?" Penwistle asked once the Captain's inspection was completed. The trio climbed through the hatch with Penwistle and his lantern in the lead.

As they emerged, Adam expected to find the upper store deck just above the waterline. But as he glimpsed into the gloom feebly lit by the lantern he saw the sweep of a deck unlike any merchantman's. Arrayed before him in powerful symmetry stretched the sweep of a gun deck. Adam counted fourteen cannon lining the deck, port and starboard, hawsed tight with block and tackle and run in. He guessed the guns to be six-foot-long six pounders, the type of supplemental armament carried by a light British war frigate or the standard armament for a sloop. They would not stand up to a ship of the line boasting twelve or eighteen pounders, but they were nonetheless serious armament.

As they entered, Adam noted that the newly cut gun ports were shrouded from the outside by the canvas draping. He ran his hand along the six-inch wales recently fitted to the port-sills to support the heavy guns.

"So she was being refitted as a privateer," Adam concluded with a chuckle.

"One of our best, a surprise to take on the British," Penwistle winked conspiratorially. "But now she won't see action, not of that sort anyway. The investors have put her up for sale."

"The ship serves admirably. But I don't need guns. A merchantman with that kind of armament! What use would it serve?"

"She sells with the guns or not at all."

"Your principals drive a hard bargain."

"With peace they have no need of the guns. You might could use them, though, doing truck with the Algerine corsairs or pirates in the Indies. The added weight will not be a bother neither. The speed of the extra canvas will more than make up. And she's still large enough to carry the standard cargo of fifty masts and more on a voyage."

"And the crew to man fourteen guns? How could a merchantman profitably run with a crew to handle fourteen long guns?" Adam asked, as he did a quick mental calculation.

"You forget that a broadside fires only one side at a time. Cut your estimate in half and you approach what a brig this size would carry as her peacetime complement. Thirty hands, give or take. It ain't a stretch. It serves."

"But I know nothing of gunnery."

"I hear it said that you are a learning man, Captain."

Perhaps it was Penwistle's challenge, perhaps it was the brig's undoubted speed and seaworthiness, or perhaps it was the added protection the guns afforded or, failing that, the extra cash they might bring if he could find a buyer for them. Or perhaps it was just the rake of the masts. Adam knew he was interested, and Penwistle sensed that interest instinctively.

"Please step into my office," Penwistle suggested, as he ushered them into a shed at the head of the yard.

Once inside, Adam opened by pleading poverty.

"You must understand, Mr. Penwistle, I have been laid up ashore these last four years, and it is only through the credit extended by cold-hearted bankers in Boston—to whom I am answerable, make no mistake of it—that I can even contemplate an offer. They would never accept your asking price. But I have a little leeway to bargain if you are willing."

Penwistle answered only with his right eyebrow arched, which Adam took to mean to proceed. Adam's gut reminded him how uncomfortable he was in negotiating.

"The cannon are a great burden, something I don't seek," he explained, though in truth he had become intrigued by them. "But in the interest of moving things forward I am willing to entertain including them as part of the package—subject of course to some adjustment in the price."

Penwistle sat in silence.

"I pray thee work with me, Mr. Penwistle. Think of this transaction as a partnership in which we both can profit, not just today but proceeding forward."

Still no reaction from Penwistle. Adam decided to unveil the sole enticement he held up his sleeve.

"And I may have need of additional services in outfitting her which would redound most smartly to your benefit."

"Let's discuss that," Penwistle allowed.

And so Adam spent the next two hours locked in negotiation with Penwistle, two penny-pinching Yankees bargaining with the full confidence of their backers and principals that they would arrive at an acceptable deal.

By noon Adam and Seth emerged from Penwistle's office with a signed contract and Penwistle's agreement to outfit the ship post haste. The guns were to sail with her.

Adam and Seth strolled to the slip to inspect their purchase with pride and exhaustion.

"I paid too damn much," Adam groused. "I'm too nice a person. I'm always taken advantage of."

"No point in second thoughts now, Fid. The deal is done, guns and all."

"Oh, I expect I'll find a use for the guns one way or another. And in truth there's not a thing I don't like about her. Except maybe her name."

"I don't know who the '*Freckled Whelp*' is," Seth admitted.

"I fear I might," Adam countered.

"Perhaps she should bear a more noble name, armed to the teeth and sleek sailor that she is. What type of name would you prefer for the brig, Fid?" Seth asked.

"Something with more gravity. Something that signifies."

Seth thought for a moment as they walked the length of the brig.

"*Atheling*," Seth said with a smile and twinkle in his eye.

Adam hesitated a moment, as if to ask why.

"An Atheling was an Anglo-Saxon prince, strong and noble of character. 'Tis but a reflection of you once you sail her. God willing, she shall make you a merchant prince."

Adam's face at once reddened in embarrassment and erupted in a smile. His son had read him all too well. Resistance was useless.

"So she shall, son, so she shall. The *Atheling* she shall be."

As they turned to leave Adam stopped. He took Seth's hand in his and shook it.

"Welcome aboard, Second Mate. Welcome aboard the *Atheling*."

3

The Queen Charlotte

1784—Part II

CAPTAIN ADAM HALE TOOK POSSESSION OF THE *ATHELING* WITH April's first fair weather—though ice still coated the freshwater creeks— and sailed her into Falmouth's harbor for provisioning. As the ship took on goods Adam walked the wharves and sloping hills of the Neck to gain a better sense of the place that was to be his family's new home. Would it indeed be a sanctuary, a city on a hill, that would welcome him and his family even as Barnstable had provided shelter? Would the law of the city permit a stranger to be a citizen, to be accepted and to flourish? Or would dangers surround and threaten the common civic life?

Adam noted that this northernmost settlement of any consequence in the newly independent colonies was but a scratch of civilization on a vast and savage land. He quickly saw that she was no Boston, Philadelphia, or Charleston. The town that stood before him covered only half the Neck and faced but two blocks toward the harbor. Beyond the ridge at the middle of the Neck that constituted Back Street stood rampant thickets of bramble bushes and high trees. Not entirely to his surprise, he learned that bear and moose wandered to the edge of town on occasion. He also learned from the residents with whom he talked that not twenty-five years before, both French and Indians had lurked in the forests that bounded the backside of the town, a constant threat to the English and Scottish settlers on the Neck.

Indeed, Falmouth could claim only two hundred and fifty homes and perhaps as many shops and warehouses, mostly of wood. And most were new and unpainted. Every so often Adam spotted a brick chimney standing like a lone sentinel on an empty lot. At first Adam wondered why. It did not take him long to find out: the British had burned the town to the ground eight years earlier. Adam had read the story in the newspapers at the time but in the ensuing years of his own trials had largely forgotten the details.

A wizened old Captain whom he met on the waterfront refreshed his memory over a tot of bumbo:

"It was a fine October morning in the year '75. Cap'n Henry Mowat's squadron hove in sight at dawn: five ships strong, off the islands in Casco Bay. The breeze failed, so they lowered their jolly boats and warped the ships up into the harbor. When they stood off the waterfront they dropped anchor. Mowat sent notice ashore that Admiral Graves in Boston had ordered him to destroy the town."

"Pray tell why? You must remind me," coaxed Adam.

"Why, for its impudence and disrespect for the King, that's why," the old Captain responded. "That is to say, for having detained Mowat six months previously when he came to collect the King's mast timbers. Mowat gave the town two hours' notice to evacuate or prepare. Now, Falmouth was a trading town and had neither the will nor the knowledge to fight. Falmouth had no Minutemen, no green at Lexington, no bridge at Concord. Her population gathered what belongings they could carry and fled into the interior. Mowat opened fire at nine thirty in the morning and raked the town with cannon balls, bombs, grapeshot, and musket fire without cessation until six o'clock in the evening. He used hot shot to set fires. The lawful government of the colonies thus reduced to ruin and conflagration a town of British subjects at the onset of winter, and this almost a year before the Declaration of Independence. In the winter that followed and indeed for years afterward families wandered destitute, homeless, and forgotten, while the country and history chose to remember only the Boston Tea Party."

"Outrageous, criminal," Adam mumbled. Adam now understood how Captain Mowat's bombardment and the ensuing fire that destroyed the town had become the North Star in the navigational course of Falmouth.

But today, as he walked the streets, both Mowat and the French and the Indians were gone. The town was partially rebuilt, and the dirt and cobbled streets leading to the wharves and warehouses in the toehold on the wilderness hummed with activity as American industry stirred from its eight-year slumber.

Indeed, in his month ashore at Falmouth, Adam took note that merchants were arriving almost daily with capital and enterprise: Thomas Hopkins, Eben Anson, the Revolutionary General Peleg Wadsworth, Richard Codman, Eliphalet Deane, and dozens of others. From Massachusetts and Connecticut they came, even from Canada, Scotland, and England. They set up their stores in India Street, Fore Street, Titcomb's Wharf, and Clay Cove with ambitious and high plans of stocking general assortments of merchandise to trade, for gold if possible, by barter if not, for the produce of the north country: masts and spars, barrel staves, flax seed, dried and salted cod, beaver pelts, pot and pearl ashes, which they would ship to Europe and the West Indies in exchange for nails, guns, fancy silk waistcoats, cocked hats, rum, and molasses.

Adam Hale also set up shop in Fore Street at the west end of town, but it was a shop more in aspiration than in fact because his first order of business was to provision and man the *Atheling* and sail for the Kennebec before any of his competitors. Adam discovered that supplies for a transatlantic voyage came dearly, and it was only through concerted effort, not to mention the assistance of the well-compensated Mr. Penwistle, that he was able to assemble the requisite casks of dried beef, salt cod, peas, biscuits, fresh water, rum, and beer in record time.

Though supplies were dear, recruitment came easily in a port town awash with able seamen and former privateers. As First Mate, Captain Hale had hired experience in Hiram Clew, a Nantucket Quaker who had served as Lieutenant under Captain John Paul Jones aboard the *Bonhomme Richard* of the American Navy. He was a toughened man, superannuated at forty-six and with one eye. But Adam judged his seamanship to be sound, and he knew the naval traditions without being a Tartar. It was a contract between like minds, for Clew gained a Captain who was not brutal in his manners, unlike so many others. Working in concert with the Captain, Clew's knowledge and example would be good instruction for Seth. What's more, Adam was pleased to note, he was expert in gunnery and could exercise the crew in that peculiar art. With him had come a dozen able seamen, foretopmen mostly, who also had seen naval service.

The remainder of the crew was an assortment of coastal hands and privateers, almost all of them Falmouth men but for a handful of Irishmen. There was not a lubber among them, unless one counted Sanchez, the temperamental but capital Azorean cook, whom the Captain recruited from a tavern on Fore Street on the strength of one lobscouse tasted and the boast that he could cook codfish three hundred and sixty-five different ways, one for each day of the year. In all, the Captain was confident that they would meld into a harmonious and contented crew, and perhaps if all went well, into a house crew that would sail his ships in years to come.

* * *

Standing alone on the quarterdeck, having relegated Seth to the main deck with the crew, Captain Adam Hale cast a sternward glance at Falmouth while the *Atheling* cleared the harbor for the channel to the open sea. It was dusk, with the ebb tide flowing and the lights of the town coming on like fireflies in the clear brisk late April evening. As she eased out of the harbor the *Atheling* was sailing close hauled on her jibs and staysails, with their leeches atwitter.

He allowed himself a smile as he stood on his natural pediment of the quarterdeck. The welcome swell of the ocean was sure to rise soon under his feet and, though they were already under way, the anchor dripped water and seaweed as it came up the side, accompanied by Mr. Clew's naval tars hauling the capstan round. They stomped in neat naval fashion and chanted as they leaned their final heaves into the licking pawls:

> *"I asked a maiden by my side,*
> *Who sighed and looked at me forlorn,*
> *'Where is your heart?' She quick replied,*

'Round Cape Horn.'
Away-away-o
Away-away-o!"

Captain Hale had approved, with somewhat reluctant amusement, Mr. Clew's suggestion that this would be a ship that followed the naval daily routine: decks washed and holystoned before dawn, all hands piped to breakfast, exercises in gunnery, polishing brass and touch-up painting, the formality of the noon observation, staggered dinner hours, with the hands eating first and the officers an hour and half later, and afternoons in general quiet. As in the Navy, the dispensing of grog was a part of the daily routine: a pint a man normally resulting in very quiet afternoons indeed. One naval tradition that Captain Hale, unlike many other merchantmen, would not follow was use of the cat. Experience had taught him that brutalization sank a ship faster than a leaky hull. Besides, its use was unbecoming a crew made of free men, largely New Englanders like himself.

"Spread the mainsail and main topsail, Mr. Clew," the Captain ordered. "And have the bosun pipe all hands."

In the gathering gloom, with just a slice of orange at the westward horizon flying over the mizzenmast like a pennant, Captain Hale stood in command of the quarterdeck, wrapped against the chill in his blue greatcoat and with his hair blowing free. He addressed his men.

"Now, lads, mind me well. That side of the channel," he said, hiking his thumb aft over his shoulder, "I have my owners and the Lord Almighty. This side of the channel," he thundered, pointing his index finger forward, "I am the Lord Almighty!"

All hands looked up, suddenly aware that this was a Captain who had worked his way "through the hawse-hole" to the quarterdeck of command.

Captain Hale listened carefully for any grumbling among the men. Satisfied that he heard none, he continued.

"Mr. Clew tells me some of you served in our Navy and fought beside Paul Jones. Others of you did not. I care not where you came from. Be you Yankee, Irishman, or Portugee, we'll have no differences aboard this ship. The same holds for English church, Papist cathedral, and Methodist chapel. Do not let any of it be a point of disagreement between you. Don't let yourselves to be heard to grumble in any way. I allow no fighting aboard this ship. Come aft to me when you have any quarrels, and I'll settle them. I'll do the quarreling for you."

And, turning to his handful of officers, he admonished, "When you call a man, see that he comes. When you send one, see that he goes. Mind those simple rules, and with perseverance," he added, his forefinger pointed to the mainmast, "with perseverance, we'll sail to hell and back. Dismissed."

Before he turned to pace the quarterdeck in solitude, Captain Hale caught the visage of Seth beneath him. His son looked shocked and troubled, for this was a side of his father that he had never before seen: not the gentle and benevolent *pater familias* of his childhood in Barnstable but a rough-edged, commanding, all-powerful despot with whom he was not well pleased. So be it, Adam thought to himself. On shipboard life was different, and the sooner Seth learned that lesson the better.

* * *

The *Atheling* slid silently into the mouth of the Kennebec, skirting a peninsula labeled on one of Spicer's maps with the Abenaki word "Sagadahoc." The only sounds that announced her arrival were the creak of her rigging and the occasional bark of the seals lounging on the rocky islands that dotted the approach. There were scores of islands, some no larger than a few yards across and others so large that their circumference could not be estimated by the naked eye. But all were of a uniformly rocky shoreline surmounted by bristling green-black spruce trees standing straight as sentinels and reflected in mirror image in the water. With its enveloping silence of wilderness, the Kennebec was as Maine must have been when the white men came, long before Plymouth Colony and even Jamestown or the nearby short-lived Popham Colony, to set up their fishing stations and drying stages for curing codfish. Ironically, Maine was one of the oldest colonized parts of North America. However, the white man's presence had been only seasonal in those early years and had vanished with the first snow of each passing autumn.

34

The *Atheling* sliced through the still and frigid bottle-black water neatly, leaving but a barely perceptible wake at her stern. So deep was the anchorage that the leadsman cast his line almost to the rockbound shore of the mainland before striking bottom. Well into the Kennebec, the *Atheling* dropped her best bower anchor in the channel not a bowsprit's length from a promontory known as Parker Head, where it grappled with the granite and held fast.

It was but a short row in the jolly boat to shore, where Captain Hale instantly spotted the shacks of the mast agent's men among the drying stages that lined the shore, just as the map had promised.

Pugh, the foreman of the mast men, was a Down Easter who had much in common with the rough fishermen who pioneered these shores over a hundred and fifty years earlier. Short, fat, puffing on a cheroot, and bundled against the cold in a flat-brimmed felt hat, white buckskin jacket, leggings, and moccasins, he smelled of bear grease and smoke. He lived with an Abenaki common law wife and brother-in-law and assorted offspring and relations in a rambling lean-to of sod and pine boughs. His brother-in-law, a tall and taciturn man, bore a horrible raw scar down his left cheek that terminated in a saturated nub where his ear had been.

Pugh was ready to do business, Adam quickly discovered.

"So, is it cod you want, Cap'n? We've cod and herring too. Drying on the stages and already salted and barreled. If you're headed for Spain or France, 'tis a valuable cargo to carry. The whole Papist countryside eats 'em Fridays, you know. I could supply you upward of two thousand quintals."

"I've come for masts, Mr. Pugh," Captain Hale corrected him as he drew out his map. "I'm given to believe you have masts here on the Kennebec."

Pugh studied him with gimlet eyes.

"You're a Yankee Captain?"

"Two days out of Falmouth," Hale responded with a nod. "I sail for myself and for a group of Boston investors."

"You don't buy for the King, then?"

"No! Rest assured, Mr. Pugh! The King's Broad Arrow no longer signifies. You do have masts, do you not, Mr. Pugh?"

Pugh laughed.

"Do we have masts? Oh, yes, Cap'n, we have masts. Only problem is they've been sitting at the bottom of the Kennebec River. Just baulked a load not a month ago, thinking a Boston merchant might appear, when over the horizon come the sails of two merchantmen heading from the Indies under escort of a frigate, all flying the British ensign."

"And what frigate would that be?"

"The *Yellowjacket* she was, of twenty-eight guns, coming from the Jamaica station. They were loitering, slowly bound for Halifax and then Portsmouth. Hove in sight, not far off from where you're anchored, and sent a party ashore. Wanted to know if we had any masts. Claimed they were the King's property and they'd come to collect them."

"What, pray, did you do?"

"What any Down Easter would have done, of course. Soon as we saw 'em coming, we broke out the axes and cracked through the ice of the river. Wrapped the logs three times around in chains and boulders and sank them to the bottom. There they lay for three days while the English lingered about, trying to figure out what had happened to 'their' masts. Mad as hornets, they were. One in particular, a slight fellow who talked venal bad, dressed in a wig and all, acted like he was in command, even though he weren't the Captain of the frigate. Came from his being a Baronet or some such aristocrat, I suppose, or so he claimed. And a damned terror he was with a sword, too. We was just standing here, like you and I now, explaining there were no masts, and all of a sudden he unsheathes his épée and slices off Squampoo's ear, just like that. No warning, no explanation. Just did it like that and keeps on talking."

"Why did he do that?"

"Don't know. Maybe because he wasn't getting the mast timbers he wanted and he wanted to scare us."

"Maybe just because Squampoo Indian," his brother-in-law interjected with a sad expression on his face.

"Or maybe," Seth observed, "he just wanted to make a show of how good he is with the sword, to impress as it were."

"Was he an ugly man," Adam asked, "with a wart on his nose, by chance? And a certain air about him . . . a certain ambiguity of compass, shall we say?"

"Aye, that's him."

"I know the man. Lieutenant Sir Ponsonby Spicer, Baronet."

"Aye, that's him."

"Sell me his timber, and you'll get your revenge."

"Well, that depends on what you are offering."

Adam's stomach tightened at the prospect that he would again bargain poorly and be taken advantage of. His bankers had given him guidelines as to pricing, but the rest was up to him. Still, he knew he was the first Yankee to appear, and he had silver for payment.

As in his negotiations with Penwistle, he made a pretense of poverty and blamed it on his bankers.

"What are you asking?" Adam opened the discussion. "I have limits, and I'm bound by my bankers in Boston."

"One hundred ten pounds lawful money of England for a stick thirty-six inches at the butt, with bigger or smaller sticks either more or less depending on size."

"Ninety," Adam countered.

Pugh laughed. Adam's complexion reddened at his discomfort with the bargaining process.

"Now, Mr. Pugh, I am in earnest. I can purchase enough to fill yonder brig, which for all I know may be your entire lot. And I sail a Yankee ship, not the *Yellowjacket*. A sale to me gives Squampoo revenge for his ear."

Pugh looked at Squampoo, who stood by expressionless.

"And I don't pay in Continental script or bankers notes. I pay cash. All in silver Maria Theresas."

"That so, Cap'n?" Pugh responded, his interest suddenly piqued.

"That is so, Mr. Pugh. And with the prospect of future orders."

Pugh rocked back and forth on his feet while he thought.

"'Tis against my better judgment. You are having the better deal of me. But, all things considered. . . . I can live with ninety. Very well, then, ninety it is."

Adam extended his hand, and they shook.

"Good, we'll load straightway."

"Can't. Timber's still wet. Can't lade it for a few more days or so until it dries out. Otherwise, it would be warped and moldy by the time you got to—where was it you said you was bound?"

"I didn't say. However, 'tis only right your question be answered. We are bound for France."

"By the time you got to France. No, you'll have to wait. Which ain't so bad. There's more sticks to be baulked upriver. Could give you a right full shipment with what we bring down this week. Should be the last of the season's harvest."

"Excellent."

"However, first I have to wind up business with the loggers. Want to travel upriver with us? Spring thaw has started. Should open the river. We leave on the flood tide at dawn."

"Where will we be going?"

"To the land of my people. To the land they call 'the place to watch the fish,'" Squampoo explained with evident pride.

"Also known as Skowhegan," Pugh added.

Skowhegan, Adam thought to himself. Had he seen it on the maps? He wasn't sure.

* * *

Leaving the *Atheling* riding at anchor, her cables drawn taut and her quarterdeck under the command of Mr. Clew, Adam and Seth Hale struck out at dawn as promised. They traveled in birch bark canoes, with Pugh and Squampoo manning the stern of each boat to provide both power and direction. The Captain and his son paddled at the bow of each craft, nervously and on the lookout for rocks and obstructions that might swamp their frail vessels. Each canoe was heavily laden with relief supplies for the loggers upriver. Atop each package of goods stowed amidships was a loaded Brown Bess musket wrapped in oiled seal skin.

They pushed up the river through the narrow, deep channel of The Chops, propelled by the incoming tide surging at two knots, which tugged and buffeted them with its turbulence and whirlpools. The laden canoes rode so low in the water that waves washed over the gunwales from time to time. More than once Adam grasped the side of the canoe, thinking it was about to capsize, and it was with no small measure of relief that they entered the gentler waters of the broad Merrymeeting Bay, where five rivers meet and flow into the Kennebec and the shoreline is softened by a blanket of tidal marshes. Overhead Adam spotted a bald eagle soaring, surely a good omen, he told himself. White pine, spruce, fir, maple, birch, hemlock, and even a few elm and chestnut trees lined the shores around and behind the marshes.

The flood tide propelled them past Swan Island and a good twenty miles upstream before meeting the downstream current. The work of hard paddling now began. The Kennebec was a great and broad river that rushed oceanward in a thousand bubbling torrents fed by the freshets. As they proceeded inland and upriver, all was green. The further they went, the more prominent spruce and fir became along the riverbanks. However, the forests were complex. They defied the simplicity of "evergreen." Rather, they were a variegated tapestry of shades of green: for starters, bottle green, lichen green, moss green, gray green, brown green, new green, sunlight-dappled green, and shadow enclosed green. As they proceeded further north and to higher elevations inland snow still chastened the landscape and ice floes raced down river, broken fragments of the sheets of ice that capped the surface of the water in the lee of clumps of trees and other dark, cool spots. The spring thaw was gaining momentum, however, and Adam sensed an increase in the current of the river as they headed upstream. Adam wondered about the thousands of unknown streams hidden in the wilderness, perhaps never seen by white man or Indian alike, which fed this drainage.

The thin birch bark hull of his canoe made Captain Hale uncomfortable. It was a far cry from the stout white pine of the *Atheling*'s sides: a membrane in fact, a skin that could be pierced by a branch or sharp rock to send the craft and all its contents to the bottom. And where was the bottom in this surging torrent? Why, even if he had a leadsman, he would have been quite incapable of taking a sounding. In all, though travel by Indian canoe was no doubt a form of navigation, a variant on his own calling, it was not to his taste. He would just as unhappily have been mounted on a hunter racing cross country and jumping fences in pursuit of a fox!

Still, the air was clear and bracing under a blue spring sky. A pure and refreshing spray stung his face and soaked his shirt with each lunge of the bow. The giant spruce and fir trees that lined the shores were noble and impenetrable. Here was a rare beauty different from that found on the high seas. Adam realized he was privileged to have this view of America that he had never before known. At length, they came to a quieter stretch of the river, where the hillsides and fir trees reached right down to the water to form two sheer walls. Silently, they glided past these forbidding moraines, pushing forward, up, up, ever up river.

For three days they thus traveled, past rocky outcroppings, through rushing narrows, evading ice floes, past distant columns of smoke from Indian campsites, stopping only to camp at night and roast freshly caught alewives or smelt for dinner, until they reached the base camp of the loggers at Skowhegan. There, some dozen men had camped out the winter in a clearing at the edge of the river. They lived off the land, their supplies supplemented by the seasonal canoe brought up by Pugh or Squampoo. For shelter they huddled in rude cabins formed in a circle round an ox pen. Here they spent the winter until all the logs were baulked and delivered to the waiting timber ships and only then would they return to their farms downstream for the spring planting.

"You've arrived in time for the felling of the Queen Charlotte!" shouted one of the men.

"Saved her for me, did you?" answered Pugh.

Captain Hale wondered about this land in which trees were addressed as ladies, royal ladies at that.

"The Queen Charlotte," Pugh explained, "is the largest white pine for miles around, perhaps on the whole Kennebec. The mast agents marked her with King's Broad Arrow well before the year '76 but never could harvest her during the war. Even your Baronet Ponsonby Spicer knew about her and tried to claim her."

The trek to the Queen Charlotte was no more than a few miles. It led upstream through the forest along one of the half dozen snow-packed roads that radiated into the wilderness from the loggers' camp like spokes from a wheel.

Adam noticed the extraordinary smoothness of the surface of the road as he and Seth accompanied Pugh to the site.

"The loggers swamped this road before the war," Pugh explained, "back when we used to work under guard of soldiers to keep the Indians and bears away. Drove oxen up pulling sledges to break down the undergrowth. Then brought spars down for a year or two, just to even it out. Put it back into shape this winter. Look at that, just as smooth as a mirror."

"Indeed, the road is most uncommon smooth, Mr. Pugh. I am reminded of those Roman roads, like the Fosse Way in England, which to this day are as straight as an arrow and all hardened, 'metaled' they call them, so that they can still bear a horse and cart," the Captain observed.

"Is your knowledge of this at firsthand, Cap'n?" Pugh inquired.

"No. I've only read of it in books—the great Gibbon or some such antiquarian. It is said the Romans hardened their roads by mixing iron ore with the rock and pouring it between the paving stones. When it rained, the ore solidified into a mass of hardened iron, 'metaled' in the truest sense."

"Aha!" Pugh cried. "We do the same here! Not with iron, but with ice. The loggers test the road for hardness with stakes. If they find a soft spot or a dip, they fill it with water. It freezes smooth and hard. 'Metaled' Maine-fashion, I'd say."

"Why do you need such a straight and smooth road?" Seth asked.

"The baulking of a great timber is a most delicate and difficult task. It is of such a size that it can turn no corners and suffer no sudden drops. You will see."

The Queen Charlotte was indeed a great timber. Between three and four feet in diameter at the butt and stretching skyward well over a hundred feet, taller than any inhabited building in the New World, she stood in a clearing all her own and head and shoulders above any other trees in the surrounding forest. The loggers had prepared a bed for her fall consisting of packed and banked snow and a latticework of boughs and branches pruned from neighboring trees. They had already notched through her trunk with their axes to prepare for her felling with a forethought and precision that, with luck, would place her atop the bed prepared to receive her. Six feet above her base, just higher than the necklace of desecration bestowed by the loggers, was emblazoned the unmistakable King's Broad Arrow pointing vertically and facing eastward, toward the coast, toward London and toward the empire.

All fell silent as the loggers began their execution. Each swing of the axe struck the wood with a crack and reverberated across the surrounding hillsides before being muffled by the snowy ground cover. One, two, a team joined in as they worked their way through the final inches at the core of the trunk, letting fly chips that, Adam wondered, might have last seen sunlight in the days when the headsman struck down King Charles I after the English Civil War.

At last the loggers finished and stood by with their axes at rest, head-down in the snow. The only sound was the heaving cacophony of their catching breaths and the rush of flannel over skin as one or two loggers wiped the sweat from their brows. Out of some unspoken respect, all waited for even these sounds to subside to absolute silence.

Adam marveled at the awe commanded by a deaf, dumb, blind, and altogether insensate tree. Surely, it felt and knew nothing of what was befalling it, and the ceremony was entirely in the eyes of the beholders. Still, to these men "it" was a "she" and no ordinary "she" at that. Adam deferred to their sensibilities on the matter.

After an appropriate pause for all to collect themselves, Pugh gave a quick nod to the chief axman. With an economical, almost anticlimactic, stroke he tapped home a wedge placed just so in the cut at the base of the tree. Nothing happened.

And then, ever so slowly, a sighing groan issued from deep within the trunk, and the ponderous timber began to list toward the intended direction. The pitch of the groan accelerated to a shearing scream as the tree rent her innermost fibers under the cant of her toppling height. Quickly, with a rush and a surge, her uppermost branches swept through the air to trace a rapidly descending arc, the chord of which was the following shaft of her trunk.

In no more time than required for Adam to inhale and exhale twice, the Queen Charlotte struck the ground with a blow that jolted him as he stood. The specially prepared bed had softened the landing only in the slightest. The deep, deadening thud of the tree striking the earth reverberated through the hills, as much a temblor to the sense of touch as a crash to the sense of hearing. Where the tree landed a cloud of fine snow and pine needles billowed.

Immediately the crew of loggers swarmed over the fallen tree. One team quickly rolled up and inserted two pairs of large wheels under the trunk, fore and aft, and secured them with chains. Another team set to work stripping the upper reaches of the tree of its branches and growth. A third group, the teamsters, appeared with oxen, some forty-four in all. Of these, thirty-two were hitched in front, with two yokes each at the sides and one at the rear.

In less than an hour all was set, and the teamsters cracked their whips.

"Yo! Yo! Up, Buster! Up boy!"

"Pull, Pasha, pull!"

"Atta boy, Samson. Lean in there!"

The teamsters and loggers bent in with their shoulders. The chains tightened. The axles creaked. Beneath the grunts of the men, the oxen's feet slithered to find a footing. After three tries, traction gripped, and the brute force of man and beast overcame the inertia of gravity. The Queen Charlotte bucked and then settled onto the axles with all her weight. Slowly the strange procession began to move.

Through the clearing and down the swamp toward the Kennebec they lumbered. No more than a few seconds would pass without the crack of whip or shout of exhortation as the teamsters hovered about their charges and urged them onward.

"'Tis a notable sight is it not?" Pugh observed.

"Aye, Mr. Pugh, I've never seen like it before," Captain Hale allowed.

So far the road held the weight without slumping. The swampers had done their work well.

As the swamp entered a decline on its path toward the river the side and rear oxen came into play, pulling back as brakes, to prevent the tree from overrunning the oxen pulling at the fore and crushing them with its mass. It was a most delicate balance of force and counterforce that was applied and adjusted moment by moment under the anxious eyes of the teamsters.

The lead oxen strained up a distant hill while the aft wheels still rolled on the decline. The procession slowed to a creeping pace under the strain. The teamsters renewed their efforts as the great bull whips cracked and shouts and slaps pierced the gathering dusk.

At last, the lead oxen reached the summit of the hill. In a surge of relief, they rushed forward over the rise to the ensuing decline. Instantly the entire aft end of the suddenly leveraged apparatus tilted skyward— tree, wheels, yokes, and oxen. The animals hung suspended in midair as they kicked frantically. The teamsters raced rearward in alarm. They clambered aboard the log and grabbed every available chain to tug downward, while their remaining cohorts in the vanguard spurred the lead oxen forward to clear the summit as rapidly as possible. The tree continued jacked skyward for five, perhaps ten seconds, as the panic-stricken oxen flailed and defecated on the snow. Then, with an abrupt and jarring crash, the entire rear of the apparatus at once re-encountered the earth.

The teamsters inspected the damage: two oxen dying with broken backs, but the rest only shaken. Thankfully, no damage was done to the wooden wheels or axles. The teamsters uncoupled the unfortunate moaning creatures. Squampoo delivered a coup de grace to each with the Brown Bess muskets. No sooner had the echo of the second shot died in the distant hills than they passed the word back up the swamp to bring up a spare pair of beasts. With barely a half hour lost, the new oxen were teamed into the old yoke, and the procession resumed.

Just at nightfall the Queen Charlotte reached the banks of the Kennebec. Driving the oxen directly into the shallows of the river, the teamsters positioned the tree for unloading. They let slip the chains that bound the great mast to the rig and with a heave launched her into the current.

"She'll travel all night and the next day from Skowhegan with the current and be at the mouth of the river before we will," Pugh explained.

Adam, Seth, Pugh, and Squampoo followed downstream at the crack of dawn two days later. Their lightened canoes made quick work of the passage. Dodging rocks and rapids, they shot by dusk the distance whose upriver passage had extorted three days of toil.

The Queen Charlotte had already arrived at the mast men's weir at the mouth of the river. They were drying her out from her downstream passage. In a few days, they hewed her into a sixteen-sided column more closely resembling the mast she was destined to become. She was then ladened on the *Atheling*'s gun deck. It was a tight fit. Hawsed to the masts at mid-deck, she allowed just enough room for the guns to be run in and out. The Queen Charlotte joined the other masts and spars from the season's harvest, which the crew had earlier stowed to capacity on the upper and orlop decks.

Seth, acting as supercargo on the voyage, carefully checked the inventory in his ledger book.

"You sure you don't want the quintals of cod?" Pugh inquired one more time as he joined the Captain and his son in the ship's cabin for the final accounting. "Five percent off the already reasonable price. Won't regret it if you take 'em."

Seth hesitated. He darted a glance at his father.

"Ready market. Easy profit. You won't regret it," Pugh reiterated.

Captain Hale gave no hint of direction to his son.

"Will you entertain an offer, Mr. Pugh?" Seth asked.

"Against my better judgment. But I'm listening."

"Fifteen percent off and I'll take the whole lot."

Adam approved the prudence of his son's parsimoniousness as Pugh silently weighed the offer.

"Done."

"Very well then, Mr. Pugh, lade the barrels."

"All two thousand?"

"Why, yes! All two thousand!" And then, in an aside to his father, "Lord knows where we'll put them."

"Thankee, Mr. Hale. You won't regret it for a minute. We'll do it straightway."

Seth counted out the silver Maria Theresas from the ship's strongbox for the timber and the fish. It was more money than he had ever seen. Still, he had it on his father's authority that the price was fair. The mast men were eager for the business and happy to trade with a fellow Yankee before another English squadron descended upon them demanding the masts for nothing.

"It was a pleasure doing business, Mr. Pugh," Captain Hale announced as he stuck out his right hand to conclude the deal.

Pugh took it and shook with earnestness.

"One thing, Cap'n. Don't forget the frigate with that Baronet cove. They're a spiteful crew. Keep your lookout sharp."

"But the war is over. There's nothing they can do to us."

"Nothing they're supposed to do to you. But, give them half a chance . . . You saw what he did to Squampoo."

"Besides," the Captain added. "They told you they were proceeding to Halifax and then no doubt running with the Westerlies home to England. We're headed nowhere near Halifax. For us, it's straight for the Azores and thence to Toulon in the Mediterranean. Our paths will never cross."

Captain Hale laughed heartily as he dismissed Pugh's concern with a wave of his proffered hand.

* * *

The *Atheling*'s final stop in the New World was Man o' War Brook, a freshwater stream that tumbled between St. Sauveur and Acadia Mountains on Mount Desert Island's Somes Sound, the only fjord in America. Adam guided the ship half a league up the deep Sound, past the sheer cliffs, dropped anchor and had his crew refresh the water supply in the casks from the waterfall. The brook was known to the Royal Navy, whose ships took on water there going back into the colonial period. Adam's knowledge of the brook came from his early days in the coastal trade.

4

Live Firing

1784—Part III

"We were so close to Flamborough Head in Yorkshire that the shepherds lined the cliffs to watch the action. The *Bonhomme Richard* was just here as she raised the signal for the chase," Hiram Clew explained as he plonked down the salt cellar to mark the ship's position. Clew was warming to his favorite after-dinner entertainment, the recounting of the engagement between the *Bonhomme Richard* and *Serapis*, as witnessed and participated in by Lieutenant Hiram Clew, United States Navy. Adam and Seth Hale both had heard the story often enough on the still-young voyage to know precisely what came next.

"We had just been raiding off the Orkneys, taking prizes right and left, when we spotted forty-one sail of merchantmen headed in convoy from the Baltic under the protection of the *Serapis*, forty-four guns, and the *Countess of Scarborough*, twenty-two guns. Captain Jones raised the signal to give chase, and the merchantmen all crowded sail toward the shore while the gunboats made the disposition for battle."

Captain Hale looked briefly at the three recently drained wine bottles that stood in a cluster in representation of the fleeing British merchant fleet. Captain Hale was grateful that the decanter of port before him had not yet been enlisted in action. Nor had the bowl of walnuts. Despite the Captain's clear orders for his favorite boiled dinner, Sanchez had served up *nuvem de bacalhau*, a singular concoction of cod fish and whipped potatoes that was as light and heavenly as its name—"clouds of cod"—implied. All had agreed that a ship had never sailed so well on its stomach as the *Atheling* this voyage. The meal over, Sanchez had stripped the Captain's table of its cloth and the three well-sated officers sat round enjoying port and leisurely conversation. Before Adam stood a large mound of cracked and shattered walnut shells, while his massive hands continued to work with immoderate zeal the remaining supply. Perhaps it was the Captain's unspoken prerogative, but neither his son nor his First Mate asked to share in what amounted to his private stash.

"To understand the battle," Clew continued, "you must realize that the *Bonhomme Richard* was a lumbering East Indiaman that had been condemned by her owners. She was slow, she couldn't maneuver, and she leaked like a sieve."

Not so the *Atheling*, thought Adam. Her stout Maine timbers and privateer's rake made her a delight of seaworthiness. Though heavily laden, her cargo of wood gave her a buoyancy and lightness that the Captain had not expected. As a result, she was making most uncommon good time. She was now well into the Gulf Stream and sailing straight before the wind under a full head of canvas. With cocked ear the Captain listened for the rush of water against her hull as she plied through the complacent early spring North Atlantic under a cooperative breeze. But all he heard were the sounds, equally reassuring to be sure, of the relaxed afternoon watch: Sanchez lounging outside the cabin door plucking a *guitarrada* on his mandolin and, farther off on the forecastle, the Irish top hands—no doubt Seamus, Padraig, and Kevin, for Adam had made a point of learning all hands' names within the first week—played a lilting and lively hornpipe. It was the time of day on one of those rare days when the thousand cares of running a ship were at rest and a Captain could find serenity in simply being the Captain.

By now, Clew was well into his narrative before Seth's rapt ears. Somehow, the oft-told story of the battle was one of those tales, like a national epic, that never lost in the retelling. That this was so for a youth, who wanted nothing more than to command a ship like his father and who thirsted for adventure on the high seas, was not surprising. That it was also so for a hardened sea dog like his father was perhaps more surprising. But try as he might to drift into reverie, Captain Adam Hale continually found himself dragged back into Hiram Clew's riveting tale.

"The ships were locked in mortal combat. The very first broadside let loose at point-blank range by the *Serapis* struck home in our gun room and exploded three of our old eighteen pounders, killing their crews. The British aimed low, trying to sink us at the waterline and destroy our gun deck. I was in command of the forward guns. It was a murderous fire, directly into us. Our gun crews began to break and abandon their stations. Then, all of a sudden, when the tide had all but run against us, Captain Jones maneuvered the ship so cleverly that the *Serapis's* bowsprit rammed across our poop and entangled in the mizzen rigging. Captain Jones himself, already astride the quarterdeck, set the grappling hooks for our boarding parties. This maneuver blocked the starboard guns of the enemy, which were behind closed ports. At that moment the English captain, Pearson he was, opened fire directly through the closed gun ports. Deadly splinters and massive eighteen pound balls, fired from not six feet away, came tearing through the gun deck. It was a showering wall of death, repeated time and time again, that mowed down scores of our gunners. The scuppers could not carry off the blood and gore, which ran ankle deep on the gun deck. Those who remained soon fled to the top deck. There we saw that the ship was on fire and sinking. Captain Jones sat atop a chicken crate on deck amid the fallen rigging and spars and shattered destruction. 'Strike! Strike! Strike your colors!' the British captain shouted through his horn. 'Should we strike, sir?' asked the ship's carpenter as he stood before Captain Jones. For a moment the captain sat without expression, as if he had not heard. Then he leapt to his feet, drew a pistol from his belt and almost knocked down the carpenter who stood by ready to lower the Stars and Stripes. 'Tell Captain Pearson I have not yet begun to fight!' he bellowed as he rallied the men and led the boarding party. That turned the tide."

"So it wasn't the guns that decided the match but hand-to-hand combat?" Seth asked.

"The *Bonhomme Richard* was no match for the *Serapis* from the start. Captain Jones had wanted to arm her with powerful eighteen-pounder long guns, but the surveyors said her timbers wouldn't support their weight. So she wound up a hodgepodge of lesser guns. It was a strange pot of chowder that fired only two hundred fifty pounds of metal on a broadside at best. This was no match to the *Serapis*'s armament of forty-four new eighteen-pounders, which threw seven hundred and ninety-two pounds of metal or almost four hundred pounds at a broadside."

"You know your gunnery, Mr. Clew. And I thought all Nantucket whalers were Quaker people who thought it against their principles to engage in warfare."

Clew chortled a ratchety cackle. "'Tis true, Captain, we are Quakers. But there are Quakers, and there are Quakers. I am, in a manner of speaking, a *practical* Quaker. Never underestimate a practical Quaker."

"I once knew a Quaker lass," the Captain mused. "Chaste and pure in her simple brown dress, the brightness of her eyes and her smile spoke most eloquent. I don't think she was a practical Quaker, though. Well, Mr. Clew, being a practical Quaker, what would you estimate our chances of prevailing against the *Yellowjacket* if engaged?"

"She being a frigate of thirty-six guns, probably eighteen-pounders?" Captain Hale nodded.

"Against our fourteen six-pounders? Why, it don't even compute. We'd be splinter board at the first broadside. Seamanship would have to carry the day if we was to engage. At least on the defensive side of the ledger. We might get a lucky shot or two. But with no weight of metal and no long-range big guns, it would likely be fatal to us were we to allow her within striking range."

"In other words, we'd better run."

"I would prepare to run and fight both. But to run first—however, lady luck does not always give the choice."

"'Tis a good thing, then, that I prevailed upon the bankers to pay for extra powder and shot. If Seth hadn't found a cheap supply at the Naval Yard in Boston because of the disbanding of the Navy I doubt they'd have obliged. Still, with no Navy to protect us and hostilities lurking about, we had no choice. The way I presented it to the bankers was that it was more economical than insuring the ship with Lloyds."

Clew and Seth both laughed.

"And Lloyds in any event have ceased to cover American bottoms," Seth added.

"We've enough for practice, live-firing, I take it?" asked Clew.

"Indeed, we do, Mr. Clew. And we shall begin gunnery practice tomorrow immediately following the noon observation."

* * *

Naval tradition has it that it is not noon until the Captain says so. Therefore Captain Hale stood on the quarterdeck awaiting the signal. As always, the sailing master took the observation, touched his hat, and reported to Mr. Clew that it was twelve o'clock. Mr. Clew then ordered Seth Hale, as second officer and in the absence of a midshipman, to approach the Captain on the lofty quarterdeck and humbly apprise him of the sailing master's suggestion.

"Twelve o'clock has been reported, sir," Seth informed his father.

"Make it so!" Captain Hale thundered according to prescribed etiquette, thinking to himself with just a hint of irreverence, "Well, indeed it must be so."

And Seth struck the bell eight times, making it noon.

"Inform Mr. Clew to commence the gunnery practice," Captain Hale next informed his son, who scurried below to execute his command.

Captain Hale removed his timepiece. Under Clew's tutelage he had run through the elements of gunnery the evening before. He had quickly appreciated that speed of fire, as much as or more than accuracy, determined success in gunnery. Beyond that, he had learned that gunnery was an art more than a science, with little in the way of prescribed formality than the fifteen gunnery orders set forth in *Falconer's Dictionary* which in turn were based on the drills introduced by Admiral Anson at the time of the Seven Years War. In an evening's study Adam had mastered these elemental details and now stood ready to inspect their implementation.

Before him stretched the seven manned guns of the port side—one complete broadside ready to go into action with live firing.

"Silence!" shouted Mr. Clew to the crews, as demanded by Anson. Not that it mattered, for each crew had long since taken its position and stood unmoving in anticipation of the next command. There at the Number One gun stood the foretopman Phelps as captain of his three-man crew—far leaner than the five or six-man crew allotted each gun on a British or American man-of-war. However, Phelps was a former Navy man, and each gun crew was captained by one of Clew's veterans. Phelps and his two subordinates stood in anticipation, stripped to the waist, their pigtails wrapped in bandanas and almost audible in their breathing. At their feet rested the six-pound shot in the wooden racks in which it had been brought up from the magazine, as well as the cartridges containing the volatile powder encased in protective boxes to guard against sparks. Also in neat order at their feet were the squat match tubs and piles of wadding, while erect in their hands like so many pikes stood the rammer, sponge and worm, and, fastened neatly nearby, the linstock with its fuming match.

All remained silent, except for the gentle swell and creak of the ship as she made her way through the water. Adam waited. A whiff from the smoldering matches made its way to his nose and infused his lungs with excitement. Adam knew in an instant that he had found a blood sport that he would love.

"Prepare for action!" Clew bellowed at the top of his lungs.

As one, the crews sprang to life. They removed the tampion from each gun, leaving it to dangle from the muzzle, and cast loose the muzzle lashing. In quick order they then inserted the quoin to depress the barrel and ran it out through the port and back in.

Satisfied that his instructions were executed by each crew, Clew then ordered, "Worm and sponge!"

Mr. Clew had told Adam that this exercise was important in the heat of battle to remove particles of burning cartridge from the prior shot before inserting the new charge. The crews ran through it in professional order. They rammed the sponge to the bottom of the gun's chamber, twisted it around to extinguish any remnant of fire and withdrew it, taking care to strike it three times against the muzzle of the gun to knock off any sparks that may have accompanied it out of the barrel. They then smartly turned the long-handled sponge downside up to use it as a rammer. Dropping the cartridge in the muzzle, bottom-end first, seam downward and followed by a wad, they drove the charge home with the rammer until it met the priming wire placed in the vent by the captain of the crew. As soon as the captain shouted "Home!" the rammer withdrew the pole.

Next came the shot, followed by a wad and rammed home in identical fashion.

"Prepare for firing!" came Clew's ensuing order. The captain of each crew pricked a hole in the cartridge with a sharp wire inserted through the touch hole. He then funneled more powder down the touch hole from his powder horn.

"Ready! Aim!" Clew screamed, once he was satisfied that all guns were primed.

On the port side of the *Atheling*, not fifty yards distant, floated a string of barrels towed in place by the ship's jolly boat. The boat had cut them loose and now stood off.

Each crew grabbed hold of the training tackle. Acting under their gun captain's orders, they ran out the gun and adjusted it toward a bobbing barrel. Inserting handspikes, the crew further adjusted each recalcitrant gun and, jimmying quoins at the breech, leveraged the muzzle to an approximation of the proper elevation. When all the nervous adjustments were accomplished, Clew looked up to the quarterdeck for Captain Hale's final order.

The Captain knew that in action the broadside should be fired on the downward roll of the ship. The theory was that if there were a delay in firing the ball would strike the surface of the water and bounce into its intended target, the enemy's hull. Captain Hale felt the ship gently rise to the top of its roll and hesitate. He counted silently to himself, "One. Two. Three."

At the count of three he gave the direct order himself.

"Commence firing!"

The captains of the gun crews touched the matches to the holes. Instantly, the entire starboard side of the ship exploded in a deafening blast. The recoil of the guns as they leapt back on their tackles sent a sharp shudder through the ship from stern to bow, and for an instant it seemed as if the forward motion of the ship were arrested as she absorbed the impact of the broadside. However, her stout Maine timbers held and bounced back with resilience.

Captain Hale strained his eyes through the smoke to see the barrels. In quick succession a string of seven plumes of water rose about the vicinity of the barrels: four short, one way long, and, dearest to the Captain's heart, two direct smashes of the targets. The result was beyond reasonable expectation and confirmed the Americans' much vaunted expertise in marksmanship.

Captain Hale checked his timepiece: an abysmal six minutes for the single broadside. His crew would have to better that rate by a third in order to stand up against a warship. And, by God, they would! From now on, there would be gunnery exercise each day, dry firing to preserve ammunition but with live firing at the Captain's pleasure. Speed must be improved! Duty demanded it. Captain Hale studied the men's excited faces, all turned toward him in uplifted anticipation of his judgment. The Captain, being Adam who had climbed the ratlines in his youth, knew when to command and when to inspire. Reaching into his waistcoat pocket, he withdrew a gold sovereign.

"Now, hear you well, my good men! Whosoever shall best the record of three broadsides in five minutes shall win this gold-piece! Each day shall we practice, and the offer shall be outstanding until it is claimed!" He held the coin up until it caught the glint of the sun and reflected it round about the eyes of the whole crew.

"Upon my honor, the sovereign belongs to the crew that fires three rounds in five or less!"

* * *

The Azores were an obligatory stop on any mid-Atlantic crossing to take on fresh water, fruit, and meat. The crew had been looking forward to raising the islands for weeks.

Ominous clouds skirted the horizon portside as the lookout cried "Land! Ho!" at dusk one evening. Captain Hale scrambled to the deck to see for himself. There in the distance stood the sentinel peak of the dormant volcano Mount Pico, which was always the first sign of the islands spotted by mariners traveling from the west.

"We'll lay off for the night," Adam ordered Mr. Clew. He knew that the approaches to the islands were too tricky to navigate in the dark.

The next morning, as they approached closer, the eight islands that comprised the chain beyond the island of Pico were at first perceptible as pencil lines on the horizon. Steering for an anchorage at Fayal, Adam observed the islands to be in fact craggy green volcanic mountains with rich black soil, lush green vegetation, and deep coldwater harbors. Two Nantucket whalers rode at anchor in the roads at Fayal while their crews engaged in "gamming" or exchanging visits. The *Atheling* took advantage of the homeward bound of the two whalers to dispatch packets of letters to loved ones in Falmouth. However, the *Atheling* did not tarry long. In its day and a half in the port at Fayal, the ship took on provisions while Captain Hale paid a courtesy call on the Governor. A wily scoundrel of no small presumption, he demanded and received a ten-dollar anchorage fee from the Captain and then hinted that a compliment for himself might be in order. The Captain declined and, pleading the press of business, rushed across town to call on the American Consul, a Mr. Dabney from Virginia. The Consul was a gentle and mannerly man with an unhurried speech and casual view of life that Adam found at once reassuring and alien. It was with no small reflection on the regional differences in temperament among his fellow countrymen that Adam rode in a donkey cart back to the waterfront and his waiting ship.

Seth had replenished the hold quickly and cheaply, and Adam was pleased to weigh anchor straightaway. As the ship left port and headed east, she passed a Portuguese brig at anchor whose deck was crowded with listless naked Africans in chains who had been brought up for an "airing" in the thin spring chill. Bought for three crowns a head in the Gambia, they were destined for the block in Charleston or Savannah. Captain Hale at first averted his eyes but then called Seth to his side on the quarterdeck.

"There, son, is the greatest shame of mankind. Preacher Wesley says that those who engage in that vile trade are doomed to hell. Doomed—as well they should be."

"Yes, Fid. God grant that we never see that sight again." And for the longest moment father and son shared the gift of intimacy.

Adam and Seth were so preoccupied with the passing panorama of the doomed slaves that they did not notice a convoy of three ships far astern slip into the roads of the islands on the western horizon.

5

The Chase

1784—Part IV

"April 2. 37 degrees 13' N. Approx. 22 degrees W. Wind strong and steady at W. Course ESE. Seven days out of Fayal."

Adam set down his turkey quill pen beside the ship's log. The cryptic entry hardly did justice to the fit and feel of the dawning day at sea. Even in the privacy of his cabin, the Captain could discern a plethora of sounds and sensations that were part of the well-worn fabric of life at sea. The aroma from the steaming bowl of Angolan coffee, rich and dark and steeped from beans procured at Fayal, rose to stimulate his senses. The glint of sunlight creeping through the cabin windows promised a clear day with fine sailing. The song of the rigging in the wind, a low hum to which the captain's ear, awake or asleep, was constantly attuned, held a pitch that was a veritable hymn of joy. Outside the cabin door, the abrading clunks of the hands holystoning the deck told him that all was well and shipshape under Mr. Clew's watchful single eye. The gold sovereign had passed from his hand to the Number Three gun crew the day before, as the five-minute mark had been met and exceeded. These joys, and many more, belonged in the log if only convention allowed. For Captain Adam Hale, however, they would be written in the log of his heart.

A loud banging at the door jarred his reverie.

"Cap'n Hadam! Cap'n Hadam!" Sanchez shouted with the annoying aspirated "h" inserted by most Portuguese before English words beginning with the letter "a" ("Hale" was all but impossible for Sanchez to pronounce, and the Captain reluctantly tolerated Sanchez's use of his Christian name).

"Cap'n Hadam! A ship! A ship!"

Adam sprang to his feet and bolted through the door to the quarter-deck. Seeing him exit, the lookout with telescope at his eye in the main topmast shouted anew for the Captain's benefit.

"Ship ho! Ship ho! Ship ho on the port beam!"

Adam strained his eyes but could see nothing.

Not one to wait, he hoisted his considerable bulk into the mainmast shroud and scrambled up the roping with startling agility, like a monkey in its favorite tree. He was panting from his rapid ascent by the time he reached the yard that was the lookout's perch.

"Is she hull up yet?"

"No, sir. But she's a three-master, square-rigged and crowding canvas!"

"Hand me the telescope!"

Adam grabbed the leather-bound brass tube and brought the distant ship into focus. She was so far away that only her sails were visible and even they were a blur which admitted of no nationality.

However, she was as the foretopman had said. Spreading canvas out of all reason, she was set on a course which would overtake the *Atheling* in short order. If only he could see her hull! Was she a merchantman racing for the Strait of Gibraltar like himself? Or was she a gunship intent on a mission? Had she seen the *Atheling* before she herself was spotted?

Adam pondered the possibilities as he let himself down a rope in the quick descent favored by top hands. As soon as his feet touched the quarterdeck he wasted no time.

"Mr. Hale," he ordered his son, "heave the log straightway."

Instantly the log crew sprang into action. They measured out the knotted rope and swung the wooden board at its end into the water. Racing to count the time as the line paid out, they quickly took the measure of the ship's speed.

"Three and a half knots, sir," reported Seth.

A tight line drew across the Captain's lips. He looked skyward and silently took the gauge of the weather.

"Spread the topgallants and topgallant studding sails," he coolly ordered. If it would be a race, he would give them a run for their money. He knew the *Atheling* was a well-built ship with good sailing qualities. Now he would find out whether her privateer's rake would give her the speed to best a charging large square-rigger hell-bent on overhauling her. If there were risks of split sails or yardarms carried away in such action, then so be it.

As soon as he voiced his order, a line of men scurried up the shrouds of each mast, spread out along the yards and unfurled the high-flying sails. They sheeted the canvas home, and the ship leapt forward with unaccustomed alacrity. Her bow-waves spread out like knife pleats as she cut through the brine. The taut rigging strained at the blocks. The wind whipped at Adam's ears. The hull creaked with a groan as she bent herself into the new burden. But those stout Maine masts with their sweeping rake stood proud and powered the ship forward without a hint of hesitation. She indeed had the sailing qualities of a privateer: uncommon speed, agility, and purpose. The only question that plagued Captain Hale was whether she had enough.

That afternoon, with the sounding of four bells and the prospect of dinner, the question of what was enough advanced like a creeping corrosion across the Captain's sense of well-being. The problem was that, like most Yankee sailors, Adam Hale did not know where he was. Seated at his charts, he confided his concerns to his two mates.

"I've fixed the latitude without problem. But there's no reckoning the longitude! Not by doing lunars under this cloud cover! Or with this timepiece!" he said as he flung his crude Boston-made pocket watch on the table. "If only I had a fine London chronometer! Is it true what they say, Mr. Clew, that every British warship is fitted out with Harrison's fine new invention?"

"Many are, I fear."

"So they know precisely their whereabouts at any given moment?"

"Undoubtedly so."

"Blast!" Adam exclaimed as he clenched his fist. "There's no way of knowing with certainty how many days we are to the Strait of Gibraltar! How many days do we have to run before that ship overhauls us? Three? Four? None of us has ever sailed these waters before. I might tell you that Fayal is 1,400 nautical miles, give or take, from the Strait, but what does it serve? We are seven days out, but I cannot calculate our position to know if we'll reach the Mediterranean and the safety of the French fleet in time."

"Assuming, of course, she is a hostile ship that follows us," ventured Seth.

"An assumption we cannot put to the test," Adam shot back. "Not with the weather gauge she has on us now. She could pick the time and place of battle and hammer us to pieces."

"Do you suppose she is the *Yellowjacket?*" Seth continued.

"I'd be willing to wager on it," replied Adam. "Remember the bad weather to our north as we came into the Azores. Those squalls could have driven the Halifax convoy more southerly as they sailed for England. And, if so, they almost certainly would have put in at Fayal."

"Where they might have learned of our passage?"

"No doubt. And that weasel of a Governor would have been just the man to have volunteered the intelligence of our visit, particularly given that I did not see fit to ante up to his demand for a gratuity. Oh, Lord, will I never learn the ways of the world?" the Captain said, as he slapped his forehead in disgust.

* * *

The next morning the Captain learned three facts of indisputable significance.

Up at first light, he immediately went to the quarterdeck to check the position of the pursuing ship. Though at some distance, she stood doggedly off the port beam, hull up now and in full view. She was gaining on the *Atheling*. Adam anxiously extended the telescope without bothering to climb the rigging for a better view.

As he did so, the second fact he learned was that she was a frigate. As Adam well knew, a frigate was the most versatile and feared ship in the

Royal Navy. With her speed and agility, she was ideally suited to cutting out expeditions and single-ship combat. Her single gun deck placed high above the waterline meant she could heel more than a larger ship of the line and carry voluminous sail for speed, even in heavy weather. With a complement of hundreds of able seamen, warrant officers, boatswain's mates, quartermasters, gunner's mates, petty officers, yeomen of the store-room, and marines, she was well and amply sailed. Even her gun crews boasted six men to the American's three. And her armament was formidable. Adam counted fourteen ports running the length of her gun deck, which meant she was undoubtedly the twenty-eight gun *Yellowjacket*, a fact all but confirmed by the now-visible British ensign that whipped at her stern through the circle of his spyglass.

The third fact that Adam learned was that the wind had freshened overnight. He would have to crowd on more canvas if he were to have any hope of fleeing. None of this news was good, the Captain knew, and he resolved to keep it to himself and his mates.

Seth and Clew found the Captain taciturn and bleak as he mulled over his coffee and the orders for the day as they met afterward in the Captain's cabin.

"Are we two, three days from the Strait?" Seth asked.

"I only wish I knew. I only wish we had a plan, for she's sure to overhaul us. Even before then we will be within the reach of her long guns. To capture such a valuable supply of timber—why I imagine it's enough to furnish the Channel Fleet for several years—would make a hero of our pursuer. If only we had a plan . . ."

Neither Seth nor Clew had a plan. They therefore crept out and went silently about their duties on deck. Every so often they would steal a glance over their shoulder at the distant frigate. Its course was unerring and tenacious. And each hour it seemed to edge perceptibly closer.

The *Atheling*, for her part, went about her routine as always. There was no choice, even though Seth overheard a forecastle hand swear he had seen a mermaid—an unlucky omen foretelling disaster, as the beautiful sirens were known to sing to people and to enchant them and to lure them to their doom.

Still, there were lines to be spliced, shrouds to be tarred, and observations to be taken. The wind had piped up even more under overcast skies, and particular attention had to be paid to the topgallants and topgallant studding sails which the Captain had ordered spread in order to gain speed. The ship was straining at full speed now with spray flying off her bow at each wave. So far no canvas had split, no spars had been carried away in the stiff wind. For that all hands were grateful. The two ships simply raced forward, silently, rapidly, on closely parallel tracks.

That afternoon the Captain took the helm. From years of practice, his hands folded instinctively about the handles, almost at ease as soon as they touched the wood, much as a master carver's would be wrapped about a chisel. Adam reflected that when one touches the ship's wheel other diversions fall away as mere distractions and false sirens.

At dinner Adam, Seth, and Clew sat silently about the table. Sanchez had served up a cold confection of salt pork, peas, and biscuits that did little to humor the officers. Washed down with water rather than beer on the Captain's order, the meal had engendered little conversation. The Captain worked his usual stash of post-meal walnuts in utter silence. His mind was preoccupied, spinning, off in some distant latitude of planning and plotting upon which neither mate dared intrude.

"What do you suppose they are thinking on board her today?" Seth asked Clew as his gaze wandered portside.

"All will be deathly quiet now," replied Clew. "They will have prepared for battle. I've seen it a dozen times: the solemn statues of the men beside their guns swallowing choked fears, the decks swept clean. On a frigate that size every bulkhead is dismantled, the netting is spread in a canopy to catch falling spars and splinters, the gunroom dining table is unbolted and stowed, all the seamen's chests are piled into the hold. Gone are the officers' quarters, gone are the crew's quarters, gone are the class distinctions by which the daily life of the ship is run. One ship emerges, in a clean sweep of deck ready for action. 'Tis a marvel to behold. And the grim preparations too! Stretchers made of rails and old sail cloth appear from the sailmaker's room and are stacked on deck. The surgeon arranges the portable amputation tables in the cockpit for his makeshift operating theatre. Fire screens are set up at strategic intervals. Cannonballs are stacked in pyramids beside the guns. Wads the size of Gouda cheeses hang within easy reach from the beams. Match tubs are set just so. Runners are stationed to convey shot and powder up from the magazine to replenish the supply during battle. And the men will be dressed most unusual, too, ready for the drama. The British officers are given to fighting as dandies dance the minuet, which is to say, attired in silk stockings. They reckon that in the event of a leg wound the surgeon can cut off the silk stocking more easily than one of cotton, which adheres to the flesh and works its way into the wound. They will fight in their best dress uniform, too. Not like our practical and frugal Yankee officer, who will wear his oldest suit into battle, knowing that if it must be shredded to ribbons far better be it an old offhand coat than one better reserved for ceremony or his own burial. And so it is aboard our British man-o-war just now. All quiet, all grim, all ready, all waiting."

"I judge us to be a pale mirror of the same," Seth observed.

"A mirror! A mirror!" Adam exclaimed as he sprang from the table. "I have it! Just so! A mirror indeed! A deceitful, lying, one-way mirror will be our plan! Thank you, gentlemen!"

Seth and Clew looked at each other in incomprehension, but before they could ask the Captain what he meant he had bounded out of the cabin.

That evening a buoyant Captain Hale honored his crew with a visit to their forecastle quarters at suppertime. The room, which housed the thirty men for the length of the voyage, was ill-ventilated and dark, save for the weak beam bestowed by a sole candle. The crew's hammocks swung in rows as straight and narrow as burial shrouds. A small table at the center of the room and the seamen's chests lashed to the floor were the sole furnishings, except for a few bottles of rum misleadingly labeled "camphor." Their utensils went no further than tin plates and a bucket of water, with a single cup for the use of all hands. The crew had just settled down to a supper of left-over longlick. The familiar aroma of its confections—tea, coffee, and molasses—rose from their bowls to greet the Captain.

So did the crew as the Captain entered.

"Keep you seats, men. I've just come by to wish you well on the morrow."

Adam studied the men's faces in the flickering candlelight as he spoke. Some were gaunt and weather-beaten, others bearded and unkempt. But to a man their eyes burned bright and attentive. They were Falmouth men and ready to revenge Mowat.

"Beggin' your pardon, sir," volunteered the foretopman Phelps who commanded the Number One gun, for the *Atheling* was not one of those rigid Navy ships where a sailor spoke to the Captain only if first spoken to.

"Yes, Phelps, what is it?"

"We of the crew, we was thinkin.' If it be any question of goin' into battle 'gainst the frigate, don't stop on our account. We've drilled, and we're ready. We'll follow where you go. We want to take her on."

"Thank you, Phelps." Adam looked about the table. All heads were nodding in agreement.

"One thing further, Captain," Phelps volunteered. "We of the crew are Falmouth men, and we have made up something special for tomorrow."

Phelps nudged one of his mates. "Show it to the Captain."

The seaman leaned over into a shot crate by the table and offered up a six-pound ball. Across the breadth of its circumference, written in bright orange paint, were the words "Remember Mowat."

"Well said, Phelps. Falmouth would be proud. Load it, and I give you my word it will be the first shot fired when we engage, be it tomorrow, be it thereafter."

"Aye, aye, sir," replied Phelps with a beaming smile.

"Now, gentlemen, 'tis dusk," the Captain admonished, "and all lights must be doused."

With that, he licked his fingers and quenched the candle flame. The velvet of darkness enveloped all.

* * *

The next day dawned dirty. A brutish mass of black clouds rose out of the west.

"They'll be bringing rain and more wind," Clew confirmed the obvious to Adam, who peered through his glass at the much closer frigate.

"No matter, as long as the canvas holds. Bye the bye, she is the *Yellowjacket*. I can smoke her figurehead painted all yellow and black like some great bee or wasp."

"She's close to being able to reach us with her long guns. We'll see action today, of that I'm certain."

"If we don't clear the Strait and find the protection of the French fleet first."

"Surely today we shall."

"Surely today."

No sooner had the Captain spoken than a plume of water rose a hundred yards off the port side of the ship, followed several seconds later by a distant boom.

"They are limbering up the long guns," Clew advised.

Adam looked skyward.

"I have no more canvas to spread."

For the next four hours the Captain paced the quarterdeck. His concentration was ruptured every fifteen minutes or so as a plume of water shot up in the vicinity of the ship, followed by an ever-closer report of the gun that had sent the eighteen-pound ball probing. Still, the *Atheling*'s canvas held as the ship pounded forward.

* * *

The ceremony of the noon observation had barely commenced when the foremast lookout cried at the top of his lungs:

"Land ho! Land ho! Land and Gibraltar ho!"

All hands dropped what they were doing, and a great cheer rose up.

Those who were close to him saw a smile creep across Captain Hale's lips and the words "Well done, *Atheling*," silently mouthed.

Indeed, there in the faintest distance rose the prodigious hump of rock like a gray whale, while the Er Rif Mountains of the Maghreb were strung out like her progeny at the horizon.

By late afternoon the line of squalls overtook both ships and lashed them with a fury of wind and rain. A string of early season thunderstorms ripped through the skies. Every few minutes, flashing sheets of lightning illuminated the gloom, only to be chased by rolling thunder that reverberated across the open ocean and cliffs of Spain and North Africa as if in an amphitheater. Against the black clouds that loomed from the western horizon to high overhead the *Yellowjacket*'s enormous spread of canvas stood out pure and white, as if she were virtue incarnate. Adam wondered how long she could keep it up. As soon as the strong westerly winds of the Vendeval had begun to scour through the passage to the Strait he had ordered the topsails, mainsails, and studding sails reefed to prevent them from splitting. The *Atheling* was thus making the passage under jibs only, with her lead over the *Yellowjacket* rapidly dissipating.

Adam stood next to the wheelhouse with his feet stoutly planted on the heaving deck. Cowled in an oilskin slicker and wet to the bone, he resembled a Dark Ages abbot whose hermitage perched on some God-forsaken promontory jutting into the sea. The Captain was no contemplative, however. He was in a high state of excitement, indeed joy. Every few minutes he could not resist reaching over and taking the wheel from the able-bodied seaman whose job it was to steer the ship.

"No, no! Just this way," he shouted over the din as he turned the wheel a few degrees. "Steer as close as possible to the African coast."

The thunder roared, and the wind howled like a pack of hyenas through the rigging aloft. As the bow plunged into the trough of each wave and rose up, the ship's fore deck was awash in seawater and salt spray. There was no longer any discerning the reports of the *Yellowjacket*'s long guns from the boom of the thunder. Adam told himself not to look backward, and for the better part of an hour, as the ship raced into the roads of the Strait, he maintained his discipline. But at last curiosity overhauled him, and he permitted himself a sternward glance. As he did, a high-pitched scream sounded overhead, and a tangled mass of spar and rigging crashed to the deck.

"Bar shot!" shouted Mr. Clew into his ear. "They're trying to take down our rigging!"

Adam carefully assessed the ships' bearings. The *Atheling* was well within the Strait now. The *Yellowjacket* lagged behind in the open sea but in a matter of time would overhaul her. Sheets of rain fell between the two ships and beyond through the Strait in the waning afternoon daylight.

"Her visibility is poor, is it not, Mr. Clew?" Adam asked.

"She can see barely beyond our bow."

"Even from her topmost lookout?"

"What! In this weather? Even from her topmost lookout, to be sure!"

"And our vision extends well into the Strait and beyond."

"On and off most surely it does."

"Just as I had calculated, Mr. Clew. Seth!" Adam called. "Raise the signal flags. Salute Admiral De Grasse's squadron dead ahead and ask his permission to fall in with their convoy."

"But Fid," Seth stammered, "there is no French squadron ahead."

"I know, I know," Adam replied impatiently. "But the *Yellowjacket* does not. Do as I say and be quick about it. Here. You will need this. I have marked the pages in the French signal book. Pray the English know how to read the French signals."

Within a minute the signal flags raced aloft. Whipping and rain-soaked but nonetheless visible, the flags proclaimed the message from the height of the mizzenmast. Adam sent his foretop hands aloft. All eyes turned to the *Yellowjacket*.

Forward she surged for a good three minutes, gaining inexorably on the *Atheling*. Then, suddenly, her jibs wavered and collapsed like deflated balloons. Next came her mainsails, hauled and reefed at once, as the ship's momentum slowed. She had bought the ruse.

At that instant Adam rolled the dice.

"Shake out the reefs, boys! Shake 'em out!" he bellowed.

High aloft, at their pitching and precarious perches, the hands cast off the reef points that held the sails to the yards. They then stood by to overhaul the rigging as the men below tugged at the mainsail halliards and braces and trimmed the sheets. A few more pulls and tugs, and the sails were sheeted home, taut and braced to catch the full force of the wind.

Instantly the *Atheling* shot ahead. There would be no looking back now. The ship was running under full sail through the howling funnel of the Strait of Gibraltar at breakneck speed. If a sail split or a yard were carried away that would be the cost of her clearing the passage without the *Yellowjacket* buzzing at her stern.

Hugging the African coast to avoid the British garrison at Gibraltar, the ship shot the Strait. In the dusk light, beyond the sheets of rain that hung like curtains before the promontories, Adam could see the faintest pinpricks of light ashore, a *vue optique* that reminded him that there was life and civilization off the high seas: a safe port that he might yet reach. But that was all far away. The *Atheling's* masts and spars bent with the stress, and her rigging fairly well shrieked in the wind. Her bow bucked and shuddered at every mounting wave it struck. The mingled waters of the Atlantic and Mediterranean anointed the Queen Charlotte, still lashed to her gun deck, as the crew, wrapped in their oilskins, lurched about on slipping and unsteady feet like drunks. But most importantly, every so often the lightning would illuminate the entire passage, and in its glaring momentary whiteness Adam saw that the straining sails held firm.

At the start of the race through the Strait, Adam cast off the seaman at the wheel and assumed charge of the helm himself. With the experience born of countless storms at sea over the years, so many in fact that they were ingrained on his character, part of the very spring in his gait, he held the wheel steady in his viselike grip, deigning to nudge it an inch to port, an inch to starboard, as his inner compass demanded. The Captain's blue eyes were bright and alive as they flickered constantly from the binnacle to the sails to the rigging to the bowsprit. The complex machinery that was a ship at sea involved hundreds of moving parts that could go wrong at any moment. Monitoring and mastering this hurtling piece of equipment, as sophisticated as anything humankind had yet devised, was an art to the Captain, as beauteous as a Haydn oratorio. Sound and feel were as important as sight, and the Captain commanded them all as the *Atheling* streaked to freedom.

However, Adam's plan held the *Atheling's* dusk-shrouded solitary passage of the Strait of Gibraltar to be only half the mission. If the *Yellowjacket* were to regain her nerve or smoke the ruse of the French "squadron," she could quickly make the passage too and resume the chase in the Mediterranean long before the Americans could raise Toulon.

Therefore the *Atheling* would have to steal the weather gauge. To this end, Adam's eye strained to spot Almina Head on the African shore at the eastern end of the Strait.

The gathering darkness and occlusion of rain made the discernment of bearings all but impossible. Because he was sailing in unfamiliar waters all the Captain could do was to steer dead ahead and hope for the best. Several times, where he thought Almina should rise, he strained for a view and went unrewarded. Had he in fact overshot it? Were his charts inaccurate?

On he pressed, heading due east. To his portside and just astern, barely visible in the distance, stood the great hump of the Rock of Gibraltar. To his starboard, much closer, rose the high outcroppings of the Atlas Mountains known as the Er Rif. It was Adam's first close view of Africa, and he wondered what marvels were hidden in the Dark Continent that lurked beyond the mountains. Even on the coast, in these very waters, he would have to be vigilant for Barbary pirates.

It came as a signal relief therefore when, the passage nearly complete, he discerned the lights of Ceuta. This walled Spanish enclave, with its back turned to the African hinterland, was where the charts indicated he could heave to behind Almina Head. Rain continued to lash the deck and shroud his visibility. Leaving Ceuta astern, he pressed forward, straining every few moments for a glimpse of the peninsula that would be his shelter.

Suddenly the dark ugly hump of Almina loomed on his starboard side. It was no more than a rude spur of the Er Rif Mountains that jutted into the sea. As the ship shot past its point Adam shouted, "Hard alee!" He swung the ship's wheel and turned to the south.

The *Atheling* responded without hesitation and changed course to head for the protection of the promontory.

"Reef mainsails and topsails!" the Captain ordered. Immediately the large sails fell slack, and the top hands spread out along the yards drew them up in bundles.

"Belay! Belay!" Adam shouted, and the sails were sheeted home. Adam turned the wheel back to the helmsman now that the *Atheling* was steady on her new course. The ship slowed and now sailed only under the power of her much smaller topgallants, which caught the high wind that circulated over the crest of the mountains.

The Captain contemplated the best position from which to heave her to. Twenty minutes into the course, and still shielded by the cape, he ordered the ship turned about once more so that her bow faced the Mediterranean exit from the Strait. She settled into place under the protection of the head, reefed all sails and dropped her lightest stream anchor, ready to be weighed on a moment's notice. Adam ordered all guns primed, loaded, and run out. He set a watch at the bow and set a watch on the watch to ensure that the first watch did not fall asleep.

That night the storm abated. Adam repaired to his cabin and opened the Bible that he kept tucked under his bunk. Cradled in his calloused hands, it fell open at a page of familiar comfort. Adam read:

"Put on the whole armour of God, that ye may be able to stand against the wiles of the devil.

For we wrestle not against flesh and blood, but against principalities, against powers, against the rulers of the darkness of this world, against spiritual wickedness in high places.

Wherefore take unto you the whole armour of God, that ye may be able to withstand in the evil day, and having done all, to stand.

Stand therefore, having your loins girt about with truth, and having on the breastplate of righteousness;

And your feet shod with the preparation of the gospel of peace;

Above all, taking the shield of faith, wherewith ye shall be able to quench all the fiery darts of the wicked.

And take the helmet of salvation, and the sword of the Spirit, which is the word of God."

And Adam drifted into a fitful sleep that lasted an hour or two. In the forecastle and below deck the rest of the crew fell into an exhausted slumber.

By the earliest hours of the morning Adam was back on deck to check the watches. The moon peeked between high-flying clouds that were the rearguard of the storm, and the air had turned cold. Seth also was on deck in command of the watches.

"Do you think she'll come?" Seth asked.

"She's come this far. I doubt she'll break off the chase now. 'Tis glory and prize money that drives a frigate Captain. And this one has smelled blood."

"What are we to do if she keeps up the chase?"

Adam chuckled.

"Pounce like a tiger. The crew know what to do. Surprise, speed, and the weather gauge will be ours."

"But we haven't the firepower to engage a frigate. Her broadside would tear us to pieces."

"I do not intend to let her fire a broadside. Always remember that the weakest part of a ship is her stern. If she comes, we will wear under her stern and pound this most fragile part of her fabric where she won't be in a position to rake us with a broadside. We'll send long scouring shots in the hope of wreaking havoc on her decks. And then we'll run."

"Will it work?"

"We haven't any choice. Now go below and get some sleep."

All the long night the Captain sat watch with his crew. The moon set, and in the stillness of the dead hours of the graveyard watch he thought he heard the tinkle of camel bells coming across the water from the nearby mountainside. Or perhaps it was only his imagination.

First light ascended in the east as Adam's head nodded in the drift of fleeting sleep. Unshaven for days and still wrapped in his oilskin slicker, the Captain had propped himself on the forecastle against the bowsprit. He intended to stay awake all the night, but fatigue and his years had overhauled him. Not that his was a deep sleep, for, as always, even in slumber his ear was attuned to the ship.

He therefore was not startled when one of the hands gently shook him and whispered, "Sir! Sir! Wake up! The frigate is clearing the Strait."

Adam rubbed his eyes and looked out. There, not a mile away, the bowsprit of the *Yellowjacket* was creeping past the promontory.

The watch had already run from their stations to awaken the rest of the crew. As the hands quickly piled on deck the Captain whispered his orders.

"Spread all sails! Weigh anchor!"

Instantly the crew was simultaneously aloft and straining at the capstan. The *Yellowjacket* had not yet cleared the point when the *Atheling's* sails billowed out to snatch the high breezes. With her anchor at her side still dripping water, the American ship gathered speed and moved out. Adam noted with immense relief that the *Yellowjacket* forged obliviously ahead for a few precious seconds. She had not yet spotted the Americans.

"Gun crews to stations!"

Then all fell silent. From his command post on the quarterdeck, Adam assessed the rare moment of expectancy that hovered over the scene like the eerie stillness that precedes a storm. The *Atheling*, still gaining speed, glided in utter silence past the promontory dead on target to intercept the *Yellowjacket*. The American gunners, stripped to the waist and unflinching, stood motionless beside their pieces. Smoke curled from their matches. Shot and powder rested in neat piles beside each gun carriage. The guns were run out for battle and their tackles belayed tight. The ship's brass bell caught a glint from the rising sun. Ahead of them, the *Yellowjacket* slipped through the strait and sailed straight into the blinding rays of the eastern sun. It was a scene, Adam judged, of uncommon grace.

And then pandemonium broke loose.

The *Yellowjacket* spotted the *Atheling*.

Shouting on deck of the British frigate carried across the mile of water to the Americans. They could see a frantic scurrying on deck as officers screamed orders and men scurried up the shrouds and ran to battle stations.

But it was too late. The *Atheling* was already wearing on the frigate's stern. Slicing through the water now, the Americans had stolen the weather gauge and were conducting the chase. The British ship began to execute a tacking maneuver to bring its broadside to bear on the Americans. But the ploy was to no avail, for the Americans' bowsprit had now drawn even with the *Yellowjacket*'s stern, three hundred yards off. The Americans had succeeded in "crossing the T." Nothing short of a complete turn would bring the British guns to bear on the American ship. The Americans' audacity—and unexpected audacity at that, for who would have supposed that a merchantman would seek out battle with a heavily armed frigate of the Royal Navy—had turned the tables, for the moment at least.

Captain Hale studied the stern of the enemy ship through his telescope. A fine single glassed gallery ran the breadth of the ship denoting the Captain's quarters. Gilded bas-relief scroll work adorned its perimeter. Above the gallery, at the level of the quarterdeck, ran an equally elaborate gold and white railing surmounted by two great glass lanterns. At the rail the Captain could discern his British counterpart whose name he had never learned: a decent looking man of his own age perhaps, solid and modest in a white wig and unbedecked blue greatcoat. Next to the Captain at the railing paced a shorter man in a gold-frocked coat and flowing black wig. In his right hand he upheld a sword which he shook in defiance at the Americans, spittle spewing from his mouth: Lieutenant Sir Ponsonby Spicer, Baronet.

The bow of the *Atheling* was now in range. Adam waited for the downward roll of the ship. As he waited he reflected on how six short months had brought him from gathering reeds on the Great Marsh at Barnstable to commanding a gunship in the Strait of Gibraltar. "I am most prodigious glad," he whispered to himself.

As soon as the railing began to descend he raised his right arm before the expectant eyes of his gunners.

"Number One Gun! Take your bead and fire on the downward roll! Other guns take your marks and fire at will! God bless America and remember Mowat!"

A terrible tongue of flame licked from the Number One Gun as its boom broke the dawn. The ball marked in orange smashed through the *Yellowjacket*'s stern gallery in a horrific shattering of glass and debris: a direct hit. Incredulous, the Captain and Spicer leaned over the railing to verify the damage. The Captain turned and shouted a series of orders to his men, and a new round of scurrying began on the quarterdeck.

On the *Atheling* all was calm, all was deliberate. The carriages of the Number Two and Three Guns leapt backward virtually in unison. Their crews had trained closely together, and the two guns were informally known to the crew as "the Twins." The blasts from the mouths of the Twins reverberated across the water. The first ball ricocheted off the water and sailed high through the rigging of the *Yellowjacket*, piercing the mizzen topsail and cutting loose a tangle of blocks, tackle, and rigging. Its mate clipped the stern railing not a yard from where the Captain and Baronet stood, sending up a spray of splinters and scattering the officers for cover. A perfect stern shot, the ball continued on its way, scouring the gun deck until it hit a gun carriage, blasting it to pieces and sending the heavy cannon flying sideways. By now the other guns had joined in and were directing their deadly fire in random sequence on the stern of the frigate as the *Atheling* glided past.

Not that the British had stood still. The ship was still trying to execute a turn to bring its guns into play. And the Captain had sent the marines aloft. Captain Hale could see the red-coated marines perched in the rigging opening up musket fire on the *Atheling*. They were just within range but could not shoot with any great accuracy. Nonetheless, musket balls sang past with alarming frequency. Some were high-pitched and whining, while others came with a fleeting "clit" sound. They snapped against the gunwales and mast behind him as if the wood had been struck with a heavy broad axe. It was clear to Captain Hale that the marines were concentrating their fire on the quarterdeck in an effort to strike down the officers. Although it was his first time under active fire (he had surrendered his unarmed blockade runner without a shot fired), the Captain was surprised at the detached analysis with which he viewed the situation. He quickly told himself that the *Atheling* would soon pass out of range of the sharpshooters.

The cannonading on deck continued at a ferocious pace. A pall of smoke hung over the ship so that Adam could catch only sporadic glimpses of the target. By now the Americans had almost cleared the stern, and the early guns had reloaded and were discharging successive rounds. A second ball from one of the Twins—Adam could not be sure which—struck the base of one of the stern lanterns, decapitating it and sending it flying fifty feet into the air. The ball continued to scour the deck for perhaps half a second until an explosion ripped through the waist of the ship. Planking blew out from the starboard side, and an entire gun carriage and crew careened through the air in the blast. The ball had obviously struck a powder store on deck. Splinters, wheels, rammers, and body parts cascaded onto the sauve-tete netting rigged over the deck. It was a lucky and terrible blow, and Captain Hale knew it.

The American crews jimmied their guns for a last shot as the *Atheling*'s broadside cleared the stern and passed out of the angle of fire. Their shots were wilder now, some overhead and others striking the water, misses all. Adam knew he would soon have to break off the gunnery and send men aloft to crowd on and trim the sails in order to make the escape.

The Number Seven Gun, the aftmost piece, had the parting word. With deliberate and careful aim her crew paced the receding frigate. Her captain squinted down her barrel, knocked the quoin with his hammer twice portside and once starboard and waited for the roll. He then dipped the linstock to the touch hole. The gun's mouth flared orange through the lingering smoke, and its carriage shot back to the length of its tackle as its ear-splitting report rocked the quarterdeck. For a moment there was no effect on the *Yellowjacket*, and Adam, surmising the shot was wide, turned to order the crews aloft. Then, a shearing, cracking sound rent the air. Adam wheeled his gaze astern in time to see the frigate's main mast collapsing onto the deck, blown clean in two and carrying with it a forest of yards and rigging. All hands on the *Atheling* stopped dead in their tracks and watched the great mast go down. A cheer rose from the American gun deck. There would be no question of the *Yellowjacket* pursuing now.

Adam paused for a moment to reflect on what he had just wrought. He had taken up arms and succeeded. To admit the truth, he had enjoyed the thrill of the chase and engagement. Moreover, it vindicated his captivity. But therein, he told himself, lay a seduction: was this to be the sole foundation of what he believed in? No, no, he told himself. There must be more: a life scrupulously lived and a *logos* to have it make sense.

The *Atheling* heeled and bent her sails ENE toward Toulon.

6

His Grace's Pleasure

1784—Part V

"WHAT, PRAY, SHOULD I CALL HIM?" ADAM ASKED NERVOUSLY TEN DAYS later as he and Seth stood in the dark, vaulted waiting room of the Abbé's country estate in the foothills of the Vaucluse Mountains just north of Toulon. The terracotta tiles of the flooring smelled of paste wax. The estate was a vast fortified palace of medieval construction, heavy and hushed, tended and orderly, far removed from the boisterous forest of masts, sailors, and supplies that comprised the King's naval yard at the harbor some twelve miles below. The brass knocker at the massive nail-studded oaken front door, Seth had noted to his father, took the form of a serpent entwined about the branch of an apple tree.

"I'm not entirely sure I know what to call him. Not 'Reverend,' I wouldn't think."

"Aren't they entitled to the courtesies of a duke or some such ilk of royalty?"

"I think so, but which one I can't say."

"Before our independence we had a 'Governor,' and here and there you would find a 'Sir.' But somehow that don't strike me as grand enough. In England they call a Duke 'Your Grace,' if I remember right. That's the highest rank I know. He can't take offense at 'Your Grace,' I wouldn't think. 'Your Grace' it shall be then. That's settled."

"He's not a proper Congregational minister, I don't think. Even though he's abbot of a monastery, he serves the state as mast agent for the King. I don't think a minister is supposed to do that, not to our way of thinking anyway," mused Seth. "Why, I've even heard that the lady on the neighboring estate is his mistress and that between the two of them they have a brood of offspring."

"Queer system."

"Perhaps. But who are we to judge? They do say he is a most well-informed and educated man and speaks English as well as you and I."

"That cannot be. It don't figure: a Frenchman who speaks the King's English better than we. Still, it should make our business easier."

The Abbé was in the adjoining *orangerie*, where he liked to work, giving dictation to his secretary. At length, a priest who apparently spoke no English appeared at the closed double doors and bade the Americans, "*Entrez-vous.*"

Once through the doors, they found a long sun-drenched arcade with brick flooring and glass panels running its length. Every yard or so stood an orange or lemon tree dripping with fruit. Adam could hardly keep his eyes off the bounty: oranges and lemons such as he had never seen. Why, each one was the size of his fist.

"Gentlemen, please come in," the Abbé bade in English as he dismissed his secretary with a wave of his index finger. The Abbé was a small and lean man well into his fifties, with gray hair, a long nose, and lively brown eyes. Adam could not help thinking that he resembled a purebred French hunting hound. But what Adam noticed most was the sumptuousness of his clothes: a veritable liquefaction of silks, folds, and ribbons with only the slightest hint of clerical sobriety. As with most foreigners, Adam noticed his shoes in particular. They were of a type much favored by the French aristocrats, with elevated heels and bows, a shoe that could never touch the mud of a road. All of a sudden Adam was acutely conscious of his own clumsy black leather American-made shoes, fine for pacing the quarterdeck, but which no doubt made him stand out in the Abbé's eyes as a rube.

If so, the Abbé did not show it, for his greeting was gracious.

"Gentlemen, please, please, come in. Do not be shy. It is I who am honored. Not every day do I receive visitors from the newly independent American states. Much less ones who have distinguished themselves by disabling a British frigate of far superior firepower."

Very well informed indeed, thought Adam to himself. The Abbé's spies in the port must have brought him word within hours of their docking.

"All France is most indebted. Your initiative allowed our Mediterranean fleet to—how would you say it?—to 'scoop up' the frigate, which is now in our custody as a prize."

"You captured her?"

"With a jury-rigged mainmast she was in no position to resist. No lives were lost—"

"And her Captain?"

"He surrendered and was our guest for several days while we awaited instructions from Paris. He's now on the stage to Paris, where he will enjoy the hospitality of Versailles before we eventually help him arrange passage home."

"There was also a Lieutenant aboard. A certain Baronet who went by the name Sir Ponsonby Spicer."

"How well I know!" the Abbé roared as he threw back his head in laughter. "We briefly considered sending him to our galleys but then concluded France would not be the better for it. What more effective retribution against *les Anglaises* than to send him straight back to London? We placed him on the swiftest packet home we could find."

Adam joined the Abbé in a sly laugh. "*De gustibus non est disputandem.*"

"Ah, you know Latin," the Abbé warmed. "How unusual for an American."

"We are not all savages, noble or otherwise."

"Indeed, I know. And now, if I understand correctly, you bring us an offer of timber masts and spars," the Abbé continued. "This might be of interest. You no doubt saw the hulls under construction at the naval yard."

"We did, your Grace. We have brought a cargo of the finest Maine timber, such as has never been seen in France before."

"My deputies have inspected your cargo and are most impressed."

"There is one mast timber in particular that would grace an Admiral's flagship," Adam boasted. "Three, almost four feet at the butt, she stands well over a hundred feet tall. So well known was she on the Kennebec that they even had a name for her before she was felled."

"Oh?" inquired the Abbé as he arched his right eyebrow and shifted his silken folds. "What name?"

"Why, they called her 'The Queen—'"

"Marie Antoinette!" Seth inserted. "They called her 'The Queen Marie Antoinette' in honor of your most gracious sovereign."

The Abbé beamed. So did Adam at his son's astute salesmanship.

"Then we shall have to have her. I have spoken with my deputies, in fact, and we will take the entire cargo of timber at your asking price. However, with two provisos. First, that you also sell us the quintals of cod at market price. And second, that you agree to establish a trade in Maine timber to satisfy the demands of our Navy and supply no other markets."

Adam smiled approvingly at Seth for his foresight in purchasing the cod. And, as for the future trade, what better customer could be found in Europe?

"We could meet both undertakings," Adam pledged.

"Very well, then," the Abbé stated as he extended his bony hand for Adam to shake. "As they say in your country, 'we have a deal.'"

"We have a deal."

"Now, gentlemen, please do sit down. You must tell me about America."

At the end of two hours Adam had not only slaked the voracious inquisitiveness of the Abbé about the American experiment but had also established that the Abbé was a man with whom he could talk as well as do business.

"Tell me, your Grace, how it is that you devote so many of your energies to the state as well as the church?" Adam at length inquired.

"The church, my son, has been here for seventeen hundred years. And so shall it be, God willing, for another seventeen hundred. So, you see, in the church we count time in millennia. States, on the other hand, are ephemeral. But a good state serves the church. So in serving the servant of my master I serve my master also."

"And thus your interest in the American War of Independence?"

"Indeed. There must be reform, and I serve my King to advocate, to agitate for, change. That is why we must modernize our Navy, so that our state may be strong enough, confident enough to change. Tell me, my good Captain, do you not believe in the perfectibility of man?"

"Why, yes, I do. Otherwise there would be no hope."

"Just so. There must be hope. The Church teaches no differently. Man can change and change for the better. We are on a progression to a better kingdom, both temporally and spiritually."

"As a voyager, I smoke your meaning."

"Look," said the energetic Abbé as he darted to one of his orange trees. "Look at the size of the fruit I have grown. It did not start out so grandly. I took ordinary stock and cultivated it. I placed the saplings in this specially created room so that it would be forever warm and inviting to growth. I prepared the soil and nourished it. I pruned. I spliced. I applied intelligence and science. I married man's gifts with God's gifts and *Voilà!*"

"They are a most impressive progeny."

"You must take a sampling of my shoots with you to the New World. Do not oranges and lemons grow in Maine?"

"I have never seen them."

"You shall plant them in your fertile soil and make them grow. A gift from the Old World to the New."

"Thank you, your Grace. You are most uncommon kind."

"You must not part without one further momento of our visit," the Abbé continued. "I wish you to protect our fruit so that you might return and tell me how they flourished in the New World."

He ushered Adam and Seth to a door at the far end of the room and flung it open. There in a vestibule leading to a cloister with a playing fountain rested two of the prettiest shiny brass four-pound bow-chasers Adam had ever seen. No more than five feet long, they bore the insignia of the Lion of St. Mark.

"Beautiful, are they not?" the Abbé whispered admiringly as he ran his index finger down the length of one of the barrels. "The finest workmanship of the Doge's Arsenal at Venice. You must take them for your ship. Your United States are a small and weak nation, beset and surrounded by hostile powers. Had you not sailed these waters under the protection of the warships of Queen Dona Maria of Portugal, who buys your corn and wheat, the Barbary pirates would have made prey of you. Do you know what they do with Christians?"

Adam shifted uncomfortably.

"Why, my good captain, they strip them naked and take them to the slave pens to be auctioned off to man the galleys. In other cases, they *roast* them. Or in some cases they hang them from walls by meat hooks, where they linger for days, alive and in the most exquisite torture."

The Abbé saw from the shock on Adam's face that his point had reached home.

"Not the fate for a free and proud people like you Americans, eh? A denial of all for which your Revolution stands? Do not be so sure. You are not immune. Take the guns for your ship. They are my gift to the cause of liberty."

Adam moved to thank the Abbé. But the cunning churchman's half smile told him that the pleasure was all his. The Captain and the Abbé understood each other implicitly.

7

Captain Hale's Covenant

1785

CAPTAIN ADAM HALE SAT ON A STUMP ON THE LANDWARD SIDE OF Fore Street, dressed in his shirtsleeves and unbuttoned waistcoat. In the breast pocket of his waistcoat, where most men kept their wallet, protruded his twice-read copy of *Pilgrim's Progress*. Overhead, gulls screed and wheeled, their cries echoing off the cobblestones and brick façades of the warehouses. In his hands Adam held for a final reading before posting a letter he had just composed:

"4 of July 1785

    My Dear Abbé Routurier,

    I could not let this day of our liberty pass without remembering your kind reception on our recent voyage to France. Through your factors in Toulon we procured a cargo for the return voyage such as has never before been seen in our rude outpost of civilization. Our worthy brig was laden with morocco kid shoes, gunpowder tea, Chinese export ware, eau de parfum, silk shawls and such luxuries as delight our ladies here in America. The shelves of our warehouse in Falmouth veritably groan with the abundance of French industry.

Your need of an additional shipment of masts before the end of the year we shall endeavor most heartily to meet. We are in contact with the mast men on the Kennebec, who have assured us of one more shipment by the end of summer, which cargo I shall place in the hands of Mr. Clew and my son for the voyage to France. The success of our last voyage requires my presence here to negotiate anew the arrangements with our creditors in Boston. Divine Providence has placed us in a most fortuitous position which brings the hope that I shall buy out my creditors and own the entirety of my ship—a risky and foolhardy proposition but one that nonetheless brings satisfaction to the heart.

Might I ask, dear Sir, whether beaver pelts would find a market in France? The mast men on the Kennebec have opened a trade with the Abenaki savages and assure us of a most prodigious quantity of the finest skins. I also will take the liberty of entrusting with my son on his return to France a bound copy of Mr. Wesley's latest sermons for your perusal. I offer this volume not with the intent to persuade, as might my father have during the late Great Awakening, but for the proper exercise of the intellect and general increase of knowledge which I know you to hold so dear.

Your humble & obedient servant, etc.

Adam Hale

Your Grace, I almost forgot. The climes of Maine do not favor lemon trees. The specimens you gave to me withered and died within a season of their transplantation. It appears that some of the glories of the Old World do not translate to the peculiar idiom of the New."

Adam, satisfied with his words, folded the letter and handed it to his son Jezreel for sealing. Adam marveled that Jezreel had grown a full four inches since their arrival on the Neck, and now at fourteen he stood a gangling and dark-haired boy with sharp features and lively, dancing eyes that hailed to some unknown ancestor. Adam suspected that he had been reading the letter over his shoulder.

"Fid," said Jezreel, pointing, "why isn't your storehouse as tall as Mr. Storer's?"

Adam looked at his own new two-story building rising across Fore Street. It was a handsome structure of brick running twelve windows in length and boasting lintels of polished gray New Hampshire granite. Notwithstanding the celebrations of the glorious Fourth, the carpenters were still at work hammering on the roof beams, each blow echoing through downtown Falmouth. In contrast, Peleg Storer's competing storehouse fifty yards up the street stood a full three stories in height and reached even further skyward with its company flag flying and white widow's walk perched atop its pitched roof for scanning the arrival of ships in the harbor.

"They say Mr. Storer is in the slave trade, son. I don't know if it is true or not. Probably not. However, I do know that I am not. I am content with two stories."

In fact, Adam acknowledged to himself, he was less than content. Despite the prospect of owning the *Atheling* outright, as reported in his letter to the Abbé, there had been the added expense of constructing his storehouse. As a consequence, he was not free of his black-suited bankers. Wealth had led only to more debt as he borrowed heavily to finance the construction of such a fine building, albeit at only two stories. And with that debt came new demands. The bankers had wanted the Captain to open a new route to the French West Indies, trading New England timber to Martinique in exchange for molasses and sugar, which in turn would be carried and sold to France, in effect creating a triangular trade between Europe, New England, and the Indies. Both Adam and the bankers would have preferred a triangular trade between Old England, New England, and the real prize, Jamaica, but American bottoms were still barred from this British trade as a consequence of the Revolution. So even as he folded his letter to the Abbé, Seth and Mr. Clew were en route with the *Atheling* and its two lovely Venetian bow-chasers to deliver a cargo of staves and building timbers to the West Indies and lade a shipment of barrels of molasses before returning to Maine to collect the mast timbers and strike out once again across the Atlantic. One winter, during his wartime years of leisure in Barnstable, Adam had experimented with inventing a perpetual motion machine. Now, he reflected, he had found it.

Jezreel, possessed of a quicksilver intuition, sensed his father's unease at his burdens.

"If making money isn't the point, Fid, why do you work so? Why do you do all this?" he asked, pointing at the rising storehouse. "What's the purpose?"

Adam shifted uneasily on his seat. What indeed was the purpose? Was his drive to succeed, coming later in life and launched by a seized opportunity—a packet of bought maps and a few lucky and oh-so-thrilling cannon shots—something innate, instinctual almost, just there to be done, part and parcel of the human condition? Or was it directed toward some eventual goal that served the improvement of himself or his family? In truth, Captain Adam Hale was not sure. His lazy self suspected it was the former, if only because that explanation was more tangible and immediate. He was not given to understanding the elusive. Still, he could try.

"Fid," Jezreel prodded. "You haven't answered me."

There would be no avoiding his insistent son. He recalled a passage, or the gist of a passage, handed down by his father and probably by his father's father. He was uncertain of its provenance but sensed that it was woven into the fabric of his life and being.

"You ask why I do it. In truth, it is by way of a contract, no, not a contract but, more than that, a covenant, Son. A covenant is not a transaction, you see, a covenant defines identity."

"A covenant? I don't follow," Jezreel responded with a frown.

"Well, the only way to avoid a shipwreck is to do justly, to love mercy, and to walk humbly. To achieve this end our family must be knit together as one. Just as in order to function a body needs arms, legs, head, and heart, all different members serving different purposes, so must our family work in concert with me the head, your dear mother the heart, and each of you children the arms and legs. We must delight in each other, always having before our eyes our duty to community and work. Only thus will we keep the Lord's blessing upon us. With the Almighty among us we will resist a thousand enemies. He will glorify us, so that each succeeding generation will say 'Make us like our forefathers' generation!' It is both our prerogative and responsibility to create a model society. To do less is to deserve justified censure. Even if other people may forgive our dereliction of duty, conscience cannot. Truly it is said: of whom much is given much is required."

Adam stopped to think further.

"But if we do not obey God and are seduced to worship other gods, our pleasures or mere profits, we will surely perish out of this good land to which we have passed over enormous oceans to possess."

Just then the bells of the First Parish Church up on Back Street, at the nape of the Neck, began to toll the noon hour, deeply, sonorously, and with the gravity appropriate to the marking of the country's birth. Adam and Jezreel suddenly realized they were late to join Nabby, Thankful, and Juvenal at the service of commemoration. With a quick step they started up the steep hill to the church. The venerable and ancient Reverend Thomas Smith, who had arrived as a missionary to the Neck in the 1720s, would deliver the homily. Settled in the pew that the Captain had purchased just the month before in the light-filled nave, Adam found it comfortable that the Hale family were but the humblest of passengers in the ship of the Almighty.

8

Theodicy

1789

THE FIRM OF HALE & SONS GREW AND PROSPERED. THE TRADE IN masts and luxuries with France flourished, with two and sometimes three voyages a year. The rhythm of the merchants' trade now pulsed throughout The Neck. Falmouth became an entrepot in the wilderness. Wagons came down from the back country of New England bearing beef, pork, butter, cheese, and other produce to be traded for fish, molasses, rum, and manufactured goods from the world over. Given its newfound status, it was not surprising that the town sloughed off its old name of Falmouth and now reinvented itself as "Portland."

Captain Hale commanded at least one voyage annually. Seth took charge of the remaining trips. Although three years earlier Hiram Clew had struck out on his own with a blessing and loan from the Captain, the Hales still sailed with many of the same crew who manned the maiden voyage of the *Atheling*. Only now speed counted for all. Adam had long since stowed the heavy guns from her maiden voyage in the cellar of his factory house on Fore Street. The brig still sported the brass bow-chasers which Adam and Seth both made a point of keeping polished and gleaming. The name of Hale & Sons became known the length of Down East, indeed from Boston to Halifax. By the year '88 Adam owned not only the brig *Atheling* outright but also held controlling interests in three Maine-built schooners—the *Allagash*, the *Aroostock*, and the

Arundel—which plied the coast, carrying the wares of Europe—perfume, brandy, and silks—to Portsmouth, Newburyport, and other towns and making the runs to the Caribbean as well. Moreover, Adam had joined with Daniel Ilsley and a consortium of other merchants to build the first long wharf into the harbor, which now extended a formidable length to accommodate the largest ships. It was known as Union Wharf. From it one could see the scores of merchants' flags that now fluttered along the waterfront of the small city of the new republic that called itself Portland.

* * *

Adam commanded the shipment of the late spring harvest of timbers to France. Upon his arrival at Toulon he received a letter from Abbé Routourier summoning him to Paris, whence the Abbé had been called by the King to attend the meeting of the Estates-General at Versailles. So Adam discharged his cargo, sailed the *Atheling* to Le Havre and took coach to Paris. As he rode through the countryside of Haute Normandie he saw the unmistakable signs of starvation: emaciated, listless peasants with sunken eyes at each village through which he passed.

The coach stopped for a fresh team of horses at Tourville-la-Rivière. Starving children approached and beat on the doors and closed windows of the vehicle.

"*Pain, pain!*" they cried beseeching the travelers within for bread. "*S'il vous plaît, messieurs! Je vous en prie!!*"

Adam's fellow travelers buried their eyes in their newspapers or pretended to nap. Adam had no bread, but he did have a handful of French copper coins—he was not sure of their denomination—in his pocket. He pulled down the window enough to extend his arm and passed out the coins to the children, who took them with gratitude in their eyes and a mumbled *merci* on their lips.

It was evident to Adam that France, though by most measures a wealthy country, had suffered a breakdown of its distribution system for basic sustenance.

The next day, as soon as his coach penetrated the ring of customs houses that encircled Paris, the second largest city in Europe, the imploring eyes and hands of the rural peasantry gave way to something altogether different.

* * *

"I give you the laboratory that is Paris," the Abbé Routourier observed with a wave of his bony hand as he and Adam rode in the Abbé's dangerously open and sleek phaeton from the Palais Royal, where the Abbé had just finished meeting with the Duc d'Orléans, to his town home or *hôtel* on the rue des Saints-Pères in the Fauborg Saint Germain late in the afternoon of July 23. Every few yards the vast and agitated crowds—young and old; men and women; destitute, working class, and bourgeoisie—that milled in the streets under leaden skies caused the phaeton to stop to await a clear path before proceeding. Adam was aware that they could be pulled from the carriage by the crowd at whim. He buttoned his greatcoat and settled himself more squarely in the vehicle. Not so the Abbé, who sat upright and positively beamed. "Do you not recall when we first met, I asked you if you believed in the perfectibility of man?"

Adam nodded warily.

"Well, here you have it. Or the beginning of it anyway."

"What, with this crowd, this mob, Your Grace?"

"Exactly, *la foule*. Nine days ago they seized the Bastille. More a matter of symbol than of substance. Those of us who seek reform will use that to press the King. His Majesty remains as popular as ever. Even as they stormed the Bastille, you should have heard the cries of '*Vive le Roi!*' Paris provides the opening to seek the reforms that the state needs to thrive and to foster the perfection of our society under a benevolent Majesty."

"You sail close to the winds of human perfidy."

"I am confident I can navigate them. See, look there!" the Abbé said as he pointed. "I said the Bastille was more symbol than substance. Those are the very prisoners freed by the mob."

Adam craned his neck to see. A solitary drummer beat a tattoo that echoed off the façades of the buildings. Accompanied by a handful of soldiers, he led a parade of seven men through the streets to the adulation and cheers of the crowd. The white flag of King Louis fluttered at their rear. Behind them paraded a cohort of street people with poles bearing wax busts of the heroes of the day liberated from M. Curtius's wax museum: Lafayette, Mirabeau, the Duc d'Orléans, and Necker.

"There you have the prisoners," the Abbé continued. "Four forgers, the Comte de Solages imprisoned at the request of his family, and two lunatics who are better off at the asylum at Charenton."

Adam's gaze fixed on one bent old man with a long white beard who looked as if he had been immured for decades. With a dazed and bewildered expression, he acknowledged the cheers of the crowd with a slight royal wave of his elevated right hand.

The Abbé sensed Adam's interest.

"That's Major Whyte, an Englishman. He thinks he's Julius Caesar. As I said, the Bastille yielded up more symbolism than substance."

With the crowd turning to accompany the liberated prisoners, the Abbé's driver negotiated an opening for the phaeton to work its way onto a bridge and cross the river to Saint Germain. Arriving at the Abbé's *hôtel*, with its deep-set courtyard, Adam found it to be the opposite of his sun-lit orangerie in the hills above Toulon. Its salon was paneled in dark wood. Heavy silk curtains blocked the light at the windows. To Adam it seemed a lair, a retreat to which to repair and shut out the world. A servant lit the candles. The room began to take on a warmer hue, with Gobelin tapestries on the walls, rich Turkey carpets on the floor, and comfortable furniture in which to relax. At the far end of the room the dining table stood before a large limestone fireplace. Above the fireplace Adam made out a fine late Renaissance painting of the Madonna and Child. Beneath the painting rested a terracotta-colored bust, perhaps a foot and a half in height. Adam drew closer to inspect. He recognized the alert eyes and enigmatically smiling face. It was a life-like rendering of François-Marie Arouet, Voltaire. Surprised, he turned to the Abbé.

"My prized possession. By Houdon."

"Oh, do tell," Adam murmured, astonished at the breadth and incongruities of the Abbé's interests.

That evening Adam and the Abbé ate an early and ascetic supper of cold cucumber soup, bread, and water—no wine—by candlelight under the faintly smiling gaze of Voltaire as they discussed revolutionary politics, the Abbé's plans to push the monarchy into reform, and the continuing need for masts for the Navy. As they finished and as Adam was about to make his good-byes to return to his lodgings, they heard a commotion erupting in the street outside, at first faint and then louder. Both Adam and the Abbé arose and went to the window. They pulled back the curtains to reveal the still daylight-touched street. A mob of hundreds of people was boisterously moving up the street, singing and chanting as it came. The front rank hoisted poles on which were impaled three brutally serrated severed human heads. They bobbed and dipped as the crowd jeered. Of one head, only the forehead remained; the visage was a shred of tangled flaps of skin and gore. On a narrower, almost delicate pointed pike rested a human heart dripping blood. The entire ensemble had taken care, attention to detail, and planning of which only the human race was capable. A porcine artist skipped along with the crowd, busily recording the scene in his sketch book for posterity.

The Abbé recoiled. What little color he had drained from his face.

"That's Foulon," he said as he pointed to a severed head whose mouth was stuffed with grass, straw, and excrement. "He is . . . he was . . . a minister in the government."

Adam stared for as long as he could stand the sight. He was not sure which repelled him more: the inhumanity of the heads atop the pikes or the leering glee with which the crowd heralded their trophies. In an instant he grasped the transmutation that he saw before him: the revolutionary impulse, started in America, had gone from wax heads of heroes on poles to a public display of deadly retribution and degradation: a perverted rite. He suddenly felt nauseated by the scene before him, thereby marking him as one whose ardor, if it could be called such, for the revolutionary impulse was limited to philosophical abstractions such as *liberté*, *egalité*, and *fraternité*. Others, of a more robust nature, whose stomachs did not flinch at the sight of blood, would make the at once age-old and thoroughly modern covenant with Satan that power could be secured by violence. But Adam knew he was different from those people. He stood on the other side of a great divide.

So too did the Abbé, who shakily drew the curtains shut on the epiphany.

"You Americans started it," he said drily.

"You French are taking it to the limits of its possibilities, however perverse," Adam retorted. "Do you not agree it is evil?"

"Yes, it is profoundly evil. But keep in mind that God did not make death. Nor does He delight in the death of the living. God created all things so that they might exist. At each step, God looked at His Creation and saw that it was good and that as a whole—and including human-kind—it was *very* good. The generative forces of the world are wholesome, and there is no destructive poison in them. Hades is not on earth. God created us for incorruption and made us in the image of Himself. Recall that it was only through the Devil's envy that death entered the world."

"Be that as it may," Adam observed, "evil in the world is not a fog bank sitting out on the horizon. It is, I fear, a multifaceted, many-splendored thing, at play and alive in the world, so much of the warp woven into the fabric of our existence, quite dazzling, really, in its proximity and manifestations."

They sat in silence in the cool darkness of the room and reflected.

At length Adam posed the question that was on his mind and which he suspected only a cleric could answer with authority.

"My dear Abbé, if God is omnipotent why does he allow evil and suffering and death?"

"Ah," the Abbé sighed. "You touch upon the vindication of God in light of the existence of evil in the world. You ask the most difficult question. But you ask it as a believer. If you thought Creation to be random and with no purpose then you would not ask. So I shall try to answer. It is in way of a dilemma of three interconnected parts, being omnipotence, goodness, and evil. Is God willing to prevent evil but not able to do so? If so, then He is not omnipotent but impotent. Or is He able to do so but not willing? Then He is malevolent and not good. Or is He able and willing but for an inexplicable reason does not? The first two of these questions are logical within themselves but the third undermines logical coherence."

"Spoken like a Frenchman," Adam averred. "I am not sure, but I dimly smoke your meaning. And what is the source of evil then in this world?"

"Why, my dear Captain, I understand evil to be of two sorts. First, that created by man exercising his will in ways God did not intend both on himself and on others, what you might call moral evil. And then that created by nature, natural evil—the Great Lisbon earthquake, for example. Not that the distinction much matters, for the effect on humankind is the same, whatever the source of the evil."

"I fear your lot may be to cope with moral evil, my dear Abbé."

"Perhaps so. We are little more than flies in amber fixed in our time and place. And my time and place are now and here. To live is necessarily to exist in a world in which there is no temporal end to evil and suffering, and every action, however good, is freighted with the potential to cause eventual evil. After all, did not the Incarnation result in the Crucifixion? But in the face of this reality, I take heart in the realization that our capacity to think is a crucial reflection of our being made in the image of God. We can exercise our freedom to shape who we are: for good or for evil. I choose to shape it for good, unlike those brutes in the street. So one should not ask 'Where is God?' but 'Where am I?' But, that said, we are victims of our time and place. And, who knows, perhaps you shall be forced to cope with natural evil and suffering as you sail the seas."

"Sometimes I fear so, but 'the sea is His and He made it,' as the Psalmist tells us. God also separated the seas and slew the primordial sea monster Rahab, so perhaps I shall be protected."

"You speak in poetry and metaphors."

"I speak from the Book of Psalms and Genesis."

"I well realize that . . . you speak in poetry and metaphors."

"That's all the balm I have."

The Abbé issued a begrudging "Hrumph."

Adam thought for a moment. "Indeed, life is a pilgrimage through a desolate and dangerous wilderness. Bunyon says as much. We need to develop our character through our responses to the destinies which confront us. There are moral examinations which we must pass in order to arrive at perfection."

"I am less sure of that," the Abbé responded. "You already have the will to act one way or another. The freedom is inherent, and it's yours today."

"But isn't there a third sort of evil?" probed Adam. "That of Satan, the great accuser, alive and active in this world? You have said as much. Did he not introduce death to the human race in a pique of envy? Did not God inflict suffering on Job on the whim of a wager with Satan? God inflicted it, not Satan, but He was finagled by Satan. And if God is good by definition, why would He have done so, much less on a wager with a fallen angel? Is that not cruel and callow?"

"I do not know," the Abbé replied. "Perhaps we, frail and unknowing humans that we are, are asking the wrong questions. It is impossible for us mere humans to know God. He is holy and separate. We don't even have the words to describe Him, much less talk to Him. For example, when we say something is good, such as God is good, it means that that particular something pleases *us*. So we set ourselves upon a judgment seat. We engage in the arrogant enterprise of wondering why God fails to please us. Perhaps God did not set out to please us, and we are forcing Him to abide by a covenant He did not sign. But, judgment aside, we are created in the image of God and, as rational creatures, invited to wonder about God's purpose in the universe. Crows and elephants do not wonder. We uniquely wonder. We are free to wonder."

And then he lapsed into silence.

From the mantle, Adam noted, Voltaire smiled enigmatically at the limits of reason.

9

En Volant

1792

THE MASSIVE WHEELS—THEY STOOD AS HIGH AS ADAM'S SHOULDER—
of Abbé Routourier's black Berline carriage turned and gained purchase
on the September rain-slickened granite cobbles of the courtyard of
his Parisian *hôtel*. Inside the closed carriage, with curtains drawn, the
Abbé and Adam Hale sat facing one another. The Abbé's face was even
gaunter than usual. Next to the Abbé on the banquette sat a wicker
hamper containing a wheel of Auvergne cheese, two loaves of bread, and
a single apple. The Abbé always was an ascetic eater, and Adam rued the
reflection that this would have to last them for much of the long trip
southward. Next to the hamper the third passenger, the terracotta bust of
Voltaire, sat on a pillow bolstered and swaddled by blankets.

The Abbé had left a message that Adam should meet him in Paris
once he had delivered his cargo at Toulon. Immediately upon his arrival
he found the Abbé directing the loading of his baggage to flee the city.
He implored Adam to join him, and he obliged. As the carriage gathered
momentum and trundled forth from the courtyard under the limestone
entrance arch, Adam recalled his dream of nine years earlier. Only this
time he was not running from the black carriage. He was in it.

"This is no more than a feint, a tactical retreat," the Abbé chortled
unconvincingly as he dismissed Paris with a wave of his hand. "I shall
return. Once things have calmed down."

"I had heard about the storming of the Tuileries and the King's arrest," Adam proffered, to show that he was *au courant*.

"Oh, worse than that my dear Captain. Just weeks ago there were the so-called September Massacres in which rampaging mobs murdered three Bishops and more than two hundred priests. And just yesterday the Convention abolished the monarchy and declared a Republic. Did you know that it is no longer the year of Our Lord 1792? It is now the Year I of the 'Era of Liberty.' Paris has gone mad. But until the forces of reason reassert themselves there is little I can do here to be of use."

"Meaning you have no monarchy or government left to reform?"

"I fear not, at least not for the moment. And far better that I return posthaste to Toulon where I can bide my time. Who knows, perhaps in three months or six months or a year at most, reason will prevail, and Paris will be Paris once again."

"I can take you with me to the United States if you wish. Think of it: you'd be the toast of New York and Philadelphia."

"Ah, to trade a violent and unstable Thebes for a law-governed Athens! I take your point. But to abandon France, my country?" the Abbé asked as he shifted the folds of his cassock. "Thank you, but I cannot in good conscience do that."

"'Twould only be a temporary sojourn. You'd be much safer in America."

"My personal safety is the least of my concerns. The safety of my country and of my faith are paramount. Somehow there is a will of God in all these developments, and I must attend in order to discern it and then act when I do. Did not your William Shakespeare have Hamlet say 'There's a Divinity that shapes our ends, Rough-hew them how we will'?"

"Is that a question?"

"Merely a rhetorical one. He did say that, and it is true."

"And what does it mean to you?"

"It means there is a Divine providence which is the means by which God leads us mortals to our destined end. To spurn this guidance is to foolishly jeopardize the achievement of one's destiny. We are assured of this providential guidance if we adhere to the will of God and faithfully adhere to His divine laws."

"Aha! So closely akin to the covenant of my Puritan forefathers! Yes, yes, my dear Abbé, but I fear that all has become political in France, and that causes me to tremble. Will you indulge me, as a New England Protestant, to make an observation?"

"By all means, proceed."

"France has become an infected country, infected by no less than the Devil himself. The Devil cares not whether man is a Republican or Reformer or Monarchist. There are equally good avenues of temptation in all three. The key is to let man treat whichever path he chooses as a part of his religion. Then, warmed by partisan spirit, he treats it as the most important part. Religion becomes merely an ancillary or supporting element of the cause, a justification if you will. Once the 'world' has been made the end and 'faith' but a means then the Devil has won, and it makes little difference what kind of worldly end the man pursues, provided that end trumps the Christian life of prayer, sacrament, and good works. 'Tis true even of you, my dear Abbé, with your talk of reform and social action under the guise of a clerical stole. Far better, and how much more important, to maintain the integrity and indeed superiority of that which is holy over that which is secular! To do otherwise is to cheapen the sublime and a sacrilege."

The Abbé sank back in his seat.

"I once had a wise old Bishop tell me as much. That is why the Church has lasted over seventeen hundred years while empires have come and gone."

"Precisely. It is pernicious, indeed the Devil's work, to mix the two."

"Well, perhaps as the great Voltaire said, it is indeed time to cultivate my own garden. In that I shall find solace and peace."

"Not to mention wisdom. If you were to revert to your lemons and legumes should I plan to bring a cargo of masts and spars next year?"

The Abbé thought for a moment.

"Oh, yes, certainly. Why not? What with the wars France is launching all over Europe, the Republicans will still need naval stores. And if they need naval stores, they will need me. Therein lies my protection. And my future as assured by Divine providence."

"Very good. I shall return," Adam replied, realizing that his comment had made hardly a dent and that the whole of Creation was groaning. The two friends sat in silent contemplation for the rest of the journey.

10

The Lawless Seas

1793

ADAM AROSE EARLY ON THE MORNING OF HIS BIRTHDAY. HE RUBBED HIS red eyes and the advancing crows' feet that creased their corners from reading too late the night before by dim candlelight: account books and ledgers, Herodotus, Sallust, Buffon, Rousseau, they all lay piled beside his bed. He hauled himself from the bed, his growing girth attesting as much to his time ashore managing his enterprise as to his station in life as a man of some importance. He turned to find Nabby already up and gone. Perhaps she had arisen to stir the embers in the kitchen fireplace and instruct the maid on assembling the family's breakfast.

As he shuffled downstairs and entered the kitchen, he found his whole family already up and assembled.

"Happy Birthday, Fid!" they shouted in unison.

It was a rare treat indeed for Adam to have everyone at home at once. Seth, at twenty-four, more often than not was at sea purchasing and loading cargoes for the *Atheling*. Jezreel, two years younger, was rapidly mastering the tricks of the Caribbean trade and often away. Their absences usually left at home only Juvenal, a studious thirteen years old, and Thankful—oh yes, sterling Thankful, about to turn seventeen, a lady of dignity like her maternal ancestors and a strong support for her mother, accomplished in conversation and needlepoint and a reader like her father. With dark brown eyes and high cheekbones, she was more handsome than beautiful and had yet to turn the eye of any of the young Captains on the Neck, of which there were now many.

"Husband dear, I have a present for you," Nabby pronounced as she cleared her voice and made an effort at ceremony.

Embarrassed, Adam's face reddened, but he made light.

"You shouldn't have made this fuss. 'Tis only another year in my life."

"But you see, I went to some effort. I ordered it from Boston," she explained as she produced from beneath the kitchen table a dark wood walking stick and placed it in Adam's hands.

"Why, thank you very much. I wasn't expecting anything at all," he said with a smile.

He inspected the walking stick closely as he turned it around in his hands. He recognized it as a fine, polished stick of Malacca wood, very dear, and with an ivory knob head in the form of a fist gripping and mastering the serpent of evil.

"It was carved by a Nantucket schrimshander," Nabby explained.

"It, it, it . . . is very handsome indeed and is more than I deserve," Adam stammered. "I shall walk with it upright and straightway this morning to Fore Street."

In truth he felt it would be with some embarrassment that he would first appear with it in the town, but he suspected he would soon grow accustomed to the swagger imparted by the prop.

"Oh, but you can't leave straightway just yet," Seth implored him. "Jezreel and I—and also Thankful and Juvenal—we too have a gift for you," he explained as Thankful and Juvenal clapped and clasped their hands in anticipation.

Also from under the table the two older boys produced a package wrapped in brown paper.

"What possibly could this be?" Adam asked as he took it and weighed it in his hands.

"Well, open it," Seth suggested.

Adam tore apart the paper. In it rested a folded flag, which he withdrew and opened in its full glory. It was a house standard that his children had devised showing the two brass bow-chasers on a field of blue.

"Oh my!" Adam exclaimed. "This is magnificent! I shall hoist it atop our establishment on Fore Street to compete with the red and gold standard of Peleg Storer and the dozens of other merchants' flags! The whole world shall know the House of Hale & Sons now that we will fly our own flag!"

* * *

Captain Adam Hale hoisted his patrician Roman nose skyward.

"I can smell it," he said, as he eyed the yellowish stain on the starboard aft horizon in early September. "Aye, I can smell it."

"Smell what, Fid?" Seth asked as he stood beside him at the taffrail of the quarterdeck of the *Atheling*.

"Why, don't you smell it? The warmth, the humidity. That terrible moist, close feeling, like the grass in Eastern Cemetery after a thunderstorm. There's a hurricane not three hundred miles from here. Bearing down on Bermuda now, if I judge right."

Adam also *felt* the hurricane—in the quickening gusts and in the alacrity with which the brig scudded before the rising waves. This would be a fast passage across the Atlantic, as early September voyages often are. The ship rode full but buoyant with her cargo of masts and spars.

Seth did not doubt the seamanship of his father. But his mind was more attuned to the business of her cargo.

"I hope we turn a profit on this run. The big sticks are harder to find now, and with Pugh charging what he did for this lot, we'll have to ask a pretty penny of the Abbé. He could turn his back on us."

"That is if he's even the mast agent any longer."

"Well, he was nine months ago when we received his order."

"But that was before we heard news of King Louis's beheading. There's much bad news out of France these days."

"Still, with the French Republic constantly at war their Navy is certain to be needing supplies."

"Let's hope so, son. In the event, I had the foresight to bring the Abbé gifts." Adam chuckled to himself at the thought of the Abbé's opening the laden chests. "Beaver pelts from the Mohawk. Tobacco from

Virginia. And a Kentucky long rifle, its stock all tiger maple. A beauty. I wish I could keep her for m'self."

Seth was at once struck by the inutility of such gifts in revolutionary France and the blessings of living in the new United States of America where, under the benevolent hand of General Washington, such goods could be used and enjoyed.

"I only hope that he's disposed to appreciate them."

"So do I, son. So do I."

* * *

True to Adam's prediction, the *Atheling* sliced through the remaining leagues in good time and not a fortnight later found herself edging her bow into the roads at Toulon.

The heat and humidity that had been their accompaniment across the ocean still enveloped them. The mole at the harbor and the yellow sandstone walls at the piers waffled in the heat. The French naval fleet still lay at anchor. It was a familiar and welcome sight.

But something was wrong, and Captain Adam Hale immediately sensed it.

"Where's the pilot boat, Seth? I don't see a pilot boat."

"You're right, Fid. There's always a pilot boat to meet us at Toulon."

"Odd that," Adam mumbled to himself as he scanned the harbor with his telescope and weighed the implications.

At length he collapsed the scope and handed it off to Seth with a shrug.

"Well, I guess we go in without 'em."

The Captain ordered the sails shortened, and the brig slid forward only under her topsails, gliding past the naval vessels and the small craft that plied the entry. As the *Atheling* nestled beside its customary pier and her crew tossed out the lines for the longshoremen, Seth, who was charged with the docking, noticed only a few sullen souls stirring to receive the lines. The harbor master's office stood boarded up and covered with graffiti. Trash littered the cobblestones. A white and brown mongrel dog, all asshole and overbite, ambled from trash pile to trash pile, sniffing. It was as if France no longer looked outward.

Adam immediately sensed the change as well. And it made him uneasy.

"Seth, you remain here with the ship," he ordered. "All crew are to stay on board."

Adam alone would seek out the Abbé and learn what had transpired in his absence.

As he parted down the gangway he gave Seth strict orders, almost as an afterthought, to allow no one to board the ship and to send a search party out for him if he had not returned by sunset the following day.

With some difficulty Adam engaged a donkey cart and driver on the waterfront to deliver him the twelve miles into the foothills above the town to the Abbé's residence. As the cart rumbled and swayed across the rough paving stones Adam was struck by the same lassitude and over-whelming filth that had marked the harbor. Trash lay everywhere, as if the populace had construed their newfound Rights of Man to include the liberty to litter. Political posters plastered buildings great and small. Parish churches they passed had been turned into storehouses and stables.

The donkey cart rattled up into the town and turned into the central square. There Adam's heart stopped as he first set eyes on the dreaded and fabled guillotine. It was a local affair, no doubt smaller than the one set up in Paris. But with its steel blade glistening in the noon sun and its tall vertical frame towering over the square it sent a chill down his spine. At its side rested a rude cart to receive the bodies. It was painted red and strewn with straw, like the gun decks of British warships, to mask the blood and gore. The guillotine stood unattended, for there were no crowds about in the midday September heat.

Adam wanted to ask the driver what was happening in Toulon and about the Abbé, but his discretion as much as his rudimentary French held him in check. He sensed that his questions might compromise his friend and that the better course was to hold his tongue.

They continued up into the foothills above the town, and Adam fell into the stride of the ponderous rhythms of the creaking leather and the donkey's inhaling and exhaling. Adam allowed his thoughts to drift. Was the Abbé still the government's mast agent? Was the Abbé well? Was the Abbé indeed even alive? Would the changes in revolutionary France mean the end of the House of Hale's market for large timbers and the need to look elsewhere?

Occasionally the donkey snorted and whinnied as if to relieve the tension. They continued upward, past broken farm carts, bales of hay, and sleeping dogs, past an ochre-colored maisonette with its shutters drawn tight against the coming of autumn and winter and past a brown-leafed pear tree drooping in the courtyard.

Arriving in early afternoon at the gatehouse to the drive leading to the Abbé's estate, Adam spotted an encampment of soldiers manning a roadblock with a simple pole as a swing gate. They were unshaven and disheveled, to judge from their ill-fitting and dirty uniforms, *sans culottes* to a man. Their only badges of alleged respectability were rosettes pinned to their crumpled cocked hats. They were in the midst of cooking dinner, and Adam suspected from their loud banter that they were already drunk.

The donkey cart stopped at the barricade. The driver explained his fare to the sergeant of the guard in rapid-fire Provencal which Adam could not follow. There ensued a great shrugging of shoulders on both sides, followed by a proffer of a plug of tobacco from the driver to the sergeant. The still-suspicious sergeant looked at Adam and poked about in the cart. The Captain plumped up his chest and drove his ivory-headed walking stick to the floor with a crack. He addressed himself to the sergeant, "*Bon jour, Citoyen.*" The sergeant took note but made no acknowledgment.

In addition to its passenger, the cart carried a jug of wine and a supply of filthy straw-flecked woolen blankets. The sergeant motioned for one of his men to remove the wine. This operation and his extraction of tribute complete, the sergeant slapped the side of the cart and motioned it forward.

Five minutes later Adam stood before the Abbé's massive door. Dust coated its timbers and spider webs festooned its iron studs and corners. Adam's heart sank at the telltale evidence of nonhabitation. He raised his right hand to the knocker but hesitated. He studied for a moment its writhing brass serpent and the branch laden with apples. The world was changing, he told himself, and there was little he could do about it but to accept those changes and adapt. He then firmly gripped the Tree of Knowledge and rapped three times in a staccato burst.

No one responded.

He rapped a second time and then a third time. No one answered.

At length, he gave up and hailed the donkey cart driver for the long trip back to the waterfront. As he headed down the hill in the silent and lurching cart, he began to parse and attack the implications of the Abbé's demise. With his largest customer gone, where would he sell his sticks? Would the revolutionary government in Paris honor his contracts? Would they deal with him in the future? Whom would he even contact to find out? Or would his business collapse for want of customers?

What of the rival powers? Britain, it was true, was increasingly nervous about the situation in France, and most surely the Navy Board in London was taking the appropriate precautions. The Netherlands too was a sailing country. Though small, she had ships that needed tall masts. And then there were Sweden and Russia, more remote and well supplied with their own stores from the Baltic.

This matter of the Abbé's fall, even at its most elemental and commercial, would demand thought and deliberation.

But Adam was suddenly struck by the realization that it was not merely a question of commercial markets. This turn of events drove home to Adam, as storms at sea had so often playfully intimated, the utter helplessness of individuals in the face of the unstoppable movements of the universe. No doubt the Abbé had come to the same sad realization as he had been carted off to a fate unknown to Adam but probably all too well known to the Abbé. Adam wondered if the Abbé's Christian faith, such as it was, had steeled him to meet his end. With a tincture of pity Adam marveled at the depravity of the creatures that had conceived and executed the deed.

And Adam wondered if he himself was falling victim to that oldest and most common of New England vices: dislike of people. In this stingy, cruel, and hostile universe, pleasure could even be derived from dislike. A New Englander's pleasures were few.

But then there was always family.

"Pirates! Pirates! Barbary pirates! They are boarding!" Scrote the fore-topman shrieked like a cacique as he flung open the door to the Captain's quarters with a lantern in one hand and a bloodied cutlass in the other.

Adam shook the sleep from his head. As a pearly glow lightened the gray Mediterranean, a glance out the window told him dawn had broken over their position not a day's sailing south of Toulon. A modest breeze rippled the waves, to Adam's immense relief.

"Get aloft to unreef the mainsail! And be fast about it!" he shouted.

"Aye, aye," the foretopman nodded and bolted back out through the dining saloon to the deck.

Adam knew instantly what was at stake: a lifetime of slavery in the galleys of the Bey of Algiers for him and all the crew and—gravest of all in his universe—for Seth. A fight, and a fight to the death, was the only option.

Adam always slept in his clothes aboard ship in case of emergency, so all he needed do was slip on his shoes and grab the cutlass that he kept mounted at the head of his bunk, which he slid between his belt and breeches. He then reached for the brace of London-made Ketland flintlock pistols which he kept primed and loaded in a rosewood box secreted under his bunk.

The Captain drew a deep breath, hunched his massive shoulders like a wild bull and charged out on deck.

Pandemonium reigned as three or four dozen pirates breached the starboard side and fought hand-to-hand with the *Atheling*'s crew, who were armed with knives, belaying pins, and, in the case of the Wampanoag hand Moses Macy, an iron trade tomahawk. The pirates were a fearsome sight—barefooted, wearing blue and white harem pants that reached to the knee, sporting two and three daggers thrust into red cummerbunds, gold brocade jackets and a variety of turbans and headgear that defied classification, their dark, bearded visages fixed by flashing eyes.

Adam quickly sized up the foe. They had arrived via two lateen-rigged dhows the tops of whose masts barely surpassed the starboard taffrails of the *Atheling*. They had boarded with lines and grappling hooks and even now were clambering into the rigging to swing themselves aboard. They came blindly, relentlessly, like the hordes Adam had read about in the great siege of Malta. Armed with daggers and scimitars, they were quickly cutting their way through the ship's defiant but overwhelmed crew. Several pirates boasted antique matchlock muskets inlaid with mother of pearl. One of those was pointed directly at Scrote as he worked to unreef the mainsail. Knowing he had but one shot for each pistol, Adam did not hesitate to pull the trigger on one of his pistols. He felled the sniper.

As he began to move amidships to the center of engagement, Adam spotted Seth on the foredeck discharging the ship's sole blunderbuss into a knot of pirates clambering over the rails. Somehow Seth had also had the presence of mind to fetch two bags of powder from the lead-lined lockers on the foredeck that kept them dry. Discarding the blunderbuss, he now strained with one of the crew to turn the two brass bow-chasers aftward while a second hand provided cover with the Kentucky long rifle intended for the Abbé. To Adam's mind Seth's maneuver was a very fortunate fact.

Less so was the sight that next greeted him: a bug-eyed, grinning pirate with a scimitar dripping blood in one hand and the severed head of Sanchez the cook in the other. Poor Sanchez—he was so corpulent and slow and well meaning he had not been able to run from the marauders. Adam hesitated for a moment. He knew this would be a wasted shot and that there would be no more. However, there was no question as to what was necessary. He took vengeful aim and squeezed the trigger. With the catch of flint on steel and the puff of the firing pan followed immediately by the blast of the discharge and a cloud of smoke, a fifty caliber ball hurtled across the deck to smash the grinning mug of the murderer into oblivion.

Quickly Adam raced to the side of his crew and set about hacking the boarding lines with his cutlass. Working methodically from aft to fore, he severed each line as he went.

Twelve lines into his task, the slash of a scimitar raked across his shoulder as a pirate swung down and into him from the rigging. The stun of the blow sent Adam reeling, and he collapsed on buckled knees. The pirate, a giant of a man with a fearsome beard and a *zebibah* or mark on his forehead from devotion to prayer, hoisted his blade over his shoulder to strike a second and deciding blow. Adam, who still retained the sinews of the topside acrobat he had once been, coiled his strength into his calves and propelled himself out of harm's way in a roll that twisted two full gyrations and landed himself back on his feet, cutlass still in hand. Now it was thrust and parry as the Captain fought the Saracen hand to hand, Yankee steel against Damascus blade. His shirt torn and blood-soaked from the shoulder wound, his sandy gray hair unbound, sweat seeping from every pore as his heart pounded through his chest, his utterances mere grunts, Adam drove his cutlass forward against the flashing scimitar, only to be deflected at every thrust. Adam knew his footwork lacked finesse—he had never been trained in the gentlemanly art of fencing. But what he lacked in style, he compensated with strength, energy, and desperation. Still, the size and reach of the pirate gave his adversary an advantage that he could not overcome, and the longer they clashed blades the more ground Adam was forced to cede. His back now to the rail, Adam slashed defensively, blocking each thrust of the scimitar, while he watched for an opening. In a split second it appeared to come— Adam was not sure—as the pirate drew back his sword for another blow. Adam saw the unprotected flank of his belly for an instant and, without thought, drove his cutlass straight in up to the hilt.

Withdrawing his blood-dripping blade from the felled giant, Adam paused to catch his breath. He noted with gratitude that the wind had just caught the unreefed mainsail, and the *Atheling* began to ease forward, disentangling herself from the two dhows and their web of boarding lines. But his overpowered crew huddled in a defensive mass amidship as the pirates pummeled and cut them.

Adam checked the foredeck. Seth had turned the two bow-chasers sternward and was ramming them full of shot and handfuls of nails. There was no question what the next move would be.

Adam bolted forward and shouted at the top of his lungs, "All hands to the foredeck! Follow me, lads!"

He raised his cutlass and ran into the mass of his men. His sudden presence energized their resistance, but he knew they could not sustain their ground long.

"To the foredeck! To the foredeck!" he again bellowed. "With me, lads, to the foredeck! Now!"

Adam interposed himself at the front of the men, his cutlass still slashing, to provide cover while they beat a strategic retreat to the bow of the ship. Checking port and starboard, he made certain all were safely forward as ordered. He caught Seth's eye, and Seth acknowledged his glance with a nod. It was almost as if an instinctual choreography had taken hold between father and son. Each was acutely aware of the other's intentions and position without having to guess or ask. The sputtering linstock hung ready.

Adam leapt forward between the two cannon. No sooner had his feet touched the deck than Seth discharged both guns, one directly after the other, with thunderous blasts that shook the ship and sent an array of hot metal raking across the deck, pulverizing all that stood in its way and letting loose showers of deadly splinters down the length of the ship.

The stunned and exhausted crew of the *Atheling* stood in silence long after the leaping gun carriages came to rest and the clouds of smoke had cleared. Before them lay a scene of carnage such as they had never witnessed before: the deck strewn with dead and dying pirates, not a one left standing—arms, legs, and hands severed about the blood-spattered deck, shredded clothing hanging from the rigging and the entire beautiful sweep of the deck of their ship, their home, pocked and scarred.

Adam let drop his cutlass in exhaustion. He looked straight at Seth with hollow eyes that were beyond emotion, lest it be the emotion of gratitude. Neither father nor son spoke for a full minute as they shared the ineffable bond of relishing—of upholding—each other's continued existence.

At length Adam moved, and he spoke barely above a whisper and only to Seth.

"Set a course for home. I am done with these troubled waters. I swear on the Holy Evangels I shall never sail them again. We must find new markets and routes in this life."

11

Know Thyself

1794

ADAM AND SETH SAT BOLT UPRIGHT ON THE HORSEHAIR UPHOLSTERED seats of the Portsmouth to London Flyer, a great lacquered yellow box of a coach with forest green wheels almost as high as a man and surmounted by a red Royal Mail box. It made easy time of the West Sussex Downs in the bright early May weather.

"So this is England," Seth mused as he gazed out the window at the passing countryside.

"It's not as I recall it," Adam admitted with a taut hollow laugh. "My previous familiarity was of a different nature and . . . well, limited."

"How is it not as you recall?"

"Why just to start, the size of the buildings and the industry of the people. Did you not see the height of the walls that surround Priddy's Hard Ordnance Depot at Portsmouth? Twelve pound cannon sunk in the ground as carriage posts at the granite gates and Marine guards in red jackets at every turn! And inside the walls, building upon building, all in stone. And thousand upon thousand of artificers and clerks! Why, I felt like the Indian who accompanied Captain John Smith back to England with an instruction from Powhatan to carve a notch on a stick for every Englishman he saw. I would have had to give up and toss the stick into the water within a minute of arrival!"

"Just so. And still, 'tis not what I expected either. For all the, the," Seth searched for the right word, "*bustle*, it is in truth familiar. Oh, there's the little turn of phrase or quirk of manner that differs from ours, but I also felt, well, at home. I could relax and breathe without the tension of navigating a foreign shoal. It makes me wonder why they were our enemy. Or perhaps, just possibly, who knows, maybe they never were?"

Adam thought long and hard about how to respond. He knew that to grow he had to revise his thinking.

"Not now, maybe. Then it was different," he grumped. "General, that is President, Washington has moved us back into better graces. There's even the prospect of our opening trade with Jamaica I understand."

"And a good thing he has," Seth replied, stiffening the resolve of his insight. "'Tis where our natural interests lie, as I have increasingly come to think. Not that our Secretary of State, Mr. Jefferson, isn't still much enamored of the French and wouldn't take us back into a dalliance with the Jacobins and regicides if he could."

"I agree a tacit resumption of our historical relationship might be fitting," Adam allowed. "And hopefully for us profitable. The Commissioner at Portsmouth received us well enough, even if we were a surprise—albeit a welcome one—showing up at his back door with our load of sticks. Of course when he bought the lot it was with his eye on France. What goes on across the Channel unnerves these English. They are in a state of high preparation now that France has declared war on them and on Spain and Holland. As always, the fortunes of our trade depend on the fortunes of politics. Events spin, and we spin with 'em."

"But it remains a dangerous game for us Americans," Seth observed.

"Aye, so it is, son. Now that Portugal has made peace with Algiers, the protection of her fleet has vanished. It'll only be time, and not much I'd predict, before the Algerine corsairs prey on our merchantmen not just in the Mediterranean but also on the Atlantic side of the Strait of Gibraltar."

"I'm glad we no longer sail those southern waters," Seth confirmed.

"Aye, but even the North Atlantic is not safe now, and that's from the British and the French. You know what happened to Anson's and Longfellow's ships: one taken by the British and the other by the French, privateers all, and their cargoes seized and crews imprisoned—and this despite President Washington's declaration of neutrality between England and France. Why, they say Mr. Jay is in London right now to try to negotiate a treaty which will oblige, which will *compel*, Britain to respect our rights as neutrals on the high seas."

"And should he not succeed?"

"'Tis for that very eventuality we are on the road to London to meet with the Clerk of the Acts at the Navy Board to seek out a long-term contract to supply the Royal Navy and the special protection it should entail. And this at the recommendation of the Commissioner at Portsmouth, no less! I think I espy opportunity here, as chancy as the proposition may be, opportunity such as we have never seen before."

"Is that all it is, Fid, opportunity?"

"How so, my son?" Adam asked, as he shifted in his seat.

"Doesn't virtue have a role?"

"Virtue? What, you mean citizenship, as understood by the Romans? That which a man, *vir*, must step forward and do?"

Seth nodded.

"Well, you mean trading in the interests of our country? Or perhaps the engagement we fought last season against the pirates? Or something more?"

"Those will serve to start."

Adam thought for a moment of his own humiliation at the hands of the British during the Revolution.

"I've fought only when I have had no choice in the matter. There's no glory or virtue in that. I'd gladly take opportunity over virtue for virtue's sake any day. I'm not one of those men who wear their country on their lapel or make ostentation of celebrating our national holiday on the Fourth of July other than by prayers of thanksgiving." Men, Adam admitted to himself, whose simplicity he at once despised and envied.

* * *

The Commissioner at Portsmouth had advised him that the Clerk of the Acts of the Navy Board George Marsh was a cagey man, self-effacing before the indolent nobles whom he served.

His office occupied a spacious suite in the Embankment Building wing of the recently constructed Somerset House on the Strand.

At a desk at the far end of the room, Adam spotted Marsh. He was a portly man, with a blandly round face, jowls, and a long nose. He was modestly attired in a maroon coat and beige breeches, both tailored to flatter the inconvenient bulges of his girth. The Commissioner at Portsmouth had also advised Adam that Marsh had been Clerk of the Acts, a position originally held by Samuel Pepys, since the American Revolution. He was viewed, as the Commissioner put it, as "indispensable." Marsh remained seated as he greeted Adam and Seth.

"A pleasure to meet you, Captain Hale. The letter of introduction from Portsmouth arrived in good time. And this must be young Mr. Hale," Marsh proffered. "Why have you taken so long to come to England?"

Adam thought of his years at the Mill and knew he would have to tread carefully here. He decided to keep his response on the political, rather than personal, level.

"Thank you, Mr. Marsh. I am a humble American merchant captain. We are still but a small and struggling nation. With no Navy of our own to protect our shipping, I sail and trade where the fortunes of great nations permit me and where my insurers will underwrite me. But, in truth, Mr. Marsh, I would have traded with Britain long ago had your ports been open to American shipping."

Marsh did not respond, knowing the truth of Adam's point. Instead, he changed the subject.

"They say you are an educated man."

"More self-educated, I'd say," Adam corrected him with a touch of humility.

"*Nosce te ipsi*," replied Marsh.

"Know thyself? I'm afraid I don't understand. . . . Oh, it doesn't matter."

"Ah, but it does, but it does, Captain Hale. You see, I am only the beginning of your quest for the mast contract with the Royal Navy. You must know yourself to know that you want it and you must be prepared to make sacrifices. This contract is not awarded lightly."

"So, it is political, is it?"

Marsh nodded. "And the House of Hale & Sons must be prepared to play the political game."

Marsh cast a long and appraising eye at Adam and Seth.

"I think it might be convenient if your son remained in England to meet the right persons," Marsh suggested. "This cannot be accomplished quickly."

Convenient for whom, thought Adam. Not in the least for himself, to be sure. Yet, if this were to be a hugely lucrative trade, the opportunity outweighed the inconvenience, and Seth would have to do his part to procure the business.

"Son?" Adam asked as he turned to Seth.

"I'll stay, Fid. I'll do whatever duty requires."

How like Seth, Adam thought. Always right, always upstanding. A man endowed with *virtue*.

But then Seth said what was for him a most unaccustomed thing,

"I look forward to it, as an *adventure*. It surely won't be more than six months. I wish to stay."

Adam looked at his firstborn son, honest, forward, admirable Seth, and wondered for a flicker of an instant if slavery did not come in differing guises. He shook the notion from his head and banned it manfully.

"Very well, Mr. Marsh, you heard Seth's decision. As for me, I will return to America to collect more sticks in the faith you will buy them. God willing, your Navy does not sink me."

Marsh indulged himself in the smallest of smiles, meant no doubt to reassure.

* * *

Ten days later Adam walked up Anchor Lane in Portsmouth to his lodgings. It was dusk on a late May evening, a little balmy. The *Atheling* lay docked below at Gun Wharf, having been laden and fitted for her departure on the morrow's tide.

He felt a prick just between his shoulder blades. He stopped. He was now certain of it. He felt the quivering pressure of a ductile blade behind the point inserted with premeditated precision.

"I've half a mind to run you through here and now," a voice said from behind him. Adam was not certain, but he thought he detected a trace of a brogue.

"You wouldn't dare. That would be murder, as I am unarmed. Besides, what kind of man would stab another man in the back, unseen? Might I turn about to see your face?"

The dancing, febrile punctilio eased off, and Adam turned. His recognition was instant: a little fuller in the face perhaps, but the same long equine visage, wart on the right nostril, eerie gray-green eyes, and black wig—Sir Ponsonby Spicer, Baronet—only this time dressed in a clean new naval greatcoat bearing the single gold epaulette of a Post Captain. The blade of his épée was extended *en garde*.

"Sir, I had heard you were interloping on these shores. Were I not a patriot I would call you out. But I know something of masts and of the King's Broad Arrow and of our needs, so I must desist—for now. But I have not forgotten the maps nor the matter of the *Yellowjacket*."

"When you were a stranger I welcomed you," Adam replied. "Why you acted as you did I have no idea. Why did you?"

"For nothing. For myself."

"As did I. Under such circumstances, I have no intention of raising the matter of the maps. Nor should you. As for the *Yellowjacket*, my ship was under pursuit and attack. I acted only in defense."

Spicer lifted the point of his épée to Adam's thorax. Adam stared hard into his calculating but unreadable eyes.

"Were you armed I would end this now as a matter of honor," Spicer threatened.

"But I am not, and you would have no honor. Besides, how have I affronted your honor?"

"I needn't explain. You stand accused. That counts for all."

Spicer hesitated and then withdrew his épée and slashed the blade through the air several times with a quick well practiced finesse that left a ripping sound in its wake.

"Until next time."

"The challenge remains yours," Adam stated and walked away.

Adam contemplated the matter of honor prorogued as he neared his inn. He cared not for honor. Such was the stuff of tempestuous souls, insecure imposters, and various sorts of small men. A truer name for it was vengeance, an emotion that constricts and stunts the soul and a word that he chose not to have in his New England lexicon. He would not allow it to be foisted onto him. Adam banished the thought of it. What, if anything, would come of the Baronet's "honor" was beyond his knowing or control.

Adam thought of Seth, who was to stay behind in London, but was yet unknown to Spicer. However, his vulnerability was within Adam's knowledge and control. Immediately on entering his room, Adam sat down and wrote a letter to Seth warning him to avoid Spicer at all costs in his comings and goings in the metropolis.

12

A Jamaican Siren

1795—Part I

JEZREEL STOOD AMIDSHIPS ON THE *DOLPHIN* AS, DRIVEN BY THE SOUTH-west trade winds, she slid into the harbor at Port Antonio in late January. There was no quarterdeck for him to pace like his father on the small schooner, even if that had been his disposition, which it was not. On this, his second voyage to Jamaica as Captain of his own vessel, Jezreel wore the comfort of familiarity in as an offhand way as his open-necked white linen shirt and bare feet. With a crew of only four hands, Jezreel shared in the labors and meals of his men and handled the sheets as readily as he calculated the navigation. At almost twenty-five, fit, tanned, and with his black hair worn long and tied loosely with a ribbon at his nape, he was at that age that still rejoiced in the attainment of full manhood, immortality, and boundless horizons.

Jezreel's blood quickened at the sights of the palm trees that waved along the shoreline and of the brilliant clear blue water that gave him a prism on the schools of yellow fish that darted and flickered among the coral reefs. Not a month earlier Jezreel had been imprisoned in the monochrome of the deep Maine winter where snow stood piled as high as his shoulder and night laid its heavy settling hand by afternoon. His parting memory of home was a slate gray hawk landing in the snow outside his bedroom window to pick at the remains of a sparrow that had fallen dead from the cold, its body frozen so solidly that it refused to bleed at the persistent pecks of the hawk, leaving only a scattering of feathers and a vague smudge of red on the crusted snow.

* * *

Great Spring Garden was an estate such as none Jezreel had ever seen before. Spread out in St. George's Parish on the north shore of the island, it bestrode the sweep of Buff Bay and the left bank of the Spanish River. The wooden great house, on a rising ground at the foot of the Blue Mountains, commanded a view of the three thousand acres that comprised the plantation: a water wheel-driven mill, the boiling house with copper vats, the overseer's house and offices, a hospital, and a slave village of thirty acres which was the home to some six hundred blacks who worked the plantation's crops of cane and ratoon, whose homes and garden plots reputedly passed from father to son and supported a lively free trade in pigs and poultry. Great Spring Garden also boasted a fine private wharf that jutted into the sea to supply its store, which was constructed of pink-white coral blocks topped by a red terracotta roof. From this wharf small boats, locally called droggers, ferried produce to the visiting foreign ships which, like the *Dolphin*, lay at anchorage eastward off Port Antonio.

Not more than an hour earlier Jezreel had ridden, with his violin at his side, in the estate's wagon sent to fetch him up a lengthy straight palm-lined drive to the great house. On the way, they passed an overseer on horseback and wearing a dusty white greatcoat leading a contingent of hoe and machete-bearing slave laborers who plodded their way home as the sun sank rapidly behind the cresting hulk of the Blue Mountains. Embarrassed at his brush past slavery, Jezreel averted his eyes. But avoidance was not so easy because in Jamaica evil coexisted with beauty and, in truth, the two were inextricably intertwined. Evening in Jamaica had a fragrance uniquely its own, Jezreel observed: a whiff of oranges, a hint of cardamom, a sweet humidity that gathered close and almost kissed him.

The great house was built to impress. It commanded an immaculately tended lawn bordered by broad leafed palms and plantain trees. Built entirely of wood, one story tall and resting on pillars of coral blocks, it was reached by a sweeping sandstone staircase leading up from the lawn. A long gallery or piazza which stretched the whole length of the house dominated the mansion's single floor and terminated at each end with a high-ceilinged square room. In between, along each side of the piazza, ran a series of bedrooms whose open windows contained dark wood slatted blinds to capture and admit any rare passing breeze. The piazza, well appointed with sofas, ottomans, tables, and chairs such as one might find in a London town house, formed the principal sitting room of the mansion, as it admitted the cooling breeze to sweep through it whenever there was a breath of fresh air. But what Jezreel noted most was the absence of carpets and the hard bread-nut floor on which he trod, as beautifully polished as the finest dining table in Portland or even, he imagined, London.

Now, as Jezreel sat at table in the teak-paneled dining room of Gabrielle Eugenie Toledano Campbell, the intimate dance between the sublime and the repellent that was daily life in the Caribbean assumed new immediacy.

"Captain Hale, we are honored to have your company," his smiling hostess stated formally but graciously to set him at ease. She spoke with a refined British accent, Jezreel noted. Unlike many white Jamaican plantation ladies, she had no Creole inflection—a trait often decried by visiting Englishmen who in their letters home mocked the indolence and drawling accents of plantation wives. It was evident to Jezreel that, even though she dwelled on the periphery of the empire, she was an exception.

"Mrs. Campbell, the pleasure is all mine," Jezreel responded with equal formality, but he meant it. Jezreel assessed his hostess in the dim light of the sputtering myrtle wax candles that flickered gold and umber hues off the polished paneling. There was no question that she was a beauty. She wore a white gauzelike dress that showed the curves of her hips and gathered her ample breasts up into an offering. The mahogany haired, peach-skinned widow with violet-hued eyes and only the hint of encroaching crow's feet to impart wisdom was somewhere adrift in her mid-thirties. Jezreel knew only the briefest outlines of her provenance—a native Creole of mixed French, Spanish, and English blood, she was the widow of a Scottish adventurer-turned-planter, Alec McKay Campbell, who had purchased Great Spring Garden fifteen years previously only to succumb to yellow fever in one of the numerous epidemics that swept the islands. Gabrielle the widow had stayed on and run the plantation for the past five years and, in so doing, had quickly acquired the reputation of an astute planter and businesswoman who was experimenting with the development of new crops to trade with the United States. Jezreel had heard that the crops she had pioneered included asparagus, barberry, beets, celery, eggplant, jackfruit, and mangoes and that her gardens brimmed with amaranthus, amaryllis, gardenia, hibiscus, and jasmine. Jezreel noted that Gabrielle was quite the industrious woman, hardly one to lounge on a settee attended by slaves who fanned her face and scratched the soles of her feet. She had chosen the bee as her personal symbol: it was woven into the golden fabric of the cushions of the chairs on which they sat. She had also acquired the reputation of something of a siren. It was for both reasons that Jezreel had sought an invitation.

However, it was an invitation he shared with a stout British army officer who sat at the end of the table opposite Gabrielle. Jezreel studied him from the corner of his eye. With his hawk nose, bushy eyebrows, and florid complexion, Jezreel guessed him to be in his late forties. Evidently he was a man who did not bend, for he wore a heavy red wool officer's tunic, gold braided and buttoned to the collar, and an anachronistic white powdered wig, slightly askew in the heat and what Jezreel suspected was his descent into drunkenness, to judge from the empty bottle of hock before him and the half-filled goblet cradled in his hand. Gabrielle introduced him only as "Major Gaskill."

"Captain Hale, what goods have you brought us in Jamaica?" Gabrielle asked as she again smiled invitingly at Jezreel.

"I've come with a cargo of staves, shooks, tobacco, capers, silks, and Spanish wine."

"Silks and Spanish wine?" Gabrielle observed, her interest piqued. "I might want—"

"Aha! I thought so," interrupted a growling Major Gaskill. "Another 'broken voyage' cargo. I could have you clapped in irons."

Jezreel thought for a second and cleared his throat.

"No, Major Gaskill, you won't, and I'll tell you why. All the New England captains use 'broken voyages' to avoid seizure by the belligerents. True, the staves and shooks are Maine produce and the tobacco hails from Maryland, but the other items were legally landed at Portland and with duties paid are now 'American' goods and, as such, neutral cargo. Besides, Jamaica needs American products, and this is a fiction your government well knows and approves."

Gaskill glared and returned to his goblet of hock. Jezreel noticed the perspiration building between his shoulder blades and beginning to soak his shirt. The heat of the exchange and of climate, the dim light of the wax candles and the black half-naked servants with grim visages who attended the dinner reminded him of Hades and caused him to imagine that he was at supper with Pluto rather than a beautiful Proserpine.

Sensing the unpleasantness of the standoff, Gabrielle moved quickly to clear the air.

"Well, you have arrived in Jamaica at a most importune time," Gabrielle observed, as a slight ironic smile formed at the corners of her sensual lips. "The Maroons are in revolt again. Major Gaskill can explain."

The besotted Major looked up with heavily lidded eyes.

"Well, if I must. The Maroons in Trelawny Parish up in the Cockpit Country think they've grievances. They're a tetchy people. You can never satisfy them."

"Well, it's a bit more complicated than that," Gabrielle inserted. "The Maroons, as you may know, descend from runaway Spanish slaves and have been a free people since Britain took Jamaica from Spain a hundred and forty years ago. They live under a superintendent appointed by the King in London, Captain Craskell. It turns out Captain Craskell is not a very politic man. He arrested two Maroons in Montego for stealing pigs and had them flogged. His mistake was to have them flogged by a black slave, not a free man. The Maroons were insulted."

"Tetchy people," Gaskill grumbled as he grasped another bottle of hock.

"But the troubles did not stop there," Gabrielle continued. "The Governor of Jamaica, the Earl of Balcarres, feared that the unhappiness amongst the Maroons would spread to the slaves and that there would be a revolt, as you know recently occurred on Saint Domingue. The Governor also saw the hand of French agents involved in the unhappiness. I don't doubt it for a moment. So he declared martial law and called out the militia. The Governor sent a message to the Maroons warning that they were surrounded and that he would attack and destroy Trelawny Town unless they surrendered. A handful of older Maroons took his terms, and the Governor immediately arrested them. The younger Maroons did not want to give up their ancestral rights once they heard of the Governor's treatment of the elders. They torched Trelawny Town and withdrew into the mountains of the Cockpit Country."

"I see why you say my timing is importune," Jezreel acknowledged. "But is there danger?"

"I should think so," Gabrielle responded with a telltale flinch of her cheek muscles. "For the last six months the Maroons have attacked and held off Britain's finest troops and our local militia. They know the terrain, and they operate by ambush. And now they have taken to brazen attacks on plantations, murdering planters and their families and carrying off slaves. London sent out a new military commander, General Walpole, who has now trained his troops to fight in this type of countryside. He has constructed a ring of armed outposts in the mountains. He is said to have the Maroons on the defensive, and yet the attacks continue. Which brings us to why Major Gaskill is here."

A somnolent Gaskill stirred from his impending stupor.

"Bloodhounds next week," he growled.

Jezreel waited for an explanation that never came.

"Pompey, serve the dessert," Gabrielle ordered one of the attendant slaves. Immediately the slaves swooped in and placed shallow dishes containing a liquid confection before the trio. "It's a syllabub," explained Gabrielle.

Jezreel caught the eye of one of the servers as he slid the saucer before him, and he reflected for an instant that what he found disagreeable in Jamaica was that the wealth of the country consisted of slaves, so that all one eats rises out of driving and whipping these poor wretches and that this kind of authority so corrupts the minds of the masters that it makes them overbearing and that this adds much to the discomfort of the place. One cannot conceive, Jezreel thought, how it strikes the mind on first arrival to have all these black faces with grim looks round about you. As for eating, Jezreel mused as he spooned the dessert, they have the names of almost everything that is delicious or in fashion in America or England, but they give them to things as little like as Caesar or Pompey were to the slaves whom they call by those names.

With dessert finished, Gabrielle turned to Jezreel.

"Perhaps you might be good enough to entertain us with some airs on your violin?" she asked. "I've heard you are quite good."

"You flatter me with your kind words. I prefer to think of it simply as my 'fiddle.'"

Jezreel obliged with a rendition of a medley of New England hymns that he had learned by ear as a boy. Gabrielle followed attentively and with a smile. Encouraged, Jezreel segued into a snatch of Scottish airs, and then, summoning ambition, he launched into *The Heavens Are Telling* from Haydn's *Creation*, which he had recently mastered with the aid of a visiting instructor from Boston.

At length, the dinner over and with Major Gaskill asleep and snoring in his chair, Gabrielle reached across the table to touch Jezreel's bow hand with her long, graceful fingers, smiling most ingratiatingly as she did so.

"We are free now. Will you join me in my chamber?"

"Are you certain, madam?" he asked with an eye to the snoring Major Gaskill.

"Though I am but a woman, I am one who from the vicissitudes of this life has learned what she wants and gets it," she purred as she stared at him with her wide-open violet eyes. "I want—and request—the pleasure of your company for the evening."

At that the rectitude of Jezreel's observations and objections melted away like an ice in the tropics as he took her arm and followed her to her great mosquito-netted mahogany bed.

* * *

The next morning Jezreel awoke to find Gabrielle already up and hard at work seated at the secretary in her bedroom going over account books and penning requests for bank drafts. Sensing that she was not to be disturbed, Jezreel observed her through half-closed eyes.

From the corner of her eye, she saw that he was awake.

"Good morning to you," she acknowledged with a quick nod and smile before returning to her business.

"And to you too," Jezreel responded and then, hoping to lure her away from her work, added, "Did you enjoy last night as much as I did?"

Gabrielle looked exasperated at the interruption as she put down her quill, but she relented.

"Yes, of course. I would have been disappointed if I had not."

"But you were not disappointed then?"

"Not in the least. But now if you don't mind, I must return to—"

Jezreel sensed that there was a practicality, a coldness even, to this woman of many parts. She had a head for figures and inhabited and mastered a world that Jezreel knew even less than he knew her soul, even if he did know at first hand the passion of her body.

A twinge of New England sensibility asserted itself in Jezreel.

"Have you no God or gods in Jamaica?" he interjected bluntly.

Gabrielle stared as she assessed his question before responding.

"They hardly figure. We in the Indies are a sea-borne people, always with our eye to the weather, to the trade routes, to the incoming ships and what they bring. Our life is a commercial enterprise first and foremost. 'Tis true we have many of the civilities of life in England: country estates, rounds of dinners, balls and parades of the militia, not to mention an established church and the official opening and closing of our legislature. But God or gods? Why they hardly figure. And 'tis just as well, for if there were a just God I would long ago have borne children."

"You cannot bear? How can you be so sure of that?"

"Ten years of marriage to Alec Campbell and not a single pregnancy. You see, Jezreel, I am barren."

"Gabrielle, I am so sorry." Somehow the cold finality of her statement conflicted with the passion she had shown the preceding night. Jezreel suspected that she needed him for reassurance of her value as a woman. If so, he little minded, for her passion in bed was ravishing, and that was more than enough.

"But, wait Gabrielle, how do you know that the fault did not lie with your husband?"

"Oh, Alec Campbell had many children. Just not by me. I suppose you have not yet had the opportunity to visit the slave village with its many spurious offspring?"

* * *

One week later Jezreel sat atop a borrowed horse at the Army's forward base camp in the Cockpit Country. The base nestled at the foot of the Quick Step Trail, one of only several paths that penetrated to the interior of the region. Just behind him lay the "Land of Look Behind," so named because Spanish horsemen who entered this region searching for runaway slaves mounted two to a horse, one rider facing forward to look for slaves and the other facing rearward to look for ambushes. As well they might have, thought Jezreel, for the Cockpit Country was an aptly named topography of high conical hills and plungingly deep valleys, all covered by an impenetrable mantle of tropical vegetation. Only the trails probed tentatively into the undulating ridges.

"Well, young Captain Hale, don't forget you are in a theater of operations," Major Gaskill said as his hefty frame creaked in his saddle and his well-lathered horse snorted. "It was against my better judgment to let you come, and it's only because I have such a high regard for Mrs. Campbell, who made such a show of insistence, that I consented. So follow close behind me and pay attention. We wouldn't want to lose you, now would we?"

"Nor do I want to be lost, Major Gaskill. I am in your hands."

"Do you see those there?" Gaskill asked as he pointed with his braided leather riding crop to one hundred bloodhounds and fifty handlers, two to a man, all the dogs straining at their chain leashes and baying. "These hounds will be the means to bring this rebellion to an end. We procured them, as well as their chasseurs, in Cuba. They use 'em there to track runaway slaves and thieves. And they're vicious. They have already attacked and killed several of our horses."

At that moment a gunshot went off, and the spooked hounds went into a frenzy of barking and lunging so that their chasseurs could barely restrain them.

"Here's to today's fox," Gaskill said as he tipped his hat and slapped the side of his mount with the crop, and off they rode.

Three hours later, high in the hills and with the bloodhounds fanned out before the troops, they came to a shanty before which an old woman wearing a turban was roasting a goat on a spit. As they stopped to ask directions one of the bloodhounds jumped to steal a bite of meat from the haunches of the goat. The woman tried to swat the hound away.

"Shoo, shoo, and off with you!" she protested as she made a pantomime of slapping at the dog.

At that the dog turned on her and lunged for her throat. The dog sank its teeth in and wrestled her to the ground. Growling and thrashing while its chasseur tried to rein it in, the dog would not let go of its prey. Blood sprayed in all directions as the dog whipped the old woman around as if she were a rag doll.

"Can't you stop it? Why don't you shoot the dog?" Jezreel asked Major Gaskill.

"No, the dog's too valuable. Besides, they're too close together. If we shot at the dog we'd probably hit the woman."

So for another three minutes the dog worked on its prey, as the woman's jugular spurted blood and the dog whipped her head back and forth with the killer's instinct that sought a broken neck while the soldiers watched. At length the chasseur brought the dog back under control and tore him from the woman with his hands. She lay motionless on the ground. Gaskill approached and, leaning down from his mount, probed her blood-soaked and dirty head with his crop, turning it first left and then right. He flicked its tip against her cheek before bringing it back up.

"Well, I'd say this one's tucked herself up. Let us proceed on our mission."

And off they rode once more. Only this time, Jezreel simmered at the depravity of Major Gaskill and of the system that produced him.

13

Jacob's Ladder

1795—Part II

Seth Hale stood with his hat in hand in the anteroom of the Grand Pump Room at Bath, admiring the life-size alabaster statue of Aphrodite as he waited. The still unfinished colonnaded building that housed the Grand Pump Room was a marvel of Palladian architecture, Seth assayed with approval. It was architecture that cowed, unlike any in America. As he entered, he spied the inscription in Greek chiseled into its architrave which translated as: Water Best of Elements. Having learned at the knee of his father, he recognized it as a Pindaric motto.

Seth hoped he was dressed appropriately in his yellow breeches, blue coat, gray-striped waistcoat, and jabot, all bespoke not a week before from a tailor in Jermyn Street. Seth justified the expenditure with the knowledge that appearing as an American rube would not likely win him the contract to supply the Royal Navy and that he had to look British in order to put his hosts at ease. Not that that did not come naturally in most matters other than clothing and speech. With his father's strong chin and profile, lively blue eyes and light brown hair tied neatly in a queue, he could pass as English, at least until he spoke. And then his American diction and mannerisms came to the fore. Although conscious of his appearance and wanting to make a good impression, he realized he would have to settle for a mythical North Atlantic look, neither definitively American nor definitively English, and yet somehow hovering in ambiguity between the two.

After months of delay and wrangling, Marsh had effected his introduction to The Right Honourable Lord Hormsby, who had come to take the waters at Bath with the Prince of Wales. Lord Hormsby, Seth had learned, was to be his channel to the Prince, who in turn, if all went well, would recommend to the Navy Board that a contract be granted to the House of Hale & Sons. Seth understood that the Prince's "recommendation" was rarely, if ever, ignored.

"Captain Hale?" the Pump House's Master of Ceremonies inquired as he opened the door to the Pump Room. "Lord Hormsby is now ready to receive you."

Seth followed the Master of Ceremonies into a long grand room in which hundreds of fashionably dressed people promenaded up and down abuzz in conversation. A chamber orchestra played from a gallery at the far end of the room. The strains of the music, the humidity of the waters, the heat of the crowd, and the buzz and hum of their conversation conspired to overwhelm Seth for an instant.

Spotting Lord Hormsby in the crowd, the Master of Ceremonies led Seth by the hand through the crowd to the ambulatory peer, who was accompanied by his wife and three daughters.

"M' Lord, may I introduce Captain Hale, who comes to us from America?"

Lord Hormsby was a tall, older man with a slight stoop. His thin, wrinkled face and lean cheekbones contrasted with the blond, blue-eyed beauty and peaches-and-cream complexion of his oldest daughter standing nearest him. Seth allowed his eye to linger for a second on her. Just shorter than himself, she was dressed in the latest style of Directoire France, with a form-clinging high-waisted *chemise à la reine* of apricot-hued silk, a bonnet of straw sporting two ostrich plumes, and a silk reticule dangling from her left wrist. The effect, as Seth absorbed it in a glance, was that of the perfect, classical beauty of an Ionic column. He wondered if she were as rigid.

Lord Hormsby acknowledged Seth with a slight nod of his head but no proffered hand.

"Ah, from America then, are we?" he asked, as his question succumbed to a phthisic wheeze.

"Yes, Your Lordship, I sail from Portland in the District of Maine, though I have been in your fair country these last nine months or more."

Seth stopped to allow Lord Hormsby to react. He did not but only stared.

Realizing he would have to seize the initiative in the conversation before he had the weather gauge of his interlocutor, Seth, who valued honesty, went directly to his point.

"I wish to speak to you about the supply of New England masts to the Royal Navy."

"A tradesman?" Lord Hormsby winced and, with a wave of his etiolated hand, averted his gaze and resumed his promenade.

At that very moment, Seth felt a hand gently asserted at his elbow. He turned to find the blue-eyed beauty of a daughter who tarried while her family moved on.

"Perhaps we should walk outside," she asserted, almost conspiratorially, in a voice at once plummy and deep, like a diapason organ pipe.

"Indeed," Seth quickly agreed.

As they exited the building, Seth saw that a passing shower had washed clean the paved piazza that connected the Grand Pump Room at a right angle to Bath Abbey.

"Captain Hale, I admire your honesty, but the way to my father's mind is not a direct line."

Here, Seth realized was a woman who was his equal in going directly to the point.

"Oh, do explain. I'd be most grateful."

"No, Captain, the way to my father's mind is through his heart. And the key to his heart is 'Dame' Rafferty."

"'Dame' Rafferty?"

"Well, she's not really a Dame. She is just called that. She is, or was, a Covent Garden actress. Now she runs a faro salon in Half Moon Street in Mayfair. And she is my father's mistress. There are some who would censure her as a Cyprian. I am not among them. No, I rather admire her pluck and enterprise. I could never do what she does because of my station, but I don't begrudge her making the most of her talents. I would do the same were I she."

"But you are not."

"No, I'm a twenty-two-year-old spinster brought by my father to take the waters at Bath each of the last five years in the hopes of finding a suitable match," she laughed as her voice romped through the octaves like the full-throated range of a cathedral's organ.

"But you haven't?"

"Not one that I would want. Oh, there are plenty of 'suitable' blades strolling about the Pump Room, or more to the point, their parents, for it really is more of a negotiation than an encounter. But I've insisted on a right of refusal."

"Which you have exercised?"

"Twice in fact."

"Well, maybe three will be a charm."

She shrugged.

"In the process I've gotten to know Bath quite well," she observed in a deliberate move to change the subject. "Do you realize that under where we are walking there is a complete Roman city, with streets and shops and all? And of course with baths. I visited it once, on a dark night with torches."

"You must be brave. Brave enough to introduce me to 'Dame' Rafferty?"

The beauty shrugged again. "We'll see. Look! Here we are at the Abbey."

The west façade of the Perpendicular Gothic church loomed before them, its magnificent window flanked by narthex towers on which carved ladders bore angels ascending to and descending from heaven. At the lowest level, barely more than the height of a man, the angels had been chiseled away in a base act of defacement.

"What happened here?" Seth asked.

"That was the handiwork of the Puritans during the Civil War. They also broke all the stained-glass windows. The Puritans were a nasty lot. Those were your people, were they not?"

Seth stumbled for an answer. The iconoclasm of furious chiselers bore no connection to the white-steepled meeting houses and propriety of New England villages which he knew.

"My forebears were New England Puritans, it is true, but I can't answer for their wrongs in the past. Look, the angels have only been defaced to the petty height of a man. The Puritans evidently could not reach higher—to heaven."

"Do you think the angels are ascending or descending?"

Seth studied the façade for a moment.

"I'm not entirely sure. Maybe both."

"Do they know where they are headed?"

"Jacob did in his dream of the ladder in Genesis: it was to the land of Israel, which God gave to Jacob and his descendants. But for us perhaps it symbolizes our chase of a ladder of beauties, all leading to the ultimate beauty, God's beauty." He shot her a glance and took in her beauty.

"Oh, you really are quite the Puritan after all," she observed with a look at once skeptical and intrigued.

"And who are you?"

"Georgette Hormsby. The Honourable Georgette Hormsby."

And as she spoke Seth saw a hint of the smile of a coquette that he would never forget as long as he lived. The column had a chink.

* * *

Two weeks later Seth and Georgette, having put the slip on her lady's maid who accompanied her on outings, stood at the bottom of White Horse Street where it spilled into the courtyard of Shepherd Market. As evening fell, the street and walkways and nooks and crannies shook off the sleep of daylight and awoke with life and sin: a chorus emanating from the rookeries to the north, prostitutes beckoning from the doorways, hucksters spreading mats for their wares on the paving stones, a drunken ruction erupting inside Ye Grapes public house, gentlemen arriving by sedan chair from the Blue Posts across Piccadilly, candles being lit in upstairs windows of the gaming rooms.

"Do you think we should be here?" Seth asked as they entered the courtyard, crab fashion, with their backs to the wall. In the Chapel Street passage to the left of Ye Grapes a gaggle of tarted-up game pullets flushed on their arrival and scattered. Georgette pulled her bonnet tighter over her head and cinched the paisley scarf that held it.

"I don't see why not," Georgette replied. "'Dame' Rafferty acknowledged my note and said to come early, before she becomes busy. Besides, 'tis a bit of an adventure, no?"

"And you have been here before?"

"Not exactly. Well, only in the daylight."

"I suspect daylight is not this neighborhood's finest hour."

"Nonetheless, here we are. It'll be just a twist and a turn now past Curzon Street. Half Moon Street is just over there."

"Are you ready?" he asked as he looked her in the eye.

She responded with a twinkle and the half curve of an ironic smile on her sensual lips. "I've always wanted to play the procuress."

A few steps later Seth grasped the brass knocker at the house with a red door and pounded. The door swung open from the inside, and Seth and Georgette gasped. Athwart the entrance stood a gigantic Don Cossack wearing black jackboots, a blue *cherkesska* tunic with cartridge loops, flowing gray mustachios, and a *papakha* sheepskin hat and with a bullwhip tucked in his belt.

"Aha, you must be the butler!" Georgette piped in quick recovery. "Now see here, we have an appointment with 'Dame' Rafferty. I am The Honourable Georgette Hormsby, and this is Captain Seth Hale, who has come all the way from America to meet with her."

The guardian of the front hall nodded curtly and with no further ado bade them enter and showed them upstairs to "Dame" Rafferty's gaming room.

Spying them from across the still unoccupied tables, "Dame" Rafferty rose to greet them and tottered forward.

Dressed in an old-fashioned hoop dress which showed off her sagging cleavage, the "Dame" was at once a broken-down wreck and ageless. She wore her dyed black hair piled high in a style long out of fashion, and her wrinkled face was a brave effort at immortality: a pastiche of rouge, arsenic, and beauty spots that would have done an Augustan Age courtesan proud. Try as he might, Seth could not guess her age but surely it was well past half a century and then some. But her eyes, he noted, were alive and dancing.

She extended a bejeweled hand in greeting.

"To what do I owe this pleasure, M' Lady? It isn't often that M'Lord's favorite daughter comes calling. But know that you are most welcome, as I am so fond of your father."

"Yes, well, thank you. And, rest assured, he of you. I would like to introduce you to Captain Seth Hale from America."

"The United States or Canada?" "Dame" Rafferty asked as she shook hands with Seth.

"Oh, the United States, to be sure."

"I don't suppose you play at cards?"

"Well, no, I don't gamble at cards."

"'Tis a sin then for you, I reckon."

"I find it idle," Seth replied, ever truthful.

"Captain Hale gambles with ships and masts and men's lives," Georgette inserted to right the conversation.

"Oh, so. Do tell," she responded as she eyed Seth up and down.

"My family controls the mast trade from New England. Following Independence we traded with France. But the 14 of July and the Reign of Terror has made that trade intolerable. We now seek the English market."

"Tell me, sir, are you a patriot?"

"I am, madam, but one like General Washington who despises the *sans culottes* and knows where the natural alignment of our nations' interests lies."

"Not like your Mr. Jefferson?"

"Just so, madam. Not like Mr. Jefferson."

"I see. So why should I help you?"

"Because we are an established house of merchants who deliver on our contracts on time and because we supply the largest and stoutest mast timbers that Britain can obtain anywhere. And at good and fair price."

"So you say."

"So I say. And I do."

"We've need of these timbers, haven't we?" Georgette interjected.

"I have heard as much, what with the French depredations on our shipping on the rise," "Dame" Rafferty acknowledged. "M'Lord has spoken of it."

"Captain Hale only needs an introduction, a word graciously planted in my father's ear, that's all we ask."

"Dame" Rafferty thought for a long moment.

"Captain, I don't know you, but I like your look and the honesty with which you have addressed me. I am willing to place a bet on you. And, by the way, I always deal the cards. I never gamble myself."

Seth smiled.

"I am most obliged to you for helping me," he proffered.

"Oh, it's not to help you. It's to help England. You see, my dear Captain Hale, I may be an old whore, but I am a patriotic old whore."

14

The Mother Country Revisited
1795—Part III

"WHAT A MARVELOUS ERA IN WHICH WE LIVE!" ADAM EXCLAIMED AS HE burst through the front door of his white frame house on India Street in Portland.

"Oh, how so?" Nabby responded, accustomed to her husband's protean interests and momentary enthusiasms.

"Nabby, today I received three letters!" He waved them aloft. "I've never before received three letters in one day. What a marvel our new Post Office Department is. Our lives are improving day by day now that we are our own sovereign country. I will open them and read them to you."

Adam grabbed the poker and stirred the embers in the fireplace, for it was still chill in the late Maine spring. He eased himself into his favorite Bargello stitched wing chair by the fireplace. Nabby took her customary seat in the Windsor chair opposite.

"The first one is from Jezreel," Adam explained as he recognized the quick, liquid handwriting on the address side. Opening the letter, Adam read out loud:

"Dear Fid and Mama, my arrival in Jamaica was safe and rapid. I disposed of the cargo without effort and have procured contracts for various Jamaican goods for the return. However, I have determined

to extend my stay in this island for some months longer. The Dolphin is in need of careening, which I am having undertaken at Port Antonio. As for the island, its flora and fauna and inhabitants, I could write you endlessly, but for now rest assured that I am most content as a guest at Great Spring Garden plantation, where the proprietress, Mrs. Campbell, has extended all the courtesies one could imagine or ask for. I shall write in greater detail later. My kisses to Thankful and Juvenal.

Signed Jezreel."

"All the courtesies one could imagine or ask for?" Nabby repeated with one arched eyebrow. "I'm glad of it, but to what does he refer?"

"I wouldn't worry about it. At least he's well and happy, even if dilatory. . . . Aha! This one is from Seth!" Adam proclaimed as he looked at the neat, almost blocklike lettering of the address. It was a much thicker letter than the one from Jezreel.

Adam opened it and read:

"My Dearest Parents, It is with the greatest pleasure that I inform you that we have obtained the contract to supply the Royal Navy, the details and specifics of which are enclosed."

Adam stopped reading and put the letter down on his lap.
"Oh, my."

Nabby saw the joy and pride in Adam's eyes and rose to put her arms around him.

"What else does he say? Please do read on," she urged as she looked over his shoulder.

Adam picked up the letter and resumed.

"These last months in England have been at once lucrative and pleasant. I have visited Bath and the Cotswolds, and my explorations of London and knowledge increase daily. My introductions have proven valuable, and I have met and become part of a most interesting set

of people. One in particular, The Honourable Georgette Hormsby, has proven most solicitous of us and our well-being. I am in her company almost daily and find it agreeable. I hope that you will have occasion to meet on your next voyage to England. As much as I miss Portland, I fear I must remain here to supervise the contract, which, as you will see from the enclosed, is the largest we have ever undertaken.

Your most obedient Son.

Signed S. Hale."

"The Honourable Georgette Hormsby, eh?" Nabby asked with both eyebrows arched.

"Don't worry. He's a sensible young man. I cannot help but reflect on how blessed we are and have been these last twelve years, how our children have grown and our fortune increased, almost without impediment, since coming to Portland. I am humbled before the Almighty for his providence to us. I pray that it shall continue."

Nabby took his hand and held it in silence. At length, Adam picked up the sheet with the specifications of the contract and read it to himself. Shaking his head in incredulity, he looked her in the eye. "This will require a fleet—or three vessels at any rate. I must get to sea. It will be good to be at sea again."

"What of the third letter?" Nabby asked.

"From the stiffness and quality of the paper I'd take it to be an official communication of some sort. What anyone would want of me I've no idea."

Adam opened the letter and read:

"Most esteemed Sir: I regret to inform you that on the 1st of March last, the French privateer Foudrier operating under a Letter of Marque issued by the Directoire in Paris seized your schooner All-agash in international waters and disposed of her and her cargo at auction at Guadaloupe. Your crew are safe and will be repatriated on the first available ship bound for New England. French seizures of

neutral American shipping, of which there are an increasing number, will not be tolerated. Rest assured that the United States has filed a protest with the French authorities, but the prospects of restitution are uncertain, and at this time you may wish to inform your insurers, if any.

Your most humble and obedient servant,

J. Pritchard, Consul of the United States of America, Basse Terre, Guadaloupe."

Insurers indeed! Adam thought. There were no insurers. The ship and her cargo were a total loss. Adam ran a quick calculation in his head: the cargo of shooks and staves, salt cod, leather shoes, London gin, and New Hampshire nails were not glamorous but amounted to $1,700, and that was on top of the value of the ship itself which easily exceeded $2,700, so a loss of $4,400. Adam had heard of the increased French attacks on American shipping. Although the United States had declared neutrality in the struggle between Great Britain and an increasingly aggressive revolutionary France, the Jay Treaty had settled most of America's grievances with Britain, and the United States had ceased payment of its Revolutionary War debt to France because that debt was owed to the French Crown, not to the bloodthirsty murderers of the Terror and Directoire. Apparently, the French took umbrage at this and had commenced preying on American shipping up and down the coast and wherever they could find American bottoms, especially those that carried British cargo.

His next voyage to England, Adam told himself, would require a new kind of citizenship. The big guns would be brought up from the cellar and refitted to the *Atheling*. Not that he had the crews trained to handle them, but maybe their presence protruding from the gun ports would deter any would-be predator. And, he reminded himself, he still knew how to handle the bow-chasers.

* * *

In mid-July Adam assembled his three ships with the *Atheling* in the van and, after stopping at the Kennebec to lade the masts, sailed north to Halifax, where he fell in with a Royal Navy convoy from the Naval Yard headed for Plymouth. At first, the ship's guns drew long stares from the British officers to whom he presented his credentials, but a quick review of his contract with His Majesty's Government allayed their suspicions, even if some of them did harbor a lingering resentment at the theft of "our" masts following American independence.

The passage was a rapid and uneventful three weeks propelled by the Gulf Stream and the Prevailing Westerlies, with Land's End raised at two bells on a late Sunday afternoon.

* * *

At exactly the same time as Adam's landfall, Nabby commenced her daily noon constitutional in the meadows atop Munjoy Hill overlooking Casco Bay. It was a splendid high summer day, crisp and clear, with the islands spread out and dotting the sparkling sea as the white sails of smacks and schooners tilted into the breeze. As always, Nabby looked eastward and tried to picture where her husband might be. But her travels years ago had gone no further than the coastal trade, so England was a mere abstraction in her mind, a land of pomp and circumstance, of great cathedrals and country houses and peers with long noses.

Although she had long ago resigned herself to the sacrifices of a seafarer's wife, she still experienced blue and moody days immediately following Adam's departure, when, alone, she found herself bursting into tears until her New England resolve reasserted itself and righted the ship. It helped that she kept a diary all their long marriage in which she recorded her moods, reactions, and speculations. Somehow the daily regularity of it, whether the entry was a few lines or a page, provided reassurance and continuity. Using this, like the ship's sandglass and bell, to set the rhythm of her life, she had learned to enjoy the daily chores of keeping the household running, of composing frequent letters to her husband and siblings, of reading many of the same books that Adam enjoyed, of socializing with the other merchants' wives and, on Sundays, taking the family pew at Old Jerusalem.

Now, at this stage of life in her mid-forties with her hair touched by gray, the integrity of the family nest she so cherished was unraveling, and there was nothing she could do about it. Seth had long ago left home on his own voyages and now Jezreel had struck out on his own. Anything she could say, any command she could give, would be as futile as whistling into a nor'easter.

Still, she was grateful that two children remained at home and constituted the family in Adam's absence. Thankful, at nineteen, was a fine and ladylike daughter with an innate goodness. Nabby enjoyed her company, and she was no end of help to her in administering the household during the men's absences. Thankful had the friendship of all the young ladies her age about town and with them attended the balls—but had no suitor with gravitas. Like her mother, she held her head high.

Juvenal, at fifteen, was a scholarly lad but, in Nabby's judgment, with something of the youngest child's propensity for dreaming and the unpredictable. Still, his tutor Mr. Weems thought he had the wherewithal to enter Harvard College, and to that end were all his efforts now bent. Juvenal had evinced no interest in going to sea, and both mother and tutor, and, if truth be told, Juvenal himself foresaw a career in the law.

* * *

Adam stood atop the high grass-covered bluff of Plymouth Hoe. He looked south, past the sweeping drama of the harbor and Devonport just to the west, to the English Channel beyond. Like a carbuncle, the high walls of the Mill Prison blighted the view to the right and behind him. Adam determined to ignore it and think of better things.

The Harbor Master had assured him that he stood on the very spot where Sir Francis Drake insisted on finishing his game of bowls before taking on the Spanish Armada. Adam blinked, and he saw the great signal bonfires of the Devon array which carried news of the Armada's entry into the channel all the way to London. He blinked again and saw the diminutive red-bearded circumnavigator in doublet and breastplate who had "singed the King of Spain's beard." Straining his eyes seaward, he saw them coming: the Invincible Armada of one hundred and sixty ships slowly, majestically moving up the channel in successive crescent formations, with the British fleet sent to intercept them nervously hovering and probing and the British fireships careening into the advancing Spaniards and wreaking havoc with their formations. Adam suddenly found his heart pounding in excitement.

Not that Plymouth two hundred-odd years later was any less impressive. From his commanding height Adam surveyed the vast naval shipyard at Devonport where his masts would be unloaded, finished, and fitted (three were destined for the seventy-four gun third rate ship of the line *Bellerophon*, affectionately known to her men as the *"Billy Ruffian,"* just back from a bruising encounter with the French). How ironic this, thought Adam, to have moved from prisoner of King George III to indispensable outfitter of his Navy. To his immediate left and right and beneath him stood the massive stone fortifications of the Citadel, while behind him spread the grassy sweep of the Royal Parade. And to the east, at the foot of the Hoe he spied the old quarter of the Barbican, with its half-timbered houses, seagulls wheeling and squealing just as in Portland, and its quay known colloquially as the "Mayflower Steps," though with no memorial or marker. It was from here that at least five and maybe more of his ancestors, all ordinary souls without pretensions, had last set foot on English soil, as they embarked on a small and leaky ship in 1620 to found British New England. How Adam had longed to visit this site—so close and yet so far—during his years of imprisonment. So Adam made a pact with himself to walk the very streets of the Barbican that his ancestors did before he left Plymouth. But that would have to be later, as he had a reunion with his son Seth and a call to pay on Lord Hormsby at his ancestral home Widgery Manor on the edge of Dartmoor.

* * *

"Fid, that is to say, my Father," Seth explained to Georgette as they strolled in the gardens at Widgery Manor, a rambling Jacobean pile of gray stone, "is an old-fashioned Captain in a rollicking sort of way. He likes nothing better than to be at sea. He is a simple man, a straightforward man but of an inquiring mind. I tremble to think of what he might say to your father. He is, at heart, an American with no airs."

"Oh, you needn't worry. My father has truck with all types and conditions of men. You must understand that here in Devon we were of the gentry. There never were peers or magnates who ran the county, other than the Courtenay family perhaps. No, it was managed by the gentry, and a prosperous, open, and upstanding gentry they were—and are—here in the West Country. In point of fact, our peerage only dates to my great-grandfather who just over a hundred years ago joined William of Orange when he landed on these shores and marched with him to London in the Glorious Revolution. 'Twas King William who elevated him to the peerage out of gratitude, and so our line is not of old or royal stock. We are proudly Devon people, with our rights as broad as our accents. And you thought only America afforded opportunities?"

"I learn something every day."

At the same time, Adam arrived before the gatehouse at Widgery Manor outside the village of Thrumbleigh Mump, having endured a hack-pulled cart ride which took him from the lush and rolling South Hams with its deep river inlets, dairy farms in the vales and sheep grazing on the hillsides, up onto Dartmoor, a barren and austere high ground with vistas that stretched to the horizon, tin works, ancient hut circles of stone and herds of wild ponies, and over clapper bridges that spanned gurgling brooks as they creased low fields dotted with spikes of purple foxglove. He was grateful that Lord Hormsby had asked him for dinner and to stay the night, for the prospect of a late day return on the moor, with its shifting moods and fogs that rolled in at eventide, did not portend well. His heart raced at the promise of seeing Seth again and of meeting the mysterious The Honourable Georgette to whom his son's letters had alluded.

And so it was with great emotion and embraces that father and son reunited, no words offered and no words needed, and introductions were made all round (though Adam's eye did linger with approval on the gorgeous The Honourable Georgette). It being but early afternoon, Lord Hormsby bade Adam and the young people to walk with him in the gardens before dinner.

"What manner of flowers are these?" Adam asked Lord Hornsby as he spied a particularly delicate flowering plant.

"Deadly Nightshade. They are poisonous. They also are called 'Belladonna' because in the old days ladies used them in eye drops to dilate their pupils to make them appear more seductive."

"Those were *Italian* ladies, Father," Georgette inserted as she blinked her long lashes.

"Do you not have Deadly Nightshade in the United States?" Lord Hormsby asked.

"No, I think not. One cannot grow them as you do in our American climate. In the North it is too cold—our clime in Maine is more Nordic, all birch and pine. Day lilies and goldenrods in the summer, to be sure, but not these. And in the Southern states it is too hot. We are not temperate enough."

"Ah, all one way or the other? It's a pity that. We are much more temperate here in England, and that allows us the civilizing cultivation of gardens such as this."

"I fear that is one of the many luxuries we don't have in America. And among the least of them. We are, as you know, but a weak republic and the orphans of the sea. We sail without protection and make ready prey for French privateers."

"I fear that will only worsen, as the predators of the French Republic feast on our merchantmen too. And now their revolutionary armies have crossed into the Netherlands and Italy. France is on the move."

"Therefore why doesn't the British Navy make common cause with us? If truth be told, British privateers are also known to prey on American shipping."

"Your hands are tied by your Neutrality Act of last year. 'Tis now illegal for an American to wage war against any country at peace with the United States, which both Britain and France are. And this notwithstanding the best efforts of France's ambassador to your country, Citizen Genêt, to outfit American privateers to attack our merchantmen. Besides, you have no Navy."

"True enough. It was disbanded with the peace in '83 and the last ship sold in '85, but until that changes—and M' Lord, I hope it does!— why not a certain measure of respect and cooperation between our sides in face of the common enemy?"

"Ah, Captain Hale, you raise questions beyond my reckoning. America is indeed an orphan, but an orphan of its own choosing. You see, the British Empire might best be viewed as a living whole. To be a British subject is to be part of a seamless web, not unlike the seamless web of the law. Therein lies our sense of citizenship. But you Americans tore the seam and tumbled out of the net. If truth be told, I don't know from what your sense of citizenship derives."

Adam thought long before responding.

"Why from volunteering, I reckon. Those of my generation stood up and demanded the rights without which the state of a rational being would be a curse."

"And did you, sir, fight? Were you a rebel?"

"Well, no, to be exact about it. I was not a combatant." Adam hesitated here, for he had to be careful about what he revealed. "But you might say that I was a rebel, as I supported those who did."

"Father," Georgette ventured, "should you dismiss so those who step forward to rally to a cause? Did not your own and much beloved grandfather do so in the Glorious Revolution?"

Lord Hormsby shot her a withering glance.

"Well, that's all very well and good," he resumed. "I know the role of your Committees of Public Safety and Correspondence in ensuring that enough rebels 'volunteered.' In the United Kingdom the aristocracy volunteers for military service, such is our citizenship."

"I'm not sure I am saying anything different. Sacrifice of self is the brick and mortar of the fabric of republic or empire equally."

"Perhaps so, but in America there was an air of retribution in such volunteerism. In America it was the Celtic fringe who manned your rag-tag militias and Continental line. It was the Scots, the Irish, and the Welsh who went out of their way to make your revolt."

"Would you so characterize General Washington?"

"No, I'll grant you that exception. General Washington was, and is, a gentleman and soldier of the highest category."

"We agree on that, then."

"But my dear Sir, I fear that you will find in time that it was only your revolutionary generation in America that stepped forward. You'll see later generations more absorbed in love of self and of wealth than of country. And that will be America's undoing."

"Perhaps, M'Lord. But I hark back to the Pilgrims—all ordinary people who did a most prodigious and extraordinary thing. They stepped forward and through perseverance overcame mighty obstacles. That blood flows thick through American veins."

"I suspect you are creating a myth of why America is an exception among all nations. But with all that boom and bust, all that 'hooray' for the individual volunteer, I would still prefer the certainty of the web of the British Empire."

"Let me posit it to you another way: Do you agree that every man is his own priest?"

"Why, yes, as a Protestant Anglican—at least a nominal believer, more like the Romans for the good of civic order—I suppose I do," Lord Hormsby replied.

"So how is it any different in the political realm than in the religious?"

Lord Hormsby pursed his lips and thought for a few moments.

"Every man is indeed his own priest, but it helps if he has a church and an episcopacy to foster and protect that line of inquiry of self. You see, I am not only a Protestant but also an Anglican."

"So were many of my forbears who left England for America. They were of the Nonconformist wing of the Anglican church, but they were Anglicans nonetheless."

"Ah, so we are in agreement?"

"Enough for the moment, I reckon."

"Good, because we must repair to dinner. And we have much to discuss on the head of why the United States does not do more to suppress the slave trade. Lord Mansfield's ruling in the *Zong* case does rather frame the issue, does it not?"

"Would that I could wage war against that venal trade."

"We can discuss this at dinner. I hope you're not a teetotaling Puritan, Captain Hale:

"I've never feared the setting of the Pleiades
Or the hidden reefs beneath the waves

Or even the lightning at sea
Like I dread friends who sit and sip water with me
And remember what we say."

Adam chuckled and replied with a grin, "Antipater of Thessalonica. And I'm not a Puritan who drinks merely water."

"Oh, your knowledge of the classics is commendable, Captain Hale. And so is my hock. Let us mix the two over dinner," Lord Hormsby responded as he took Adam by the arm and led him into the house.

* * *

His business done at Plymouth, Seth parted with his father and returned to London. With the three ships laden with bone china, Moroccan kid gloves, paisley shawls, Plymouth gin, Seville orange marmalade, and all manner of luxury goods for the American market, Adam fulfilled his promise to walk the cobblestones of the Barbican. It was a warm but blustery evening, well past nine o'clock, and still lit by the north European sun so that the harbor and quays glowed with a golden glow that contrasted with the dark green of the rising hills of the South Hams inland. Adam found the Mayflower Steps and walked to and fro, with humility and gratitude, trying to picture the scene when his ancestors left for the desolate wilderness that was America. He pictured them huddled on the quay with their belongings stacked and waiting to load, gravely aware that this would be the last they would see of their native land. The sighs, the sobs, the prayers they must have uttered. And the embraces and leave-takings. They knew they were to pass a vast ocean with a sea of troubles before them and with no friends to welcome them on the other side, an unknown coast with no inns to refresh them and no houses to repair to. When they arrived, what could they see but a hideous and desolate wilderness with wild beasts and wild men of unknown numbers? Wherever they turned their eyes, except to Heaven, there was no solace. If they looked forward, they saw a whole country full of woods and thickets and with a wild and savage hew. If they looked back, they saw a mighty ocean they had passed which now was a bar that separated them from all of the civil parts of the world. Such was the price of citizenship in trading tyranny for the freedom to worship as they pleased.

Sobered, Adam sought refreshment in the nearest inn, the Admiral Benbow, which faced the quay. The inn was a sailors' pub, crowded, noisy, smoke-filled, and with the smell of stale ale permeating all. Adam bought a tankard of ale and seized a seat in the corner of the room to watch the crowd. Sailors English and American, indeed the world over, he observed, were alike. There was something in the gait, in the hands, in the gestures that made them all of a fraternity. And how better off they were at sea than on land. Here, there were only wages wasted on drink and whores, boasts and quarrels. Like children they were, at their worst. But perhaps he was being too harsh. Adam reminded himself of some of the American sailors he had known, sober men from Maine and New Hampshire who sailed as a profitable calling and maintained wives and families ashore in neat and trim houses with their wages. These were men he respected, his neighbors in the democracy of America.

Adam ordered another pint of ale and listened to the cacophony of British accents among the crowd. Some were round and clear, easy to comprehend, others were West Country broad and not far off the American English that Adam spoke; a few, from East Anglia, or so Adam understood, were indistinguishable from the way Bostonians talked, tight and nasal, while others, fast and swallowed, were incomprehensible to his ear.

Suddenly a great hubbub filled the front of the tavern. Dogs barked, women screamed, and a crowd shoved to and fro. Adam craned for a look. A dozen brawny sailors in blue jackets and red kerchiefs and bearing belaying pins had pushed their way into the room amid protests and resistance from the customers. Acting under the orders of a blue-coated Royal Navy Lieutenant with a drawn sword, they quickly ordered all able-bodied seamen against the wall and demanded identification papers.

So this was one of the dreaded press gangs about which Adam had heard so much.

"Ye thar," the Bosun who led the gang shouted as he singled out a sailor in the room. "I can see ye are as able-bodied a seaman as ever I saw. Look at ye, now. Show me your hands. That's it, palm up, like a good lad now. Been handling sheets for years, haven't we? I'd say you're a foretopman."

The sailor struggled to protest.

"No, sir. I'm a tailor now. I gave up the sea two year ago last April."

A buxom wench, great with child, darted from the crowd and threw herself at the feet of the inquisitor, sobbing.

"It's true, Your Worship," she begged between sobs. "He's an apprentice tailor with Mr. Yeo over in Friars' Lane. And we're married an' with a little one on the way. I beg you, please let my Jimmy stay!"

The Bosun shook her free of his leg to which she clung. Withdrawing a silver shilling from his pocket, he pried open the sailor's tightly closed right hand and placed the coin in it.

"The King's shilling for ye, foretopman," he said as one of his gang members grabbed the unfortunate sailor by his lapels and dragged him from the room.

And so on did the gang work through the crowd while Adam watched. Growing up as a boy, he had heard of the naval press gangs that had haunted American ports earlier in century. He knew of the Knowles Riot and other spontaneous portside risings of the citizenry in the 1740s that had at last driven the press gangs from American shores. They had not been a part of life in America for the last fifty years.

Eventually the gang reached the corner of the room where Adam sat. He stayed seated.

"'Evening, Gov'nor," the Bosun said as he eyed Adam up and down with a malevolent and skeptical eye, taking particular note of his weathered complexion and well-worked hands. But there was something about Adam's appearance he could not smoke: he was built like an able-bodied seaman but dressed in the blue wool coat of a master and his face was that of a man born to command. An awkward moment ensued as Adam judged how to respond.

"I am Captain Adam Hale of the United States of America, at your service, Bosun. What may I do for you?"

Adam made sure his American accent was unmistakable.

The Bosun shifted about on his feet. "Uh, uh, have ye any able-bodied seamen about ye'd know?" he asked. Knowing that officers who were not

British subjects were off-limits to the press gang, although some gangs were known to turn a blind eye to the legalities, Adam sensed he had evaded whatever ill intent the man harbored.

"Why no, my good man," he declaimed. And then he decided to have some sport. "But I have a question for you: What sort of excitement do turtles have, their little flippers atwitter propelling their bulky selves about fetid and murky waters? What pleasure, I ask you, sir? To eat, surely. Perhaps to lie on a log in the sun. But what is their difference with us? Have they sailed into the wind, have they read a book, have they ridden a horse? I ask you: do they not lead a life of unremitting boredom in which they are only dimly aware of their existence?"

The Bosun looked toward his Lieutenant, who shook his head as if to say, "This man is mad, let's leave."

"Thankee, Gov'nor. Have a good night now," the Bosun said as he quickly retreated.

Adam did not allow himself the luxury of a chuckle after they had departed. He remained in his seat and finished the last sips of his ale, all the while telling himself in silence that the practice of the press gang was as abhorrent as slavery for it equally deprived men of their freedom.

"May God forbid this scourge from ever returning to our shores," he mumbled to himself as he put his drained tankard down and left.

15

The Triangular Trade

1796

LOUNGING IN BED UNDER THE MOSQUITO NETTING, JEZREEL HELD THE letter from his father in his left hand while the index finger of his right hand traced the trade winds on the orb of Gabrielle's left breast.

"It appears that I have been summoned," Jezreel remarked with a sigh.

"What? Back to Maine?"

"Yes. I must make haste." A twinge of guilt lurked in Jezreel's heart. The *Dolphin* was long since careened and sent back to Portland with a cargo of molasses and sugar under a contract Captain and now, in late April, was back in Port Antonio awaiting lading. Jezreel had lingered all the while in Jamaica, indulging in Gabrielle's inviting company.

Jezreel realized he was little more than a guest. True, he had been living in the main house with Gabrielle, and he had managed to involve himself in a small way in the day-to-day operations of the plantation. Every morning Gabrielle would arise, dress, and ride the grounds, side saddle, conferring with her overseers. He would go into town and super-vise the import of supplies and loading of the plantation's production. It was a felicitous division of labor. But he wondered whether he would ever fully move into her soul and possess this woman with a history, as much as he enjoyed her physical presence. Perhaps her reaction to his news would provide a clue.

Gabrielle's plucky countenance dissolved as lines of concern began to form about her brow.

"Jezreel, what am I to do? I shall miss you so. And you've become so much a part of Great Spring Garden. It's not just that I'll be lonely without you. To be honest, I'm uncomfortable when you're not here. I know, I know. I've lived here for years and made my way as a planter. But each year I stay here I fear my luck is running lower. Someday there will be an uprising. We are outnumbered more than ten to one. It's going to burst someday. I just feel it. And when it does it will be as if the Maroons were a mere distraction."

True, enough, Jezreel thought, she was right about the slaves. But how could one predict with accuracy if or when a revolt might erupt? It was not by chance that Major Gaskill also lingered at Great Spring Garden, living in one of the dependencies. Once the Maroons had sued for peace in the face of Walpole's encirclement, the island uttered a collective sigh of relief, and life returned to what passed for "normal" in Babylon. The army remained to guarantee the peace and to intimidate any slaves who might be tempted to revolt. However, things had not worked out so tidily. The treaty of surrender signed by the Governor and the Maroons in December of the previous year required them to hand over any runaway slaves and to ask the King's pardon for the revolt. In return, the Governor promised they would not be deported. They complied, but the Governor forthwith abrogated the treaty and deported the surrendered Maroons to Nova Scotia. Jezreel was incensed at the government's perfidy.

Jezreel folded the letter from his father back up.

"I'll be back," he assured Gabrielle as he tossed the letter aside and embraced and kissed her. "I promise you I will return as quickly as I can."

Among many things that Jezreel did not know was that Seth had received an identical letter.

* * *

Seth held the open letter in his hands while sitting at a picnic on Hampstead Heath with Georgette and her two younger sisters, all of whom were attended by their maids. It was a bright and sunny late April

Saturday afternoon, with the first hint of the summer weather to come. A breeze rustled the soft new green of the trees.

"Pardon the rudeness of my reading," Seth offered, suddenly aware of his manners, "But it is from Fid. Duty calls."

"Meaning what?" Georgette asked.

"Meaning I must return to America to meet with him."

Seth immediately detected a downcast look on Georgette's beautiful face. It cut him to the quick, affirming how much he had fallen for her looks, her shifting moods, her complex being, which he read as if a map.

Oblivious, the younger girls, with much laughter and glee, began to launch kites they had brought and the ladies' maids looked on. Seth and Georgette used their activity as an opportunity to walk alone.

"It won't be for long," Seth reassured her, summoning a brave front but knowing in his heart that he would miss her.

"But why just now?" she asked. "Just when we . . ."

"I know." He too could feel the tug.

"But what if you don't return? There's always risk in a crossing. I can't bear the thought of losing you. I know such emotions are wild and crazy and inappropriate. Then there are the circumstances of our birth. And society, my society in any event, is aligned against us. But I so want to spend the rest of my life with you."

"And I with you," Seth affirmed, again from his heart.

"Could it work out?"

"We must make it so. And when I go I shall carry you with me at all times in my heart and in my mind. There won't be an hour I won't think of you."

Georgette broke into a radiant smile. At length she spoke.

"I suppose it's settled then. You must go, and I must be patient. I respect your honoring duty. Come, let's join my sisters then in the moment. Can you fly a kite?"

Seth watched her trip off ever so lightly across the grass of the Heath in all her glory, herself like a kite in full flight, shimmering and with joyous tails aflutter. He knew he must possess her and never let her go.

"Georgette!" he shouted after her. "Upon my return will you marry me?"

* * *

Five weeks later Seth stepped onto the planking of Union Wharf from the deck of the *Three Brothers*, a small swift Yankee-built brig he bought in England and named for himself and his two male siblings. It was good to be home. Though Portland looked small after London, it had prospered in ways he could not have imagined. The harbor was busy and full of large, deepwater ships in addition to coastal traders. The town itself could be called "handsome," with many fine new brick mansions replacing older wooden houses. There were perhaps four hundred houses in addition to the numerous mechanics shops, storehouses, and shipping depots, not to mention three rope factories, two distilleries, four meeting houses, two schools, a courthouse, and a jail. Portland remained a compact town, though, easily walkable, and Seth had no problem in directing himself to his father's storehouse at the northeast corner of Fore and Union Streets.

* * *

"I've called this meeting because we are facing a new and uncertain world," Adam pronounced as he eyed each of his three sons in turn. Seth, looking like a younger and more refined version of himself, sat upright and with hands folded in a Windsor chair opposite Adam's paper-crammed desk in the office of the Hale storehouse. Jezreel, tanned from the tropics and with his dark hair flowing, paced back and forth. And Juvenal, young and slight, sat in a corner fidgeting with a watch fob.

"The way we have done business must change."

The boys waited for their father to continue.

"America has tried to steer a course of strict neutrality in the war between France and England. But the depredations against our shipping have only increased. French privateers prowl up and down the East Coast, and even English ships are known to attack us. Insurance rates have risen five hundred percent in the last year. And it is now too dangerous to sail without insurance. We learned that lesson with the loss of the *Allagash*. Therefore all the Portland merchants are cooperating in order to spread the risk. With the insurance costing so much, we have agreed to take shares in each other's voyages, so the capital is raised and the risk is fanned out. But capital is tight here, tighter even than in the past."

"Nonetheless," Adam continued with finger pointed skyward, "there's money to be made because we Yankees can out-sail and out-trade anyone on the high seas. Our ships are stout and fast, and we have markets established in the West Indies, England, and even the Mediterranean—though I choose not to sail there any longer. Which brings me to the House of Hale & Sons. With war between England and France, the mast trade will only flourish. But to prosper we need to perfect and strengthen a triangular trade and run it with clocklike precision. We also need the insurance, as it were, of another spare trade. I've thought greatly on this head these last few months. From the Indies we will bring molasses to Portland, where we will distill it into rum and sell it at a profit. In return, we'll supply the Indies with wood, barrels, salt fish, corn, and other produce from the interior. To England we'll take masts and sticks, as before, and bring back fine luxury goods for the American market. But if one leg of this triangle were to break we would be in trouble. We therefore need to devise another, parallel leg for this trade."

Silence froze the room as everyone thought. At length, Seth broke the quiet.

"I've got it! The port wine trade! I can break the British monopoly on the port wine trade. I operate out of London, and with my ships laden with British manufactured goods, I can open business with Portugal and supply America with wine directly, cutting out the British wine merchants."

"If only they'll let you. I don't think they'd cede that trade without a fight. Don't forget the Navigation Acts which require shipment on British bottoms and payment of customs duties in England before wine can be re-exported."

"No, no, my scheme is to eliminate the British middlemen. We have something the wine producers in Portugal need in order to age and ship their port: barrels. Specifically, 'pipes,' those long and extended barrels, exceeding narrow, which the wine producers favor to ship their wares. Our New England white oak serves admirably for these 'pipes,' just as our red oak is used to ship rum. I've heard this talked of in London.

England does not produce these staves, heads, or hoops; we do. So we have leverage."

All eyes in the room were on Seth in amazement at his insight.

"I'll get introductions to the British wine producers in Portugal," he continued, "and if they don't want to cooperate I'll deal directly with the Portuguese producers. Whoever said wine had first to go to London or Bristol before it came to America?"

Adam nodded. "Worth a try. Now, Jezreel, if you will stand still for just a minute, I'll explain your role in this. You will need to run the *Dolphin* or one of the other schooners to Jamaica three times a year. No more extended dalliances in the Caribbean. I'm not asking why you did what you did, but I can readily speculate, though I know you'd never tell me. I will need you involved, on board, at sea and answerable to me."

"Very well, Fid." Jezreel acceded, knowing he had no choice. "But with the privateers up and down the coast, I'll need protection."

"Agreed. I'll lend you four guns from the *Atheling*. Those should fit on the schooner and deter an aggressor."

"Six," Jezreel shot back. "And a letter of marque so that I too may sail as a privateer. And instruction in all you know of gunnery. And this winter buy up all the ice from Maine ponds. I want to take ice to Jamaica. We could make a killing."

"Oh, you are audacious. . . . So you want to go on the offensive and be a privateer, then? Could be the ruin of us. 'Tis true the United States has begun to issue letters of marque in retaliation against the French depredations. I'll see what I can do to arrange one. And very well, six guns, but that leaves me with only eight, plus the bow-chasers. Then again, as often as not, I'll endeavor to voyage in convoy with the Royal Navy or other merchantmen. But I can spare no more; the mast cargo is too valuable to put at risk. Seth, I fear, will be more exposed as he sails the Portugal run and to America. You well know by now that the seas are lawless."

"The *Three Brothers* is an uncommon swift ship," Seth responded, "and Portugal is but a short distance from England. First, let's see if we can make a market, and then we can worry about how to secure it."

"Agreed then," Adam proclaimed.

"Oh, I almost forgot. Though he has evinced no interest in life at sea, Juvenal is here so that he can understand our family's business. And he has an achievement worthy of celebration. Tell your brothers, son."

"I have been admitted to Harvard College. I shall study Classics and Jurisprudence."

Adam's heart swelled with pride at his youngest son's academic achievements, and his older sons joined in congratulating Juvenal with warmest wishes.

"Oh, and Fid," Seth inserted when the joy of Juvenal's moment had died down, "I have more news worthy of celebration. I have asked for Georgette's hand in marriage, and she has assented. More to the point, though it took some tact and negotiating, I obtained Lord Hormsby's blessing before I left England. We are to be married upon my return."

Another round of joyous cheer erupted in the room.

"I can't wait to tell your mother!" Adam thundered. "But first, all hands to the middle and on mine."

The four Hale men formed a square and extended their right hands so that each was on top of the other, with Adam's serving as the base, where they held them, tight-pressed.

"All hail the House of Hale & Sons!" Adam bellowed, even as he felt a twinge of guilt at the sin of pride.

"Huzzah! Huzzah! Huzzah!" they all responded.

Only Jezreel felt the expatriate in Portland. Like many expatriates, he carried his sense of place within him. And that place was Jamaica.

As his sons moved to leave, Adam turned to Seth.

"One further matter: have you encountered Captain Sir Ponsonby Spicer yet in London?"

"No," Seth replied. "I have not. But I do understand that he is held in much esteem by the Admiralty. With the growing hostilities between Britain and France he is viewed as, well, *effective*."

"I see," Adam grunted. "Keep away from him."

* * *

"It's a point of indifference to me," Adam grumbled. "No, that's not true. It's sinful to spend money on a house like this."

"But I like it so," Nabby countered.

Adam, who was at heart more interested in extravagance in outfitting his ships than in extravagance in a home, judged the house with a critical eye. It was a spacious three-storied white frame house, a mansion even, newly constructed in the latest Federal style at the northern edge of town on Cumberland Street, with a center hall, parlor, airy symmetrical windows, and a graceful fanlight over the front door. It had been built as a speculative venture, buoyed by the booming economy of Portland which attracted carpenters and artisans from all over New England. Those not employed in the shipbuilding industry on the Presumpscot served the town's insatiable demand for housing.

"I know it is a handsome house," Adam conceded, "but we must be practical. With Seth and Jezreel at sea and Juvenal at college in Cambridge, what need have we of such a grand and commodious house?"

"It's the home of my dreams. You do want me to be happy, do you not? I spend so much of the year alone without you, and surely the wifely consolation of a fine and proper home would set your mind at ease when you are across the seas."

Adam sensed that resistance would be useless.

"Very well, you shall have the house, and it will be our new home."

"Thank you," she smiled as she took his arm in hers. "I love you."

"And I you," he conceded as he softened his mood, ever the malleable clay in Nabby's adept hands.

* * *

Months later, on a hushed and hot Saturday afternoon at the end of August, Seth and The Honourable Georgette Hormsby were married in St. Petrock's Church on the edge of Thrumbleigh Mump. The small Norman stone church was more a chapel of ease than a proper parish church. A swag of garlanded white and barely yellow flowers softened the entrance arch at the church door and proclaimed the joy of the day. Inside, the church was cool and musty. To the south of the short nave stood a double white alabaster tomb with the effigies of a fifteenth-century knight and his lady, their hands folded and forever at peace—"my ancestors," Georgette had explained. Other than the "ancestors," the only people in attendance were Georgette's parents and two younger sisters. Knowing he had little choice with his strong-willed daughter, Lord Hormsby had acceded to the marriage with an American. However, he saw no reason to celebrate it with his friends in a public way. So as The Honourable Georgette Hormsby made the brief walk down the aisle, her footsteps echoed off the whitewashed walls. The vicar read the office of Holy Matrimony quickly and without fanfare and pronounced them man and wife. Afterward, at the door, Georgette balanced her spray of baby's breath flowers in her left hand, lifted her veil with her right, and kissed her American merchant prince, as he drew her in his arms and kissed his English lady, sealing the deal.

As they stepped outside, there were no cheers, no backslaps, no hearty congratulations, only the deep country, high August hush of a half dozen unshorn sheep shambling about and chewing at the unkempt grass in the church yard.

16

Hobson's Choices

1797

"ARE YOU SURE THIS IS SAFE?" SETH ASKED. THE SPRAY STUNG HIS FACE as he crouched in the stern of the *rabelo* cargo boat shooting the rapids of the Douro River. Like his father, he distrusted rivers.

"Absolutely!" Dom Antonio Perreira shouted over the din.

Beneath them surged the snaking, snarling Douro hemmed in by high hills on either side at the narrow passage at Cachão da Valeira. The *rabelo* that sheltered their lives shuddered as the currents buffeted its hull. Seth reflected that the *rabelo* was a curious boat—perhaps fifty feet in length, lateen-rigged, with oars for steering and a high pointed prow and stern that harked back to its Phoenician origin. Amidships it was laden with two dozen pipes of port wine making the voyage from the Upper Douro vineyards to the lodges or *armazems* of Vila Nova da Gaia opposite Porto for eventual shipment across the bar of the Douro to destinations around the world. At its helm navigating the rapids stood Dom Antonio, who knew the river intimately. A native of Porto, Perreira was five years older than Seth and the scion of one of the few Portuguese-owned port wine houses. He spoke fluent English, but Seth had made the effort to teach himself rudimentary Portuguese in his company during their sojourn the prior two weeks along the Upper Douro. He now put it to use.

"*Vamos ver.*" We shall see.

Dom Antonio merely smiled.

Seth enjoyed the September fortnight in the remote and elevated Upper Douro country—at once hot and dry but with steeply terraced hillsides planted with vines. Seth had accompanied Dom Antonio on his rounds as the annual harvest, or *vindima*, got under way. For days he had inspected the laden and low-hanging vines awaiting the exact moment to initiate the harvest (determined by the moon, Dom Antonio swore, but as much by intuition, Seth inferred). He watched the harvesting teams work the hillsides, filling their great wicker baskets with grapes and then lashing them to donkeys or carrying them themselves down the hillsides on their heads, a veritable army of bobbing ants. He watched the crush of the grapes by treaders in the cool stone *lagars* in the valleys as they sang a cadenced march. And in the evenings he savored the gathering dark in the deep pit of the river's trough while the golden rays of the setting sun still kissed the brows of the hills.

"When can we sign the contract?" Seth shouted to Dom Antonio.

"As soon as we reach Gaia!" he replied as he steered the boat to avoid an outcropping of jagged rocks. Seth gasped as the boat shot past the protrusion with inches to spare. Dom Antonio gave Seth an amused glance once he had cleared the rocks.

"I just did that to keep you awake."

"Not to worry. I am wide awake. And worrying that the English producers won't like it when they hear about our arrangement."

"Bugger them," Dom Antonio shouted and laughed.

As satisfying as the prospect of the contract was to Seth, he had also gained a friend in Dom Antonio. Vigorous and wiry, with dark curly hair, deep-set eyes, and an infectious smile, Dom Antonio was easy company. He shared with Seth the role of the outsider, though in Dom Antonio's case he was an outsider to the cartel in his own country. Not that that diminished his love of his land. He was connected by his own blood or by that of his wife to what seemed to be every Portuguese family of consequence from Coimbra northward. Seth had come to appreciate Dom Antonio's passion for his native land as together they climbed through the vineyards, chatted with the locals, and traversed the rapids of the Douro. "This is Portugal!" Dom Antonio exclaimed at one point with a sweep of his hand as the two of them stood on a bluff high above the

Douro and enjoyed a vista that stretched from horizon to horizon. To Seth Dom Antonio was a man almost spiritually connected to his native soil.

And all this was attributable to an introduction given him to a Portuguese wine house "just in case." Indeed, "just in case" had proven the difference between failure and success. Before meeting with Dom Antonio and his trip to the Upper Douro, Seth had courted the British wine producers in Porto. Oh, they had received him politely enough in their Factory House on the Rua Nova dos Ingleses, a handsome Palladian building, not unlike the Pump Room at Bath, which functioned as a cross between a gentlemen's club and cartel. There the factors who held membership colluded on pricing, shipping, and marketing and generally advanced the British monopoly on the port wine trade. Needless to say, the few independent Portuguese producers, such as Dom Antonio, were not welcome.

The building was designed to impress, and impress it did. From entering the granite-floored entry hall to having his breath taken away by the monumental cantilevered granite stairway that defied gravity to the elegant dining and ball rooms done in the finest Adam style, Seth was transported back to London, or at least the illusion of London imparted by this little piece of England plopped down improbably near the docks of Porto. The factors had hosted him at dinner, which ran through the cheese course accompanied by a tawny port. Then, according to custom, the group arose and reassembled in a second, identical dining room set end-to-end with the first one. There, free from the aromas of the meal, they blind tested a vintage port selected by the Treasurer; the game was to identify both the shipper and the vintage. At this challenge Seth failed miserably, as, it turned out, he also did in his quest to trade barrel timber for direct shipment of port wine on American bottoms. When he broached the subject the factors made clear, politely but firmly, that this was simply "not done."

Thus, it was with gratitude that Seth had taken advantage of the introduction to Dom Antonio, gotten to know him and had obtained agreement to supply Perreira's wine directly to the United States on his ships without paying British duties. In return, he would provide to

Perreira the aged wood required for production of barrels. It was a small inroad into the potentially huge wine trade but one that was neatly profitable and promised to grow. It also established the precedent of American ships competing fairly and openly with the British cartel. All that remained to be done was the execution of a contract when they laded the *Three Brothers* with pipes from the Perreira wine lodge across the river from Porto in Vila Nova da Gaia.

* * *

"Let me see the glass," Jezreel ordered his mate.

Putting the telescope to his right eye and squinting with his left, Jezreel studied a sail that had suddenly peeked over the horizon. It shimmered in the hot and humid air off the coast of Georgia.

"I don't know. What do you think?"

"Could be one of our merchantmen. Or she could be British from Jamaica or one of the islands. Or French from Guadaloupe. It's too soon to tell."

"Well, we'll learn soon enough. She's hell bent on a course nor'nor'east looking, no doubt, to catch the trade winds and we're beating sou'sou'west. We're headed direct for each other."

The *Dolphin*, loaded with lumber bound for Jamaica and with her guns run in and their ports wrapped in canvas as camouflage, plowed forward in the swell under an ample spread of sail.

A half hour later, Jezreel extended the telescope and surveyed the vessel, whose hull was now visible above the horizon.

"Aha!" he cried as he spotted the tricolor at her stern. Snapping the telescope shut, he turned to his mate.

"She's a fat-bottomed French merchantman heading home! Oh, this will be fine pickings. Load the guns for action but leave the wrappings. Tell the port gunners to prepare for action in a half hour. We'll commence with a shot across her bow."

"Should we strike the ensign?" the mate asked as he looked back at the oversized American flag at the stern.

"No, I want them to know who we are—a Yankee merchant ship. And never to forget who is taking them."

"Aye, aye, sir."

As the two ships came within a mile of one another, almost within hailing range, Jezreel ordered the number one portside gun uncanvassed.

Standing next to the gun's crew, he looked them in the eye, pointed, and spoke.

"Now see there. She's bearing down fast. We haven't much time. After I give the order to fire, wait for the downward roll and touch the hole. Make certain the shot is forward of her and over her bowsprit. Understood?"

The crew all nodded.

Jezreel silently counted to himself. One. Two. Three.

"Fire," he ordered in a soft voice.

The gun blasted forth its ball and rocked its carriage back six inches.

Jezreel strained to see the result through the cloud of smoke wreathing the muzzle. The Frenchman sailed on toward them for another ten seconds, which seemed like an eternity. Then, suddenly, she wore off to the starboard and her sails exhaled a great sigh of wind, deflated, and stood fluttering in submission.

"Uncanvas the other guns," Jezreel ordered as he drew closer to the waiting ship. This has been almost too easy, he told himself, and he wanted to ensure that the evidently unarmed French merchantman was in no question as to his firepower.

Grabbing the ship's trumpet, he called out to the other captain.

"I am the *Dolphin* out of Portland, Maine, sailing under letter of marque. Jezreel Hale, master."

His counterpart responded in heavily accented English "I am *Tante Louise* of Bordeaux, France. Dumas, C*apitain*."

"Permission to board!"

"*Allez-y!* Go to it."

Once on board, Jezreel found a short, pot-bellied stove of a captain perspiring in the humidity. He seemed genial enough, given that his luck had just run out and he was about to lose his ship and all its cargo.

Jezreel showed him the letter of marque, which Captain Dumas fingered with indifference and handed back with a shrug.

"What cargo do you carry back to France?" Jezreel asked.

"Casks of sugar and molasses."

Jezreel's mate quickly confirmed the veracity of his statement with a glance below. This would be a valuable cargo to take before a prize court in the United States.

The three men got down to the business of occupying the prize. Jezreel split the small French crew in two, with half to the *Dolphin* where they could be watched, and half to remain on the *Tante Louise* to help the prize crew from the *Dolphin* sail her to the nearest American port at Savannah. Jezreel would remain with Captain Dumas on the *Tante Louise*, as that was where the greater danger of mutiny or surprise resided, while his mate would take charge of the *Dolphin* to make the fifty-mile run into Savannah. Both ships were to sail in tandem.

Before they got under way Jezreel, accompanied by Captain Dumas and one of the men from his prize crew, went below to inspect the cargo. Just as Captain Dumas had said, there were row upon row of tightly stacked casks of sugar and molasses from the French West Indies. Satisfied, Jezreel turned to leave. Just then he heard a deep moaning from below the deck—human to be sure, but mournful and despairing.

"Give me the lantern," he ordered his seaman. Searching about, he found the hatch leading to the lowest deck, where normally a bed of ballast would lie.

He lifted the hatch and inserted the lantern.

A blast of fetid stench knocked him in the face so that he recoiled in a fit of coughing. He regained his composure, held his breath, and peered down again. That was when he spotted the whites of their eyes—twenty pairs of twitching eyes deep in the hold dazed and pained by the light from the lantern held in his hand. Their owners, all black, raised thin manacled arms to try to shield them from the light.

Jezreel immediately withdrew.

"Who are these people?" he asked, turning on Captain Dumas.

"Prisoners en route to France for trial."

Jezreel studied Dumas's face to try to understand.

"You mean you would keep people under these conditions? Even if they were prisoners? Why didn't you declare them?"

Dumas was impassive and did not respond.

"If they were prisoners being transported for trial, wouldn't they be on a French naval vessel? No, I don't think these are prisoners. I know your revolutionary government in Paris abolished slavery three years ago, but this is still the Indies and a long way from Paris. Orders often don't get obeyed. These men may have been free on paper but they never knew it. You are slave trading. You knew what these Africans would fetch in the pens at Savannah or Charleston and decided to market them before they learned they were free men."

Dumas, now soaked in perspiration, shrugged.

"Free these men and get them topside for air and fresh water."

Back on deck, Jezreel found his head reeling. If he took the prize in to Savannah, the men, without papers showing them to be free men, would be enslaved right away, just as if Dumas had completed his mission. If he sailed to Jamaica or any other port in the British West Indies the result would be the same, for slavery was still the law of those places. And he would lose his prize because he needed an American admiralty court to declare the award. Oh, he was right—this had been too simple! The only course was to turn around and head for a northern port where he could find an admiralty court and the men could be set free. Philadelphia came to mind. Or New York. Either was a long way off.

As Jezreel contemplated what to do, the lookout from the *Dolphin*, which lay alongside, shouted.

"Sails ho! Astern!"

Jezreel looked up.

"She's hull up. French man-of-war! I think, I think, yes! A ship of the line. Could be seventy-four guns!"

The lookout turned to Jezreel for instruction. Jezreel stood in stunned silence. At length, Jezreel turned to Captain Dumas, who had just led the unfortunates onto the deck, where they performed an involuntary spasmodic dance, at once shaking and shielding their faces from the glare. It was a scene of utmost depravity and absurdity. Sensing Jezreel's unuttered question of how the warship knew to find them, Dumas, once again, shrugged—but this time with a faint smile on his lips.

Slowly it dawned on Jezreel that the *Tante Louise* was an outlier in a naval-escorted convoy. From their perch on the much taller masts of the ship of the line, the lookouts may have heard the cannon shot and almost certainly had watched the whole prize-taking occur. Their field of vision was such that they could see the *Dolphin* and *Tante Louise* but not vice versa. Perhaps the enchained blacks really were prisoners, given the naval escort. Not that that mattered, for now their fate lay in the hands of Captain Jezreel Hale, privateer.

Jezreel quickly did the calculus. The options were not good. He stood no chance against the man-of-war. He could capitulate and lose the *Dolphin*, her cargo, the prize, and the prize's cargo and hand the blacks over to whatever ugly fate awaited them. He could sail for Philadelphia and safety, but the distance was too great. The man-of-war would overtake him handily, and he would lose all. He could make for nearby Savannah, with luck outrun the pursuer and collect his prize. The blacks would be enslaved as collateral damage.

Jezreel thought hard for several minutes. There was no choice between practicality and morality. If only he could think of another way out!

His weighing of options and morality was rudely interrupted by the man-of-war's long-range guns which began to pitch cannonballs toward them. For now, they hit wide of the mark. Jezreel had to act and to act now.

"Set a course nor'nor'east!" he shouted. "Bear straight for Savannah! And pile on all sails!"

The *Dolphin* and her prize swung about and gathered speed as the wind filled their sails. First one hour and then another and on into the afternoon the two ships strained before the wind on a rhumb line course to Savannah while their pursuer slowly, almost imperceptibly, gained on them. Being a schooner, the *Dolphin* was able to extract every measure of speed by sailing close to the wind. The *Tante Louise*, being a square-rigged merchantman, lagged behind, but Jezreel's seamanship kept her within close proximity to her leader.

Late in the afternoon, as sunset approached, the man-of-war, which by then had drawn into something approaching accurate gun range, commenced firing at the *Dolphin*. The shots tore past, followed seconds later by the distant thunderous reports of the cannon. As dusk descended, a ball punctured the taut mainsail of the *Dolphin*, high up and narrowly missing the mast.

Still, the ships bore on, desperately racing toward their port in a stiffening breeze. As welcome darkness enveloped them, they tore on with all lights doused so that they were swallowed up in the embrace of the night which mercifully bore no moon. At length, the French man-of-war ceased firing because she had lost her target.

Later still, Jezreel spotted the lights of Tybee Island, and the two ships groped their way into the Tybee Roads and up the river to the safe port of Savannah.

* * *

Three weeks later the *Dolphin* slid into Port Antonio borne in on the trade winds that were the lifeline of the Caribbean—behind schedule but with its strong box bulging with cash. Jezreel slipped into Port Antonio with the excitement of seeing Gabrielle again in her exotic world of beauty and violence and with the shame of having traded in slaves. On the cruise down he reminded himself when the subject crossed his mind, which it did daily, that the matter was thrust upon him and not of his own choosing. Were it not for him the blacks would not have enjoyed even their fleeting moment of freedom aboard the ship and would have proceeded to who knows what dismal and grisly fate. But there was no escaping the fact that he had opted to snuff out their liberty, albeit for the greater good. He simply had no choice, he told himself. He might have purchased their freedom, but to what end? To return them to Jamaica and slavery? Or to leave them to an uncertain and no doubt short-lived liberty in Georgia? And yet the consequences of his actions ate at his conscience and attached a small but, he feared, growing corrosion in his soul. He realized his career as a privateer was over; he would return his father's guns.

So it was with resolution to enjoy the moment that he found himself that afternoon back in Gabrielle's arms in her great mahogany bed. It was as if he had never left.

"Oh, I've so missed you, my handsome Yank," she whispered into his ear in her plummy English voice as she stroked his chest and arms.

"Oh, and I you," he responded as he delighted in her dancing violet eyes and plush lips which he drew to his own and kissed.

The rest was a rush of passion as they ravished each other with the hunger of the separated now united. And then sleep, deep foggy sleep.

When Jezreel awoke it was late afternoon with the sun low in the sky. Gabrielle was still asleep. Their reunion had been reaffirming. He did not know if their feelings for one another would evolve and mature, nor did he care. It was enough to be together in the moment.

He went to the window. It had been left half-opened to allow a breeze. He now smelled the fragrances it bore—a sea breeze mixed with hibiscus. Beneath him a yellow monarch butterfly fluttered among the banana leaves. In the distance of the dark canopy of vegetation that mantled the mountains beyond Major Gaskill's cottage a macaw screeched to its mate. The brilliant turquoise blue of the sea stretched out before him to the horizon, punctuated by the spanking white sail of a schooner heading eastward around the island.

Jezreel savored the moment and delighted, with thanks, in his return.

17

The Stranger

1798—Part I

"THEY SAY HE'S FROM NEW YORK, MAMA," THANKFUL TOLD HER mother as they stood on the curb at Middle Street in the center of town.

"No, I don't think so," Nabby responded. "I've heard he's from Boston or thereabouts. His manner of speech signifies Boston, or so Mrs. Longfellow and other people say. Your father met him. But then he asks questions which are most un–New England-like. They say he's called on all the merchants in town, one by one, to size them up. For what purpose I have no idea. If it's for loyalty, he's wasting his time, as there are no French sympathizers here. Maybe he has other reasons."

"I don't know who he is or where he's from, but he's quite dashing," Thankful allowed.

"I'll grant you that."

Brigade Major Gideon Sewell made his entry into Portland society, or at least what passed for Portland society, with great parade and cunning. The occasion was the annual Independence Day celebration, which now had evolved into a martial demonstration. With President Adams's undeclared but hot war against France, defensive forces were mustering throughout the American states. Nowhere was the concern more acute than in Portland, where fear of French raids or even an invasion gripped the populace. As a result, the Massachusetts militia had set to work rebuilding and expanding the Revolutionary-era breastworks at the seaward edge of Munjoy Hill. They now mounted twenty large cannon that commanded the entrance to Casco Bay, a barracks for the permanent detachment of Portland Light Infantry and a parade ground boasting an oversized American flag.

Major Sewell led the Portland Light Infantry as they marched up Middle Street to the beat and blare of a military brass band and the rippling applause of the gathered citizens. He was indeed an impressive sight atop his prancing, snorting, lathered black stallion. He was a fine, broad-shouldered man in his late twenties, with dark brown hair, penetrating eyes, and a sharp profile. Everything about him exuded the confidence of his military bearing. Atop his head he wore a Roman-style helmet crowned with waving black horsehair. His red blouse was faced with black lapels, a theme that continued with the black cords that ran down his white pants legs until they culminated in his spit-shined black officer's boots.

"I've heard he designed the uniform of the regiment himself," Nabby observed.

"Very smart they are," Thankful said as her heart fluttered within.

"He must be a man with a singularly particular eye for detail," Nabby replied more wisely.

As Major Sewell and his troops drew even with Thankful and Nabby his horse balked, whinnied, and clattered from side to side as the procession stopped. He quickly brought the horse under control with his reins. Spotting the two ladies at the curbside, he withdrew his sword from its scabbard and raised it in a vertical salute between his two flashing dark eyes directed at them.

"Mrs. Hale and Miss Hale, if I am correct! The joy of the day to you!"

They both blushed and nodded in acknowledgment. As he rode on, Thankful turned to her mother.

"Oh, my goodness!"

* * *

Social events hosted by the regiment had quickly become the talk of the town and the most sought-after invitation. The levies and balls were deemed "exceedingly attractive" by the universal consensus of all the families that mattered.

So it was with particular delight that Thankful responded to a pounding of the brass knocker in the form of a dolphin at their front door to find a private in the uniform of the Portland Light Infantry bearing a silver salver with a stiff, cream-colored envelope addressed to "Captain and Mrs. Adam Hale and Miss Thankful Hale." The messenger stood at parade rest and waited while she opened it and read:

"Brigade Major Gideon Sewell

requests the pleasure of your company at the Mid-Summer Ball

of the Portland Light Infantry

at eight o'clock Saturday July 28, 1798

The Armory"

Thankful put the invitation down and looked at the private.

"Tell Major Sewell that we will consult our calendars and reply."

"Ma'am, the Brigade Major ordered me not to return without an answer and that the answer had to be 'Yes.'"

"Oh, I do see. Your Major is quite an insistent man."

"You don't want to tell him 'no.'"

"You don't want to or I don't want to? Oh, very well, tell him that he's very persuasive. Tell him 'Yes.'"

* * *

Two days before the ball Thankful practiced her dance steps before the long pier looking glass in the parlor of the Hale house and reread her copy of John Griffith's *Instances of Ill Manners To Be Carefully Avoided by Youth of Both Sexes*. She therefore was well prepared when the regimental band warmed up the assembled guests, consisting of all the best families in Portland, with a wheezing rendition of *To Anacreon in Heaven*, followed by a spirited *Road to Boston*.

With her brown hair arranged in the latest Roman fashion, a touch of rouge on her cheeks and wearing a diaphanous gown *à la mode française* with fluttering blue ribbons, elbow-length white kid gloves, and white dancing pumps, Thankful, in presentation if not natural beauty, was easily the equal of any of the young ladies in the room. Or so Nabby reassured her just as her father turned to fill three glasses at the punch bowl.

Moving away from her parents to the company of her peers, Thankful made small talk with her friends as each waited in feigned indifference for a dance partner to approach. In Thankful's case she did not have to wait long. Brigade Major Sewell, in clanking sword and boots, made a straight line for her.

"Miss Hale, may I have the pleasure of this dance?" he inquired with correct formality.

"But Major Sewell, we have not yet been introduced," she responded, mindful of the etiquette of dancing only with a partner to whom one had first been formally introduced.

"Not so, Miss Hale. I introduced myself to you on parade. So there you have it."

Thankful's eyelashes fluttered and a faint smile formed on her lips. Even with his presumptions, this *was* a man who took charge, unlike the bumbling and awkward young men talking with their friends and warily eyeing the ladies from across the dance floor.

"I don't know if that counts," she replied. "But now that you've asked, it would be my pleasure."

She offered her hand, and he took it lightly to direct her to the dance floor.

As they lined up with the other couples for the longways country dance known as *Stony Point* in honor of the Revolutionary War battle of that name, Major Sewell decided to reconnoiter.

"Your father, I believe, is a merchant in Portland? I had the pleasure of meeting him when I first came to town."

"He is a merchant and a Captain, Major Sewell. He sails his own ships, as do my brothers."

"In the West Indies trade, if I am not mistaken?"

"You are not mistaken. But there are other angles to it. As a lady, I'm not involved in the business, but our voyages take us to England and Europe as well."

"I see," he observed blandly.

Suddenly aware that she might have given away too much too soon, Thankful decided to change tack.

"And you, Major Sewell, from where do you come?"

"From Boston of course," he said as he looked at her with his penetrating dark eyes. Evidently he had heard a rumor of questions about his origins.

"Oh, I see," she smiled. "From Boston town itself, born and bred?"

"Well, to be more precise, we're originally Scituate people."

"South of Boston then. The Old Colony. Not North Shore, not the Bay Colony," she said as she smiled with the approval of recognition. "I'm glad we've established that. So are we. From the Cape."

Just then the regimental band struck up *Stony Point*, and the line of dancers sprang to life. The top lady and her partner quickly danced down the line, and any chance at further conversation flew as Thankful and Major Sewell awaited their turn to join in the frolicking steps while whoops of cheer greeted the couple traversing the line. Soon their turn came, and they too ran the gauntlet of the weaving and bobbing line of dancers as if buoyed by the bounding waves of the brass instruments.

A half hour later they caught their breaths.

"What is your profession, Major Sewell?" Thankful asked. "You are an officer of the militia, are you not? And therefore arms are only a part-time affair?"

"In Boston I apprenticed to a merchant, Mr. Fish, while a junior officer in the militia and then set up my own establishment. But with the coming of the troubles with France, I have been called to duty. I think that I should like to return to commerce someday."

"But for now you are Major Sewell."

"That is how I am known."

Just then the band struck up a rousing Scotch reel.

"May I have this dance, Miss Hale?" Major Sewell asked as he took her hand.

"But, Major Sewell, a gentleman is supposed to dance with as many ladies as possible."

"I am not a gentleman," he replied with a twinkle in his eye as he led her into the line of dancers heying and setting.

And so the evening continued as Major Sewell danced with Thankful in the *Fisher's Hornpipe* and five ensuing numbers. Thankful was flattered by his undivided attention and, if truth be told, enjoyed his company. Her friends at the punch bowl and sitting in chairs at the perimeter of the ballroom noted the rush, as did Adam and Nabby who watched but did not dance.

At last, as the evening neared midnight, the dancers assembled for a *boulanger*, a circular dance performed by groups of eight. Traditionally the last dance of the evening when the guests were tired, it was nonetheless a lively strip-the-willow. By the end of it, Thankful's head was spinning as much from the attentions of Major Sewell as from the music and motion.

"I suppose I must return you to your parents now," Sewell said. "Alas, the evening is over."

"Yes, but I wish it weren't. Or maybe I am just being giddy. One cannot live a life of fun and hot air. "

"And why not? At least one can try."

At that, he took her kid-gloved hand and pressed it to his lips while he penetrated her eyes with his piercing brown ones.

* * *

At the same time that Thankful and Major Sewell were dancing in Portland, French privateers swarmed like bees up and down the waters off the East Coast of the United States and throughout the Caribbean, inflicting stings on American merchant shipping on an almost daily basis. With only a handful of revenue cutters to oppose them, the United States was defenseless. And no privateer was more feared than *L'Italie Conquise* commanded by Captain Gautier and named after General Bonaparte's victories on the Italian peninsula.

As a speculative venture Adam and Jezreel had jointly purchased the one-hundred-and-five-ton schooner *Hunter*, built at Cape Elizabeth in 1796 and outfitted her for the Caribbean trade in partnership with fellow Portland merchants John and Rufus Horton. On a voyage to Martinique, which was then controlled by the British, in July of 1798 she carried a cargo of beef, pork, beans, fish, lumber, staves, hoops, and shooks. The cargo was owned one half each by the Hales and the Hortons. Her return voyage was to bring sugar, cotton, and molasses to Portland. Jezreel acted as her master while the *Dolphin* was laid up for repairs.

Thirty days into the voyage, on approaching Martinique, *L'Italie Conquise* cut out the *Hunter* and took her to Guadaloupe, where ten days later both vessel and cargo were condemned by the French authorities for the technical excuse of not having a *rôle d'équipage* or crew list. The value of the vessel was $4,220 and of the cargo $1,758. It was a total loss. When Jezreel made his way back to Portland penniless and without the vessel some weeks later, Adam slumped in his chair on hearing the report.

"What can I tell the Hortons?" Adam asked, as his first thought was for the welfare of his venture partners. "I committed to them that this would be a profitable voyage."

"It wasn't your fault, Fid," Jezreel responded. "The attacks on our shipping are so intense that American commerce can hardly operate. Where it will end I cannot speculate."

"Yes, yes, I know. But we can't afford these losses. When, how, can we ever be made whole?"

Adam stared off into the distance as he thought. With the responsibilities of operating his factory house and store in Portland, and with his sons captaining the voyages, Adam had increasingly spent time at home.

"The only answer is that I must return to sea. I must redouble the mast trade with England."

Thus it was that Adam determined to return to active command, and, while at sea, he never learned that the U.S. Marines aboard the new twenty-four gun frigate *Connecticut* stormed and took *L'Italie Conquise* off Guadaloupe.

But he was never made whole.

18

They That Go Down to the Sea in Ships

1798—Part II

"MR. SPURLING, I GIVE YOU THE PLAYGROUND OF THE NORTH ATLANtic," Adam said as he snapped his telescope shut and handed it to his First Mate. "Look at the *bacalhau* boats out there. That one's Basque. See there, he's a Frenchman, and that one's Portugee," he added as he pointed. Spurling was from a Maine seafaring family but only in his mid-twenties, so he was still learning.

Adam had always liked the Grand Banks, with their teeming fishing boats from all of Europe and America, their swirling birds—gannets, shearwaters, and sea ducks—living off the catch as it was hauled aboard and their tricky tentacled fogs conjured up by the colliding warmth of the northbound Gulf Stream as it met the cold Labrador Current heading south. The Grand Banks were a long-established fishing grounds, with their own rules and etiquette, a last outpost of civilization before jumping off into the surly and lonelier reaches of the North Atlantic.

Adam was glad to be at sea again with the deck rising and falling under his feet. He had been right to realize he had been too long ashore. He belonged at sea. The *Atheling* was loaded with sticks for the Royal Navy, tight packed and riding high, in an early September run across the Atlantic to Plymouth. Given the winds, Adam calculated a good and easy passage, with landfall, unlading, and return before the bad weather set in.

At sea Adam was at one with the realm of the ocean, enveloped and cut off from the land. Astride the fragile ark that was his ship, he stayed topside late on clear nights so that he could also be at one with the stars.

As they neared the eastern reaches of the Grand Banks and rode the Gulf Stream to the Flemish Cap, Adam noted the disappearance of the birds that accompanied the fishing fleets. They had gone, and Adam asked himself why. Adam noted the fact in his ship's log.

The next day, Adam noticed a rising swell in the ocean. It was perhaps of three to five feet and coming in every eight seconds according to Adam's calculations, nothing to be remarked about, but discernible nonetheless. Adam duly recorded his observation in the ship's log.

On the third day Adam felt a rising breeze and increasing swells of perhaps ten feet. He timed them as coming every seven seconds. On the horizon he spotted a mass of white cirrus clouds slowly spreading its veil over greater swaths of the sky.

"I think we are in for dirty weather, Mr. Spurling," he told the Mate. "Make sure the sticks are secure."

And he entered his observations in the ship's log.

The next morning brought a strong wind that whistled through the rigging and strained the sails. White caps flecked the waves and streaks of foam frothed in their troughs as the swells accelerated to five seconds apart.

"Reef the mainsails," Adam ordered, and the men scurried up the ratlines to haul in canvas.

By early afternoon the low clouds had thickened and overtaken the ship, and rain began to fall in squalls driven by gusty winds against which Adam found it difficult to stand. The canvas covering on the ship's jolly boat whipped about, and the few loose items not tied down or stowed below flew off the deck. The rising waves and swell now pitched the bow of the ship skyward and then plunged it in a baptism of water, from which it emerged dripping but firm.

"This is a hurricane, Mr. Spurling," Adam shouted as his Mate struggled to command the wheel. Adam had weathered hurricanes before, early in his career, in the West Indies. They were not to be trifled with.

"Reef all sails!" Adam ordered the men. He then ducked below to get two mugs of hot coffee from the ship's cook, who had just doused the cooking fire. He emerged in a hooded oil skin slicker, with an extra for the Mate, and bearing the coffee. He knew this would be a long night.

The two men stood at the wheelhouse dressed like medieval monks and enjoying the last sips of warming liquid in their bellies before the onslaught. Adam took the precaution of fixing two harnesses of rope so that he and the Mate were loosely tied to the wheelhouse in order to prevent their being swept overboard.

By what passed for dusk the dark ceiling of clouds had descended and enveloped the sky all around. Gale-force winds whipped past them as they struggled to maintain their footing before the wheel. As the evening wore on the squalls became constant, with the accelerating winds driving sheets of rain horizontally. The ship pitched and creaked as it rode the fifteen-foot waves, but so far its cargo below deck held tight. The night became so dark that Adam could no longer see the waves, only feel them. Or he thought he could not see them. He was not sure. Sometimes he discerned a dark looming mass rising high overhead crested by foam and sure to swallow up the ship as it bobbed and pitched and yawed like a cork lost in a vast and angry ocean.

Running without sails, the ship was off course. All Mr. Spurling could do at the wheel was to try to keep the ship headed forward so that it could ride the waves and not fight against them. As each monster wave approached the *Atheling*'s bow heaved up at a forty-five-degree angle to mount the crest and then as it passed beneath the hull the ship dove into a gut-wrenching fall that seemed to know no end, while at the same time foam-flecked ocean water surged over the deck and hurricane force winds tore through the rigging with a thunderous roar.

So it continued for three hours. Sometime in the wee hours Adam relieved Mr. Spurling, who fell into a crumpled heap in a crevice behind the wheelhouse, enveloped in his slicker and numb with fatigue. Adam grasped the wheel and held firm, against powerful resistance, to keep the ship moving forward in a line that kept her afloat.

"Don't fight the waves. Don't fight the waves," Adam told himself repeatedly as he struggled at the wheel. As the night wore on, his hands became stiff and numb as they gripped the wheel. The insensitivity began to spread to his forearms as well. But he did not dare take his hands off the wheel. To stay awake he recited aloud to himself Marc Antony's Funeral Oration and other fragments of learning from earlier days. When those gave out, he found himself reeling off childhood verses—"Ring around the rosies" and "Humpty dumpty"—as his mental discipline began to flag. Realizing the unraveling of his focus, he fell silent. Several times he found his head beginning to nod, but he always brought it up again with an involuntary jerk. And then he blacked out.

When he came to his hands were still frozen to the wheel. He had no idea how long he had been out. It may have been minutes or only seconds. But as his consciousness snapped back into gear, he immediately saw the mortal danger in which the *Atheling* had fallen while he was out. Unable to guide the ship, she had been allowed to broach to, veering to windward so that her broadside met the wind and sea.

Now slammed sideways by the incensed waves, the ship was in imminent danger of swamping and sinking. Adam fought furiously at the wheel to try to right her trajectory.

As he did so, he realized that he had not mastered the sea and never would. Nature in all her awe-filled majesty reigned supreme. Oh, he could play at the margins of her rules, such as he understood them, and bend his luck here or there. But he had committed the sin of presuming intimacy when in fact something less, sufferance maybe, had been extended. And now he was paying the price for his hubris. The North Atlantic stripped bare Adam's guilt.

At last, desperate, Adam cried aloud for Divine intervention. As a free-thinking Christian, Adam had never held much store for the doctrine of the elect or the contorted gymnastics of the sentences of St. Paul or even the Greek subtleties of the Trinity, but he had a personal relation with his God. And now he called on it. He uttered up a prayer, explaining that he had always lived in a covenant with God and that God had favored him and should not cease to do so now. If spared, he would enter into a new covenant with the Almighty, a different sort of personal relationship with God. And from somewhere in his consciousness, he dredged up and recited aloud lines, snatches and no more, from the

107th Psalm that he had heard in a seamen's Bethel in some coastal New England town in his younger days and later memorized:

"They that go down to the sea in ships, that do business in great waters:

These see the works of the Lord, and his wonders in the deep.

For he commandeth, and raiseth the stormy wind, which lifteth up the waves thereof.

They mount up to the heaven, they go down again to the depths: their soul is melted because of trouble.

They reel to and fro, and stagger like a drunken man, and are at their wits' end.

Then they cry unto the Lord in their trouble, and he bringeth them out of their distresses.

He maketh the storm a calm, so that the waves thereof are still . . .

So he bringeth them unto their desired haven."

As he recited the verses, three times through, Adam nudged the *Atheling* inch by inch, foot by foot, back into line between the waves that assaulted the sides of the ship. He looked up, and the winds began to slacken. The sky started to brighten with the coming of dawn. The ocean proved itself yet again as a force that is capable of swallowing but also of casting up again, at once cruel but merciful.

One half of the bargain was fulfilled, with alacrity. Ever the dutiful servant, Adam gave thanks. But he failed to ask what constituted the other half of the covenant—his obligations.

* * *

That autumn was a time of unsettled weather up and down the coast of New England. The coming of winter coincided with the wreck at the mouth of the Portland harbor of the *Grand Turk*, a five-hundred-ton merchantman bound from India to Salem. Her cargo of silks, teas, spices, and other rare merchandise from the East scattered upon the shores of Cape Elizabeth and the islands in Casco Bay. A particularly festive Christmas season ensued as ladies little accustomed to such luxuries promenaded up and down Fore and Middle Streets clad in silks and holiday tables were all the more festive with turmeric and Lapsang Souchong.

Despite war and losses, riches were to be had by those willing to seize them.

19

Pressed by His Majesty

1799

SETH HAD SETTLED INTO A LIFE DIVIDED BETWEEN THE BUSTLE OF London during the season and the respite of Georgette's family's lands in the West Country during the summer. September traditionally brought their return to London, where Georgette and Seth resided in a Georgian three-story yellow stuccoed house with a red door tucked into the north-east corner of Berkeley Square. It was a house of modest proportions, one of Lord Hormsby's properties, but location counted for all. The City and its bankers were a hackney ride away, while St. James's was but a short walk and even Whitehall was but a little further. Often Georgette and Seth would stroll, arm in arm, through nearby Green Park. It was thus little wonder that Seth found departures increasingly difficult. No more was this true than on the initiation of his autumn voyage to Portugal and America to uphold his leg of the triangle. On the eve of his sailing Georgette had informed him that she was three months with child. His remorse at departure was thus acute, and he determined to make a light-ning run to Porto to fill out his cargo of English manufactured goods with one hundred and twenty pipes of port wine, dash across the Atlantic to discharge his load, and return to England empty if need be to speed his return.

It was therefore with trepidation that he saw the cannonball fly across his bow, followed by the report of the gun that discharged it. Both emanated from a British frigate a mile on the starboard side of the *Three Brothers*, which he had just overtaken in indifferent wind heading west three days from Portugal. The frigate was the rear ship in a squadron consisting of two other frigates, two fifth rates, and a bomb ketch, all hovered about the mother hen of a massive third rate ship of the line boasting seventy-six guns and flying a swallow-tailed broad pennant of a Commodore.

Seth immediately ordered his ship brought in irons. The sails fell limp, and the *Three Brothers* slid to a virtual halt, rocking side to side with the swell of the sea. Through his telescope Seth saw the frigate's cutter lowered loaded with a dozen uniformed men. He waited patiently while their long oars magisterially swept them slowly toward him.

"Mr. Morse, I wonder to what we owe this pleasure?" he said to his Mate.

When they were in hailing distance, Seth spoke through the ship's trumpet.

"I am the American merchant ship *Three Brothers*, Seth Hale Captain."

The cutter responded. "HMS *Resolute*, Sydney Loring Captain. Permission to board!"

It was not a question but a command. Seth had no choice given the collective firepower hovering menacingly before him.

"Permission granted. Stand by."

The boarding party was a rough lot: tough, seasoned seamen, muscle-bound and tattooed, bearing belaying pins and knotted and tarred ropes a yard long, backed up by sheathed broad knives.

The young Ensign in command, barely old enough to shave and with a weak chin, spoke as soon as he set foot on board.

"I am to enquire if any seamen who are His Majesty's subjects are aboard, and I demand all such."

"We're a Yankee crew," Seth replied. "Unless you count old John Davy over there," as he nodded toward the ship's sixty-eight-year-old Welsh cook. "You can 'ave him."

A ripple of laughter spread through the crew, who by now had assembled on deck. Seth knew full well that cooks were not sought by press gangs and in any event they would not have taken a decrepit old man. They were after topmen.

The Ensign, annoyed at the impertinence of the response, sucked in his chin and redoubled his efforts in a higher pitched voice.

"I invite any volunteers to step forward."

None did.

Silence greeted the Ensign until from somewhere in the loitering crew an audible fart issued forth.

The Ensign reddened with rage and spittle sprayed from his mouth as he shouted in an even higher pitched attempt at command, "I demand to see your crew list! Bring me your crew list immed--ji--ately!"

"Mr. Morse, please fetch the crew list from my quarters for the Ensign," Seth said to his Mate in a calm, almost matter-of-fact voice. He conveyed equanimity and confidence but was not about to leave the deck and his men to the press gang to get it himself.

While the Mate went below Seth stared in silence at the Ensign. Seth maintained his face as blank and stony as the Old Man of the Mountain in New Hampshire. There was no place for small talk in this encounter.

After what seemed an interminable interlude, the Mate returned with the papers and handed them to Seth, who in turned passed them to the Ensign, who studied them with a close eye. At last he looked up, with a hint of astonishment in his face.

"See, I told you. We're an all-Yankee crew," Seth gloated before the Ensign could say anything. "Foreigners, masters, and chief mates of all merchantmen over fifty tons are exempt from impressment, are they not, Ensign? I believe we fall into such a protected class."

The Ensign rocked back and forth on his feet trying to decide what to do. He grimaced and shoved the papers back into Seth's hands.

Wheeling to leave, he turned back for an instant and stared at Seth.

"And you, Captain Hale. You say you are a Yank, but you speak in a most plummy manner. How long have you lived in England?"

"I am at sea most of the year."

"How long have you lived in England?"

"Five years, but I don't see how that's either here or there. I am an American."

"I see a wedding band on your finger. Is your wife a British subject?"

"I don't see how that's any of your business, but as a matter of fact she is. She is—"

"Aha! I thought so. Foreign seamen are liable to impressment if they have lived in England for two years or if they have married a British subject. You qualify on both heads. You are a naturalized Briton. Seize him!"

"No, you don't understand. I am not a seaman. I am an American Captain! And my wife is the daughter of—"

"Belay it! Take him!"

The press gang surrounded Seth as they pulled their belaying pins and knives from their belts.

"Wait! Let me at least get my chest from below. Mr. Morse, come with me."

Followed by two of the burliest members of the press gang, they went below to fetch the chest. As they did, Seth whispered to his Mate.

"I haven't much time. I'll have to go with them. You take the ship and head straight for Plymouth. Inform Georgette and Lord Hormsby about what has happened. Tell them I've been impressed by HMS *Resolute* under Captain Loring. They will know what to do to secure my release. Tell Georgette that I will contact her as soon as I am able and that I love her."

The Mate nodded in comprehension.

Then Seth pulled out his sea chest and quickly gathered up all the charts and maps he had at his desk, as well as a small compass, and stashed them under his folded clothes in the chest. He carefully felt for the oil skin covered packet that he always kept at the bottom of his chest. In its velvet lining were sewn twenty gold sovereigns in case of an emergency. With these he knew he somehow would be safe. He closed the chest, locked it, and tucked it under his arm.

"Farewell, Mr. Morse. Godspeed and sail like a fury!"

As Seth stepped into the cutter he addressed the Ensign.

"I want a word with your Captain. This is a misunderstanding that I am sure we can clear up."

The Ensign glared at him.

"I'm telling you this one time and one time only. As a seaman in the Royal Navy you speak to an officer only when he asks you a question and then only to respond to the question. You have no right to talk to an officer. Do you understand?"

Seth remained silent.

"Do you understand? Respond to my question."

Seth remained silent.

And at that, the cutter pushed off and headed not for the frigate but for the three-decked seventy-six gun ship of the line, HMS *Neptune*.

* * *

Seth was assigned a hammock on the dark and low-ceilinged orlop deck in the fo'c'sle of the massive man o' war, more of a teeming and unsleeping city than a ship Seth thought. The next morning he was put to work at the lowest form of manual labor—holystoning the main deck. As he did, he asked himself if his father-in-law, in some fit of Manichean vengeance, had set him up to be impressed. But he reassured himself that would make no sense because in fact Lord Hormsby needed his masts and spars. Perhaps, more plausibly, the British cartel at Porto, jealous of his breaking their monopoly, had ordered him seized. But, the more he mulled it, that too was far-fetched. He had happened on the naval squadron by chance. His present circumstances were the fruit of his own navigation. He was the author of his own misery.

The next day being Sunday, and the winds nonexistent, the entire seven-hundred-and-fifty-man crew was ordered assembled for divine services on the main deck amidships. Under a sail spread out as a tent overhead, the Anglican chaplain, viewed by many as an unlucky accompaniment on a ship, droned on while all the crew stood at attention. The Captain of the ship of the line, who also bore the position of Commodore of the squadron, attended, or more precisely presided, from the quarterdeck: a remote figure with an old-fashioned black wig, beefy and dissipated face marked by a warted nose and encumbered by a pot belly. He wore a sword, even at what passed for church. Finally, the service concluded with a hymn, "O God Our Help in Ages Past, Our Hope for Years to Come."

Expecting the midday dinner, the men began to shuffle away when the Bosun blew his whistle and shouted, "All hands to stand by to witness punishment!"

At that, a poor shirtless wretch was frog-marched by a squad of red-coated Marines to an upended hatch and lashed to it. There was a quick roll of a drum, and the Bosun laid into him with a whistling cat-o-nine-tails that lacerated his back with the sickening thud of leather and lead shredding flesh.

"What was his crime?" Seth whispered to the sailor standing next to him.

"Tried to jump ship in the Cape Verde Islands."

The thrashing continued until the man's back ran in sheets of blood and his rib cage was visible through what was left of his back. By what Seth counted as the twenty-fifth blow, he could watch no longer and averted his eyes. The punishment so exceeded the crime that he felt outrage in his heart. When the flogging ceased, the Marines threw a bucket of salt water on the man's back, causing him to cry out and writhe in agony. They then cut him down and bundled him into a jolly boat to row him to each ship in succession, where the procedure was repeated.

"He'll be dead by the time they're done," Seth whispered to the sailor next to him.

"Sometimes they are," he replied and shrugged.

That night, when work was done and the men were at leisure after a supper of cold salt pork and hard tack, Seth offered his rum ration to the sailor who owned the hammock next to his. He learned he was a former London wharf rat named Blee, impressed into service six years earlier.

"Right, gov'nor, they come and took me in Canary Wharf back in '93."

"Did you not think of escaping?"

"Oh, I thought o' it, all right. But to escape, you 'ave to 'ave an opportunity. I never 'ad the opportunity. You see, it's like this. Those that escapes, they do it right away. In the first few weeks. Once they's been on board longer, well, they get used to it. And it becomes a sort of way o' life for 'em."

"So where are we headed?"

"Don' know. They say the West Indies, to fight the Frenchies. Maybe Guadaloupe or Martinique. But mos' probably Jamaica first."

"Jamaica?" Seth asked as his ears perked up.

"Aye, Jamaica. The Commodore will want to call there."

"And who is our Commodore?"

"Oh, he be Sir Ponsonby Spicer."

Seth flinched. He felt the tautness at the corners of his mouth as he tried to mask his shock. He prayed his eyes did not betray his recognition of the name. He did the simple calculus. He would have to keep his head low. His name must not come before the Commodore except in the most superficial way. And yet Jamaica might provide his means of escape. Despite great distances, he and Jezreel had maintained contact through regular letters to one another. He knew all about Great Spring Garden Plantation and Gabrielle Campbell. He judged it a reasonable calculation that Jezreel might be there at this very instant. Even if he were not, he could seek out Gabrielle Campbell and surely she would shelter him until Jezreel arrived. The challenge would be how to make his escape. Aboard the *Neptune* he had seven hundred and fifty sets of eyes on him at all times. Escape would be well-nigh impossible. No, he would have to make himself useful in order to devise a moment more discrete in which the odds would be more in his favor. This would be a most difficult needle to thread indeed. For now, he would make himself useful, gain the trust of his overseers and look and observe.

And so he did as the squadron made its desultory passage across the mid-Atlantic. The usual trade winds that blew in that part of the ocean had tapered off to a whisper. Whole days the squadron lay adrift in the hot sun. As ordered, Seth occupied his time on his knees holystoning the deck and making five yarn sennit by braiding rope yarns together for use in the rigging. Each day followed its regulated routine, with changing watches, the noon calculations by the officers, dinner of increasingly fetid fare and evenings generally at leisure. Each day following the officers' dinner the Commodore, freed of his coat and in shirtsleeves, sparred in bouts of fencing with a rotation of his Lieutenants and Ensigns on the quarterdeck. Though he was far away and high up, it appeared to Seth that he always won.

As a rule, Seth shunned the company of his fellow seamen, who were a profane, brutal, and superstitious lot.

"This is a haunted ship, it is," observed a red-bearded Irish sailor named O'Malley as they sat about when the day's work was done. "And the proof of it is I saw my chest fly across the room."

Seth pretended not to be listening.

"Did ye not see the open coffin floating by with an open Bible in it as we left the Channel?" asked another.

"Aye, the sure sign of shipwreck coming," the Irishman agreed, and all heads nodded.

In an exception to his rule, however, Seth cemented his relationship with Blee by handing over his half pint of rum to him each day.

One evening, when he thought it safe, he broached the subject of the Commodore with him.

"So, Blee, what do you think of the Commodore?"

"Ole Spice Cake? 'e's as bad as any of 'em, I reckon. A very particular one, 'e is. Rules by the cat."

"Didn't he lose a ship to the Americans during our war of independence? How did he go from there to Captain and now Commodore?"

Blee looked at him with hooded eyes for a moment deciding whether to respond. At last he spoke.

"Aye, that he did. He lost a ship. The A'miralty raised a hue an' cry, but it seems back then all the powers that be wanted to bury it an' move on, so Ole Spicey got off scot free."

"That was all he was tried for, loss of the ship? Nothing else?"

"No, jus' the ship. Warn't nothing else."

"I see," Seth observed with a faint and relieved smile. It seemed that the sale of the timber maps remained a secret.

"So back to Ole Spicey. 'e retired on half pay, jus' like so many others after the war. But it seems retirement wasn't Ole Spicey's cuppa tea. So he goes an' joins up as an officer in the Russian Imperial Navy, sailing in the Baltic Fleet for the Empress Catherine. There he makes Post Captain.

An' Catherine likes 'im and gives 'im some medal for valorous service. So when war breaks out with the Frenchies, 'e comes highly recommended, as it were. The A'miralty calls 'im back to duty on full pay an', low an' behold, Ole Spicey makes Cap'n in the Royal Navy. Such is the wheel o' fortune. Why d' ye ask?"

"Oh, just curious, that's all. Just curious."

During his long hours of servitude Seth had ample time to reflect on his current condition. Not only had he fallen from the status of Captain of his own ship and an aspiring merchant, more importantly he was robbed of control of his property and political say and the last badge of an independent adult American, his freedom of movement. He was now no more than a child or a slave. Spending hours on his knees and with head perforce bowed in servility before the uneducated brutes who commanded him, he was no longer an adult or a man. To Seth's mind, nothing brought into clearer focus the distinction between being a subject of the British monarchy and a citizen of the American republic. By fighting and evading his impressment he would define for himself what it meant to be a citizen of the United States of America. Being such a citizen was an exercise of free will, not a duty or an obligation.

On one particularly hot and still day, after the squadron had been stalled the better part of the week, Seth noticed that the Commodore had taken to visiting the other ships aboard his barge. Seth also noticed that the barge was rowed by twelve young and fair sailors, all the same height and attired in red striped jerseys and straw flat brimmed hats with ribbons.

That evening, he asked Blee about the Commodore's barge.

"Oh, Ole Spicey be most particular about his barge. An' those who man it. He likes a smart an' comely appearance."

"Who selects the men?"

"The Master-at-arms knows Ole Spicey's preferences. An' he recruits 'em."

"What are the qualifications? A strong arm and experience with the oar, I suppose? Anything else?"

Blee looked at him once again with a long and weighing eye.

"Well, I don't know. But what I've heared, well, if Ole Spicey, that is the Commodore, speaks to ye, ye 'ave to answer. Night or day, if ye follow."

"I follow."

Two days later Seth let slip within hearing of the Master-at-arms that he was an experienced rower. It was a lie of course, and he was not sure he had heard. So the next day he spread the word among his mess mates. That evening, sure enough, the Master-at-arms approached him after supper as he was repairing a rope.

"I hear ye have experience rowing."

"Aye, sir, I do."

"How old are ye?"

"Just turned thirty, sir."

"That's older than we like for service on the Commodore's barge, but ye are well built and in good shape," he said as he apprised him. "Fair and comely too. I'll keep ye in mind. Now back to work."

One week later, as dusk fell, the squadron arrived at Kingston, Jamaica. They dropped anchor off the ruins of Port Royal, the "richest and wickedest city" in British North America until the sea swallowed most of it in a catastrophic earthquake in 1692, as if in retribution. The Commodore entertained aboard ship that evening. At once close and yet a world away from the white tablecloth and hock in the Commodore's quarterdeck cabin, Seth swung in his hammock in a gloomy corner of the orlop deck, both anxious and determined. If only he could nudge Fate to act, he thought to himself. But Fate is what it is and beyond his control, he realized. And with a resignation borrowed from his reading of the Stoics, he drifted asleep in the stifling heat.

All hands were piped on deck early the next morning to turn out for the Commodore's disembarking for the port. Pennants had already been hoisted in the rigging, and the British ensign at the mizzen hung in the heat.

The Master-at-arms grabbed Seth by his shoulder and spun him around.

"Here, take these and change," he ordered as he handed him a red-and-white-striped jersey and straw hat. "You're to take the number five starboard oar. Just follow what the other rowers do. And you're to report to the Commodore's cabin after he returns from town at eight bells. Understand? Now be quick about it!"

This would be a very thin needle indeed to thread, Seth thought to himself.

"Aye, aye, sir," Seth confirmed as he grasped the clothes and ran below.

Once on the empty deck below, he pulled out and unlocked his sea chest. Fumbling through the charts and maps, he found a map of Jamaica, which he stuffed, along with his compass and the oil skin packet containing the sovereigns, inside his shirt. He then pulled on the striped jersey over his shirt, donned the hat, locked his chest, and shoved it back in the corner.

Seth took his seat in the barge and, watching the other rowers for instruction, raised his oar vertically when they did to salute the boarding of the Commodore. They then rowed him the half league to the quay, tied up, saluted him again on his disembarking and fell out while they awaited his return. Most of the men were anxious to set foot on land after so many weeks at sea, so they followed the Bosun ashore and milled about the docks taking in all the sights and sounds of the old pirate's lair that was Kingston, now grown into a prosperous city of thirty thousand people with three thousand brick houses laid out in a grid pattern like a Spanish colonial city and dwarfing Philadelphia and Baltimore, not to mention Portland. Seth lingered at the periphery of the group. The other sailors rapidly became distracted by the bustle of the hawkers, prostitutes, and stevedores. The Bosun and two of the men wandered to a wharfside tobacconist's shop to replenish the supplies for their pipes. Sensing this was his moment, Seth slowed his pace behind the knot of talkative sailors with whom he was walking so that he fell a few steps behind, loitered as he gazed into a shop window and then, approaching a street corner, he ducked right and into the town. He zigzagged through a series of right and left turns along the streets, darted up an alley and tried to remove himself as quickly as possible from the district of the waterfront taverns. He calculated once they discovered his disappearance they would look first for him there, thinking him a simple seaman. Five minutes into his peregrination, he removed the jersey and hat and stuffed them in an empty barrel beside a warehouse. He now was any man afoot in the teeming port city of Kingston.

Seth consulted his map and compass and soon was on the high road leading out of town toward the Blue Mountains. He calculated his journey at sixty miles, give or take, as the crow flies. But he knew his trip would not be as the crow flew because he had to surmount and pass the Blue Mountains. At the edge of town he found a dealer in horses. For one gold sovereign and change he procured a jade with saddlebags and enough oats to last three days and struck out along the road. An old woman selling jerk chicken by the roadside provided his next purchase, which he knew would be his last meal for a day or more. Seth figured he would have to ride without ceasing in order to clear the Blue Mountains before a patrol was sent out looking for him. So he did not tarry. He also knew that the trip was not without other risks as well. From his correspondence with Jezreel he had learned that Maroons who lived in the mountains often captured and returned naval deserters, while, in contrast, runaway slaves assisted them. Altogether, he determined to avoid people if he possibly could.

The road climbed steeply into the mountainous terrain, evolving into a series of switchbacks as it tackled the rising elevation. By sunset Seth had cleared the hamlet of Newcastle, and the rising hulk of Catherine's Peak stood guard over the Blue Mountains past his right shoulder. Shortly thereafter the road gave out to a trail. His saddle creaked, and he swayed as the horse put one foot in front of the other in a monotonous rhythm. Seth marveled that the horse could follow the trail in the pitch black of the night. All the jungle about him was as quiet as death save for the occasional call of some exotic bird high up in the canopy. Many hours later—Seth was not sure how many for he had no timepiece—he reached the Hardwar Gap leading over the Grand Ridge of the Blue Mountains. The trail forked. Seth stopped his horse. How he wished for a light to consult his map and compass. It was a dark and cloudy night, and there was no moon to aid him. He would have to draw on his instincts as a navigator to judge which way to go. Those instincts told him to take the starboard fork. So he did.

In the early morning hours fatigue began to take its toll. His head drooped, and he found his hands letting loose of the reins. Still, the horse plodded forward, following the trail as if by rote. At one point in the depths of the night the clouds unleashed a torrential shower which soaked him. With all his clothes drenched and at the high elevation and with the nighttime temperatures plummeting, he was cold to the bone and began to shiver. He wanted to stop, to lay down, to sleep, but he knew he could not. He told himself he must keep going. So he did.

Step followed step. Minute followed minute. Hour followed hour on the interminable journey.

Just when he thought he could stand it no longer, the sky in the east began to lighten, and Seth saw the crown of John Crow Peak outlined against the horizon. He reminded himself that he was on the eastern side of the island and, as in Portland, Maine, would be among the first to see the rising of the sun. At this altitude he would be among the very first indeed.

The sky lightened further and as the sun's first rays extended themselves into the new day Seth first sensed and then saw that he was on the descent. He had cleared the Blue Mountains. The trail continued down the mountainside in a series of zigzags. By what he guessed to be about seven o'clock he had skirted the village of Wakefield, which had begun to stir. The chickens and roosters were long up, and a dog barked at his passing. He took care not to enter the village for fear of the Maroons. From there it was an increasingly straight path to lower elevations. By midday he had cleared Rose Hill. And then he saw the ocean. He stopped his horse and surveyed with wonder, excitement, and relief the north coast of the island spread out before him and the deep blue of the water in Buff Bay beyond.

In late afternoon a weary, sore, aching, and unshaven Seth checked his map and compass one final time. They promised him that Great Spring Garden plantation lay only a mile ahead. Although he had been fighting off sleep for longer than he could reckon, he rallied with excitement at reaching his safe harbor. He nudged the horse to pick up the pace as he found the entrance to the estate and headed up the long drive.

Within minutes he was at the main house. He dismounted, approached the front door, and knocked.

Footsteps sounded from within, approaching. The lock disengaged and the door swung open to reveal his brother.

"Jezreel! Brother!" Seth shouted.

An incredulous Jezreel could only stare.

And then he held out his arms and cried, "My brother!" as Seth collapsed into the enfolding succor of his embrace.

* * *

"Where to, Captain?" Seth asked Jezreel in humor as the *Dolphin* nudged its way out of Port Antonio harbor less than two days later.

Jezreel replied with a wink:

"LATITUDE 43.66

LONGITUDE –70.25."

"Aye, aye, Captain, set the course straight and true!"

The previous day had allowed Seth to sleep and clean up. When he finally emerged for dinner he regaled Jezreel and Gabrielle over several glasses of wine with his tale of woe. Jezreel in turn told him how he had brought a shipment of freshwater ice from the ponds of Maine, packed in sawdust in the hold of the *Dolphin*, only to find a gelatinous blob below deck when he arrived in Jamaica. Still, he managed to chip enough off to cool a bowl of flip that Gabrielle had prepared to celebrate his arrival. At the end of the evening both Jezreel and Seth agreed that they had not a moment to lose, and so the next morning Jezreel canceled the lading of his ship and set sail for Portland with a partially filled hold but the most precious cargo of all.

As Jezreel bade good-bye to Gabrielle, he took her hand and squeezed it. Jezreel sensed a veil of concern descending over her eyes.

"Darling, I understand why you have to go, but I feel so much . . . safer . . . with you here."

So that was the glue which now cemented their relationship: a sense of security that Jezreel provided. That and physical passion.

"I'll have to tackle the improvements to the mill house that I have been putting off," she reasoned as her thoughts turned to another compartment.

"That's right. You have the plantation to attend to. Once I'm over the horizon, you'll be just fine. And besides, Major Gaskill is still about to keep an eye on things."

"Promise me you'll return quickly."

"I promise."

* * *

The homecoming of Seth and Jezreel brought great joy in the Hale house. The news of a prospective grandchild and of Seth's delivery from impressment provided causes for celebration. But that was not all, as Juvenal was home from Harvard College and, with the whole family reunited and in attendance, the Reverend Doctor Deane from the First Parish Church married Thankful and Major Gideon Sewell in the front parlor of the house at one o'clock on a cold and bright Saturday afternoon in early December.

Following several rounds of celebratory toasts, the young couple ventured out into the banked snow and mounted their one-horse sleigh. Major Sewell adjusted the fur lap robe, gave the belled reins a shake and off they sped to a friend's farm in Gorham to spend the night. Adam and Nabby waved good-bye, and the three boys chased after them, huzzahing and waving, and continued into town to keep the celebration alive at Colonel Burnham's tavern on the waterfront.

Adam and Nabby returned to a still and empty house in the waning light of late afternoon. Adam stirred the fire with the poker, sending a flurry of sparks up the chimney and rekindling the heat. He took Nabby's hand and held it.

"Well, a good job, Mrs. Hale," he said.

"A good job, Captain Hale," she responded.

And the only sound remaining in the house was the pendulum of the tall case clock in the front hall as it swung back and forth.

20

The New World of Major Sewell
1800

THE NEW CENTURY OPENED ON A SOMBER NOTE. IN JANUARY NEWS OF the passing of President Washington the previous month reached New England, and the country went into deep and profound mourning. Commerce ceased, ships lay still in the harbor, and people gathered only at church.

For Adam and Nabby the prevailing gloom grew only worse with the arrival at the end of March of a letter from Seth advising that his young daughter, named Abigail after Nabby, had lived only one week.

It therefore came as a surprise to Adam when Major Gideon Sewell approached him soon after with a plan to float shares for a new syndicate to purchase and export corn. He asked him to lend him the money to do so. Adam was skeptical at first but eventually relented, as much to appease him as for the soundness of the investment. But the investment proved sound indeed. Adam's shares rose in value, and Sewell had flipped his shares within a month, making a three hundred percent profit.

Now, emboldened with this money, he explained to Adam that he intended to set himself up as a merchant in town.

"But, my dear Major, you have never gone to sea," Adam protested.

"Nor do I intend to. Going to sea is a waste of time. I can better profit by managing and contracting with others to sail ships and letting them tie up their time on great, long voyages."

"But what do you know of being a merchant? Most sons in merchant families start out as 'purchasers' on a commission basis and then graduate to 'agents' so that they can establish contacts for later successful careers as merchants. You have not followed that route."

"I know the process—I saw it when I was in Boston—but I haven't time for that. I know exactly how I am to go about this."

"I don't doubt that for a moment," Adam allowed.

"So will you back me as a silent partner?"

Adam stroked his chin as he thought.

"It could be a glorious opportunity. And I won't ask twice," Sewell warned.

Still, Adam weighed the proposal and hesitated. Something in Sewell's brash approach raised a warning flag deep in his mind.

"No, Major, I think it better that our business affairs not intertwine. I wish you the best of fortune with your endeavors, to be sure. How could I not for the sake of my daughter? But I would not want commerce to complicate our family relationship. Family comes ahead of commerce. Such matters have a way of standing in the way of true friendship."

"I see," Sewell responded as he stared with a cold eye. "Very well, then, I'll raise the money on my own. I shall not forget this."

* * *

True to his word, Major Sewell raised the money in partnership with another aspiring merchant, Parker Ilsley, and set about revolutionizing the way business was done by the old sailing merchant Captains. Major Sewell set up a factory house in Fore Street and never went to sea. He had an unerring instinct for his fellow man: those to whom he should defer, those whom he could manipulate, those whom he could dominate. And he played them like an organ. Although he was deprived of a family alliance to launch his career, he nonetheless operated, at least at the start, under the penumbra of respect that the town held for his father-in-law. He quickly analyzed the intense competition, suspicion, and mistrust that characterized other leaders in Portland's merchant community and played one off against the other, striking alliances here, out-maneuvering there. He leased ships and hired Captains. No detail was too small for his attention. Knowing that the keys to success were economy, efficiency, and attention to detail, he informed himself about market prices and conditions, sought the best possible prices for the sale of his goods, personally chose which supplies to put aboard, and instructed his masters with care on policies to be followed on voyages. Using his accounting acumen, he devised elaborate and impenetrable systems of debits and credits that squeezed sailors on their slop chests and cost of food. The slop chests, which contained personal items, shoes, clothing, and the like, were valued at twenty to twenty-five dollars each, but he sold them to the sailors for as much as seventy dollars and the privilege of sailing on his ships. They were charged for them before they left port and could not open them until well under way. He squeezed the bounds of the "lay" system by which sailors were given a percentage of the profits and assumed some of the risk of the voyage but had no say in the assumption of risks.

Within the year, these tactics, small in themselves and often not readily perceptible, began to pay off. Major Sewell was on his way to becoming a successful merchant.

His timing was impeccable. By the summer, the fledgling United States Navy and Royal Navy, as well as a more conciliatory policy by the new government of First Consul Napoleon Bonaparte, had curtailed the depredations of the French Navy and privateers. By the end of September, the Quasi War with France had ended. And Portland, and New England in general, were set to embark on seven years of unparalleled prosperity that would send American ships to the four corners of the globe and bring the riches of the world to American shores.

* * *

The year which had begun on somber notes ended happily for Adam and Nabby. Thankful and Gideon joined them for Christmas dinner. Before the roaring fire, they each recounted their blessings—their health, safe passages by the Hale sons, growing wealth, an America at peace and, as Thankful let slip, the expectation of a grandchild in the coming year.

21

Te Deum

1801

By June the Hale household was in an uproar. Adam had delayed a long-planned voyage to England and was in an irritable mood. Each day he skulked about the house until Nabby made him walk down to the office in his storehouse on Fore Street.

"It won't be today," she advised him as she eased him out the front door.

"But when?" he asked. "I wish to be here, but I can't make the whole world stop spinning just because a child is about to be born."

"Soon, my love. Now off with you."

Upstairs, with the windows thrown open to admit the fresh summer breeze off the ocean, Thankful lay in the four-poster bed in the spare bedroom waiting. Nabby had insisted that she move to their house, with its more spacious accommodations and servant girl, for the birth. It had been a difficult pregnancy, accompanied by morning sickness and several false alarms of the imminent loss of the child. Dr. Noyes had checked in daily.

Now that she was three days overdue, all they could do was wait.

That night, well past dark, a violent thunderstorm shook Casco Bay. Highly electrical, its lightning flashes illuminated the town as if it were a stage set. Its rolling, restless thunderclaps cracked like Mowat's cannons every thirty seconds. Discomfited by the noise and her time finally having arrived, Thankful went into labor. Nabby and the servant girl attended her, working by flickering candlelight, while Adam kept an anxious pacing watch and Gideon waited in the study below. The labor was short and violent. Thankful tensed and heaved with each strike of electricity. Her cries and groans screamed in counterpoint to the claps of thunder. And from the mass of flailing limbs and twisted and sweat-soaked linen faintly illuminated by the candlesticks on the nightstand between flashes of blue that exposed the bedroom and its frail and terrified inhabitants, new life was born: a baby girl. Adam cradled her in his arms and held her up for all to see as the booming *Te Deum* of God's Creation sang in full-throated cry.

Thankful named her Hephzibah, for she took delight in her.

22

Mrs. Campbell's Lapdog

1802—Part I

JEZREEL NEVER QUESTIONED GABRIELLE ABOUT HER OWNERSHIP OF slaves. Although he made three voyages annually to Jamaica to fetch molasses for the insatiable American rum market and to barter goods, and each time lingered in her company as long as he could, he sensed that it was a topic better not broached. He knew it would only lead to disagreement. He understood that she was a widow and an astute businesswoman and that she had not chosen her lot—or perhaps she had? Still, she enveloped him each time on his return to the island, and he fell anew under her, and its, spell. But the topic was a many-headed beast, and it would not lie still.

Or so it seemed to Jezreel as he accompanied Gabrielle and Major Gaskill to a reception in late March at Government House in the garrison at Fort George that bestrode the point jutting into the sea at Port Antonio. Built by the same architect who designed the Royal Citadel at Plymouth, England, it was in fact a small reproduction of its parental model. Constructed of granite and boasting ten-foot-thick walls and twenty-two naval cannon, it warned off invaders and Maroons alike. Huddled within the fortification, but trying to present a festive spirit, were all the planters of the north shore of the colony, the military brass, and the senior government officials, up to and including the Governor who was up from the capital at Spanish Town.

They were, to a person, on edge.

"This virus will spread, I fear," the Governor warned. "First it was the revolt on Saint Domingue. And all the slitting of white throats by that Louverture chap. Encouraged of course by the Jacobins in Paris."

"Aye, it's coming here," Major Gaskill agreed. "I see it in their eyes. The way they look at you. The way they move. There's insolence in the air."

"That's why you are still here, Major," the Governor confirmed. "The garrison has become permanent and it must be augmented."

"Unless . . ." Gabrielle spoke up. "Unless First Consul Bonaparte retakes Saint Domingue. I understand he has sent a force of over twenty thousand men under General Le Clerc to crush the revolt and retake the island."

"Well, I suppose we all wish 'im well," the Governor replied. "Here's to First Consul Bonaparte!" he said as he raised his glass.

"To Bonaparte! To Bonaparte!" all in the room responded as they lifted their glasses, even while their faces betrayed their prolonged anxiety.

All except for Jezreel, who stopped to ponder the puzzling equation of "my enemy's enemy is my friend."

The cold eye of the Governor noticed and stared at him. Major Gaskill immediately picked up on it and moved in for the kill.

"So why doesn't Mrs. Campbell's lapdog drink with our Governor?"

Jezreel bristled. His face grew flushed as he struggled for words.

"Because . . . because I don't . . . I don't agree," he stammered.

All the room now stared in silence.

Gabrielle moved toward him and took his arm in her bare one, whispering *sotto voce*, "Dearest Jezreel, not now."

Jezreel brushed her aside.

"No, no! I deplore slavery in all its forms. There are certain rights which are self-evident and common to all men—life, liberty, and the pursuit of happiness."

A sardonic and patronizing smile curled at the edges of the Governor's lips.

"I've heard those words before. But they are only words. Far be it for you, an American who comes from a slave-holding country, to lecture us."

"But our country is split on the issue. And I'm from New England, where we don't countenance slavery."

At this the Governor let out a loud roaring laugh.

"You don't countenance slavery, my dear American tar? What! You come here and spend months at a time or so I hear. You buy up our slave-produced molasses and sugar. You take them to New England and sell them at a profit while at the same time making money for your New England compatriots by selling their goods here. Oh, no, my friend. You are part of the system! A necessary evil and a little shitty one at that."

Stunned, Jezreel shrank back, not knowing how to respond to the looking glass thrust in his face.

Jezreel suddenly envisaged all the persons in the room, except himself, as characters in a play that they had written for themselves and as trapped in the theater they could not leave.

"But . . . but . . . I can always leave, and you can't."

"Oh yes, you can always weigh anchor and sail north," the Governor replied. "But you'll come back. Of that I'll assure you, you'll come back. Come, now, let's all move to more pleasant topics."

All heads in the room nodded and murmured their agreement, leaving Jezreel standing alone.

23

The Stork

1802—Part II

THE SOARING ANTHEM OF ORLANDO GIBBONS SUNG BY THE CHORIS-
ters of the Chapel Royal filled the barrel-vaulted arch of the Queen's
Chapel and lifted up the praises of the hundreds of joyful worshippers
who filled the delicate, light-washed sanctuary in St. James's Palace on a
bright but chilly Saturday morning at the close of March. The nave was
filled to capacity for the christening of the baby son of one of Georgette's
childhood friends. Georgette was one of the godmothers. The venue could
not have been more appropriately selected. The Queen's Chapel, built for
the private use of the Catholic Queen Henrietta Maria, had since the
Glorious Revolution been the home church for Protestant diplomats
from Denmark, Germany, and the Netherlands resident in London.
Georgette's friend had married a young Dutch aristocrat, Govert Kruijs-
bergen van Couwenhoven, who had come to London in, as it turned out,
an abortive attempt to resurrect the Dutch West India Company. He had
stayed on. The failure of his venture did not matter, for he had vast wealth
and connections and, by all accounts, enjoyed leading a cosmopolitan life
in London. Georgette's circle had dubbed him "the Dutchman" because
of their inability to pronounce his tongue-twisting names (and, in Seth's
view because of an innate English laziness at foreign languages, not that
Americans were any better). And so Seth and Georgette stood at the
sanctuary of the chapel along with the other godparents, including the

rotund Prince of Wales himself in yellow breeches and waistcoat framed by a dark green surcoat, all enveloped in the joy and rightness of being *there* for the flower-scented, organ-piped, and royally-assented affirmation of belonging. The Ton had gathered.

Seth noticed a tear running down Georgette's left cheek. He slid his hand over hers and held tight. He had told her they would try again after losing Abigail, and now he reaffirmed it in silence and with the strength of his all-enveloping grip.

"None can enter into the Kingdom of God, except he be regenerate and born anew of water and of the Holy Ghost," the minister intoned in a stentorian voice without inflection that reverberated off the blue plaster walls of the chapel.

"Almighty and everlasting God, who of thy great mercy didst save Noah and his family in the ark from perishing by water; and also didst safely lead the children of Israel thy people through the Red Sea . . . and by the baptism of thy well-beloved Son Jesus Christ in the river Jordan, didst sanctify water to the mystical washing away of sin . . ." he droned on.

And Seth's mind began to wander. What of Jonah and the whale? Does that figure?

"We beseech thee, for thine infinite mercies, that thou wilt mercifully look upon this Child; wash him and sanctify him with the Holy Ghost; that he being delivered from thy wrath, may be received into the ark of Christ's Church; and being steadfast in faith, joyful through hope and rooted in charity, may so pass the waves of this troublesome world . . ."

Seth allowed himself the irreverence of speculating which came first: the Royal Navy or the English Church? Perhaps they were twins born of the same parents. The English and the Dutch, he observed, were good at institutions: the British East India Company, the Muscovy Company, the Hudson's Bay Company, the Dutch East India Company, the Dutch West India Company, all mercantilist monopolies that eliminated competition. America had nothing comparable. In the United States, it was every man for himself: thousands of individual or family-owned ships, fleets, and building yards scrambling in a chaos of competition against each other and against the statist leviathans from Europe.

Seth eyed the bulging figure of the Prince of Wales whose very physical presence lent favor and legitimacy to the proceedings. In the United Kingdom's monarchy without a constitution, the personal role of the monarch—one man, or in this case his son—was the glue that held the state together, Seth reflected. How this model contrasted with the American constitution without a monarch, where ideas and checks and balances, rather than a physical presence, cemented the integrity of the state. Therein lay the weakness of the British model, Seth figured, for the monarch had gone mad a few years earlier, and the Prince of Wales acted as Regent pending his father's recovery. Or was this weakness any worse than that in the American system that had allowed the ascent of the partisan Mr. Jefferson? Seth's mind wandered.

Before Seth knew it, adrift as he was on the "waves of this troublesome world," the christening was over with the child baptized, a few mumbled prayers and a great shuffling of chairs and feet before the organ opened up in an exultant postlude.

The entire congregation, including the Prince, ambled en masse up the incline of St. James's Street to a reception at the Palladian stone pile of Broodles Club. There, in the dark green walled library and with the grates in the fireplaces throwing off an acrid heat from their coal fires (an odor to which Seth's nose was still unaccustomed, having been raised in proximity to New England wood fires), Seth found himself shifting his feet uncomfortably under a portrait of Banastre Tarleton while the conversation swirled around him. To be sure, Seth had borne well the humiliation of his impressment and had been accepted back seamlessly into the friendship of Georgette's circle. Indeed, the matter was never mentioned, almost a taboo, which made Seth in his darker moments all the more suspicious. He was accepted, but was he *really* accepted? Alas, he did not know the answer, much as he would like to. So his only choice was to muddle on.

Leaving the unwelcome gaze of the Butcher of the Carolinas, Seth and Georgette found themselves drawn to the Dutchman with his towering frame, lank reddish-blond hair, and blue eyes. He was dressed richly, in a flattering but sober suit.

Georgette whispered admiringly in Seth's ear, "He's quite the Corinthian."

Seth merely grunted. He wondered why Dutchmen were always so large. But then so were Danes and Latvians. Perhaps it had something to do with coming from a small country.

"My country is under water, both literally and figuratively," the Dutchman boomed in his *basso profundo* voice to a knot of listeners. "First it was the Spanish and the Duke of Alba. Then it was the Batavian Republic imposed by the regicides in Paris. And now it is First Consul Bonaparte who won't leave. Of what value is the Peace of Amiens if our country remains occupied? Bonaparte says he brings 'civilization.' But what need have the United Provinces of 'civilization'? Were we not 'civilized' over two hundred years ago when our ships and traders tapped the wealth of the East and West Indies and our trading houses spanned the globe?"

Seth moved closer and listened as the Dutchman inveighed against Bonaparte and the French ambassador to the Netherlands who had just engineered a coup d'état in support of the French occupying army. All heads nodded in agreement. The threat that Bonaparte posed to Britain was implicit but growing more explicit every day.

"Tell me, sir," Seth ventured, "do you ever visit Amsterdam?"

The Dutchman shot Seth an admonitory glance from on high that stated, without saying so, that he was both taller than and superior to the American. Seth felt increasingly discomfited as the Dutchman looked down his aristocratic nose at the upstart American, deciding how to respond.

"Yes," the Dutchman at length replied in a guarded manner. "Why do you ask?"

"I would like to see your country at first hand. Perhaps when I sail to Portugal later this spring, I might stop en route. Might we coincide?"

The manners to which he was born and in which he was raised reasserted themselves, and the Dutchman humored him with a thin smile.

"Come. I shall be there from mid-May onward. Come and see for yourself—if you are so inclined."

"Perhaps I shall."

That evening, after Seth and Georgette had walked home to Berkeley Square and she had retired Seth closed the door of his study, lit a candle, and took a seat at his secretary desk whose cubbies were jammed and overflowing with papers. Taking the diplomatic cypher book supplied him only two weeks before by the United States Department of State, he began to compose his first message to the United States's Minister Extraordinary and Plenipotentiary to the Court of St. James and his fellow Mainer Rufus King.

"Dear Sir,

It has come to my attention that an elevated level of discontent with French rule now pervades the Netherlands. With your consent, I propose to travel to Amsterdam to gather information and report on the situation there.

Your humble servant,

Cincinnatus"

Seth set down his pen and read the message before encrypting it. Perhaps it had been the stain of his impressment or the nascent commitment to his native country that it stirred which, the month previous, led him to volunteer his services to his country as an extra set of "eyes and ears." Both he and the Minister agreed that his position was too delicate and important in London to apply his services in the British capital and that therefore his efforts must be confined to third countries he visited. Still, he was well traveled, observant, and knowledgeable about shipping and trade and could report on items of interest. The Minister had offered him pay. Seth refused it.

* * *

Seth arrived aboard the *Three Brothers* at Amsterdam on Ascension Day. It was a bright and warm late May day and a national holiday. The mouth of the Amstel River swarmed with small pleasure craft with leeboards—*punters* and *botters* and *schokkers* and others whose names he didn't know or could not pronounce. So too were the canals that laced the city, with family barges and boats hosting convivial groups quaffing beer and gorging on sausages. It was as if the whole city had shaken off its wintertime indoor malaise and come outside to greet the spring.

After docking, Seth wandered the streets to get a feel for the place. He marveled at the stout burgher architecture and the steep, narrow houses with hip roofs some five or six stories high that faced the *grachts* or canals. He observed that the skyline was dominated by church steeples, not simple ones as in America or England, but wedding cake confections with five or more courses, clocks, armillary spheres, and flagpoles. He walked all the way from the Damrak to the Rokin imbibing the wealth and sophistication of the cosmopolitan and polyglot entrepot which seemed at times as if it should sink into the sea from the weight of all the riches that it had accrued starting in the Golden Age. Indeed, Seth began to understand why Amsterdam was known as the "keyhole of Europe." But, in Seth's estimation, the city's charm lay not just in the richness of its architecture or the prosperity of its well-fed populace but also in the vast tobacco warehouses that lined the Grimburgwall canal near the Rokin and the clean and simple interior of the Nieuwe Kerke into which he ducked for a respite: Amsterdam, and by extension The Netherlands, were a triumph of muscular Protestantism, a world power to be reckoned with.

At length, at the appointed hour as the nightshades began to fall Seth found the "brown café" on Spook Steeg, a dark and dodgy alley in the Centrum, that was to be his rendezvous with the Dutchman. Entering through the thick door, he surveyed the dark wood paneling and ceiling stained with tobacco smoke—the Dutch still smoked long-stemmed clay pipes. Casks were stacked from floor to ceiling, covered in dust and marked with chalk "10 j" or "20 j" to denote the age of their contents. A few of the lower ones were tapped with spouts. At the far end of the room stood a vat and maze of copper tubing that gleamed in the candlelight, for the cafe had once served as a distillery. On the bar stood rows of clay gin bottles and, in a twist of incongruous humor, a stuffed stork about whose neck hung a sign reading "*De Ooievaar.*" Seth memorized the word, his first Dutch word. He said it softly to himself: "*De Ooievaar.*"

Cincinnatus was dead. From now on he would be the Stork, a bit awkward perhaps, stuffed, silent, perched on a chimney pot or ledge and watching all the goings-on. His new identity was appropriate, he figured, because his mission had assumed a new dimension when Minister King responded to his message by instructing him to ingratiate himself with the Dutchman and report in detail on his connections and activities. Evidently the Dutchman had already come to the attention of the Minister's never-sleeping eye.

"*De Ooievaar,*" he said it once again. "The Stork."

But his words were drowned in the hum of the crowd gathered around tables engaging in chattering conversation. The room vibrated with a warm coziness of *bonhommie* that Seth was to learn was quintessentially Dutch.

Seth spotted the Dutchman at a far table in the corner with six other men, all sober suited and plump with civic pride. A wench was serving them plates of oysters and tankards of frothing beer. As Seth approached, two men looked up with a startled, interrupted look.

"Ah, Captain Hale! So you did come," the Dutchman acknowledged Seth as he waved him forward. "Please feel free to join us." He did not rise to greet him.

"Captain Hale is all the way from America," the Dutchman explained as he introduced him around.

One of the company, a well-fed burgher, welcomed him. "But first you must have a glass of *jenever.* Two glasses of *oude jenever!*" he shouted as he beckoned to the wench. She brought two thimble glasses filled to the brim with the liquor.

"We drink like this. Just so," the burgher explained as he placed his hands behind his back, leaned over, and sipped from the glass on the table.

Seth, who normally did not drink, did likewise. The potent flavored gin burned his lips and throat but, he had to admit, was tasty and convivial.

"Oude jenever!" he proclaimed. "I like this so much I will have to purchase a supply to take to America along with my port wine."

The men at the table smiled and murmured their assent, but the Dutchman remained aloof. Seth entered into the scrum of their conversation, which shifted from Dutch to English for his benefit. It started out where they had left off, discussing grain prices and shipping, but it quickly turned to politics and the pernicious meddling of the French in their country. There was a decidedly conspiratorial edge to their observations on how to oust the French. Seth shuddered to think what might happen to them if a French, rather than American, intelligence officer happened to be overhearing.

Seth did not emerge until late, late that night with his head crammed with names, observations, and intrigues, much of it loose talk and bravado, that he knew nonetheless would make interesting reading for Minister King.

* * *

Juvenal graduated from Harvard College that spring, and Adam and Nabby sailed by coastal schooner to attend. Like his father, Juvenal had shown an early proclivity for the classics, but he also excelled in rhetoric and religion. Jurisprudence seemingly had fallen by the wayside, though it had extracted an extra year and a half from his academic career and his graduation was long overdue. In truth, his tutors were well pleased with his performance and prospects.

As they walked about the arboreal grounds of Harvard Yard and looked up at the stately academic buildings, Adam studied his youngest son. Never robust like his father and brothers, Juvenal had a cerebral intensity about him that his years in academia had only accentuated. He dressed simply, almost indifferently, and wore his thin brown hair tied back in a queue. His skin was pale and fair, and he had his mother's eyes. Being thin, his dominant facial feature was his Adam's apple, which bobbed about as he spoke.

Adam broached the subject.

"Now that your formal education is complete, it is time to learn other things of a more practical nature, matters of the world. To this end, I have spoken with Mr. Titcomb, and he has an opening in his counting house on Fore Street for just such a young man as yourself. What a marvelous opportunity this will be!"

Juvenal winced and kept on walking without responding.

"But surely you appreciate how fortunate you are to have such an opening?" Adam asked.

"Yes, yes, of course," Juvenal assented. "But, but, I'm not sure . . . I'm not sure I wish to go into business. I have been talking to my professors."

"And?"

"And there may be other options. My interests don't lie toward business."

"Well, you could always go to sea as I did. Sailing is in your blood and is a noble calling."

"Fid," Juvenal addressed his father as he stopped and squared off in front of him. "I have determined to attend divinity school here at Harvard. I wish to be ordained a minister."

Adam stared, not sure how to respond.

"A minister . . . a minister," he mumbled as he weighed the implications. "Well, son, the clergy is a learned calling and one that is held in high respect. I could be proud of you in your choice. But there's no fortune in it, mind you. Of course, if you were to land a prosperous congregation, say in Boston or another large coastal town, the perquisites do add up."

"It isn't for the money that I do this. I have talked for hours with my professors on this head. It is because I *want* to do it. It is because I *belong* there. I feel the call. And they agree I am a good candidate."

"Setting aside that you didn't consult with me, dear son, I will support you in whatever you choose," Adam concluded as he put his arm around the slight but determined frame of his youngest son.

* * *

"Still no messenger!" Gideon Sewell exclaimed as he snapped shut the case of his gold pocket watch and stood bolt upright from the upholstered wing chair in his sitting room. "I'll just run up and have another look." At that he raced up the stairs to the widow's walk atop his house on Elm Street to survey the harbor.

"He's anxious," Thankful explained. "The Schooner *Pemaquid* is a day late in arriving and with it a cargo of nails."

"Nails?" Adam huffed. "This is Sunday, and we are here as guests for dinner." The aroma of a New England boiled dinner on the simmer, all beef and carrots and root vegetables, mixed with the sweetness of an Indian pudding baking in the oven, wafted into the sitting room.

"I know. Gideon has become obsessed with his business interests. He even talks of resigning his commission because he hasn't time for the militia and, besides, he now says it does nothing to advance his career."

"But this is the third time he has run upstairs to have a look!" Adam protested. "Doesn't this greed of his approach idolatry?"

Adam instantly recognized that he had gone too far.

"He is a good provider. He is so . . . committed," Thankful noted as she tried to place the best face on her embarrassment at her husband's inattention to her visiting parents.

Sensing the edge in Adam's judgments, Nabby shifted their year-old granddaughter Hephzibah in her arms and changed the subject.

"Adam, would you like to hold Hephzibah for a spell?"

Adam looked at the sweet-smelling, bubbling and gurgling little pile of joyful flesh before him, and his heart softened. He took her in his powerful arms and caressed her forehead, moving a few stray strands of reddish blond hair back in place. He looked into her wide blue eyes, she looked into his weather-beaten blue eyes and she smiled. It was as if they were one, and Adam was as putty in her hands.

As he rocked her back and forth in his arms, Adam began to think. He barely understood such a "commitment" as exhibited by his son-in-law: a commitment that trumped personal relationships, the joy of shared conversation, indeed even the sanctity of the Sabbath. Nor, at times, did he understand the peculiar commitments of his own sons. Possibly it was a generational difference. Business was all fine and good, and so were religion, philosophy, study of the classics, and attention to citizenship, but first and foremost was family. Without the arch stone of family, none of the other pieces of the edifices of life made sense or mattered. No, Adam told himself, he was not a man of "commitments" other than to that one fundamental.

24

A Demand of Honor

1803

"Major Gaskill has taken to the field," Gabrielle explained as soon as Jezreel entered the house at Great Spring Garden on a bright early November day fresh from docking the *Dolphin*. "I suppose you have not heard, having just arrived. The slaves are in revolt just west of here, in St. Mary's Parish. They burned three plantations and slit the throats of all three owners and their families—men, women, children, everyone."

"Are you safe here?"

"I don't know. They say it is spreading," Gabrielle replied with a distracted look, numbed by years of anxiety. "This is what we get for the failure of Bonaparte's army on Saint Domingue. They pull out, and the disease spreads here."

"I can take you to England if you want."

"To England?" she shrugged. "If I, a Jamaican, were to go to England I would only be ostracized and left to socialize with other absentee planters from the Indies. I would never fit in."

"I could take you to Maine or, if you don't care for that, Charleston, New York, wherever you choose."

Gabrielle shrugged again.

"But then what? My whole livelihood is here. I can't abandon my plantation. Perhaps this shall be but a passing bubble that will swell a bit and then burst. And all will be well again."

Jezreel gathered her in his arms.

"Assuredly so. Now, now. I have missed you so these last months. 'Tis joy to see your face again."

Gabrielle allowed herself a tentative smile.

"Put your concerns aside. We have the moment. Shall we?"

Jezreel sensed he had struck a chord: she remained alive to joy, still an inhabitant of a land where little restraint was placed on the passions of the moment.

Gabrielle nodded, and they repaired to her great mahogany bed.

* * *

They were awakened before dawn by dogs barking and roosters crowing. Then the cries of men and the thunder of horses' hooves. They cast off the mosquito netting and ran to the window. Jezreel opened the louvered slats. The scene was one of utter chaos: hundreds of slaves bearing torches and spilling down from the mountainside through the grounds of Great Spring Garden, stopping only momentarily to set fire to the outbuildings of the plantation. Behind them, barely visible in the pre-dawn light, advanced the red-coated troops of the mounted Major Gaskill. It was as if the soldiers were chasing them to the sea. A rivulet of running slaves, flowing like lava down the incline, made straight for the house.

"Do you have weapons?" Jezreel asked a visibly terrified Gabrielle. "A musket, a pistol, a sword—anything?"

"In the storage room. Pistols. Unloaded," she stammered.

"Damn! No time!"

Jezreel cast about for what next to do.

"We must lock the bedroom door and barricade it with the furniture! That might buy time. And, damn it, clothe yourself!" he ordered.

Gabrielle pulled on a shift while Jezreel bolted the door and piled chairs and tables behind it. Only then did he pull on his breeches and shirt.

They returned to the window. It must have been no more than a minute or two later, but the scene had dissolved and re-formed. This time, the slaves were spread out in a half moon and much closer to the house. Less than a quarter mile behind them Gaskill's troops advanced with bayonets fixed. When the troops approached to within fifty yards of the wavering and flickering line of slaves they let loose a volley from Brown Bess that echoed off the mountains. In the smoke and dim light Jezreel thought he saw a dozen or so slaves down. Still the line surged and quivered, unsure whether to advance on the house or flee. Then came the bayonet charge as the troops cried at the top of their lungs and ran headlong into the mass of mutineering slaves. The engagement was over within three minutes at best. The troops cut through them like a knife through suet, and everywhere about the property slaves lay writhing and screaming and begging for mercy.

At once relieved and repelled, Jezreel turned away from the window. A more hardened Gabrielle stayed to watch the mopping-up operation before turning her gaze back to the room.

"Well, thank God for Major Gaskill," she sighed.

* * *

That evening, after the troops had restored calm in the vicinity of Great Spring Garden, Major Gaskill had sent word that the area was secure. Jezreel and Gabrielle ventured out to inspect the damage. A sugar mill and a half dozen store houses, together with their contents, had been set to the torch and were still smoldering, but there was little further damage visible. The plantation's slaves had for the most part stayed indoors out of fear of the marauding mutineers from the neighboring parish. A few had joined in, but the overwhelming majority had calculated, wisely as it turned out, that the odds of success, at least this time, were not good.

Mounting a buckboard wagon, Jezreel and Gabrielle rode into Port Antonio to assay further the situation. Gabrielle wore a dark red hooded cloak under which she hid two loaded pistols. Jezreel brought his violin and bow, for reasons perhaps only he could fathom. All along the coastal road soldiers stood guard at intervals, and even in the dying light there were incessant, frantic movements of troops and supplies up and down the highway. They passed through three roadblocks before entering the town. What was normally a quiet provincial outpost had now become a hub of nocturnal activity with soldiers bearing torches moving to and fro, post riders galloping through the streets and windows shuttered tight. It was an eerie scene, disturbing in its upending of normal life. Jezreel and Gabrielle looked in vain for familiar faces. All they found was a town under occupation.

At length, they ran into the slave pens by the waterfront. There, the captured surviving rebels had been herded: hundreds upon hundreds jammed into three small, fenced rings surrounded by armed guards. Light from the flickering torches around the perimeters lit the holding pens and illuminated their inhabitants. Some wore torn clothing. Almost none had shoes. All were dirty and sweating. They were male and female alike and even some children.

Mesmerized, Jezreel stopped the wagon and alighted for closer inspection. Gabrielle followed. Jezreel slowly circled the first of the rings as he studied the slaves' faces. Some were passive, numbed almost, while others showed fear and terror in their eyes. As he passed, several thrust forth their arms toward him begging mercy in an African dialect he did not comprehend. In the encroaching blackness of the night and the heat and the flames from the torches, Jezreel felt as if he were glimpsing into a Hades inhabited by half people, spirits even, with whom he could never communicate. The prospect of inviting one of these tormented souls to dinner or of having a rational discourse on the rights of man was beyond contemplation. Surely, these people should have those rights, Jezreel thought, but he conceived of it solely as an abstraction—the right thing to do—and not as a practical dictate of personal intercourse. And he found that failing within himself an epiphany.

Not knowing what to do, he clutched his violin. Walking around the perimeter of a pen, he mounted it and began to play the first movement of Beethoven's *Sonata Pathétique*. He played with passion as he slowly carried his small gift of music to all three pens. At first the slaves did not know what to make of it. A mockery of them, perhaps? But then they fell silent and realized it was a lament offered by a white man rendered mute by his station in life and place in history. Tears came to the slaves' eyes, joining those that Jezreel already was shedding as he leaned into his bow. Jezreel bestowed a balm over the open sores of the pens, if only as a passing gesture and one that could never change the reality of the world in which he and they lived.

At length, when done, he turned back to look at a speechless Gabrielle, who stood in her red hooded cloak masking the tight grip her hands held on the cocked pistols beneath its folds.

"What will they do with them?" Jezreel asked.

"They'll probably hang ten percent of them at random as an object lesson and deport the rest to Cuba or someplace worse."

"Suppose I tried to free them?"

"You must be jesting. You'd be shot."

"I have some means. Could I not buy the freedom of at least some of them and transport them to the States? In New England they would be free."

"These are mutineers. They must receive stiff punishment. Major Gaskill would never allow it."

The muscles at Gabrielle's mouth began to tighten as she stared long and hard at Jezreel, as if she were calculating the distance that had grown between them.

"Screw Major Gaskill," Jezreel sputtered.

The muscles that commanded the corners of Gabrielle's mouth drew as taut as anchor chains.

"Indeed, sir, I do."

* * *

Jezreel stared down the barrel of the cocked dueling pistol.

The previous thirty-six hours had raced like the Roaring Forties: the white hot fury that had surged up his spine and annihilated his reason—the storming into Major Gaskill's tent while he was conferring with his officers—the annoyed look Gaskill had shot at him for the intrusion—the slap Jezreel delivered to Gaskill's jowly cheek—the demand for satisfaction—Gaskill's demurral—Jezreel's insistence and then Gaskill's plodding calculation that here was a way he might rid himself of his rival once and for all—Gabrielle's hysteria when she realized she would lose no matter what the outcome—her pleas with him to reconsider—the return of the white hot fury—a night spent alone aboard the *Dolphin* playing his fiddle until sleep overtook him in the wee hours—and, now, standing barefoot on the white sand beach at Buff Bay with the sun rising over the horizon and gilding the stately palms, armed, alone and with no second, facing down the red-coated might of a commissioned officer of His Majesty King George the Third whose second and batman stood impassively by while his sixteen-hand warhorse impatiently whinnied and pounded the sand with its hoof.

"Present!" Gaskill's second commanded.

Jezreel looked down the plane of his extended right arm and at the Purdey dueling pistol wavering in his hand. Just minutes earlier he had admired the pistol, one of two identical pieces cased in a mahogany box with green felt lining and all the accoutrements for their use, the property of Major Gaskill. Jezreel knew by instinct the delay between flint striking steel to ignite the firing pan and the actual discharge of the ball. Whoever found his bead and fired first stood the greater chance of prevailing. To wait was to court preemption. The muzzle of the pistol in Jezreel's hand danced about Major Gaskill's upper torso, which stood erect and at a right angle to diminish its profile as a target. If only he could get his mark and hold it to squeeze the trigger on which his forefinger drew ever tighter. The gun wavered ever so slightly as he began to bring it under control and then—Bang!—the flint dropped against the steel unleashed by the hair trigger he had not expected. The shot fired before Jezreel was ready, and in a sickening split-second he realized it would not find its mark. Indeed, as he dropped his arm and the smoke cleared Jezreel saw Gaskill standing tall and now at an oblique angle and with his own pistol aimed with the killer's instinct at his head.

Jezreel felt the nerves tighten in his throat. He waited. Perhaps Gaskill would do the decent thing and raise his pistol and fire into the air. Perhaps he would sail the *Dolphin* again. Perhaps he would find his way back into Gabrielle's bed.

Gaskill tickled the trigger and sent a forty-five caliber lead ball hurtling toward Jezreel. It caught him in the forehead, and the cruel and unforgiving wings of oblivion enveloped him.

* * *

News of Jezreel's death reached Adam five weeks later in the form of a note penned by Gabrielle and carried north by a Yankee Captain. It lay crumpled in Adam's powerful right hand as he sat slumped in his wing chair, sobbing. Jezreel's violin and bow, which accompanied the letter, lay in his lap.

Adam's immediate question was, "Was she worth it?" He would never know the answer to that question, but his heart told him she was not.

For once in his life Adam felt vulnerable. He was on the cusp of becoming a fallen man, out of sorts, disconnected with the order of the universe: fodder for the Devil. When would he fall into the abyss? Adam asked himself. If not now, it was only a matter of time.

"God, why is this happening to me?" he asked aloud. "Why have I lost my son?"

No answer came.

Adam shakily wiped away the welling tears at his eyes with the forefinger of his right hand. He opened his Bible at the 15th Psalm and read:

"Lord, who shall abide in thy tabernacle? who shall dwell in thy holy hill?

He that walketh uprightly, and worketh righteousness, and speaketh the truth in his heart."

So this was the basis of the bargain: a blameless life. Adam thought he had lived a blameless life, but now he resolved to live one impeccably so.

* * *

Gabrielle saw to it that Jezreel's body was buried in the Anglican cemetery in Port Antonio, and so the atoms of this son of old New England stock and cold New England weather mixed forever with the fetid, teeming soil of Jamaica. His grave was quickly forgotten and became overgrown, and it disappeared. The Governor had been correct: he would come back. And he never left. In due course the government condemned the *Dolphin* and broke her up for lumber. Some of her planks found their way into shanty housing on the hills outside Port Antonio where they remained until scattered by Hurricane Ivan in the twenty-first century. Gabrielle succumbed to a cholera epidemic five years after she buried Jezreel. Major Gaskill returned to England and was promoted to Colonel.

25

Restoration

1804

APRIL IS THE KINDEST MONTH, ADAM THOUGHT AS HE PACED THE quarterdeck of the *Atheling*. The trade winds filled the top gallants, blowing fresh and strong on the starboard quarter with a following sea and a broad reach. There had been no need to tack or wear. April was always the month in the Great Migration when the emigrant ship captains judged it safe enough to weigh anchor at Sandwich, Weymouth, or Plymouth and depart for America. April was the month the lambs were born on the inland farms Down East. April was the month of hope. April was the month Adam regained his life after a long, desolate, and despairing winter.

For ten days after leaving the Kennebec with a cargo of mast timbers Adam had stood at his post of command while his Mate Mr. Spurling handled the ship. The gentle spring weather, the rolling troughs of the waves, the endless horizons all had done their work abrading his cares. Each wave was different. They varied from black-bronze nearest the ship to blue further off, save where the newly risen sun to the east off the starboard beam had temporarily plated a pathway in glittering silver. Adam had stared at them for hours, as they worked like tumblers smoothing out the jagged edges of his life until he now had an equilibrium, an acceptance even, of his loss. It took little to remind Adam that his surest footing was astride the quarterdeck of the ship he loved as it plied the North Atlantic.

But there was another dimension to his journey, Adam confessed. He made haste to see, touch, and be with Seth. It was as if the loss of Jezreel had injected a need, an urgency even, into re-establishing his paternal bond with the remaining son whom he had always understood best.

The week before he departed Adam and many other New England ship owners had received news of a settlement with France whereby, in exchange for the purchase of Louisiana, the United States Congress assumed responsibility for their claims for seized ships and cargo during the Quasi War. There was jubilation along Fore Street in Portland at the prospect of resolution of the so-called Spoliation Claims. It would only be a matter of months before the Congress honored their just claims and provided restitution! But as welcome as that news was, in Adam's estimation it was secondary to the prospect of being reunited with his son Seth.

Adam gripped the taffrail and stared hard into the eastward rising sun. Only twelve more days, he told himself, only twelve more days.

* * *

"Aren't you a sight for your old father!" Adam gushed as he embraced Seth. "Let me see you!" he commanded as he held him in his arms and looked him up and down. "My, you've put on weight! And look at those cheeks! Georgette's cooking must please you. But your hair," he said as he ran his hand across his son's forehead, "is growing thin. I hope 'tis not from worry."

"Oh, no, Fid. Not worry. I find life here agrees with me. Come, let's walk together. This is a most propitious spot, Hampstead Heath, the very place I proposed to Georgette. Do you not see the city of London below?"

It was a bright and clear May day, and indeed the metropolis with its church spires and din and bustle spread out before them in the distance. But on the parklike Heath all was green and quiet, save for the chirping of songbirds.

"And Georgette? How is she? Has she surmounted the loss of little Abigail?"

Seth nodded and spoke deliberately. "It took awhile, as she took to her bed. But she's a pillar, as you know. She came back as determined and as cheerful as ever. We never forget, but all is well now."

"I hope it hasn't discouraged you from trying again."

"No, but 'tis out of our hands. We do all we can, but Divine Providence plays a role, and so far . . ."

"Just so. Divine Providence will surely not let you down."

"And you, Fid? And Mama?"

"The loss of Jezreel was a blow. The last winter was long, cold, and dark."

They walked in silence. Adam weighed whether to raise so quickly why he had hastened to Seth's side. Always a man of direct honesty, he decided to ask.

"Son, do you ever consider returning to Portland? Not just on the occasional voyage, but permanently. Now with Jezreel gone I could use some help."

Seth's mouth turned up in faint amusement, almost but not quite a smile. He thought as he walked.

"Fid, I miss Portland and you and Mama, but my life is here now. I have fit into Georgette's set in most respects and tolerably well like it here. Look at my clothes and hear my accent," he said as he stopped and pointed at himself. "I am an American but one accustomed to living here, and with each passing year I fear that America recedes further from me."

"Perhaps that is in part why I asked the question. You see, at the end of the day you risk being neither American nor British."

Immediately Adam regretted the harsh words he had delivered, father to son.

"Not that your service here is not appreciated," he hastened to add.

"Yes, I do think I am needed here to continue to assure our contracts with the Royal Navy. That's our life's blood, after all. And of late I've spent considerable time on the Continent, in places such as Portugal and the Low Countries, pursuing other ventures. Have you not appreciated the shipments of port wine and Amsterdam gin?"

"Yes, and for that I thank you. But with Jezreel gone I feel as if one leg of our three-legged stool has been kicked away and we are teetering."

"I know we can never replace him, but as a make-do can you not arrange a contract Captain to step in or, better yet, what about Gideon Sewell?"

"That is not so easy."

"How so, pray tell?"

"Major Sewell and I have different approaches."

"Have you parted ways?"

"No, it's not that. He works hard and provides well for Thankful and the baby. For that I am grateful; you know that I always look for the best in people. But his singularity of purpose doesn't admit of other thoughts or speculations. He does not read. Perhaps it's best left at that. And he has bought up and controls all the good contract Captains in Maine."

"So the Caribbean leg of the triangle is defunct?"

"For us it is, for the moment. Sewell trades there ever more intently. 'Tis highly profitable, as you know."

Seth nodded. "But so is the mast trade. And war is brewing, which means more demand for naval stores. Bonaparte tore up the Peace of Amiens, and Britain is rearming. The Netherlands, where I have just been, is in turmoil. I foresee a long period of hostilities in the coming years. So perhaps we should simply continue to do what we do best."

"Aye, events spin, and we spin with 'em."

"Aye. Besides, we are to join Georgette and Lord Hormsby this evening. She is most excited about seeing you again. She says you are her favorite father-in-law."

"Well, I guess that makes her my favorite daughter-in-law. I have no choice."

* * *

"Fid! Welcome to London," Georgette effused as she bent forward on the Westminster Stairs on the Thames in invitation for Adam to kiss her on both cheeks. Her beauty, which Adam had noted on their first meeting but the memory of which time had dulled, struck him anew. Her blue eyes danced and her fair skin glowed. She wore her blond tresses long, almost to the middle of her back. Over her white gown she wore a fashionable dark green pelisse coat fronted with red lapels, collar, and cuffs and sporting shiny brass military buttons. Atop her head, and at a jaunty angle, rested a broad-brimmed straw hat fronted with knotted grosgrain ribbons. She carried a riding crop under her left arm—for effect rather than use, Adam assumed. Behind her stood Lord Hormsby with "Dame" Rafferty pressed to his side like a scabbard—Lady Hormsby, conveniently, was in the country—and, of course, Seth.

With the greetings made all round, the party embarked just before dusk in a taxi boat for the short trip upriver to the Vauxhall Pleasure Gardens on the opposite, Surrey side of the river. The river crossing, with its hint of danger and "crossing over," set the stage for the experience that was Vauxhall. They alighted at the Vauxhall Stairs and after paying the price of admission entered the Grove or central area of the gardens. Adam had never seen anything like it before, certainly not in America and not even in his travels. Beneath the stately trees and *allées* stood a confection of rococo, Chinoiserie and Levantine pavilions, orchestra boxes, ruins, arches, statues, and a water cascade. To his left stood a polished marble statue of the composer Handel lounging as if at home. Lining the walks were private open-air dining salons, called "supper boxes" Lord Hormsby explained, each capable of holding up to fifteen people. Some were already full, while others awaited their guests. And through it all milled an enormous crowd of thousands of people, many of them families and well-dressed but also, Adam spied, the occasional prostitute or pickpocket.

"Look at this," Lord Hormsby stated as he waved his hand over the scene. "This could never exist in France. See how the crowds conduct themselves with dignity and decency and with none of the tumult and disorder that disturb the public diversions in France."

Adam had to agree that indeed it was so.

"Ah! Here are the 'dark walks,'" Georgette exclaimed as they penetrated further into the grounds. "See those dark, winding paths just over there. This is the place where young lovers go for privacy. They lose themselves, but find each other, in the windings and turnings."

"Did you ever do that?" Seth asked.

"Why, me, no. But I have it on the best authority."

They arrived at the exotically decorated Pillared Saloon on one flank of the central Rotunda building. They entered, and Adam looked up to find four huge canvases on the walls, each easily twelve by fifteen feet.

"Scenes from the Seven Years' War," Lord Hormsby explained.

Adam studied them up close and with a critical eye.

"Can't say as I see anything I recognize. But then we called it the 'French and Indian War.'"

With darkness descended, they found their way to Lord Hormsby's supper box as the orchestra struck up a lilting tune. They took their seats, and, to Adam's astonishment, unseen servants placed throughout the gardens simultaneously set an elaborate network of fuses which illuminated—at once—thousands of glass oil lamps hung among the trees that lined the walks. The effect was magical, as if the heavens had descended to the earth. Never had Adam seen such a sight, which he appraised with an approving eye.

As they waited for dinner to be served Lord Hormsby leaned over to engage Adam in conversation.

"Now that I am of a certain age, Captain Hale, approaching seventy and more advanced in years than you, I have come to realize that there are proper occupations for each stage of life, and old age has its own appropriate tasks. The trick is to keep oneself usefully occupied so one doesn't notice the gradual process of extinction. I find solace in study, writing, friendships, quiet contemplation, observing nature through changing seasons, mentoring the young, counseling the Navy Board."

"Indeed, M'Lord, to be respected is the crowning glory of old age."

Lord Hormsby nodded in agreement.

"The alternative, I fear, is irritability and moroseness, both of which must be guarded against with constant vigilance. Old age frees us from lustful pleasures that cloud a man's judgment," he said as he nodded toward "Dame" Rafferty. "Conversation and companionship are more important for the old. Food and drink need not be lacking, but they too diminish with age. We can set aside such sensual pleasures along with ambition, rivalry, quarreling, and other passions in favor of a quieter, more tranquil life."

"Spoken as if by Cicero."

"Just so, Captain Hale."

"Your words provide comfort at the prospect of growing old and are wise. I too, though only in my mid-fifties, have begun to find the world a less interesting place."

"So you would consider abandoning your endeavors to lead a contemplative life?"

"Not just yet, but perhaps someday I shall. I can see that day on the horizon: a safe port and haven. Indeed, by reading, a philosopher in retirement can share the company of the greatest minds and is never alone. Power, office, and wealth are of little account compared to such wisdom."

"But," Lord Hormsby riposted, "would not Cicero also say that each of us has an innate feeling for his fellow man which causes us to do good and to defend the well-being of the community? In short, the most important field of engagement is in government, and one should not abandon the republic for a contemplative life."

"Ah, Cicero was fond of glory. So, was his praise of civic duty merely a screen for his own ambition? An attempt to justify what he would do anyway?"

"Perhaps so, and therein lies the uncertainty, the tension if you will, between the contemplative life and civic duty. I doubt we shall solve it this evening."

"Moreover, Cicero was a convinced and dedicated atheist," Adam inserted as a parting shot to discredit the ancient.

"Should that matter?" Lord Hormsby responded with arched eyebrows. "The Roman gods were not your God."

"No, they were not my God. But one's God or gods always matter, whatever the epoch."

"I am not so certain of that," Lord Hormsby observed. "*Fortuna* or luck plays a role out of all proportion."

"Luck, my dear Lord, is no more than the name we give to nice things we don't understand. It is a pagan concept, much delighted in by your beloved Romans. Luck is random and, as such, an abnegation of God's purposefulness in the universe."

"Ah," Lord Hormsby sighed as he withdrew a thin leather-bound volume from his vest pocket. "You might profit from this. Take it as my gift to you and read it at your leisure. Drink deeply of the spring of knowledge."

Adam took the book in hand. It was titled *Meditations*. The author was the Roman emperor-philosopher Marcus Aurelius.

"Thank you, M' Lord. I shall."

* * *

While Adam and Lord Hormsby discussed Roman wisdom, five supper boxes away on a separate but parallel walkway and unbeknownst to them, the First Lord of the Admiralty, Henry Dundas The Right Honorable Viscount Melville, entertained a party in his own supper box. Guests of the tall, beetle-browed Scot included Lady Melville, the Secretary of the Admiralty, assorted Admirals and their ladies and, the odd man out, Vice-Admiral Sir Ponsonby Spicer, Baronet. Melville had summoned Spicer, who commanded the white squadron at Portsmouth, to London for consultations. His inclusion in the evening's entertainment at Vauxhall was in way of a courtesy extended to a visiting, but lower ranking, colleague after several days' work. From Spicer's optic, the evening was a rare opportunity to impress and seek advancement. However, the evening had not cooperated. The Irish Baronet sat at the end of the dining table, on the periphery, engaged in a faltering conversation with the blowzy wife of one of the Admirals whose imperial jowls admitted of no joy. Sensing his guest's isolation, Melville called out.

"I say! Spicer! How long before Lord Nelson defeats Boney?"

"Soon, my Lord. I'm certain of it."

"Come, sit by me, and let's talk."

With that, the guests shifted about, seeking new conversational partners about the table, and Spicer took the seat next to the First Lord.

"And if Nelson smashes Boney and peace breaks out, what plans have you?" Melville inquired.

Spicer shifted uncomfortably on the narrow seat.

"Well, I don't think I'd be content to retire on half-pay, M' Lord. I'd like to retain my command."

"Well, of course. But we can't always have what we want, now can we?"

"So, you are asking me what else I would like, when, if, as you say, 'peace breaks out?' Well . . .," the Baronet responded with his right wrist supinated as he thought.

The First Lord watched the gray-green eyes sit stagnant like some primordial algae-clogged pond. Suddenly they shifted, focused, and locked.

"I know much about America. I served there during the war of independence. And I know about Americans too. They delude themselves into thinking that they fought for something higher, their so-called inalienable rights. Deluded self-righteous fools, the lot of them."

"Go on."

"Once we have cleared the seas of Napoleon—and defeated him on land—we will be freed up to deal with the Yanks."

"How so?"

"We can regain our supply of timbers for masts and spars, the great Maine timbers. They are rightfully ours. We shouldn't have to pay for them. You see, a lowly American sea Captain stole the maps back in '83. Stole them right off the deputy mast agent when he and I were held prisoner on a hulk in Newport. Robbed him in the night while he slept. But . . . not before I had taken the precaution of memorizing the maps and preparing copies."

"Good man. But they're old, then, are they not?"

"Yes, but they still serve," Spicer averred. Warming to the task, he grew animated. "And I know where other mast timbers, large beyond belief, are hidden unmarked with the King's Broad Arrow. I added them to my maps."

"You tempt me. But just because you say it is so does not make it so. What proof have you?"

"It is so. My copies of the maps are the proof. They show the best. The best beyond what even you might have imagined. And, under the right circumstances, they will be there for our taking."

"And how would you go about that?"

Spicer thought for a moment.

"I have a plan, I confess. War with the States is inevitable. When it comes, and under cover of hostilities elsewhere, we seize the ports and river mouths along the coast of Maine. They are undefended, except by ragtag militia. From there, we can control upstream, into the interior, where the great timbers stand. We annex Maine to Canada. The inhabitants there bear great grudges against their masters in Boston. They might even join us willingly. So we take advantage of the fissures that already exist and split the colony away and back to us. Who knows, maybe it will even cause the larger union to splinter. All to the good and a fine piece of work."

The First Lord thought in silence for a minute, his chin cupped in his right hand.

"Tempting, as I said. I shall have to think on it. But we are not yet in a position to lay such plans."

"Aye, it may take years. File it for now in your portfolio marked with my name. And, to be sure, I too would have to tidy up some loose ends—even in particular one here in London."

"No doubt. I shall think on it."

Spicer's eyes suddenly bore in on Melville's as if they had come from far, far away.

"M' Lord, you would not want to be accused by those who wish you ill that you did not seize the initiative. Therefore, when the time is right, *carpe diem.*"

* * *

"Minister King recommended you. But then he might have, as you are both from the District of Maine in Massachusetts," James Monroe, Angus King's replacement as Minister to the Court of St. James, observed coolly as he eyed Seth from across the desk in his study at his official residence on a late December afternoon.

Minister Monroe was a tall, lanky man with a prominent nose and dimpled chin and the reserved, smooth manners of the Virginia planter class, polished no doubt by his prior years of service as American Minister in Paris. He intimidated Seth, not only because of his physical presence and reserve but because he was of his father's generation and, unlike his father, had accompanied General Washington in the Christmas crossing of the Delaware and had taken a ball in his shoulder at the Battle of Trenton. He was one of the Generation of Heroes. But there were other gaps between them.

"Sir, although I am from Maine, my allegiance is not to a single state but to the United States," Seth replied dryly. He was well aware that Monroe earlier had fought Virginia's adoption of the United States Constitution on the grounds that it vested too much power in the central government at the expense of the states, or so he thought.

Monroe winced almost imperceptibly.

"Well, I suppose your generation's sense of citizenship is lodged more at the national level than mine, which is probably a propitious thing given the grave challenges our young republic faces," Monroe responded.

Seth was aware of the chameleon-like nature of Monroe's character. He knew that he was of mixed Scottish and French Huguenot descent. He knew that he had studied law under Thomas Jefferson and that he owed his position as Minister in London to Jefferson, who had just been re-elected for a second term as President. He knew that Monroe was a staunch friend of the French Revolution whom President Washington earlier had dismissed from his Ambassadorial post for being too pro-French and not protecting American interests. He knew that he was an absentee slave owner whose overseers ran his plantations by the whip and separated families with impunity. Monroe was not, by nature or circumstance, Seth's kind of man. But he was the American Minister in London, and he was asking a favor.

"Minister King spoke well of you and the reports you have rendered. We have continued need of your services. Spain has just joined France in war against England. With all Europe teetering on war and with the circles you inhabit and the visits you make to the Continent, your functioning as an extra set of eyes and ears serves the United States well."

"You're not asking me to report on the British? That I will not do."

"I might ask you to do that, but your government will not. No, we are aware of the delicate position you hold. The greater concern is with the opposition to Bonaparte, in the Low Countries, in Portugal. Of course, any stray information on the efforts of Britain to exploit that, well . . . that would be always welcome."

Seth did not respond.

"You appreciate, I'm sure," Monroe continued, "there are those of the view that Bonaparte is a force for good. He has spread the Enlightenment. He promulgated the Napoleonic Code, a most marvelous body of laws."

"And he has just crowned himself the first Emperor of France in over a thousand years, while his armies are on the march all over Europe."

"Quite so. And that is why our republic is marshaling every asset to stay informed. We must preserve our neutrality. There are many in Britain who would lure us in, and I dare say they would succeed in doing so were it not for the torments they inflict on us daily with continued attacks on our shipping and their pressing of our sailors."

Seth, in turn, winced almost imperceptibly.

"So what need I do?"

"Continue with your reports and seek out opportunities for new insights. Report directly to me, as you did to Minister King." Monroe reached in his desk drawer and retrieved a small book. "Here is the latest code book. Take it and guard it well. We are taking the precaution of changing it thrice yearly and may do so more often, as tensions are aboil."

Seth pocketed the book.

"I am prepared to compensate you for your services. I have an account for 'Extraordinary Expenses' upon which I draw."

"That won't be necessary," Seth replied. "My citizenship is of the voluntary kind and not for sale."

Minister Monroe stared at Seth for a couple of seconds, trying to fathom his New England federalist mind.

"As you wish," he said with a shrug and extended his hand. They shook, and Seth departed.

* * *

Major Gideon Sewell replaced the sputtering and exhausted candle on his desk with a fresh one. It was eleven o'clock at night on New Year's Eve, and Fore Street was shrouded in darkness and quiet. The windows of his office were the only ones aglow with industry and light. Thankful and the baby would be long abed, but he had accounts to go over and contracts to read. He knew that the extra hours were the currency convertible into success.

An hour later, as the tall case clock in the corner of the room struck midnight and as he completed the addition of a column of figures, he set down his quill and allowed a faint smile to gather at the edge of his lips. He was on the cusp of being in a position to dominate the market and drive out competition. It would not be long before he could pay top dollar, such as five percent commissions, in order to control resources. The next step would be a vertically integrated business in which he held a privileged position enjoying a wide choice of markets.

At that, he moistened the forefinger and thumb of his right hand with his tongue and snuffed out the candle, a good day's work done in his inexorable drive to the top. The new year 1805 promised to be a bumper year for Major Sewell.

26

Continental Intrigues

1805

SETH STARED OUT THE WINDOW FROM HIS ROOM IN THE HEEREN Logement. The Logement was a handsome three-story brick edifice, with six tall windows gracing its façade at each story, finely dressed quoins, and three tall chimney stacks atop its pitched roof, more Palladian than the hip-roofed Dutch architecture of the buildings in the neighborhood. For one hundred and fifty years it had served as Amsterdam's "gentlemen's hotel" for visiting dignitaries and directors of the Dutch East and West India Companies. Even Tsar Peter the Great of Russia had lodged there during his sojourn in Amsterdam studying shipbuilding. The mid-February dusk on the drizzly afternoon had already encroached on the Grimburgwal that lay before his window, effacing all the right angles in its gloom. Its relentless march devoured the nooks and crannies between the houses and cast its mantle over the sidewalks. Only the pinprick of light from the candle on the table before him stood in sentinel defiance of the Low Country depths of winter sadness and served as a beacon while Seth collected his thoughts. A full ten minutes later he put pen to paper as his unencumbered thoughts began to flow freely.

"Dear Sir," Seth wrote. Somehow the formal salutation seemed more appropriate to his relationship to Minister Monroe than a more familiar *"Dear Minister Monroe."*

"I have been in the company of the Dutchman and his friends these last two weeks. The Batavian Republic totters on the brink of collapse. Bonaparte has ordered the French Navy and customs officials to police Dutch ports and confiscate cargo independent of the Dutch authorities. In response the Dutch have forbidden any of their officials to take orders from the French. Bonaparte refers to The Netherlands as 'the alluvial deposits of the French rivers,' and there is increased concern of an outright annexation of The Netherlands by France. At the same time, rumors abound here of a renewed effort by Bonaparte to invade England, using the naval patrols here as a screen. I have walked the docks and seen much French naval activity. If they were to strike at England, the betting among the merchants here is it would be by the end of May."

He signed the message *"The Stork."*

Seth read over his note, the twenty-fourth he had written to the American Minister in London, he noted to himself. Satisfied with it, he withdrew the code book from his breast pocket. He painstakingly encrypted the message in invisible ink interspersed between the lines of an in-clear report he had prepared about shipments of pilchards. He then sealed the secret message and burned the draft of the letter with the candle. The next day he traveled by carriage to The Hague, where he posted the letter with an American merchantman bound for London. As an added precaution, he addressed the letter to Georgette in London in the hope that inquiring eyes might be less likely to open correspondence of a domestic nature. Georgette knew to deliver such letters personally to the American Minister. More she did not know.

Seth also posted a separate personal letter to Georgette. The night before he left, she confided in him that she was pregnant again. Seth had lain with her in bed, caressing where she had begun to show. But his impending departure sundered their joy. Seth cursed and railed against fate, duty, and the fact that the tide waits for no man. He had left elated at her news but agitated. The letter was an attempt to make amends, to set things right, to reassure Georgette that even though he was absent his heart was near. Seth knew he would not return for many months. He had a cargo of wine to load in Porto and then a trans-Atlantic voyage to Portland before returning to London with a hold full of barrel staves, spars, and ash for making soap, all routine stuff but profitable. Besides, he had promised his father before he left London the prior year that he would return at least briefly to see his mother, sister, and niece.

So Seth returned to Amsterdam the next day, boarded the *Three Brothers*, and weighed anchor for Portugal.

Within a week he crossed the rain-lashed bar at the Foz de Douro and docked on the channel side of the River Douro at the Cais da Ribeira in Porto opposite the port wine lodges of Vila Nova da Gaia. A lighter quickly took him across the river. Huddled in his woolen greatcoat, he immediately entered the Perreira *armazem* and, after the customary bear hugs and *abraços*, found Dom Antonio Perreira in a state of high agitation.

"I tell you, my friend, there's going to be a war right here!" Dom Antonio thundered as his curly black hair shook. "France and Spain have allied. It is only a matter of time before they have designs on Portugal. It may not happen today. It may not happen tomorrow. But mark my words, it will happen soon!"

"*Vamos ver.* We'll see. *Nos esperamos que não*," Seth replied with a shrug. He had become passably proficient in Portuguese in the years since he had started trading with the country. "Are there others who feel as you do? If so, I'd like to meet them."

"Yes! Yes! I can arrange it. There are many, all smart, people of *categoria*: the Mayor, members of the city chamber, journalists, merchants, even the Bishop! We are all very concerned. You see, Bonaparte still wants to take England, and Portugal has long allied itself with you British."

"I'm not British," Seth reminded him.

"Oh, yes, I forgot. British, American . . ." he waved his hand and smiled. "*Os bifes*, the beef-eaters, the same all of you."

Dom Antonio, and then Seth, allowed a small laugh.

* * *

Dom Antonio sliced a serving off the roast suckling pig as it turned on a spit in a fire pit at his *quinta* on the outskirts of Porto. He handed it on a tin plate to Seth, who tasted. The steaming meat had a crispy bite on the outside but was succulent, greasy, and comforting on the inside.

"*Gostoso*. Delicious," Seth acknowledged and nodded his approval.

Dom Antonio carved and passed pieces to his other assembled guests, a dozen or so leading citizens of Porto, all wearing hats and wrapped in drab capes to ward off the early March cold as they stood by the fire.

All, that is, except one.

The exception was an Army officer, perhaps two or three years older than Seth, tall and with curly, sandy hair, and a weather-beaten complexion. He wore a bicorne hat and scarlet tunic with the insignia of the 15th Light Dragoons, an ivory-hilted hangar, impeccably polished black hip boots, and spurs. Of his two blue eyes, the right was direct and focused, while the googly left had a tendency to wander.

"Captain Garnett, meet Captain Hale," Dom Antonio offered.

"I am mighty proud to meet you," the officer said as he extended his hand. "Tayloe Garnett the Fifth, at your service."

Seth was taken aback by his accent: Tidewater Virginia, if Seth were correct, with a drawing out of words—deep, sonorous, slow—and so thick he wanted to bottle it.

"Why, you're a fellow American!" Seth blurted despite himself.

"Why, I do declare, sir, so are you!" Captain Garnett beamed.

"Yes, Seth Hale from Portland, Maine. Well originally, Portland, Maine. I've lived these last ten years in London. I am a Yankee captain and, in a manner of speaking, a merchant."

"Captain Hale is married to Lord Hormsby's daughter," Dom Antonio interjected.

"Oh, I do see. I do see."

"And you, you, sir? You are a Virginian, if I am not mistaken."

"Why, sir, indeed I am from Essex County in the Old Dominion."

"That would be by the Rappahannock River, am I right?"

"Yes, sir. My daddy had a tobacco plantation right on the River."

"And so how . . .?"

"How did I find myself here? Well, my mommy was English, from Berkshire. I was born and grew up in Virginia, though. It was my lot to be the third son, you see, so I had no hope of inheriting the plantation. Instead, I attended the College of William and Mary."

"So you are a college-educated man, Captain. I am most impressed. In my family only my youngest brother, also the third boy, has that distinction. And in what year did you graduate?"

"Sir, I did not graduate. Book learning and I did not get along. The Dean and I had a falling out, a contretemps if you will, over grades and drinking and gambling. So I withdrew and went on the Grand Tour. When I was in England I looked up some of my relatives, and they suggested I get a commission, which I did and I've been in the service ever since."

"Well, I'll be. I guess our paths are similar. I too washed up on England's shores and stayed. 'Tis a pleasure to meet. We'll have to dine together when you are next in London."

"It would be a pleasure, sir."

"That is, when your duty is done here."

"Oh, that's only temporary. I'm seconded to the Portuguese Army to observe and make recommendations for training. We have an alliance, you know."

"Yes, I do. A very old one at that."

"Come, gentlemen, let's talk of that alliance and what needs to be done," Dom Antonio interrupted.

As he spoke one of the caped guests loosened his covering to reveal a purple cassock.

Seth began to see the making of his twenty-fifth report to the American Minister in London.

* * *

"Would you care for a glass of sherry?" asked the Dean of the Divinity School at Yale in New Haven.

The newly minted Reverend Juvenal Hale stood erect and thin before the seated mass of the black-clad Dean in the faculty common room.

"Why, yes, I think I might," he piped. After all, he had graduated and now was an adult.

"Good, then," replied the rumpled old Dean with wispy white hair as he cast a benevolent smile and poured a tumbler full of Dry Sack for each of them. He handed Juvenal his. "Cheers, then."

"Cheers."

"So to business, then. All your professors at Harvard, but most particularly Dr. Cogan, who is an old friend, speak highly of you. It seems you have distinguished yourself in all your courses but most especially in homiletics. After careful consideration and much discussion, I am pleased to inform you that the faculty here at Yale is prepared to offer you a position as Instructor in Homiletics. This is a position that, though junior, could lead in time to a Professorship if all goes well. You would be free to study, write, and preach, as well as to teach. We look forward to welcoming you into our little family of scholars here at New Haven. So what do you say?"

"I am flattered and honored. I could think of no place I'd rather be. I accept."

"Good, then. Here's to The Reverend Hale at Yale. Nice ring to that then, eh?" he guffawed as he raised his glass.

* * *

At fifty-six years, Adam's life had assumed a comfortable rhythm. His business in the mast trade had prospered with Portland's rise as a major shipping center, and his warehouse brimmed with luxury goods from Europe that readily found a market inland and southward to Boston and beyond. Still vital enough to command a ship, he sailed the *Atheling* up and down the coast at will and gloried in the occasional trans-Atlantic crossing. He made it a point not to allow a week to pass without being on the water. Thus, even when shore-bound in Portland, each Saturday afternoon he took his sixteen-foot gaff-rigged catboat out alone into Casco Bay and tacked for hours in solitude between the many islands. These were hours for contemplation, away from contracts, markets, and the perfidy of men. They were hours in which Adam embraced the beauty of nature, of pine, rocks, and waves, and in which he allowed the fingers of his free hand to dangle in the frigid wake as the boat slipped effortlessly and silently forward.

So with Adam, so also with Portland. In twenty years, the town had gone from destitution to prosperity. In the last ten years alone her wealth had quadrupled. The Neck had now filled out with many fine new brick homes. She supported a small army of merchants, sea captains, mates, seamen, stevedores, longshoremen, sail makers, rope walkers, carpenters, blacksmiths, chandlers, victualers, money lenders, insurers, accountants, innkeepers, tavern owners, and even a dancing master. Foreign visitors who came to Portland commented on her industry, wealth, and sophistication.

Prosperity had also brought a burgeoning sense of civic pride. Everywhere, it seemed, the town's citizens came together to found and support worthy institutions: a Benevolent Society to relieve the destitute, a volunteer fire department complete with a horse-drawn pumping engine, and all manner of institutions to foster self-improvement, including a public library styled the Atheneum, musical societies, and philosophical discussion groups. The town veritably hummed with betterment.

Adam's role in these endeavors was reluctant at first. But, realizing his isolation might be less than charitably received by his neighbors, he assented to serve as first president of the Seamen's Aid Society and set about with his usual vigor to raise funds for the relief of widows and orphans of those lost at sea.

But more importantly, Adam's life at fifty-six was a time to embrace his family as the most precious possession he had. His love and respect for Nabby only grew with every passing year, and they had by now long settled into a life in which each instinctively felt the needs and moods of the other and in which so much more was left unsaid as spoken. It was as if Nabby had become a *presence* in his life upon which he depended. It helped that he found her still beautiful and charged with grace, even though her hair had grayed at the temples and beyond.

And then there was his granddaughter Hephzibah, now four years old, and so much the image of her grandfather. Each Sunday morning when the weather was good he and Nabby stopped by Thankful's house in their open chaise and picked up Hephzibah and Thankful for church. Hanging from a large beech tree in the yard beside the church was a swing, and each Sunday after services Adam would place Hephzibah in the seat of the swing and push her back and forth, higher and higher, until her squeals of delight resounded through the windows of the church.

Finally, there was life itself for which Adam was most grateful. At fifty-six, he knew that he had outlived many men and that mortality lurked just over the horizon toward which he inevitably sailed.

Thus, it was with a sense of fulfillment and joy that Adam answered the knock at his front door one Saturday morning in early June to find Seth standing at the threshold.

"My son! Oh what a joyous homecoming! Nabby, come quickly! Seth has arrived!" he shouted so that all the house could hear. Nabby, who had not seen Seth for six years, rushed down the staircase in a bustle of silk and threw her arms wide open to embrace him.

"Oh, let me see you," she murmured as she looked him up and down. "Now, you've put on weight, but, oh my, it's good to see you. Welcome home, my dear son."

The ensuing days were a hubbub of activity, as Seth updated Nabby on Georgette's pregnancy, as Adam steered Seth by the arm up and down Fore Street to chat with the other Captains and merchants and show off his prodigal son, and as Seth met for the first time his little niece Hephzibah and regaled her with stories of life beyond the waters. So buoyed was Adam at having his eldest son home that he splurged and purchased sixty acres of country land at Back Cove that he had been eyeing as a retreat for Nabby and himself. The whole family piled into the chaise and drove out on a sunny afternoon to inspect the land and the little frame cottage that it held nestled in a field of grass overlooking the water.

"Now, here I'll plant beans," he explained as he walked down the hillside. "And here English peas. I think we could even grow some Indian corn. What do you think, Nabby?" It was a question that she knew needed no answer, as the excitement on her husband's face said it all.

Despite the pleasures of his familial dalliance, Seth grew restless and anxious to return to England because of Georgette's pregnancy. He had received only one letter from her, addressed in care of his father. It was written not long after his to her and acknowledged the same. She complained of morning sickness but kept up a cheery note, talking of walks in Green Park, of the upcoming season, and of gossip from her friends.

Holding her letter in his hands, written in her flowing script and touched by her own hands, made him long for her and for home. Within a week his ship was laden for the return voyage, and he told his parents that he must leave. However, Thankful implored him to remain one further week.

"Gideon and I are just putting the finishing touches on the ballroom we have constructed at the wing of our house," she had effused. "We want to host a small assembly in your honor. 'Twill be just a few friends and neighbors, our maiden voyage, a trial run, if you will."

So he stayed one week longer to humor his little sister, whom, he suspected, was in turn humoring her husband.

Seth's extended week in Portland only made his departure harder for all members of the family. Nabby had tears welling in her eyes as she bade him good-bye. Adam drove him to Union Wharf to take ship. He found himself choking up as they spoke hard, distant words.

"Weather's clear. Should be good sailing."

"Yes, Fid. Good sailing."

"Should make the crossing in less than three weeks, I'd think."

"Yes, I'd think. Less than three weeks."

"Say hello to Georgette for me."

"Take care of Mama."

Suddenly the dam broke and Adam could take it no longer.

"Don't you want to stay, son? I can set you up here and bring Georgette over. We could all be together again, for now and forever. Think about it, boy."

"Fid, I just . . . I just can't," Seth stammered as tears welled in his eyes just as they had in his mother's. "Fid, I love you," he declared as he hugged his father. "But I must go. I just must."

He alighted from the carriage and walked a straight line out along the wharf and never looked back.

Left alone in the carriage and holding only the emptiness of the reins, Adam at once resented the hardness of his son's heart, realized the small death that had invaded their sacred bond, and cursed himself for having provoked it. He was failing to lead a blameless life.

* * *

Three weeks later Seth inserted the key in the lock and eased open the red door of his house off Berkeley Square.

"Georgette!" he called. "I'm home."

No answer.

"Georgette!"

No answer.

Perhaps she had just stepped out, Seth speculated. The house looked the same as he had left it earlier in the year. All was in order. He dropped his sea chest at the door and entered the dining room. There, on the dining table, he found a note in Georgette's hand. It was dated six days previously. He read:

"Darling Seth: I despair of your return before I shall have to give birth, which should be any day. I find each day I grow weaker and in greater discomfort. Oh, I do so wish you were here. I have determined that I cannot face this ordeal alone and therefore I have decided to remove myself to Mimsy Walker's house in Cheyne Walk at Chelsea, where she has agreed to attend me and make me comfortable in my labour. Lord H. knows of my whereabouts.

Love, Georgette"

Seth left straightaway for the water taxi up river to Chelsea. Mimsy Walker was an old friend of Georgette. He knew she would be in good hands with her. Perhaps her date had already come and she had delivered. Perhaps he was already a father.

The water taxi docked right at Cheyne Walk, which fronted the river, and Seth made a straight line for Mimsy's house, which he well knew from previous visits. He knocked on the door.

A haggard-looking Mimsy opened the door.

"Seth!" she exclaimed. "Thank God you've arrived! It has been an ordeal. Three days ago . . . yes, was it three days? Yes, three days ago Georgette gave birth. The child . . ." she stumbled for loss of words.

"The child?" Seth prompted her.

"The child was stillborn. I am so very sorry."

"And Georgette?"

"She is resting upstairs. We thought we might lose her too, but she survived."

"Thank God," Seth heaved a sigh of relief. "The child, was it a boy or a girl?"

"It was a little boy. Lord Hormsby has made the necessary arrangements. He has already taken him to be buried in Devon."

"I must see Georgette right away," Seth declared, as he made for the staircase. As he mounted the steps two at a time he cursed himself for the extra week spent in Portland. Had he only been here for Georgette and his son. Damn Gideon Sewell and his obscene ballroom.

* * *

The private grief of Georgette and Seth was fated to be short-lived, however, for it was soon subsumed in the sweep of world events, as a mortally wounded Lord Horatio Nelson led the Royal Navy to a smashing defeat of the French and Spanish fleets at the Battle of Trafalgar off the coast of Portugal in late October, and all eyes turned to the mix of national elation and public mourning over the loss of such a conquering hero. It was as if private cares ceased to have any place in the nation's psyche.

27

A World Turning Upside Down

1806

FROM SUNDAY JANUARY 5 UNTIL WEDNESDAY JANUARY 8 THE BODY OF
Admiral Lord Nelson lay in state in the great hall at Greenwich Hospital down river from London. Thousands of mourners filed past to pay their respects while thousands more waited outside or were turned away disappointed. The coffin lay on a catafalque over which hung a canopy of black velvet festooned with gold braid and ornamented with the Admiral's coronet and the *chelengk* or plume of triumph awarded Nelson by the Sultan of Turkey for his victory at the Battle of the Nile. On the back field, beneath the canopy, blazed an escutcheon of His Lordship's arms: a helmet surrounded by a naval coronet, a trident and a palm branch circled about with silver stars and, surmounting the whole, upon a cloth of gold and embraced by a golden wreath, sable-colored letters proclaimed the single word "TRAFALGAR."

At precisely half past seven on Wednesday morning, a procession of honor assembled at the Admiralty and proceeded down river to Greenwich to escort the body. It was a cold and blustery day with wind-beaten white caps clipping the tips of the waves of the Thames but with shafts of sunlight reaching out from between the clouds to illuminate and gild the dignity of the drama. Lord Hormsby, Georgette, and Seth sat in the barge of the Lord Commissioners of the Admiralty as it moved down river.

With the body collected and shipped, the first barge, bearing the Royal standard, led the return procession up the river riding on the incoming tide. A barge carrying Nelson's sword and military regalia followed. The third barge bore Nelson's body. In the fourth sat the Chief Mourner and his entourage. Then came the Royal barge followed by the barge of the Lords Commissioners of the Admiralty and a procession of city barges bearing the Lord Mayor of London and other officials. All the barges flew their colors at half-staff.

As the procession inched up the river from Greenwich minute guns fired in succession. Both the shoreline and the decks, yards, rigging, and masts of the hundreds of ships on the water were lined with multitudes of spectators with their hats off and their visages grim. Normally a hive of activity, of loading and unloading and with colliers, lighters, and taxi boats plying to and fro, the Thames stood deathly still. Not a boat dared move out of respect for the procession as it slowly made its way up the river.

As the solemnity of the occasion sank in, Seth could not help but marvel at the contrast of the scene with the normal mien of the river. It was as if this lifeline of the empire, with all its industry and bustle, had decided to show its darker, more sinister, more ancient side: a River Styx whose highest calling was to convey the dead.

The procession passed the Tower of London and arrived at the Whitehall stairs at half past three. The casket was landed surrounded by attendants from the principal mourning barges. The remaining barges lay upon their oars. The discharge of minute guns, the only sound audible on the water, heralded the arrival. The procession then reconstituted itself on land and marched through lines formed by Guards units to the Admiralty, where Nelson's body was to pass the night.

The following morning, at eleven o'clock, the final, land-bound funeral procession began to move from the Admiralty. The Admiral's casket was borne upon a horse-drawn carriage built to resemble his flagship the HMS *Victory*, complete with a full-sized stern ensign and surmounted by a plumed canopy, but minus the towering masts of Maine timber under which the *Victory* herself sailed. A veritable army accompanied the casket as it clattered through the streets of London to St.

Paul's Cathedral. Over eight thousand soldiers, many of them veterans of the Egyptian campaign, marched in the procession, as well as Light Dragoons, Scots Greys, and flying artillery from Woolwich. Carriages followed bearing the Prince of Wales, Dukes and Barons and then came carriages full of naval officers. The entire procession took over three and a half hours and did not reach the cathedral until the last light of day wanly shone.

Inside the cathedral, Lord Hormsby, Seth, and Georgette had long stiffly held their seats, waiting. In the down time Seth, Georgette, and Lord Hormsby scanned the crowd to see whom they knew, who was seated where, and what political messages the seating arrangements implied. In a forward section of the nave occupied by senior officers from the Admiralty Seth saw many new faces, Captains and Admirals who had been at sea or commanded port installations scattered about Great Britain but who had returned for the funeral. One in particular caught Seth's eye: a short Vice-Admiral with an equine visage and a wart on his right nostril. He wore a hopelessly old-fashioned black wig.

"That fellow over there in the black wig," he whispered to Georgette. "Do you know who he is?"

Georgette shrugged as if to say no and then relayed Seth's question in a whisper to her father. He nodded and responded to her behind a cupped hand.

"That is Vice-Admiral Sir Ponsonby Spicer," Georgette explained. "He recently commanded the white squadron at Portsmouth but has now been elevated to a posting at the Admiralty. Lord H. wants to know if you'd like him to introduce you after the service."

"Thank Lord H., but that won't be necessary, as we are already acquainted," Seth deflected the offer.

At last, in the dim and dying light, the casket slowly was borne up the aisle of the nave to the great crossing and was placed on a catafalque covered in black velvet bearing gold tassels. All who formed the procession took their places, including the Prince of Wales who sat to the right of the Bishop's throne. The doors were inched closed, and the service began. Solemn chants, the *Magnificat*, and other anthems rendered by the choir resounded through the arches. The great crossing where the body lay was illuminated by an octagonal lantern containing nearly five hundred lamps suspended from the overhead cupola. From the arches surrounding the great crossing hung oversize captured French and Spanish naval ensigns tattered and lacerated by cannon balls.

As the choral service ended the Bishop read the burial office, save for the final prayer. The body was then moved to a platform in the crossing of the nave, and, as the Bishop intoned the prayer of commitment, the remains of Admiral Lord Nelson descended, solemnly and by balanced weights, to the vault beneath the crossing to rest forever in the bosom of England.

Seth marveled at the gravity and sumptuousness of the pageantry and was humbled by his acute awareness, yet again, of the chasm that separated England from America.

* * *

"There you have it, gentlemen!" Gideon Sewell exclaimed as he held out his hand and rubbed the first drops of liquid gold between his thumb and forefinger as they dripped from the mouth of the copper pipe.

A half dozen investors rudely wearing their fashionable beaver skin hats indoors nodded their approval.

The moment was the culmination of a year of planning and construction. Before Gideon stood the shining copper vats and coils of his new distillery. The apparatus stood two stories high and was housed in a fireproof brick warehouse specially built on the flats on the far side of the Neck by Back Cove. It was fueled by a mountain of cord wood cut from the Maine forests and brought in by sledge. Behind the complex of vats and coils an army of puncheons stood at parade rest, stacked floor to ceiling to receive the rum. Sewell never ceased for a single day to think of the significance of the investment, which he shared with his assembled guests, but he reminded himself that it was an investment that would pay off. He had eliminated the middlemen in supplying the insatiable New England thirst for rum. From the newly opened Louisiana cane plantations to the shipping of the molasses, to the distilling and to the distribution, he now commanded it all. Together with its adjoining tannery which cured imported hides for use by shoemakers all over New England

and his storehouse on Fore Street, Major Sewell was well diversified and positioned to prosper and survive any adverse economic winds.

* * *

"Adam, I'm concerned about Thankful," Nabby ventured as the two of them sat at supper of cold beef and potatoes leftovers washed down by a glass of porter.

"How so?"

"She seems tense, almost distant, sometimes."

"I haven't noticed."

"You wouldn't," Nabby responded as she allowed herself a faint smile.

"Probably just having to attend to the child."

"I don't think so. Hephzibah is, what, almost five now and much more self-sufficient. It's something else. I can't quite put my finger on it. You'll have to observe for yourself."

"Well, I guess I'll soon get my chance. Their May Ball is coming up next week."

"Just so. A week from tomorrow."

* * *

The May Ball thrown by Gideon and Thankful was a chance to show off their new ballroom to a hundred or so guests who constituted Portland's merchant and seafaring elite, thereby cementing their, and in particular Gideon's, own place within that society. But it was more than that. Simply to have hosted a ball to celebrate May Day and the coming of spring would have been too pagan and profligate for Portland. Instead, the May Ball was also a fundraiser at which the guests, by participating, had purchased subscriptions for the new maritime Observatory signal tower to be built atop Munjoy Hill. The Observatory, long desired and planned, would allow merchants to see their incoming ships while still far out at sea, beyond the islands of Casco Bay which blocked the view from the wharves. It would guide those ships safely home on dark and stormy nights. In short, the May Ball was for a good cause.

On entering the ballroom, Adam had to admit to himself that it was most pleasing. Constructed as an addition to the house, it was a long and spacious room with carved wood paneling boasting Roman vases and floral patterns in the finest taste, all painted cream and gold. The high ceiling surmounted a molding of carved eggs and darts pattern, also delicately painted to match. Tall pier mirrors interspersed the paneling. They reflected and magnified the light from the many wall sconces bearing candles, making the room appear much larger than it even was. About the perimeter of the room stood a dozen delicate ballroom chairs with rush seats and backs in the form of five arches. They, like the room, were painted in cream and gold.

Adam quickly found himself by the punch bowl engaged in a conversation with other Captains, while Nabby congregated with a gaggle of wives at the far end of the room. Gideon, resplendent in his late military uniform but looking something of the stuffed goose, and Thankful, stunning in a white linen *empire* gown and bearing a fan of white ostrich feathers, greeted the guests as they entered. Adam observed her, mindful of Nabby's earlier comments. Certainly, she played the proper hostess. She smiled and nodded to greet the guests by name and make each feel welcome. Only occasionally, when she was not engaged with a guest, did Adam catch a certain tautness in her cheeks and a distant gaze. But to what to attribute it?

At nine o'clock the musicians at the head of the ballroom commenced the festivities with a medley of Scots reels. Gideon and Thankful led off the dancing and were soon joined by others. Adam and Nabby even participated in a couple of rounds until, overheated, they begged off for a cup of punch and the conversation of their peers. The reels gave way to country dances like *The Black-eyed Milkmaid* and those in turn to *The Duchess of Devonshire's Reel* and, in a nod to something more patriotic, *Rhode Island*. Adam and Nabby returned to the dance floor.

At midnight the musicians struck up the newly imported *Mdme. Buonaparte's Waltz*. Its moments of intimacy, if not scandalous, proved uncomfortable for the older generation, who peeled from the dance floor to watch the younger generation dance.

Adam noticed an animated Gideon Sewell performing the waltz with a raven-haired beauty wearing a scarlet silk *décolleté* ball gown. Though attractive, her dark eyes, sharp nose, and high cheekbones imparted a certain lapidary quality to her face.

Turning to Nabby, he whispered, "Nabby, who is that in red?"

"That would be Bathsheba Quimby from Stroudwater. The daughter of Captain John Quimby."

"He who owns so much property here and about?"

"I do believe so."

Adam took note and filed the fact in his mind.

* * *

"Have you seen 'em?" asked one old Captain as he sat at his grog in Colonel Burnham's tavern late of an afternoon.

"Can't say as I have. But I know people who have," replied another as he sipped from his cup.

"That's right," piped another. "They say they dart from alleys and swing from trees. There are maybe a half dozen of them, dressed all in tights like medieval fools and with their faces painted."

"Well, I did see one," Adam stated. The room fell silent and all eyes shifted toward him.

"I was walking on Middle Street yesterday morning. All of a sudden this figure popped out from between two buildings. He leapt and did a somersault and waved his hands about in a most exaggerated gesture. He said nothing. I didn't know what he wanted. I was too embarrassed to look so I just stared at the ground and walked on. I think they are called 'mimes.'"

"Mimes—whatever might that signify?"

The Captains all shook their heads in disbelief.

"I'd wager they're from France."

"Aye, they must be from France. One way or the other. Either through the front door of our port or the back door through the wilderness from Quebec."

"Either way it bodes no good."

All heads nodded in agreement.

"We'd best get Constable Tucker to look into this right away."

Constable Tucker did as he was asked. It turned out the mimes were not from France but were advance men hired by a theatrical entrepreneur in Boston to stir up interest in opening a theater in Portland. There had never been a theater in Portland, but the town's growing prosperity had caught the attention of the entrepreneur who thought it might support a resident company of actors. This revelation promptly sparked a debate among the citizenry: should the town accede to the entrepreneur's request and allow a theater or adhere to the old ways. The debate raged in the taverns and coffeehouses, and even churches, for weeks. It culminated in a town meeting devoted solely to the topic. Each side offered heated arguments. Adam took a somewhat more blasé attitude, as he had dipped into the pleasures of Covent Garden under the tutelage of Lord Hormsby while in London. He therefore rose to offer a reasoned defense, but to no avail, as the sentiment tipped squarely against the idea of a theater in Portland. The issue was resolved by the adoption of a resolution disallowing the opening of a theater in the town or even supporting a theatrical troupe without a license from the Superior Court, which of course would never issue such a license. The entrepreneur and his mimes left town.

For all its wealth and sophistication, Portland had not forgotten the old New England custom of "warning out" undesirable elements.

* * *

While Portland danced, made money, and warned out mimes, whole armies were on the march in Europe. Bonaparte was on the move. On August 6 the last Holy Roman Emperor abdicated, ending a state that had stood for a millennium. Prussia declared war on France. On October 14 Napoleon defeated the Prussians at the Battle of Jena, and ten days later French forces entered Berlin. In November Napoleon declared a Continental Blockade against Britain, closing all of Europe's ports to British shipping. But it was a blockade that he did not have a Navy to enforce, thanks to Lord Nelson. On land it was another matter. Next he invaded Poland and entered Warsaw. The world was turning upside down.

28

Raked by a Broadside

1807

"Oh, my goodness, Nabby, how it does reach almost to Heaven," Adam marveled as he looked up at the new Portland Observatory. "I wonder if it shall, like the Tower of Babel, offend the Almighty and invite retribution?"

The Observatory had arisen quickly under the expert guidance of Captain Lemuel Moody. The eighty-six-foot-tall signal tower stood over two hundred feet above sea level and dominated the eastern end of the town. It rested on a ballast of large boulders culled from the shoreline. The shingled wooden tower, painted a russet brown, was octagonal in shape to withstand high winds. It tapered as it rose, culminating in a cupola that housed a Dolland Achromatic Refracting Telescope that commanded a sweeping view from York to the south to the mountains of New Hampshire to the west. It allowed the viewer to identify ships forty miles out at sea. Three flag poles rose from the cupola. The subscribing merchants stored their house flags at the Observatory. When the keeper of the Observatory spotted an incoming ship he would run up the appropriate merchant's flag. It would be visible from the wharves and alert the merchant to prepare to receive the vessel and its cargo.

Adam Hale longed for the day his blue flag with the two bow-chasers would wave from the Observatory to signal the arrival of one of his ships. Just that morning he had received a letter from Seth in London advising of a particularly rich cargo of British luxury goods—fine bone china, Wedgewood ware, black and white beaver skin hats, shawls, and silks, as well as kidskin gloves and precision scientific instruments—that was bound his way under a contract Captain as soon as the winter storms abated. Adam had already contracted for a goodly supply of masts and spars from the Kennebec to reciprocate on the ship's return voyage. But for now the North Atlantic was too rough to cross, as subfreezing temperatures gripped, and winter winds lashed, the coast. Snow stood piled shoulder high in front of Adam's storehouse. No matter how many layers of wool Adam wrapped about his body, the cold assaulted him every time he stepped outdoors and made life a series of uncomfortable dartings to and fro, volelike and with hunched shoulders, in the dim light of the New England winter. Even these outings became problematical as an ice storm swept across Maine coating all the bare tree branches in a brittle gossamer frosting and rendering Fore Street and other byways lethal passages for uncertain and aging feet. In the lee of the shoreline stretches of the harbor froze, locking the Portland merchant fleet in sheets of crusty ice.

Then the grippe rampaged through the populace. Where it came from no one knew, but some called it the Russian grippe, as if to assign it an exotic origin because it was so terrible. It heralded its arrival to a victim with high fever, coughing, and unbearable pressure on the lungs so that the sufferer thought he could no longer breathe. In the more severe cases uncontrollable effusions of blood as well as mucus were emitted. The disease lingered for weeks in some victims, gradually wearing them down and resulting in death. The town's doctors had no cure.

Adam and Nabby both weathered mild cases, but Thankful fell ill to a virulent strain and lay in her bed coughing and groaning for a week. Nabby, who deduced she herself was by now immune, visited every day bearing hot tea and sweets. Thankful could hardly touch them and each day grew worse. By the tenth day she was greatly weakened and sank into delirium. Nabby and Gideon took turns in attending her. Unable to breathe and writhing in agony in her storm-tossed bed linens, alone but for Nabby at her side and holding her hand, she died at ten o'clock at night on the thirteenth day of her ordeal and in the thirtieth year of her life.

The loss was enormous for her mother, to whom she had always been closest. Nabby walked home in the darkness alone, oblivious to the cold and ice. She removed her woolen cape and fell exhausted into Adam's arms.

"Thankful has succumbed," she mumbled, and Adam flinched but quickly recovered as his great frame steeled itself to uphold and envelope her body, which he held without letting go until the early hours of the morning.

When Nabby was at last in bed asleep Adam took the candle and repaired to the parlor. Sitting in his customary wing chair, he once again found himself teetering on the verge of the abyss of becoming a fallen and bitter man. No tears came, only numbness. He asked his God why he had lost his only daughter.

No reply came.

Adam railed at the absence of God, this Deus Absconditus.

Was this loss retribution for some failure in his character, for some slight unknown to him but known to The Almighty? Adam thought he had lived a blameless life based on the knowledge he had gained with the loss of Jezreel, but perhaps not so.

With unsteady hands he opened his Bible to the 130th Psalm and read:

"Out of the depths I have cried unto you, O Lord;

Lord, hear my voice: let thine ears be attentive to the voice of my supplications.

If thou, Lord, shouldest mark iniquities, O Lord, who shall stand?

But there is forgiveness with thee, that thou mayest be feared.

I wait for the Lord; my soul doth wait, and in his word do I hope.

My soul waiteth for the Lord more than they that watch for the morning: I say more than they that watch for the morning."

Adam took some small, pitiable solace in the knowledge that others, even in antiquity, had asked the same questions as he.

* * *

The next morning Adam walked to the house where Thankful lay still in the bed. After allowing himself a fleeting glance at her corpse, he met with Major Sewell in the parlor and made the necessary arrangements. Because the ground was frozen her body would be placed in the aboveground holding vault at Eastern Cemetery to await interment after the spring thaw.

Before he left, Adam visited Hephzibah in her room. She sat on the edge of her bed in the darkened room with the shades drawn, sobbing.

He gathered her in his arms.

"Grandpapa and Grandmama need your help. Grandmama especially needs you now. Will you come stay with us for a week? You can help Grandmama cook. And I can take you down to visit the ships. Now that will be nice, won't it? And then you can come back home to your Papa once you have helped us out."

Hephzibah nodded weakly. He took her by the hand, and they departed together.

* * *

"Napoleon has attacked Russian forces in East Prussia. This is madness," Seth observed to Georgette as he read the newspaper over breakfast on a chilly but bright winter's day in the light-filled morning room that overlooked the dormant garden behind their house on Berkeley Square.

Georgette gathered her dressing gown about her, and teacup in hand, came to Seth to read over his shoulder.

"The Monster is insatiable. He simply does not know when to stop. It's all in the name of '*Gloire*,' I fear, and nothing more," Georgette observed. "At least we had the backbone to respond to his 'Continental Blockade' with our own of Europe. Excepting Portugal of course. Good old Portugal. Our oldest ally. I wonder how much longer she'll be able to hold out."

"Indeed. I have an apprehension that soon we'll all be drawn in, like a piece of flotsam at the edge of a whirlpool. And for what?"

"The Enlightenment run amok? You Americans started it, lest you forget."

Seth looked up. Georgette was smiling teasingly, to his relief.

"But, ho! Look here! All is not doom and gloom," she said as she pointed her well-manicured finger at an article on the left-hand side of the page. "It says that the Commons, as well as the American Congress, are both advancing bills to halt the slave trade. So we do progress."

"And long overdue, I'd say. A not insignificant step for mankind. Still, one step forward, one step backward, and all at the same time. What a world in which we do live. I think I shall have to dine with Captain Garnett to get his views."

"You spend entirely too much time with Captain Garnett as it is. I fear he is an evil influence on you. The Dutchman is even worse. I dread to think of what you conjure up, especially when the three of you meet, as you so often do now."

"How so, my dear?"

"Well, you always seek their advice on world events and what they mean. It's as if you have ceased to think for yourself."

"No, no, that's not it at all. I simply like to obtain as wide a source of views and insights as I can. It makes me a better-informed citizen."

"I think you should spend more time with Lord Hormsby. He is wise and objective."

"Granted so."

"Besides, I do not trust the Dutchman. I know from his wife that he has vast resources, even now—as well as friends at Court. He acts only in his own interests."

"Or in those of his country?"

"They are largely one and the same, I would think."

"Well, he does play his cards close to his chest. He is hardly forth-coming."

"So perhaps you should be equally circumspect in his presence."

"And is your assessment of Captain Garnett the same?"

"From all I can tell, he is a different case. More of the gallant. Unlike the Dutchman, he acts rather than thinks. But he could be dangerous as well."

He stopped to admire his wife's still fair beauty and caring eyes.

"Thank you. Sometimes you see things I don't."

"Call it a wife's intuition. So no meeting today with Captain Garnett or the Dutchman?"

"Not today," Seth acceded.

She smiled.

"But maybe tomorrow."

* * *

Adam paced up and down the length of Union Wharf in the chill April air. Mr. Spurling was overdue in arriving with the *Atheling*. Five days previously he had sent her under his command to the Kennebec to load timber for the New York market. Under most circumstances Adam would have sent Mr. Spurling directly to New York with the cargo, but he had determined to take command himself and call en route at New Haven to visit Juvenal. The loss of Thankful had taken a silent toll on Adam, and he felt the need to see and touch the remaining child who was within reach.

Adam occupied himself by surveying the harbor. Union Wharf, which he owned with a handful of co-investors, was by far the longest and grandest, stretching two thousand two hundred feet into the water, able to accommodate the largest ships and boasting more than fifteen stores and warehouses. But others also jutted into the harbor: Titcomb's, Ingraham's, Long, and Commercial Wharves, as well as the newest one, the Pier, under construction and owned by Gideon Sewell and his syndicate. The total square footage of Portland's wharves rivaled that of major ports in the United States and even Europe, and the tonnage of shipping they served placed Portland as the third or fourth most active port in the United States, depending on how one counted.

Adam looked up toward the Observatory, and his heart leapt. There, on one of the poles, flew his house flag and the red, white, and blue striped pennant signaling the arrival of a single brig. Mr. Spurling would soon arrive.

In the days that followed, the voyage from Portland to New Haven was all fair sailing as Adam directed the *Atheling* around Cape Cod, past Rhode Island and, clearing Montauk Point, into Long Island Sound. It was no time before he docked at New Haven and found himself face-to-face with his youngest son in the faculty common room at Yale.

"Dear son, if you are not a welcome sight for an old man's eyes!" he gushed on seeing Juvenal.

"Fid, welcome to New Haven!" his son reciprocated as he grasped his hand and they briefly embraced before realizing the unseemliness of it all. "You look well. And how's Mama? I know the loss of Thankful has been a most terrible blow."

"As it has for all of us. But she's slowly recovering her feet. Grief has its own life span, and one cannot hurry such things."

"No, indeed not."

"But what news of you, Reverend Hale?"

"Oh, Fid! I don't know where to begin. The last six months have been such a whirlwind. I apologize for not writing. But I have been most uncommon blessed. First, my repute as a homilist has grown both here at the seminary and beyond. I have just been offered the pulpit of the church in nearby Weathersfield, which I am minded to accept."

"Congratulations, dear son. Is it a large parish with a living?" Adam asked with an eye to the practical.

"Yes, very much so. But with something even more important. The retiring minister, Doctor Goodrich, has a most comely daughter Anna, and she and I have just become engaged to marry next year. See, here is a miniature portrait of her which I wear about my neck at all times."

Adam took the gold chain and examined the oval portrait painted on ivory and framed in gold. The sitter, Anna, was a doe-eyed beauty with light brown hair, fair skin, and a most pleasing countenance.

"She's lovely, son. I cannot wait to meet her. I'm so pleased for you and for all of our family. This does call for a celebration!"

Juvenal turned to the cabinet in the corner of the lounge and broke out a flagon of sherry to pour two glasses. Father and son toasted each other and sat talking for hours until the ravages of distance and time faded to the periphery and their lives became as one. Before they parted Adam and Juvenal agreed that he would bring Anna to Portland at the earliest opportunity to meet Nabby.

* * *

On a bright sunny Sunday morning in mid-July Adam and Nabby sat in their pew at the First Parish Church listening to a guest preacher's sermon too long by half. It thus was with some relief on their part that the sermon ended and the organ began to pump and wheeze through a hymn in which Adam, Nabby, and the entire congregation joined with full-throated vigor:

> "*O for a thousand tongues to sing*
>
> *My great Redeemer's praise,*
>
> *The glories of my God and King,*
>
> *The triumphs of His grace!*"

Then the regular minister, the doddering Reverend Samuel Deane, mounted the lectern to make the weekly announcements.

"I have just been handed this message," he stated.

Everyone stirred to attention.

"'On June 22 the British warship HMS *Leopard* attacked the frigate USS *Chesapeake* off Norfolk, Virginia. The *Chesapeake* surrendered after firing only one shot. The British boarded and removed four crewmen from the *Chesapeake* and will try them for desertion.'" The minister paused and then stated drily, "It seems that the scourge of the press gangs has returned to our shores."

A pervasive rumbling began throughout the congregation. When it subsided the minister continued with the regular announcements. They were the usual fare of housekeeping items: a bake sale, time to renew pew rentals, a listing of those ill and in need of prayer, and so forth.

"And, to conclude," Reverend Deane added, "banns have been posted for the marriage of Major Gideon Sewell and Miss Bathsheba Quimby of Stroudwater."

Adam pivoted to look at Nabby. Her face was in utter shock.

"How could he? How could he do this so soon?" she blurted audibly to Adam.

Adam looked about. All eyes in the church were upon them or so he thought.

"Shh, I'll explain later."

He did not have to, for within days the town buzzed with rumors about the flurry of deeds and conveyances being filed at the courthouse making Major Gideon Sewell a major property owner, in addition to his already confirmed status as a major merchant, in the town.

* * *

Seth knew the voyage to Portugal was a gamble because French privateers still plied the English Channel and Bay of Biscay. But he also knew, or at least suspected, that this would be his last chance to load a cargo of port wine before hostilities broke out. Because of the risk, he partnered with the Dutchman on the finances of the voyage. The arrangement brought the added benefit, despite Georgette's warning, of drawing him closer to the Dutchman, whose activities remained a matter of interest to the American Minister in London. Thus, the two of them stood on the quarterdeck as the *Three Brothers* slid safely across the bar of the Douro and into port alongside the Cais da Ribeira under leaden late November skies. Once docked and disembarked, a lighter quickly took Seth and the Dutchman across the river to the port wine lodges at Vila Nova da Gaia.

Seth observed that Porto looked different this time. There was a hubbub of activity beyond even the normal. Bales of hay and barricades were piled up along the docks. Soldiers milled everywhere. Boats were busy loading and unloading their cargoes as if they were about to weigh anchor at any moment.

"*Que passa?*" Seth inquired of the lighter man. "What's happening?"

"*Os franceses estão à chegar*," he responded with a wary look over his shoulder. "The French are coming."

Dom Antonio immediately confirmed the worst.

"As you know, in July Bonaparte demanded that we close our ports to British trade, but we refused. Then Bonaparte issued an ultimatum: close the ports or France would invade. Still we kept them open and held our breath. Bonaparte then bought off the Spanish with his plan to partition Portugal between them. In October General Junot entered Spain with a French army of thirty thousand men. As a result, Junot has now been joined by a Spanish army twenty-five thousand strong. It was only a matter of time. It is now Portugal's turn to be invaded. The attack is already underway."

"And what's happening?" Seth asked with a hint of urgency in his voice.

"A two-pronged invasion of Portugal, as best we can figure it out. Junot crossed the border at Castelo Branco just days ago and is marching on Lisbon. The Spaniards breached our frontier at the same time and are headed straight here. Our forces are impotent to stop them. That is why they have fallen back on Porto. You saw the soldiers as you landed, no?"

"Indeed so. But what happens next?"

"Our correspondents in Lisbon advise that extreme measures are being taken to save the government. The King and Royal Family plan to depart in a few days with the Portuguese Navy and merchant fleet and as much wealth as they can stow. They will sail for Brazil, where they will establish a government-in-exile. The French will be left only with the crumbs under the table."

"And what about you?"

"The wine trade is dead. I have a warehouse full of vintage port. And I and many of my friends need passage to England."

"How much port and what is its value?"

Dom Antonio drew a paper from his pocket and scribbled on it with a pencil. He showed it to Seth and the Dutchman.

"Can we afford that?" Seth asked his business partner. Seth knew that Dom Antonio was desperate to protect and cash out on the inventory before the French arrived and so had discounted its value by a solid twenty percent, but the volume was high and it would be a major invest-ment. Still, he also calculated that it would be the last shipment of port wine out of Vila Nova da Gaia for a long, long time and its value would soar in the coming years.

"Allow us to confer," the Dutchman asked. Dom Antonio nodded. Seth and the Dutchman retired to a corner of the room.

"I feel we are taking advantage of an old friend. That isn't right," Seth protested.

"Yes, he is in dire straits, but he has no choice. It is a most heavy investment for us."

"You can afford it. I know you have lines with Barings."

"Of course. But it still must make sound economic sense for me to engage. Perhaps another solution?" the crafty Dutchman speculated.

"What do you have in mind?"

"We take it at a twenty percent discount but rebate that discount to him upon its successful transport and sale in England. That way he would venture with us on the risks of the voyage. We would still make out handsomely, and this would give him and his friends additional funds with which to operate in England and do whatever it is they have up their sleeve."

"Do you think he has anything up his sleeve?"

"Most men who have lost their country do."

"Well, you should know."

"Just so. Could we carry it all on your ship?"

"A good bit of it, maybe not all. But enough to make it very, very worth our effort. And his."

"Done?"

"Done."

Dom Antonio's weary face broke into a smile when Seth explained the terms.

"*Obrigado.*"

"*De nada.* How quickly can you load?"

"We will start immediately and work day and night. We have only two days at best."

"And how many of your friends need passage?"

"At least a hundred. Two hundred—if you can take them."

Seth and the Dutchman looked at each other in disbelief.

"Two hundred?" Seth stammered.

"Yes, they are the cadre of our northern army in exile. Others are securing passage as best they can. We expect hundreds more, maybe thousands, to make the passage. We will reunite in England. We planned this in advance with Captain Garnett, whom you know."

"Well, some of you may have to sleep on deck," Seth chuckled as he realized what a singular report the Stork was about to write to the American Minister in London.

At dawn's light two days later the *Three Brothers* cast off its moorings at Porto and caught just enough high breeze to fill its topgallant sails and warily ease itself at high tide over the bar into the ocean. An observer would have seen a ship low in the water and dangerously overladen as she groaned to transport the fleeing wealth and talent of northern Portugal. Later that day the Spanish army entered Porto and the Royal Family set sail for Brazil. Three days later Junot entered Lisbon. Portugal had fallen.

* * *

Juvenal regretted that he and Anna had not been able to travel to Portland as soon as he had promised his father. The exigencies of his new position at Weathersfield had proven overwhelming, as he strove to learn the name of every member of the congregation and establish his credibility with conscientious pastoral work and eloquent preaching. He and Anna had married in Weathersfield in July. She was given away by her father the former minister and with the cheerful support of all the congregation as guests. Neither Adam nor Nabby had undertaken the voyage to Connecticut to attend. So now it was incumbent upon Juvenal to bring his young bride to Portland to meet, at long last, her parents-in-law.

Juvenal and Anna embarked at New Haven on the *Saratoga*, one of the innumerable passenger and mail packets that plied the New England coast. It was the first week in December, and their intent was to spend ten days in Portland before returning to Weathersfield for Christmas. The trip was long overdue, and Juvenal had arranged it with a letter to his parents announcing his anticipated date of arrival.

The weather was cold and overcast as they left. One day out, as they were on the open ocean somewhere off New London, snow squalls began to spit precipitation and the sea took on a churlish turn. The Captain adjusted his sails, and the packet plowed forward on its course nor'nor'east. By dawn the next day the squalls had accelerated into a full-blown nor'easter, with howling winds, driven snow, and waves that tossed the packet about like so much flotsam. Juvenal and Anna stayed in their cabin clutching each other as the ship heaved and tossed with a violence at once sickening and shattering.

The Captain determined to try to make for port, for Newport or New Bedford, for any port in the storm. But his efforts were for naught, as the storm only intensified through the day and he lost control of her direction. By late afternoon, when darkness fell, the ship veered off course and further out to sea. The Captain decided to try to make for Nantucket with what little sails remained aloft that had not been shredded and torn away by the screaming winds.

The waves by now were the size of houses. The ship pitched and yawed in helplessness. One minute the cabin floor pointed skyward and the next it dropped downward as if there were no bottom. All crockery, chests, and loose items on board flew and slid with each violent lunge. The waves began to assault the starboard side of the ship, rolling it not just fore and aft but sideways. Juvenal and Anna huddled in the corner of their berth wrapped in each other's arms in the pitch darkness. Juvenal began to pray for deliverance. Anna closed her eyes and held fast to him.

Water began to penetrate the cabin from above following one particularly dramatic roll. Juvenal and Anna heard the groan and crack of wood in the superstructure of the packet. They realized that the ship was breaking up under the pounding.

They both prayed in unison and clutched one another for as long as they could. Within minutes, the *Saratoga* had broken asunder, taken on water, and slipped beneath the waves somewhere in Nantucket Sound.

News of the loss of the packet spread rapidly through New England. Adam first suspected a problem when Juvenal and Anna did not arrive on the appointed day. Or the following day. Adam sent out feelers through the few coastal Captains who still plied a trade. Within two days the news came back that the *Saratoga* had gone down with a loss of all on board somewhere off Nantucket during the terrible storm.

Adam was sickened at the news. He told Nabby, and they both took to bed for three solid days, unable to rise or face the daylight. The third loss of a child in such a short time overwhelmed them. Adam cursed himself for living, and Nabby cursed herself for having given birth. Adam edged once again onto the by now familiar ledge that lined the precipice of the abyss of lost faith and bitterness. Still, the prospect discomfited him. God first owed him an explanation or at least a dialogue. Adam asked himself why his God had forsaken him. Nabby asked herself if she should have done anything differently.

No answers came.

On the third day, with shaking and uncertain hands, Adam opened his Bible and read from the 139th Psalm:

"O Lord, thou hast searched me and known me.

Thou knowest my downsitting and mine uprising, thou understandest my thought afar off.

Thou compassest my path and my lying down, and art acquainted with all my ways.

For there is not a word in my tongue, but, lo, O Lord, thou knowest it altogether.

Thou hast beset me behind and before, and lain thine hand upon me.

Such knowledge is too wonderful for me; it is high, I cannot attain unto it.

Whither shall I go from thy spirit? or wither shall I flee from thy spirit?

*If I ascend up into heaven, thou art there; if I make my bed in hell,
behold thou art there.*

*If I take the wings of the morning, and dwell in the uttermost parts
of the sea;*

Even there shall thy hand lead me, and thy right hand shall hold me."

Once again Adam pulled back from the abyss. He slowly stirred
himself from the bed.

"Well, we still have Seth," he consoled Nabby.

Her lips trembled, and fatigue had drained all the customary sparkle
from her eyes.

"Yes, we have Seth. And we have Hephzibah," she responded flatly.
And she thought for a moment.

"Perhaps some good shall come from all this."

"I have faith that it must," Adam replied.

But privately he wondered, judgmentally, what a benevolent God's
will was in his loss of three children. Try as he might, Adam had no
answer, and he found himself irked and irritable, angry even, as if a blotch
of corrosion were gathering in a nether corner of the escutcheon of his
character.

* * *

The somber-faced Captains and merchants, both Adam and Gideon
among them, crowded into the ground-floor large room of the Observatory wrapped in their great coats and mufflers. Christmas was past, and it
was cold outside and growing dark too in the late afternoon. They shifted
about from foot to foot to keep warm, whispering among themselves in
anticipation of what possibly could be up. Captain Moody had urgently
summoned them with runners who had fanned out about town earlier in
the day: news was at hand from Washington. Captain Moody mounted
the steps leading to the top of the tower to address the crowd. The throng
fell silent.

"Gentlemen, I received today a report from Washington. Congress has passed and President Jefferson has signed into law the Embargo Act. Henceforth all outbound American shipping is made illegal. No American vessel is to dock at a foreign port unless authorized personally by the President. Each trading vessel now must post a bond of guarantee equal to the value of both the ship and its cargo to ensure compliance. The law is to be enforced by the Navy and revenue officers."

The crowd stared in stunned silence as the implications of the measure sank in. The Embargo Act went far beyond any previous measures. It imposed a total embargo on all American international commerce.

The assembled Captains and merchants began to murmur among themselves, and then the murmur grew in intensity to a grumble, and finally it fell back to a dead and steely silence. All filed out into the cold staring straight ahead at the enormity of having lost their livelihoods. Only Adam tarried. He climbed the steps to the cupola alone. He swung the great telescope seaward. With squinting eye, he made out the twinkle of Portland Head Light in the distance but, beyond that, nothing in the gathering gloom.

29

The Embargo
1808

IN THE ENSUING MONTHS THE WORST NIGHTMARES OF PORTLAND'S Captains and merchants came true. By April more than twenty-five merchant houses failed, including some of the largest concerns. One house, Taber & Son, were Quakers whose reputation for honesty and liquidity was so impeccable that their promissory notes were treated like bank bills and passed as currency. With their collapse, all holders of the notes found themselves with unredeemable paper, further spreading distress and a new wave of bankruptcies. The Portland merchant fleet sat dead in the water, its masts topped with "Jefferson's nightcaps," inverted barrels of tar to combat rotting. By early spring grass was growing on the wharves. As the effects of the embargo rippled through the economy thousands who serviced the mercantile economy, from artisans to sailors, lost their livelihoods. The town set up a soup kitchen to feed the destitute.

> *"Our ships all in motion once whitened the ocean,*
> *They sailed and returned with a cargo;*
> *Now doomed to decay, they have fallen prey*
> *To Jefferson, worms, and embargo."*

So lamented the *Portland Gazette*.

Those who had built up reserves, such as Adam Hale and Gideon Sewell, survived for the moment but with no relief in sight. Some merchants reflagged their ships or filed papers to sail to another American port but found themselves suddenly "disabled" and put in for "repairs" in the West Indies or Europe. With loads of timber selling for less than eight dollars in Maine but for more than sixty in the West Indies, the temptation was great. Others attempted to divert their efforts toward the coastal trade, trying to establish markets in Boston, New York, Philadelphia, or Charleston, but they had few contacts in those American ports, for Portland had always been a hub for international commerce, and in any event there was little demand for Maine goods, as those ports too were in collapse because of the embargo. Still others turned to out-and-out smuggling through the town of Eastport tucked conveniently close to British New Brunswick. Rumors began to circulate in town that Major Sewell had connections in smuggling circles, but nothing was ever proven. All of these efforts were put to naught as Congress passed new legislation tightening the embargo to prohibit even coastal trade or fishing outside the harbors of American ports and as the Navy cracked down on smugglers. Eastern Maine erupted in open revolt, and demonstrations filled the streets of Portland.

The aged Reverend Deane at the First Parish church declared a week of fasting and prayer. Adam and Nabby participated along with many of the established merchants and their wives. But their prayers went unanswered.

And then came the news that Bathsheba Sewell was pregnant.

* * *

The days wore long for Adam, as he had no work to occupy himself, and his outings to Fore Street or the wharves only brought discouragement. Consequently, he took to staying at home and burying himself in his books, much as he had done during the Revolution thirty years earlier. It was a cold spring, and the fireplace in the front parlor struggled to keep the house from freezing. Each morning Adam arose and wrapped himself in a blanket for warmth. He rambled in solitude to the parlor to read and take notes. Most mornings he found the ink frozen in the glass ink well. Nabby would eventually join him in the chair opposite his and occupy herself with busy needlework. And there they sat in silence for hours on end.

By mid-afternoon Adam would grow restless at the hiss of the green wood in the fire and the waning sunlight. Nabby would decide it was time for her to take a walk. Enveloping herself in her hooded sad-colored wool cloak, she would brace the cold for an hour's perambulation. Adam never objected. He just buried himself deeper into his books.

"I am worried about Hephzibah," she announced as she returned from her walk on a particularly raw day. "I went by Gideon's house."

"And what happened?"

"Bathsheba answered the door but would not let me in."

"Pray tell, why not?"

"I don't know. She simply said it was not 'convenient.' She has a hard way about her sometimes. I don't know what to make of it. She has become quite the doyenne of Elm Street I have heard. She's repainted the front hall and several of the rooms, to 'brighten them up.' And moved new furniture in. It's been weeks since we've seen little Hephzibah. I hope she's all right."

"Is Bathsheba showing?"

"Oh, yes, quite."

"Then I think this bears watching. We may have to act in the interest of the family."

Adam and Nabby exchanged long, cold, knowing stares.

* * *

"As a sailor, I distrust horses," Seth confessed as he stared out from the spectator stands at the newly graded and raked parade ground at Horse Guards. "I once rode one clear across the island of Jamaica. I did not enjoy it."

"As a cavalryman, I distrust boats," Captain Tayloe Garnett responded. "But y'all will see some mighty fine horsemanship here today, sir."

"I don't doubt it. I understand the Prince of Wales will receive the salutes."

"That's right. He'll be just over there on the reviewing stand."

"It's terribly kind of you to have invited us," Georgette effused.

"Oh, the pleasure's mine, ma'am," the ever-courteous cavalier responded. "I'm anxious for you to see the fine work we do in this branch of the service."

"And what news from Iberia, Captain?" Seth inquired.

"Much is in the works. It simmers like a cauldron. Our allies still trickle out, and they bring word that Junot disbanded the Portuguese Army. What's more, the French occupiers treat both the Spanish and Portuguese like animals. They make sweeping arrests in the middle of the night and torture civilians. We hear the French firing squads are busy night and day. But here's the interesting part: Spain has grown out of sorts with its French allies. The city of Madrid is in revolt, and the uprising has begun to spread all over Spain and even seeped into Portugal—to Bragança, the Upper Douro, and Porto. Bishop Pisões of Porto has taken command and rules in the name of the Royal Family."

"Why, that's astounding. Is there an opening to be of assistance?"

"'Deed so. We spotted a chink in Boney's 'Fortress Europe,' and we're moving fast to exploit it. I'm serving to train a Loyal Lusitanian Legion right now in Plymouth. They're three battalions of light infantry supplemented by light artillery and cavalry. They're to be what you'd call a 'rapid strike force,' officered under Portuguese command but with British advisors and trained to British standards. Your friend Dom Antonio is Lieutenant Colonel of the Legion. Thousands of Portuguese refugees have signed up. We expect to have 'em deployed within a matter of months. They're right good soldiers. You'll see the first battalion on parade today. What's more, an English force under Sir Arthur Wellesley, late of India, is gathering with plans to land in Portugal. So, yes sir, we are on the move."

"I'm glad of it, Captain," Georgette interjected. "We'll show those Frenchies what we're made of. Hearts of oak, as they say in the Royal Navy. Hearts of oak."

Garnett chuckled. "Hearts of oak. I like that. . . . Look here come the Household Cavalry," he said as he pointed off into the distance.

The Household Cavalry advanced toward the parade ground with a pounding of hooves, clatter of metal, and squeak of leather and with bugles blaring and kettle drums pounding. Other units followed in order of precedence until, near the end, the Loyal Lusitanians stepped forward. Dressed in dark green uniforms of British manufacture with coatees trimmed in white cord and lace, they wore plumed shakos with brass bands stamped "LLL," and each man shouldered an old but serviceable Indian pattern Brown Bess musket and was armed with a sword.

"I must say they march smartly," Georgette observed.

"Thank you. I've a rather proprietary view of them, if I do say so myself," Garnett responded.

"Ah, they can march, but will they fight?" Seth asked.

"Yes, Captain, they will fight. Of that I can assure you."

* * *

In the ensuing months Seth struggled to arrange a cargo of goods to send to his father in Portland, since the American embargo, perversely, was one-way and did not prohibit British ships from calling at American ports, only the other way round. But with the economic collapse in New England and no easy access to naval timbers and with Britain consumed by its preoccupation with the rapidly evolving events in Iberia, his efforts came to naught and, like his father, he found himself with time on his hands. Unlike his father who resorted to a renewed interest in the study of the classics, Seth read the newspapers and passed hours at Broodles talking with refugees from Continental Europe and British military officers in various stages of deployment. It was a heady mix, which at once excited him and made him envious of those able to take part. Georgette's "Hooray Harry" brand of patriotism only fanned the flames and caused him to feel that he must prove himself worthy in her eyes.

From the newspapers Seth learned of the vicious French massacre of women and children at Évora in Portugal in July, of Napoleon's toppling of the Spanish government and placing his brother Joseph on the throne as King of Spain, of Wellesley's landing at Figueira da Foz on the Atlantic coast of Portugal and the two ensuing stunning victories over Junot at Roliça and Vimeiro, of Wellesley's replacement by a more senior general and the signing of the Convention of Sintra by which Junot was allowed to evacuate his army intact, and of the recall of both Wellesley and his successor to England for an inquest. From his contacts in the military, he learned of the dispatch of the Loyal Lusitanian Legion, along with Captain Garnett, to Porto to support the rebels and of a larger reinforcement of the British bridgehead in Iberia under Sir John Moore.

In late October he received a letter from his father announcing the birth of a baby boy named Henry to Gideon and Bathsheba Sewell. It was a dark and brooding letter in which his father lamented the strangling consequences of the embargo, the loss of American cohesion and destiny, his own personal financial woes and, finally, his and his mother's concerns about the well-being of Hephzibah in the household of the newly empowered Bathsheba. Several times Seth took pen to paper to try to respond, but each time he gave up because of his own preoccupation with events in Europe, by which events in America, depressing though they were, paled in comparison.

Oddly, for all the concern over building war clouds, London had assumed a frenetic, almost festive air. Its streets thronged with soldiers, its clubs and pubs overflowed with gaudily uniformed officers, and its buildings were bedecked with strings of pennants bearing the red, white, and blue of the Union Jack. It was a time of mutual encouragement, of putting on a brave face, of standing up to be counted. Such was patriotism, and, were Seth to admit it to himself, he rather enjoyed the elevated spirits that it entailed.

It was in this mood that Seth received news that Napoleon had personally taken command in Spain and had arrived in the country with two hundred thousand fresh troops, thereby swelling the total French force to over three hundred thousand. What's more, Bonaparte was accompanied by his Imperial Guard, an artillery train, and some of his best marshals, including Soult and Ney. Aiming straight for Madrid and ultimately Portugal, they swept aside all Spanish opposition. Spain was about to fall, except for one complicating factor: Sir John Moore had advanced his army of twenty-five thousand from Portugal into Spain and had joined forces with the Loyal Lusitanian Legion, which was already conducting hit-and-run operations against the French.

Seth sat explaining these developments to Georgette as they had morning coffee in the sunroom at their house.

"I am told that the General Staff at Horse Guards are very concerned for Moore and his army. There is a risk they will be caught as between meat grinders."

"And the Lusitanians?"

"They will too, I suppose. But they might be viewed in a more collateral way. The Admiralty has issued an emergency call for a relief task force to sail at once to the north coast of Spain should Moore's army require evacuation. They also need to carry provisions to the army headquarters in Lisbon. There's a need of all available ships. My merchantman would serve well. I also know the country and speak Portuguese. Your father strongly hinted that my participation would be welcomed."

"Would you do so?"

"I don't know."

"How can you not know?"

Seth stared at his wife, who by now was standing erect with her blond hair flowing and her blue eyes welling in tears of passion, like some latter-day Boudicca.

Seth could not answer as he groped for words.

"This is for England!" she whispered as she touched her hand ever-so-gently and persuasively on his shoulder, almost as if she were knighting him. At once, Seth was reminded that he was married to a lady and a formidable one at that.

"Yes, yes. For England. I will think about it," Seth stammered.

Three days later Seth received a writ from the Admiralty. The writ ordered him and the *Three Brothers* to join the Royal Navy's rescue convoy to the Iberian Peninsula.

It bore the signature of Vice-Admiral Sir Ponsonby Spicer, Baronet.

Seth placed his hand against the slight bulge of the latest code book, received only days before from the American Minister, that lay hidden and sewn in the lining of his waistcoat. If the man who stole his freedom through impressment could now order him to Spain, he was no longer bound by his code of not reporting on the British. He would go and report on the Baronet and anything else he saw.

30

"Over the Hills and O'er the Main, To Flanders, Portugal and Spain"

1809—Part I

THE BRITISH TASK FORCE OF TWO HUNDRED AND FORTY-FIVE SHIPS, comprised of men-of-war, troop transports, supply ships, hospital ships, packets for speedy communication, and merchantmen, was a forest of masts as it stood off La Corunna on the northwest coast of Spain in January. The passage had been storm-tossed and close-reefed as a series of bad weather fronts made its way across the Atlantic and brought gales, snow, and bitter cold to the Iberian Peninsula. It was one of the harshest winters in years. Seth's ship, the *Three Brothers*, was laden with provisions for the Portuguese Army at Porto: barrels of salt beef, oats and dried peas, horse shoes, blankets, and, not least, a menagerie of animals to supply the forces, including spare cavalry horses and cattle and goats for food. In what Seth judged to be a gratuitous maneuver by the Admiralty to lessen the risk to naval vessels, his ship also held on its lowest deck one hundred and thirty-six barrels of gunpowder. The prearranged plan was for most of the naval vessels to evacuate Moore's troops and return to England, while Seth would accompany several merchant ships in the company of a small protective convoy, which would peel off to discharge their cargoes at Porto.

Seth was already busy penning his initial secret report to the American Minister as he sat at his desk on the *Three Brothers*.

"Sir," he wrote:

"Arrived at La Corunna the 14th instant. Situation disastrous. Bonaparte unleashed an avalanche of fire and steel and destroyed the Spanish Army. Moore's field army was in danger of being trapped near Salamanca, so went into headlong retreat across Galicia to try to reach Portugal. Forced march of two hundred and fifty miles beginning December 25. Bad weather, mountainous terrain, sickness, break down of discipline, and French chasseurs in pursuit almost undid the army. Bonaparte outmaneuvered Moore with forced marches over ten days in blizzard conditions and cut off planned retreat to Portugal. Moore diverted to Vigo but was unable to reach because of disintegration of his army, so diverted to La Corunna. Moore lost more than a quarter of his army and a fortune in stores and horses. But Bonaparte failed to bring him to battle and left the field for Marshal Soult's II Corps, supported by Ney, to try to finish him off. Moore reached La Corunna, and we began process of embarkation. Unable to ship many military stores, and British had no choice but to destroy 12,000 barrels of powder, 300,000 cartridges in two magazines outside La Corunna, and 50 fortress guns and 20 mortars intended for Spanish allies. While embarking Moore's army, Soult marched up and forced him to give battle on the 16th. Moore prevailed and drove off the French but at the cost of Moore's life when he was felled by a cannon ball. Such was the only glory, if that is the word, in the affair. That, and the bulk of what remained of the army was saved. Last evening after nightfall British began to withdraw in silence from their lines, leaving behind pickets and watch fires. Completed embarkation throughout the night, and last of the pickets withdrew and are taking ship at daybreak. There is no question that Soult will invest La Corunna as soon as he smokes the ruse."

Seth transcribed the letter into code with invisible ink between the lines of an anodyne letter to Georgette in-clear, signed it "The Stork," sealed the missive, and burned the draft.

No sooner had he completed the task than a knock came at his cabin door. Opening it, he found a courier who had just arrived via fast mail packet.

"How fortuitous!" he exclaimed as he handed the courier his letter. "Kindly carry this back to London."

In exchange the courier retrieved from his leather satchel a letter addressed to Seth, which he handed him. Once the courier departed and Seth closed the door he examined the envelope. To judge from the size and the handwriting, it was a coded instruction from the American Minister in London.

Withdrawing once again his code book, Seth went about the laborious task of decrypting the message. When he completed it almost an hour later he held the message up to the candle and read:

"Sir—

You are ordered to rendezvous with Captain Garnett and accompany the Loyal Lusitanian Legion, reporting in detail on its activities. You are then ordered to attach yourself to Wellesley's army when it lands and to report in detail on its leadership, composition, strategy, and activities. You are not to return to London until you have accomplished these missions."

"Holy Angels!" Seth blurted out loud.

"Ordered to?" By what right did the Minister "order" him—a volunteer—to do anything? Seth held up the letter and read it again. Who was ordering him? Was it the Minister personally or the government of the United States? Unfortunately, the letter provided no clue.

Slowly it dawned on him that the Minister might have misled him all along and now that he had him where he wanted him, he switched the rules of the game. Or maybe the instructions came at the connivance of Vice-Admiral Spicer, who wanted him compromised and sent out to the slaughter like Uriah the Hittite? Certainly, Spicer had ordered him and his ship into the danger of the theater of war, but it would be a stretch to think that he had colluded with the American Minister to change his orders. No, this must have been the work of the American Minister. Oh, why did he ever trust anyone? In this wicked world his only true friend was Georgette. And of course Fid.

But what if there were a real need for his services as postulated in the instructions? Circumstances do change. His country might be calling, and he could hardly return in defiance and empty handed. Well, he could of course, but what would his fellow Americans think of him were they to find out? What would he think of himself even if they did not find out? Seth spent a sleepless night pondering these and other questions to which there were no clear-cut answers.

What was clear was the decision that lay before him: he was either in or out as a citizen of the United States. There was no halfway point or means to obfuscate the matter any longer.

At first light in the morning Seth resolved to opt in. He did so as an act of faith in doing the right thing. Like any act of faith, it was by definition unproven and its consequences unknowable. But his inner New England self told him to take the hard right against the easy wrong.

He grabbed two leather satchels with his personal belongings and the few changes of clothing that he had with him. On deck, he instructed his Mate to sail the *Three Brothers* to Porto as planned and explained that he was going to proceed overland. He disembarked at La Corunna. On the waterfront teaming with British soldiers waiting to evacuate he had little trouble finding Lieutenant Colonel Dom Antonio Perreira, his advisor Captain Tayloe Garnett, and seventy Loyal Lusitanians accompanied by a band of partisans or *caçadores* in slouch hats and blankets.

"We are not embarking," Captain Garnett explained. "Our orders are to go back in and rescue a missing part of Moore's artillery train. This could be risky, but you are welcome to come along."

"I'll ride with you," Seth volunteered. Garnett arranged to spare a saddled horse, and the Loyal Lusitanians were ready to proceed on one of the few remaining escape routes before Soult took the city.

The contingent nervously made its way past the still-burning watch fires abandoned just a few hours before by the British pickets and headed up a narrow steep path into the hills that lay inland from the rocky promontory of La Corunna. They heard the stirring of Soult's army to their east and picked up their pace in order to move clear of danger. They counted on the likelihood that Soult's attention would be directed solely to taking the city.

Within an hour they reached a bend in the path, well within the rising foothills, that afforded a sweeping vista of the harbor and the departing British fleet. When Soult realized that the British had left their positions along a ridge, he placed six guns on the heights above the southern end of the bay and began to fire on the departing ships. Seth uncased his telescope to watch the action while they rested. The French guns caused panic among four of the transport ships, which ran aground. He watched as their crews set them afire to prevent their capture. He strained to find the *Three Brothers* in order to be sure of its safe escape. At length he located it under sail within the circle of his scope. Several British warships accompanying the transports sailed smartly into position and silenced the battery with their return fire.

Perreira signaled that it was time to move on. The weather grew colder at the higher altitude, and sleet began to fall. Perreira, Garnett, and Seth huddled in silence on their horses as they plodded forward. The *caçadores* also were mounted on horses, old jades from what Seth could tell, but better than the mules the noncommissioned officers rode or marching on foot like most of the Loyal Lusitanian rank and file. So they continued all day until as dusk fell they found an abandoned shepherd's cottage with its roof collapsed but its stone walls intact, where Perreira directed that they camp for the night. Only when they had settled, posted the pickets, kindled a campfire, eaten a meager supper of warmed-over hash, and lit three cigars did the three friends begin to talk. Seth, as the newest member on the mission, was full of questions.

"Where are we going exactly?" he asked.

Garnett pulled a folded map from his vest.

"Over yonder is La Corunna," he explained as he pointed with the glowing tip of his cigar. "And we sit here, just to the southwest. The artillery train broke up just there, catty-cornered by Orense, as Soult gave chase. It looks like those who did not reconnect with Moore's retreat probably got lost somewhere in the vicinity. So we have to go back and find 'em and lead 'em to safety."

"How do you know they weren't captured by Soult?"

"We don't know. But we'll find out."

"The *caçadores* are a freely flowing people," Dom Antonio explained. "Those with us today may not be the ones with us tomorrow. They move in and out of the French lines. They know this terrain because it is their home. They know all the back roads and paths. We should have intelligence on the artillery's whereabouts within the next day or two, three at most."

"Well, I'm glad of that. It does seem a bit preposterous to stake the safety of these seventy men on a will-o-the-wisp rescue mission."

"These men can handle themselves. They've been conducting raids on Soult's army for months. We will of course be leaving the mountains as we head toward Orense," Dom Antonio observed.

"What does that signify?"

"Up here it is rocky and hilly," Dom Antonio explained, "with many stone walls, gullies, and small farms, what we call *minifundia*. Not good for cavalry. Closer to Orense, which is in a river valley, it will be flatter, and the French heavy dragoons maneuver more freely there. We'll have to be alert. General Franceschi's *cuirassiers* will be out in force. Our intelligence tells us they are over three thousand strong: the 1st Hussars, 8th Dragoons, 22nd *Chasseurs à Cheval*, and the Hanoverian *Chasseur* Regiments, not to mention de la Houssaye's 3rd Dragoon Division and Lorge's 4th Dragoons."

"Are they as fierce as they say?"

"Aye, they're monstrous fierce," Garnett interjected. "They call them the *cuirassiers*, the heavy cavalry. They come on you all of a sudden in a passel, mounted on seventeen-hand war horses, with sabers drawn, breastplates gleaming, and *cadanettes* dangling."

"*Cadanettes?*"

"Those are the braids of hair they wear. It gives 'em the look of something fierce, like a Frankish warrior or some such. Or so they'd like you to think."

"How do you stop them?"

"Best not to meet 'em in the first place. But, that failing, one thing only stops 'em: grit and the bayonet."

"How's that? Sorry, I'm a sailor and don't know of such things."

"Horses are afeared to charge bayonets."

"Oh, I see," Seth mumbled, realizing he had much to learn.

* * *

Three days later, while Dom Antonio's Loyal Lusitanians still clung to the mountain paths before descending into the valley at Orense, the *caçadores* brought news that Soult had captured the missing remnants of the artillery train weeks before. Moreover, they brought intelligence that Soult had seized huge supplies of munitions and provisions at El Farol, had refitted his army and was on the move south.

The implications for the Loyal Lusitanians were ominous: they were at risk of being surrounded and cut off.

Dom Antonio called a council of war as a half dozen officers squatted shivering around a campfire at their bivouac in the ruins of a *citânia*—a lichened rock-strewn Bronze Age circular hut settlement atop a mountain. Snow fell and caused the fire to sputter.

"We have a choice to make," Dom Antonio explained. "We can stay in Spain and look for opportunities to harass the II Corps. But we are only seventy men against tens of thousands. And our supplies are dwindling and the weather is against us. Or we can retreat to Portugal, hopefully before the French find us and cut us off."

"That's right," Garnett weighed in, "it'll be a race. We don't know exactly where the main body of Soult's army lies, just that they are heading south toward Portugal and not tarrying. Most likely they could be moving by the Pilgrim Road south from Santiago de Campostela, but just as easy they could be headed for the old invasion route at Chaves— not named "Keys" in Portuguese for nothing. With luck we can get shut of 'em and cross the border where we can meet up with the rest of the Portuguese forces and whatever the British have left in the area."

"Porto would be the objective. That's where the main Portuguese resistance is centered. Captain Hale, that's where your ship is to rendez-vous, am I not correct?" Dom Antonio asked.

"Yes," Seth confirmed.

"Good then. That is our recommendation. Gentlemen?"

The officers chatted among themselves for only a minute or two.

"We see no choice," their spokesman announced.

"To Porto it is then," Dom Antonio confirmed. "Dismissed. Captain Garnett, stay with me a moment to discuss the best routes."

* * *

The next morning they awakened before dawn. The campfires were dead, and the mountaintop was enveloped in a blizzard. The snow had already accumulated a foot and a half and showed no sign of abating.

"We can't bide here," Garnett advised as he shook the snow from his blanket. "Soult will steal the march on us."

"Nor can we continue over the mountains, as we had planned," Dom Antonio added. "The going will be too slow. Our only option is to seek lower ground where it will be warmer. Maybe we can skirt the base of the mountains and slip through the valley of the River Lima."

"Pray Soult took the Pilgrim Road," Garnett added.

Accordingly, the green-jacketed Loyal Lusitanians and the ragged band of *caçadores* descended the mountain and found what appeared to be a path leading south toward the Lima. They proceeded slowly, foot by foot, yard by yard, taking care to try to pick out the path in the fallen snow. Within two hours their altitude had decreased sufficiently for the snow to have tapered off into the occasional flurry and then, as they descended further, into a dull and numbing freezing rain. They crossed innumerable mountain streams engorged by the precipitation as they tumbled from the surrounding mountains. Stone walls delineating farmers' fields began to appear. And then bare and gnarled vineyards, their vines supported by vertical granite shafts. Onward they marched through the unceasing rain until dusk overtook them. In the dwindling light they spotted a gray granite *armazem* or barn in the foothills. They approached it cautiously, in a half circle and with muskets loaded. The scouts quickly determined it to be unoccupied, and with exhaustion and relief the entire shivering force entered the edifice and took shelter for the night. They stabled the horses and mules at one end of the barn, where they found, to their immense relief, badly needed bales of hay for their mounts. Only after feeding and settling their mounts did the Loyal Lusitanians consume the last of their cold rations and bed down for the night.

The next morning Captain Garnett saddled up a foraging expedition to probe further down the valley. The detachment consisted of six horse-mounted troopers with muskets and panniers to accommodate the food. Seth rode with them. Before mounting, Garnett turned to Seth.

"Do you prefer a sword or pistol?"

"I'm sorry?"

"What's your preference: a sword or a pistol? You'll need to be armed."

Seth thought for a moment. He was proficient in neither.

"What about both?"

"Just in case?"

"Just in case."

"Very good."

Garnett ordered one of the sergeants to bring up the weapons, and Seth mounted his horse with a dragoon saber clapped to his side and a sixty-nine caliber Army issue flintlock pistol bearing the proof marks of the Tower Armory jammed in his waistband.

At first they rode in silence. The only sound was the dull plod of the horses' hooves and the clatter of tack. In the dawn's light the weather was misting and cold. Drops of water formed on Seth's nose. Visibility was poor.

Garnett and Seth rode side by side at the head of the detachment.

At length Seth spoke.

"Ever miss America?" He felt foolish that his manner of speaking had assumed the same staccato tone as the Stork's reports increasingly had. How odd he had grown in his nation's service.

"Why, in truth, sir, I must say I do," the more florid Garnett responded. "I miss the little things. The Rappahannock River on which I hunted ducks as a boy. The old brick county courthouse. The long dusty lane that led to our home. The taste of sweet corn and butter beans in the summer. And the refreshment of cool buttermilk. Aunt Emma, who ruled the kitchen house and made the best fried chicken and spoon bread you have ever tasted. And Uncle Mose, her husband, who fished the river for catfish and bass and whatever else he could catch and who taught me how to set traps for muskrat and beaver in the pocossons."

Seth sensed Garnett's youthful formation was far different from his own.

"So you owned slaves?"

"Not I, sir. But my daddy did. He was the 'buckra,' as the Negroes say. Not many slaves, but enough to help plant and harvest and run the household. Most had lived on the place all their lives and were the children and grandchildren of slaves who had been with the property since long before Independence. My daddy did not believe in breaking up families. Even when they multiplied so that we could hardly gainfully employ them or feed and clothe them or when they got old and needed care. It was all he could do with a system that was just 'there.'"

"But you never freed them?"

"For what, might I ask? Where would they have gone? How would they have taken care of themselves? It would have been their ruination to let them go."

Seth sensed that Garnett falsely justified financial necessity by a myth of benevolence, which he no doubt truly believed. But he held his tongue.

"And you, sir, I take it your family holds no slaves?"

"No. Certainly not," he replied tartly before realizing his response might have sounded harsh and self-righteous. "In New England," he explained, "we don't hold slaves. At least most of us don't. It's not the done thing. It's looked down upon. It's a point of morality."

"That's easy for a Northerner to say, as you've no economic necessity. Morality don't cost you."

Seth gave a short begrudging laugh. "I suppose you have a point. In any event, with the slave trade now abolished, maybe our two societies in America can grow closer together."

"I'd think that a right good idea, but I'm not thinkin' it'll be happenin' soon."

"Why not?"

"Well, let's put it this way: what do you New Englanders do to kill time?"

"Well, I can say that I never thought of time as something to be killed. It's something to be treasured and taken advantage of, turned to good use. Work is all."

"Aha! Just so! Sir, have you no steeplechase races, no cock pits, no gander-pulls, no shoots, no wagering at cards, no blood lusts? Life's a bore without those pastimes." Garnett was beginning to smile now. "So you see, 'tis far more that separates our two American societies than the slave."

"Well, here we are nonetheless together as volunteers on the same side in a foreign land."

"Yes, Captain Hale, we are all volunteers. We are all volunteers."

"The next question is why."

"Why? Why? I suppose for equal measures of adventure, glory, the chance to be part of something larger than yourself, and, if truth be known, havin' nothing else better to do. At least that's the brew in my case. What about you?"

Seth thought long and hard.

"Duty," he at length said and offered no further explanation.

In the distance a small *aldeia* or village came into view. Garnett raised his hand to stop both the conversation and his advancing troops. He listened.

"I don't like it," he whispered. "Everything is too quiet. Either an army has been through here or is about to come. Everyone has left."

The only sound was a dog barking in the distance. He had heard them approaching.

Garnett signaled to proceed. Slowly, cautiously they edged toward the *aldeia* with muskets pointed. When they reached the edge of the settlement, which had less than a dozen dwellings, they stopped again. Indeed it appeared to have been recently abandoned.

They approached the largest house and unlatched the plank door and eased it open. Whoever had vacated it had done so only shortly before because the embers still glowed in the large cooking fireplace. The foraging party knew where to look for food, and they quickly found five hams hanging to cure on the interior of the chimney shaft. In the larder they discovered several dozen heads of cabbage, loaves of bread, and, most precious surprise of all, dozens of eggs resting in straw in two crates.

Garnett toted up the inventory and withdrew a handful of silver pieces from the money pouch he carried. He dropped them on the kitchen table.

"If the farmer had been here we would have asked to purchase the food. But since he is not, we cannot ask. However, we pay for what we take. And we pay well. Unlike the French, who steal it. This war is all about respecting and winning the people," he explained to Seth. "Inch by inch, farm by farm. It'll be a long war."

The party similarly entered and scavenged the remaining houses and barns in the deserted *aldeia* and soon filled their panniers to capacity, leaving small piles of coins on the table at each house.

The laden foraging party, following the road by which it had come, mounted a hillock on its return trip to the base camp. Suddenly Garnett held up his right hand, signaling it to halt.

"See down there," he whispered as he pointed to a river ford a mile distant. "*Cuirassiers.*"

Seth strained to see the enemy fording the river at the bottom of the valley: perhaps a dozen heavy cavalry on patrol.

Garnett did not wait further.

"Quick, get the horses off the road and behind that wall before they see us," he ordered. "Move fast!"

The soldiers did as he told them, hiding the horses behind a high stone wall fifty yards up a hillside and to the left of the road.

"Keep those beasts quiet, and maybe the Frogs will pass without knowing we're here. Just in case, each man take your mark on a soldier as they come up."

The Lusitanians hunkered down behind the wall, with their muskets at the ready.

"Do you think they saw us?" Seth asked as he crouched behind the wall. "The mist has lifted."

"Truly, sir, I don't know, but I reckon we'll find out," Garnett replied.

The Lusitanians waited anxiously as the *cuirassiers* completed their fording of the stream below, regrouped on the road, and started up the hill. It was not long before Seth heard and felt the pounding of the heavy horses' hooves on the roadbed. They appeared to be proceeding at a trot. Seth told himself that if they were proceeding at a walk they likely would not have seen the Lusitanians, but that at a trot, well, that was hard to say. . . . Maybe they normally patrolled at a trot through relatively open countryside such as this. At least by moving at a trot they would pass more quickly and might be less likely to notice anything amiss.

The French mounted column approached the crest of the hill. The Lusitanians cocked their hammers. Seth withdrew his pistol and did the same. Each took a mark as the Frenchmen came within range.

The pounding of the hooves, the creak of leather tack, the jangle of scabbards were all that punctuated the silence.

The van of the column moved past, and the Lusitanians exhaled a silent sigh of relief.

The remainder of the column trotted by until the rear guard came even with the hidden Lusitanians.

Suddenly one of the Lusitanian's horses behind the wall whinnied.

The rear man in the French column stopped his horse and turned around to look, his *cadanettes* visibly dangling by his cheeks.

He scanned the hillside for a second, and then he shouted.

"Arrêtez-vous! L'ennemi à droit!"

The other *cuirsassiers* stopped and turned their mounts around.

"Fire!" Garnett ordered.

Five muskets and two pistols discharged at once from behind the wall. Five of the shots found their mark, for as many *cuirsassiers* slumped in their saddle or fell to the ground. Seth aimed at the rear rider who had sounded the alarm, and he fired. His shot clipped the cavalryman in the right shoulder. He spun around, bent in agony, trying in vain to regain control of his horse.

The remaining seven *cuirassiers* immediately grouped into a formation and bounded from the road up the hill toward the Lusitanians, who were scrambling to reload their weapons. Although the wall was too high for the French to jump, it would be only a matter of seconds before they found a way to circumvent the barrier, come from behind and charge downhill on the Lusitanians who had their backs to the wall and thus no means of escape.

Garnett wasted no time.

"Fix bayonets!" he ordered.

His men immediately complied and then went back to reloading their pieces.

Sure enough, the seven *cuirassiers* found a breach in the wall not a hundred yards distant and accelerated into a fast trot until they gained the terrain advantage, at which point they wheeled and immediately charged down on the embattled foraging party at full gallop.

"Fire at will!" Garnett ordered.

The Lusitanians did not wait and let loose a rolling fusillade that cut down another three of their attackers. Well trained, the Lusitanians immediately bunched and knelt. They drove the butts of their muskets into the ground so that the bayonets protruded at sixty-degree angles at the charging horses. Seth stood behind the cordon with his sword drawn.

The remaining four *cuirassiers* hurtled down the hill brandishing their cutting sabers and shouting oaths in French. The Lusitanians held fast. Not ten yards from their position the steeds saw the band of steel and the wall they could not mount and pulled away to the side. The *cuirassiers* fought for a fleeting second to regain control of their mounts and then wheeled them inward to the huddled Lusitanians from the side, galloping parallel to the wall. The Lusitanians shifted to try to redeploy their bayonets against the reformed French attack.

Onward the French came, still at a gallop. The Lusitanian line was more ragged this time, and their bayonets were not in place quickly enough to prevent the *cuirassiers'* horses from smashing into the front of the Lusitanians. Desperately the Lusitanians lunged at the horses with their bayonets to try to bring them down, while the heavy, razor-sharp French sabers cut at their heads and shoulders with practiced precision. Horses stumbled and fell, bringing their riders into bayonet range. Blood, screams, and chaos gripped the scene. In an instant Seth saw next to him a mounted *cuirassier* with pistol drawn and pointed at the head of Garnett, who, oblivious, was fending off with his own sword the savage blows of another attacker. Seth leaped forward and brought his sword up against the wrist of the shooter, sending the pistol flying and discharging aimlessly as it went. He then drove his sword into belly of the *cuirassier* before he could react.

The skirmish was over almost as soon as it began. One *cuirassier* lay dead on the ground, two remained mounted but wounded, and the fourth, unscathed, broke off the engagement and fled with his two wounded comrades. The Lusitanians counted many slashes about their upper bodies but no deaths.

They made haste to reload and pull together their scattered equipment. Garnett ordered them to corral their horses, which had scattered at the first sign of the attack, and to remount. There would be no tarrying on this road. They had been discovered, and the French could return at any moment with reinforcements to finish them off. More to the point, the patrol was the firmest evidence they had that Soult had not taken the Pilgrim Road, was not far away, and was moving to enter Portugal via Chaves.

Within an hour the foraging party reached their camp with the eggs intact.

"I know of a road," Dom Antonio said. "It goes over the Serra de Gerês. It is steep and not easy, but it is almost certainly not known to the French. It is an ancient Roman road that ran between Braga in Portugal and Asturgas in Spain. It should take us away from the valleys where the French patrol and get us back into Portugal."

All agreed it presented the best available route into Portugal while avoiding the roving patrols and main body of French troops. So they struck out southward, climbing ever so slowly the vast hump of the Serra de Gerês. The mountain was only one of many undulating, barren, and rugged ridges that stretched as far as the eye could see and that defined the border between the two countries. The mountain was all but impenetrable save for the ancient road. The road on the Spanish side of the border was more a trail than a proper road. Dom Antonio stopped the column frequently to consult his map and compass. Once past the summit the next day they began to descend into forests of gnarled and stunted oaks that blanketed the Portuguese side. The Roman road took on more definition. Like all Roman roads, it ran in a straight line oblivious to the terrain and wilderness. It consisted of large flat stones which were deeply rutted from two millennia of wheeled traffic. Upright granite mileposts inscribed with the names of Roman emperors lined the road. At one point Seth stopped to marvel at the abutments of a Roman bridge over a surging stream. Although the span had long since collapsed, the perfectly dressed granite stones of the abutments still stood, almost as if they had been constructed the week before. Seth pondered the impressive accomplishments of Roman civilization.

On the downward side of the mountain, as they entered the more populated areas of the northernmost Portuguese province of Entre Douro e Minho, the oak forests and wilderness gave way to *minifundia* landholdings indistinguishable from those in Galicia across the border: the same small walled fields, the same ubiquitous vineyards and corn cribs, the same rushing streams. Even the dialect of Portuguese in the region bore a close relation to *galego*. But all with a welcome Portuguese hominess, a familiarity that bade them welcome. They knew they were home when they saw the four graceful arches of the stone bridge at Arcos de Valdevez spanning the River Vez nestled in a rich and gentle valley.

* * *

General Baron Friedrich Christian Freiherr von Eben und Brunnen, sitting in nearby Braga, Portugal, was in trouble, and he knew it. The Prussian-born commander of the Loyal Lusitanian Legion, who held a commission in the British Army from King George the Third, had learned that Marshal Soult had invaded Portugal at Chaves, had annihilated a small Portuguese force at Póvoa de Lanhoso just to the east, and was headed straight for Braga and, from there, to Porto.

What is more, he had just watched helplessly as the Portuguese militia in Braga had revolted and lynched his predecessor because he had advocated retreat. Now he was in charge of a rabble of twenty-five thousand Portuguese militia armed with muskets, pikes, and assorted agricultural implements such as scythes, hoes, and spades. His Loyal Lusitanians were few in number and the only professional leaven in the mass. So he was relieved to see Lieutenant Colonel Dom Antonio Perreira with his detachment of Loyal Lusitanians stumble into Braga on a cold and rainy morning, thereby providing reinforcements that more than doubled his core complement of veteran professionals. He determined to try to make a stand against Soult at Braga.

Their arrival had been none too soon, for already the ground shook with Soult's army on the march. Von Eben hastily arrayed his artillery—a dozen and a half light field pieces—to cover the road from Póvoa. He hoped the sight of the guns and the impact of their first volleys might deter Soult. Behind them he placed the thin line of Loyal Lusitanians, with their bayonets fixed, to break or divert any cavalry charge. And in the third layer of defense swarmed the militia, who were to engage the French in hand-to-hand combat to prevent them from investing the town.

Dom Antonio, Garnett, and Seth all stood in the center with the Loyal Lusitanians, waiting.

Seth soon heard the chilling, unmistakable beat of the French drummers hammering "Old Trousers" as Soult's II Corps advanced in column up the road. It grew louder and louder. The Loyal Lusitanians crouched over their guns, hammers cocked, their breaths visible in the cold air. A ripple of movement ran through the line as the soldiers crossed themselves. Seth, whose unsteady right hand gripped his pistol and whose left hand nervously fingered the hilt of his sword, looked at Garnett. His teeth clenched an unlit cigar, and both of his hands clutched loaded and cocked pistols. The drumming grew louder still.

"Don't worry, we'll give 'em as good as we get," Garnett mumbled.

The French drummers and the stomp of boots only grew louder. But the enemy was still not visible to the defenders of Braga.

"I'd say a half mile off," Garnett observed.

Then the drumming ceased.

As Seth turned to Garnett to ask what was happening, all hell broke loose as thousands of *cuirassiers* suddenly unleashed a charge with bugles blaring and horses' hooves pounding the roadbed. Within seconds they were in view, sabers drawn and pointed, helmet plumes flying, and blood-curdling screams on their lips.

The Lusitanians' artillery fired. A few horses and riders went down. But on they came, so quickly that the gunners had no time to reload before the French were upon them, slashing and trampling the artillery-men. The impact of the collision was so severe that the entire Portuguese defensive line buckled. The Loyal Lusitanians held their ground, however, and got off one round at the charging dragoons, dropping a handful. Seth and Garnett both fired their pistols but instantly found themselves knocked flat on the ground by the onslaught. The speed and power with which the French attacked allowed no time for the Lusitanians to jam the butts of their discharged muskets into the ground to set up a protective cordon of steel. The *cuirassiers* simply ran right through them and into the mob of militia, whom they hacked mercilessly.

Seth and Garnett both shook a cloud of disorientation from their heads and regained their feet. They looked about for their fellow Lusitanians. Dom Antonio saw that resistance to such an overwhelming force was futile and that they would only be butchered. He was busy rallying the surviving Lusitanians to try to retreat by a side road, away from the town. Seth and Garnett fell in with them, and in some weak semblance of order they marched at quick time away from the battlefield and into the surrounding hills that lay between Braga and Porto. As soon as they had cleared enough distance to stop in safety, Dom Antonio counted his losses and conferred with his officers.

"We are lucky. I only count five men missing. But we must make Porto as quickly as possible. We'll march straight there with no rest."

All agreed. They regained the main road from Braga to Porto just as a cold, wind-driven rain blew in off the ocean to the west, soaking them to the bone as they marched. The terrain through which they progressed was a rolling one with small family-owned farms delineated by networks of stone walls, spindly stalks of cabbage growing in the fields, elevated wooden corn cribs resting on stilts of granite, and vineyards, everywhere vineyards, many smaller than a single acre, of vines trained along man-high trellises for production of the region's famous young white wine, *vinho verde*. Every so often they spotted gracefully arched stone bridges in the distance spanning the swollen and rushing streams that ran down from the mountains to the east, while along the road a gathering hoard of peasants walking and riding in ox carts began to flee to the relative safety of Porto ahead of Soult's advancing army.

31

The Bridge of Boats

1809—Part II

SETH AND THE LOYAL LUSITANIANS REACHED THE NORTHERN LIMITS of Porto at dusk the following day. The city was in turmoil. Its population teemed with refugees from the surrounding countryside. All through the streets of the upper town people milled about bearing torches against the gathering darkness and jostling one another as they jockeyed for space on the avenues leading to the waterfront. Shopkeepers were busy boarding up their windows, and hand carts, ox carts, and donkey carts rumbled through the streets piled high with personal belongings in a desperate bid to escape the coming onslaught. In the midst of it all, an organ grinder with a monkey wearing a chained rhinestone-studded collar made music.

Midway through the city, amid the thronging refugees and fleeing soldiers, a procession led by a crucifer and comprised of an aged priest in vestments and a half-dozen altar boys exited a chapel and calmly walked up the hill, in harm's way. Seth stopped in his tracks to marvel at the transcendent importance of God's progress through the clamor and strife of the world until he lost sight of the small epiphany.

The Loyal Lusitanians made for the Bishop's Palace overlooking the Douro, which was the command center of the uprising. Dom Antonio, Garnett, and Seth ascended the staircase to the Bishop's office. The high-ceilinged study was strewn with papers, maps, and people. There they found the frenetically pacing cleric dressed in a purple cassock and issuing orders to his minions as they came and went with astonishing rapidity, many of them flushed and breathless, no more than in their twenties. The trio had to wait their turn. At length, the Bishop spotted their presence and turned to them.

"Dom Antonio. Gentlemen. What news do you bring?"

"Braga is falling or has already fallen. We don't know the fate of General von Eben," Dom Antonio responded.

"So it's only a matter of time before Porto is threatened," the Bishop said in a sad, resigned voice.

"That is a safe assumption," Dom Antonio confirmed.

"What plans do you have for defense of the city?" Garnett asked.

"Look here," the Bishop responded as he turned to a map spread out on his desk. "Generals Lima and Parreiras are in command of three battalions of the Portuguese Army, forty-five hundred regulars, spread out along the northern approaches to the city but concentrated on the Braga road. They are supported by ten thousand militia and nine thousand armed civilians."

Garnett looked at the deployments on the map. It looked like a recipe for confusion, but he realized little more could be done under the circumstances.

"Any artillery?"

"One battery across the river on the heights by the Convent to cover the river."

"At Braga," Garnett started to explain, when suddenly there was a rush of cold air and bustle at the door to the Bishop's office. In strode a bloodied, bruised, mud-splattered, and rain-drenched General von Eben with two aides.

"Gentlemen!" the red-cheeked portly Prussian announced. "Braga has fallen! I have ridden straightway here. Our losses are enormous: four thousand Portuguese killed, four hundred captured. All our artillery gone. Our army disintegrated and fleeing. I expect Soult to be here within a matter of days. You must prepare to evacuate Porto. "

"Evacuate or defend?" the perturbed Bishop asked.

"You can try to defend, but against three thousand *cuirassiers* and the whole II Corps . . ." von Eben's voice trailed off.

"We must defend. We've no choice. Besides, there is no route for escape, except by ship, and there's nowhere near the tonnage available to transport the army, much less the refugees who swarm into our city. Don't forget that Porto lies between Soult and the Douro, and there is no bridge to cross the river." He looked out the window at the swollen and surging river below.

"But if only we could get what remains of the Portuguese regulars across and eventually to safety we would live to fight another day. There would be greater numbers, and assistance and reinforcements from England . . ."

"General, General," the Bishop protested with raised right hand, "I don't doubt the logic of what you say, but we have no bridge. There is no way to get across."

Seth crossed the room and looked out at the river below. He spotted the masts of the *Three Brothers* at the far end of the Cais da Ribeira amid a fleet of beamy *rabelo* river craft. Suddenly he had an idea.

"I can build you a bridge," Seth announced.

"I beg your pardon?" the startled Bishop responded.

"I can build you a bridge. It would be a pontoon bridge of boats lashed together and laid with planking for a roadbed. It could stretch from the Cais da Ribeira to Vila Nova da Gaia. You could evacuate the refugees and the army over my bridge."

Seth looked at Dom Antonio and Garnett for validation. Both nodded tentatively, as if to say "Well, it might work . . ."

"Interesting," the Bishop conceded.

"Captain Garnett and I could work with the Loyal Lusitanians to assemble it if you can 'borrow' the *rabelos*, of which there are plenty along the waterfront, and arrange the planking," Dom Antonio offered.

"You must do it. It is the only hope," General von Eben stated emphatically.

"Very well, then, you had better get to work immediately if Soult is knocking at our door."

* * *

That night, working under Seth's direction and by the light of burning torches that reflected on the water, the Loyal Lusitanians began to construct a bridge, laboriously and one boat at a time. Seth initiated the project by removing the kedge anchor and extra line from the *Three Brothers* and asking to be rowed to the middle of the river.

"This will be the reference point," he announced as he swung the anchor overboard and paid out the line until it grappled the riverbed and held fast. After being rowed back to the Cais da Ribeira, they started by anchoring the line and the bridge along which it would be built to the stanchions that lined the quay. They brought the first boat up, tied it to the line, and secured it to the stanchions with cables. They then extended the bridge out into the stream by dragging up and aligning one boat after another and tying them together with stout ropes. From every third boat they dropped smaller anchors upstream to steady the floating bridge against the strain of the swollen current. More than once the churning river swept away the boat with which they were working, and the growing string of boats swung out in a precarious, straining arc that threatened to snap at any moment. But at last they completed the chain, anchored it to the opposite shore, and laid the planking. It was past four o'clock the next afternoon. Seth walked the bridge to test its soundness. Although taking considerable pressure from the rapid river, it held tight. Dom Antonio and Garnett agreed that, treated properly, it would serve.

The thousands of refugees who had fled to the waterfront began to cross immediately. Before departing with Captain Garnett for the line of defense on the northern limits of the city, Dom Antonio stationed a small detachment of Loyal Lusitanians to maintain order and ensure that all the refugees did not mount the bridge at once and swamp it. Slowly the city began to drain itself of the pent-up masses of people and belongings that had congested its streets.

That night the Loyal Lusitanians encamped under the stone arches of the warehouses that lined the quay, and Seth fell into bed exhausted in his own cabin aboard the *Three Brothers*.

In the ensuing days Seth supervised the unlading of his cargo in a cold, driving rain. He was particularly glad to be rid of the gunpowder. In return he shipped various military supplies that the army wanted removed to Lisbon for safekeeping, and he began to take on, as paying passengers, some of the more well-to-do citizens who wanted to evacuate to the capital. He tarried to complete the lading of the ship and intended to destroy the bridge and weigh anchor at the last minute before the city fell.

Porto remained a nervous city as it awaited the expected assault from the north. Rumors of an impending attack swept the city every day. The procession of people and vehicles crossing the bridge of boats never ceased during the daylight hours: a steady line of people huddled against the rain threading their way precariously across the bridge to safety. Each day, twice a day, Seth checked the cables that held it to either shore and ventured out onto the bridge to test the anchor lines and lashings that held the boats together. So things continued for five days.

On the sixth day Seth was awakened before dawn by a thunderous cannonade from north of the city. It shook the ground and echoed off the amphitheater formed by the steep hills on either side of the Douro. He realized instantly that the action had started and that Soult was pounding the city's defenses with artillery before attacking. Within minutes the first waves of new civilian refugees began pouring onto the Cais da Ribeira to cross the river. The cannonade lasted over an hour, and the frantic mob on the waterfront swelled to enormous size so that people were backed up into the streets leading up into the town, all clamoring to cross. The Loyal Lusitanians stationed at the head of the bridge struggled to maintain order. Seth paced back and forth the length of the bridge keeping a close eye on its integrity as the civilians pushed and shoved their way across.

From his vantage point at sea level Seth could not see what was transpiring in the northern outskirts of the city. In fact, in a reprise of the action at Braga, Soult hurled the full force of his three thousand *cuirassiers* under Franceschi, de la Houssaye, Merle, Heudelet, and Mermet at the weakest point in the Portuguese lines. The Portuguese force rapidly dissolved, and what was supposed to be a battle degenerated into a rout as twenty-five thousand soldiers, militia, and armed civilians fled in great confusion back into the city. The *cuirassiers* chased them through the streets, cutting them down right and left, and the rout turned into a massacre.

The first of the fleeing units to reach the Cais da Ribeira were mounted Portuguese militia soldiers. They came shouting, waving their swords, and cursing the civilians to move aside. They ran down those who did not comply.

At the same time the Portuguese artillery battery atop the hills opposite opened fire, apparently aiming at the pursuing French forces within the town on whom they had fixed a bead. Cannon balls flew overhead while chaos reigned on the quay below, all as sheets of rain off the ocean drenched the scene and engorged the river to the bursting point.

The horse soldiers forced their way onto the pontoon bridge, already crowded with civilians. The Loyal Lusitanians guarding the bridge ran onto the span after them shouting "Stop! Stop!" as they continued to plow through the lines of refugees attempting to cross. Midway on the bridge, Seth instantly saw the danger and positioned himself to block their advance, all the while waving his arms and screaming at the lead horseman to stop: *"Pare-se! Va embora! Va embora!"*

Panicked by the horse soldiers, more refugees poured onto the bridge in a mob, all clamoring to get on, shouting and screaming and waving their arms. The bridge began to rock and sway.

Still the horsemen plowed forward, oblivious to the entreaties or to the obvious danger they posed.

Then the inevitable happened. The rocking became so violent that several pedestrians lost their footing and fell into the river, where the churning brown water instantly swept them away. Seeing this, the crowd on the bridge began to scream in terror.

The rocking and swaying continued. The shearing force of the current began to exert itself on the bridge. Seth held his breath. Seconds later Seth heard a sharp crack. Then he heard a deep groaning noise. It accelerated and drowned out the screams, as the lashings holding the boats together broke in sequence up and down the length of the span and the entire bridge burst apart with a violence so sharp that it capsized many of the boats and hurled the planking, boats, persons, and animals on the bridge at that instant into the surging current.

As Seth went over, he saw horses flailing, human arms grabbing into the air but finding no purchase and large planks tossed by the river and striking people in the head as they struggled against the current.

Seth fought to keep his head up and make for shore. But with the river almost at flood stage a powerful undertow kept sucking him downward. He struggled against it and surfaced once more. He managed to surface his head to clear his lungs with a draught of fresh air. His thoughts raced by as to what meant most to him in his life.

"Fid! Fid!" he gasped.

"Georgette!" he cried.

His wife's name was the final word on his lips as the current sucked him under again. He never resurfaced. The river carried him downstream, across the bar at the Foz, and into the effacing enormity of the Atlantic Ocean which embraced him.

* * *

News of Seth's death reached Georgette in London a week later when the *Three Brothers* docked at Canary Wharf. She immediately wrote Adam of the news. Inconsolable, Georgette never remarried during the long life that it was her lot to have, sustained by unending interest earned on Lord Hormsby's vast portfolio of Consols.

A little over three weeks after the collapse of the bridge of boats, Sir Arthur Wellesley landed at Lisbon, retook Porto, crossed the Douro at the site of the earlier disaster, defeated Soult, and at the head of a combined Anglo-Portuguese army launched a four-year campaign that drove the French from the Iberian Peninsula and caused Napoleon to abdicate. Dom Antonio Perreira lost his lower right leg to a French cannon ball at the second battle of Porto but, invalided, survived the war to become a major force in the port wine industry. Captain Tayloe Garnett fought with Wellesley across Iberia. Following a string of battlefield promotions, Brevet Brigadier General Garnett died from bayonet wounds in the fierce fighting at Hougoumont during the Battle of Waterloo. His fate was shared by the Dutchman, who served as an aide to Prince William of Orange and who was killed by a stray French bullet later the same day.

32

Facing the Abyss
1809—Part III

ADAM LET SLIP THE KNOT THAT TETHERED HIS GAFF-RIGGED CATBOAT to the Union Wharf. He was in the company of his old friend, the day sailer with whom he had spent so many hours sailing about Casco Bay. When alone in the boat he often talked to himself, well, to the boat really, as if it were an old friend. It was a mild eccentricity and one forgivable in a Captain who treated vessels as if they were women. This time, how-ever, Adam sailed in silence. It was a sparkling day in late May with the sun rising high in the east and glimmering off the gentle waters. A fresh breeze filled the sail, and the boat heeled as it gathered speed. A fine spray of salt water caught Adam in the face. He licked his lips and bore on with his right hand on the tiller. He cleared the harbor and headed straight for Diamond Island Pass which ran between Great Diamond and Peaks Island. He sailed past Pumpkin Knob and Soldier Ledge, all familiar bearings. He headed into the Hussey and through the Green Island Passage. He pushed further still, until he reached Halfway Rock, a barren outcropping where gentle Casco Bay kisses the brusque North Atlantic: the edge of the abyss. He lowered his sail and dropped anchor in the lee of the Rock. He was alone in a marine amphitheater surrounded at a distance by the islands and promontories mantled in thick green pine trees. He sat in silence at the realization that he was but the latest inductee into the reluctant spiritual club of parents who outlive their children, a club with many rituals but with no *bonhommie* and no meeting house but in the lonely prison cells of the minds of its members.

Adam waited for an answer to the question that he held in his heart. He waited patiently.

No answer came. The tomblike silence of the watery wilderness enveloped and smothered him.

Adam strained his ear to hear. Perhaps he was not listening properly. Still, nothing.

Was God absent, hidden, or simply silent? Adam did not even know which. He yearned to receive a revelation. He was, if nothing, receptive.

Adam began to grow agitated. He spoke, softly at first.

"Why, God? Why me? Why did this happen to me? It cannot be punishment for my sins, for I have few. Have I not loved you all my life and walked in your ways? Haven't I striven to lead a blameless life?"

Only the gentle slosh of the waves against the hull as the boat rocked at anchor whispered back in mockery.

"God! Do you not hear me? Why don't you answer?" Adam pleaded peremptorily.

Still, nothing.

Adam withdrew his Bible from his pocket and angrily tore the pages open to the 17th Psalm. He read aloud:

"Hear the right, O Lord, attend unto my cry, give ear unto my prayer, that goeth not out of feigned lips.

Let my sentence come forth from thy presence; let thine eyes behold the things that are equal.

Thou hast proved mine heart; thou hast visited me in the night; thou hast tried me, and shalt find nothing; I am purposed that my mouth shall not transgress.

Concerning the works of men, by the word of thy lips I have kept me from the paths of the destroyer.

Hold up my goings in thy paths, that my footsteps slip not.

I have called upon thee, for thou wilt hear me, O God: incline thine ear unto me, and hear my speech."

He closed the book and waited. No answer came.

Adam sank back into the cockpit of his boat and wept for his son and for himself. Had he not in fact sacrificed his son by opening the mast trade with England? Even the most well-intended actions eventually have lethal consequences. And was it for this sin that God punished him by not responding?

Then Adam had the harshest insight: the silence of God to the last words on the Cross: "My God, my God, why hast thou forsaken me?"

Would Adam now, at long last, fall into the abyss of faithlessness?

33

The Guano Voyage and Stepmother Dear

1810–1811

ADAM FACED A PANEL OF BLACK-SUITED BOSTON INVESTORS WHO SAT before him like a flock of crows.

"The opening of the Ohio lands to settlement provides a need for fertilizer," one of the investors explained. "That means there is a market for guano from Peru."

"Guano?" Adam replied with curled lips at the thought of a cargo almost as inglorious and unaesthetic as whale blubber. "Is there no prospect of a voyage to the Indies?"

"They remain closed. Guano can be highly profitable. There's a trade opening up there. Why, Captain Colby from Salem has already been out and back with three ships and to great profit. "

Adam well knew the backdrop. Congress repealed the Embargo Act in 1809 because of its predictably disastrous effects on the economy. However, three days before Jefferson left the Presidency he signed the Non-Intercourse Act to replace it. This Act allowed trade with all countries other than England and France or territories they controlled. It did little to alleviate Adam's economic bind or that of most Portland merchants and Captains. Still, it provided some small glimmer of hope as the New England merchant class sought to get their ships to sea again. In Adam's case the pickings were slim.

"Well, guano it is then, I reckon. My ship is a timber hauler, but I suppose she'll serve."

"Actually, Captain Hale, she's rather old, and this voyage entails two passages of Cape Horn. We cannot take the risk with an old vessel like the *Atheling*. We were thinking more along the lines of a newer ship, of which there are many sitting idle."

Adam did not take the insult to his ship lightly but decided it would be impolitic to protest.

"Well, then, if not my ship, what is my role to be?"

"A contract Captain, to be sure. With your experience . . ."

"Gentlemen," Adam cut off the discussion as he raised his hand. "I've never served as a contract Captain before. I would have to think about this."

"We'll make it worth your while. But if you decide you'd rather pass, there's no shortage of other experienced Captains in Portland and elsewhere who'd leap at the chance."

"I will have to get back to you on this," Adam grumbled at the twinned thoughts of the truth of their statements and of his helplessness before the buffeting waves of economic adversity. Still, he was determined to get back on his feet, and he knew in his heart that, at age sixty-one, he had no choice other than to accept the offer.

* * *

"I like a happy medium," Bathsheba Sewell explained to Hephzibah as the two of them sat on the edge of the bed in Hephzibah's spacious, light-filled corner bedroom on the second floor. Bathsheba had grown gaunt following her pregnancy and the birth of Henry, and a hardness that never left had settled in about her eyes and at the corners of her mouth. Her earlier beauty had proved fleeting. Her mien was reinforced by the black silk long-sleeved, ankle-length dress she wore with a small gold pocket watch pinned to the left breast and a belt cinched about her waist from which dangled a handful of keys, like some sort of latter-day chatelaine. In contrast, Hephzibah had grown plump from overeating as she tried to cope with the grief attendant upon the death of her mother and the shock of her father's remarriage and the birth of a half-brother.

"As I said, I like a happy medium. It is therefore my duty to tell you that there are to be changes made around here to achieve that end. Things are different now. I am fed up with your lounging about like a little princess. There are schools in England and France for children like you. It is my regret that we haven't one available here. As it is, stuck in this wilderness, we will simply have to make do."

"But Papa . . ."

"Papa is busy at work, and I am in charge of the house. Now that Henry is two, he no longer needs to share our bedroom. Henry will be moving into this room starting tonight."

"But where am I to sleep?"

"You will move to the spare room between the pantry and kitchen on the ground floor, near the room that the two servant girls share."

Hephzibah knew the room well. It was hardly large enough to accommodate a single bed, chair, and dresser. It was lit by one small, high window.

"What's more, you will have duties, which will make your placement there all the more appropriate and convenient. Each morning you will arise at five o'clock to kindle the fire in the kitchen. Every third day you will remove the ashes. Each evening, after supper, you will work with the servant girls to wash and dry the pots and dishes. This will not interfere with your schoolwork, as they will occur at either end of the day. Of course we will pay you for these chores. A penny a day. You will learn thrift as well as industry."

"But Bathsheba—"

"That brings me to two simple rules. First, the name Bathsheba is never to issue from your lips again. Henceforward you are to refer to me as 'Stepmother Dear.' Second, you are to confine yourself to the ground floor of the house in your room and the kitchen area, excepting the dining room for meals, unless summoned by name. You are not to be seen when guests call. Do you understand?"

"Yes, Bath . . . Stepmother Dear," she mumbled half-comprehendingly.

"Good. I will now give you a taste of what will happen if you don't follow the rules. The choice is yours. It is entirely in your hands. Now take this," she ordered as she produced a coin silver tablespoon and glass vial from her pocket and poured a spoonful of a yellow oily substance.

"What is it?" Hephzibah asked.

"What is it, *Stepmother Dear*. Castor oil. Now drink it."

Hephzibah brought the spoon to her mouth and ingested the noxious oil. She wanted to spit it out and vomit.

"Don't spit it out. Drink it. Drink all of it."

She did as ordered.

"Good. Now I think we have the basis for a happy medium in this household."

* * *

"We have to do something!" Nabby exclaimed in an uncustomary furor as Adam packed his sea chest. "Hephzibah's treated as little more than a scullery maid."

Adam slowly folded a shirt and placed it on top of his sextant before answering.

"I know. The question is what to do. We've no legal right to interfere. I've already consulted with Attorney Longfellow about it. Our rights are limited and truly secondary as we are not the parents."

"Perhaps we could pay for her education and thereby gain a right?"

"With what? I'm in narrow straits, as you know. I've already pledged my compensation from the guano voyage as surety for bills to purchase dry goods to restock our store in anticipation of better times. But until then . . ."

"The guano voyage! Don't even talk to me of the guano voyage! Here you are leaving home when our granddaughter needs us."

"I'll be back in six to eight months. Can you not deal with it in the meantime?"

"How so, dear husband?"

"I don't know. Insinuate yourself somehow."

Adam folded his breeches and stockings and laid them in his chest alongside the case holding his two pistols and their accoutrements.

"I must make this voyage, you understand. Otherwise, we've no hope of regaining our fortune."

"I know," a subdued Nabby replied as she looked at the floor. "It's just that I worry so. Family is so dear to me."

Moved, Adam embraced her in his arms and kissed her forehead.

"And to me too. Especially after all we've lost. Hephzibah is all we have. Know I'll be back as quickly as I can and that then we'll be in a better position to devise a plan."

"I pray so."

"I shall miss you dearly."

"And I you."

* * *

The days of Adam's absence passed slowly for Nabby. Each day she took her customary walk atop Munjoy Hill overlooking Casco Bay and made a point of strolling past the Sewell house on her return. As tempted as she was to knock on the door, she knew she would gain no admittance or at best a hurried and uncomfortable sit-down in the parlor with Bathsheba straining at a stilted conversation and in a rush to have her leave. So she walked on, wondering what was transpiring inside the house.

One prerogative Nabby refused to surrender, however, was picking up Hephzibah each Sunday morning for church and dinner at her house, just as she and Adam had done since the child was little. Each Sunday she stretched these visits a little longer, as Hephzibah was in no hurry to leave and she was in no hurry to have her go. They would sit by the fire in the parlor, often in silence, working at needlepoint, a gentlewomanly art in which Nabby encouraged her granddaughter. After a month or so of this shared company, it occurred to Nabby to interest and instruct her granddaughter in her own family history. And so, as they sat by the fire with the tall case clock ticking away the seconds, she began to recount the heritage to which Hephzibah was heir. She told tales of the Siege of Louisburg in '45 and of her uncle Nathaniel Bacon who was a Lieutenant in Rogers' Rangers during the French and Indian War and who skated the length of Lake Champlain with his musket slung across his back and who fought at the Battle of the Snowshoes and witnessed the massacre at Fort Edward. She told stories of her aunt, Priscilla Bacon, who had emigrated with her husband to western Massachusetts, only to be captured during an Indian raid and marched through the winter snows to Quebec where she worked as a slave to the French nuns at a convent for two years before making her escape aboard a visiting merchant ship which brought her home to Cape Cod. She told of Bacons who ran the British blockade during the Revolution and of the disastrous Battle of the Penobscot in which her brother had captained a ship. She told hazier stories of her emigrant ancestor Deacon Philemon Bacon and of her family back in Old England. Some of these tales were twice told or more and embroidered more than the needlework on which she toiled as she spoke, but they were all grounded in truth, and it was essential for Hephzibah to know the truth in order to know her own self.

After several months of this weekly Sabbath monologue Hephzibah raised an interesting question.

"Grandmama, I enjoy history at school. And languages. Maybe someday I'll be able to read Latin and Greek like Grandpapa. But in the meantime, do you think I might be able to borrow some of Grandpapa's history books?"

A faint smile crept across Nabby's face. The seed had germinated.

"I think he'd like you to," she advised as she went to the secretary that stood against the far wall. "Hmm . . . why don't you start with this? Caesar's *The Conquest of Gaul*. It is an English translation. It is short, and he writes very well and clearly too."

She handed her the well-thumbed volume, fully aware of the seditious undercurrent of intellectual inquiry.

"I've never read such a serious book before," Hephzibah acknowledged.

"Not to worry. You can do it. And when you have, bring it back and tell me about it. There are many more here that await you. Caesar's *The Civil War*. Tacitus's *The Histories*. And one of Grandpapa's favorites, Seneca's *Letters from a Stoic*. The world awaits you."

In addition, consistent with her husband's admonition to "insinuate" herself, Nabby enlisted the help of the Widow Gookin. The Widow Gookin, a prominent widow of means who had time on her hands, was the neighborhood busybody. Nabby conspired with her to call on Bathsheba from time to time and to report to her on what was transpiring within the house. Nabby calculated that Bathesheba would never turn away a lady of the Widow Gookin's standing. Nor did she. The Widow Gookin invented pretexts to call on Bathsheba every several weeks, and her reports provided complementary insights into what went on behind closed doors—observations to which Hephzibah, at age nine, would have been oblivious. Her reports only confirmed the basis for Nabby's concerns and cemented her determination to free her granddaughter from Bathsheba's domain.

* * *

"All hands ahoy!" Adam shouted from the quarterdeck of the sprightly and aptly named brig *Hercules* as she beat against the prevailing winds and garrulous head sea, making slow progress on his maiden westbound rounding of Cape Horn. Before him loomed a mass of black clouds rolling toward the ship from the west. "I think we've arrived!" he shouted to his Mate.

Already the churning gray water in the Drake Passage, where Atlantic meets Pacific, was heaving in waves that drenched the bow of the ship with each roll and in vortexes that spun counterclockwise. Adam had previously taken the precaution of close reefing his mainsails and topsails and was proceeding only under his jibs: such was the reality of the "Furious Fifties" prevailing winds as he drove the ship to latitude 56 degrees south to round the Horn. On the advice of several old China trade hands he had consulted at home before undertaking the voyage he had steered well clear of Cape Horn and was far out into the five-hundred-mile passage to allow greater room for maneuver as the winds changed.

The black clouds rapidly descended on the ship, bringing with them gale-force winds and mounting waves that combined with the surging eastward current through the Drake Passage to make the progress of the pitching and lolling brig all but imperceptible. Adam wondered how the great Elizabethan seafarer had made the passage in his tiny high-castled vessel. He told himself he could have it worse.

Worse soon came as the mass of brutish clouds unleashed torrents of sleet. Adam, his Mate, and his helmsman donned oilskin slickers but remained at their stations as they plowed slowly forward and kept the lookout for icebergs, which even in the summer at this far southern latitude posed a hazard.

The sleet froze as it hit the deck, and soon the entire ship—masts, spars, rigging, and deck—was encased in a covering of ice. Each roll of the oncoming waves plunged the forward part of the ship underwater, and the sea poured in through the bow ports and hawse-hole threatening to wash overboard everything that was not tied down. Even the salt water began to freeze and locked the bow in an ever-thickening case of ice. The violent lunges of the ship and the slipperiness of the deck caused the three experienced sailors to hang on for their lives.

And so it continued for four hours until the light began to seep from the day. During the long and dangerous hours Adam reminded himself that the voyage would be worth the trouble because when he returned before Christmas his warehouse would already be full with the newly purchased goods he had bought on credit and he would be the first with the most to meet the demands of consumers and take advantage of the reawakening New England economy.

"Iceberg portside!" shouted the Mate above the howling of the wind as dusk began to settle over the Passage.

Adam snapped open his telescope. Sure enough, not a mile or two distant but well clear of the ship, looming in the dwindling light rode a massive blue-gray shard of ice.

"We'll have to keep a close eye all night," Adam shouted to his Mate and helmsman.

By the fifth hour, as darkness replaced dusk, Adam noticed the winds abating. The sleet stopped, and the sea, though still churning, threw waves of diminishing size against the hull of the brig. The storm had passed.

* * *

"I've finished *The Conquest of Gaul*," Hephzibah announced when she handed the book back to Nabby two months later.

"I'm so proud of you for having read it. Might I ask: did you enjoy it?"

"Parts of it. I've never read such a book before."

"But you've read it, and that's to be celebrated."

"Yes, I suppose so. In fact, I enjoyed it and would like to read more."

"Can you tell me what you enjoyed most?"

"In truth, Grandmama, I'd like to, but we are late for church, and it's a beautiful day. I'd like for you to swing me in the old swing in the churchyard if we have time. It reminds me of when you and Grandpapa did that when I was little."

"Certainly, my dear, we will have time. We can discuss books later when we get home. I've baked you a special treat, Indian pudding, for dinner. Now come along. As you say, we are late."

* * *

Adam collected the cargo of guano from an island off the coast of Peru in good time and headed back southward through the Roaring Forties and into the Furious Fifties for his second, return passage of Cape Horn. Only this time he was anxious to arrive home, and he navigated closer to the Horn. Even though he was now rounding the Horn in late summer at that latitude, the current and prevailing winds were with him, and the *Hercules* maneuvered through the gale-force winds and frolicsome sea without incident. By now the Drake Passage was littered with ice floes, so he ordered the watch to keep an especially alert lookout for impending danger.

The passage was quick given the winds and current. Under cloudy gray skies the brig rounded the Horn within sight of the craggy, inhospitable, weather-beaten rocky promontory of the Cape that jutted into the ocean. Adam paused to admire it if only to be able to say he had seen it. In truth, he found it disappointing. It hardly compared to the Rock of Gibraltar or other sights he had seen in a lifetime of sailing. He shrugged and turned back to checking the set of the sails aloft. Perhaps he had become jaded with age and harder to impress, he told himself. If so, so be it, he concluded.

* * *

"Fire! Fire! Fire!" the boys shouted, running through the town.

Adam roused himself from the drifts of sleep. It was the wee hours of a frigid morning not long after Adam's return from Peru, and he had allowed himself a late night and extra glass of toddy the evening before.

Still wearing his night shirt, he bundled himself into his woolen greatcoat and stiffly descended the staircase. He saw neighbors spilling out their doors and everyone running toward the waterfront. For good measure he swept the Turkey carpet off the dining table and wrapped it about his shoulders as he headed out into the frozen night. As he did, he noticed that the tall case clock by the door struck four o'clock in the morning.

The mob raced swiftly down Center Street, which was piled high with banks of snow on either side. Adam pursued them riding a wave of adrenalin and curiosity as to what was afoot. He could see the glow from the waterfront illuminating the nighttime sky. At the foot of Center Street the mob took Adam with it as it turned eastward onto Fore Street. There Adam stopped, riveted by the scene: eight blocks of warehouses, including his own, ablaze while hundreds of panicked people milled about shouting or just staring. The flames licked high above the roof of his store, sending sparks flying over the town. The inferno shown through what was left of the windows in his brick building and cast a glow over the faces of all present witnessing, while a fireborne wind sucked in off the harbor to fuel the contagion. Adam spotted the town's sole horse-drawn fire engine trying to reach the destruction, but the shoulder-high piles of snow impeded its progress. At length, the fire brigade stopped the engine short of its goal and started working the two parallel pump handles, but the streams of water it ejected fell short of the buildings and began to freeze as they spread out on the street. From somewhere up the hill a bucket brigade began to form, and leather fire buckets began to snake their way down to the scene of destruction. But there was little they could do to quench the raging flames. Adam quickly calculated his storehouse a total loss, together with the wealth of all held in it. Meanwhile the flames moved further up Fore Street to a warehouse holding paint, and the night sky took on garish tones of copper, blue, and yellow as the paint fed the fire and bathed the scene in the mockery of a rainbow.

Adam stood like a post staring at the conflagration until the morning's first light showed the fire burning itself out once it had finished gutting the adjoining buildings and had reached open space. Adam's storehouse stood a smoldering ruin with its walls still standing but its interior and collapsed roof a charnel house of ash and blackened timbers.

With hunched shoulders and his head buried beneath the folds of the Turkey carpet he slowly made his way back up the hill to tell Nabby of his utter loss. God evidently had not finished playing with him yet.

* * *

The new year of 1811 brought little solace to Adam.

"I'm destitute, broken," he explained to Nabby once he had added up his losses from the fire. "I had not yet purchased insurance on the inventory when the fire came. All is lost. The entire guano voyage was for naught. . . . All my life's work has been for naught."

"So you would give up hope?"

Startled, Adam thought for a moment. God had played havoc with his life. But it was still his life and, as such, precious beyond all measure. Adam's faith, though buffeted and battered, still somehow survived or so he told himself. Though his hope of reward in this life had dwindled, it was not extinguished. And quite apart from that, for a person of faith, there remained the overwhelming promise of the Resurrection.

"No, as long as there is life and faith, my hope remains. As long as I am able, I will have hope," he responded. "Even if I go down to the grave I will sing 'Alleluia.' But there will have to be changes. I have debts I cannot meet. We will have no choice but to sell the house."

Nabby winced.

"Perhaps you could ask Major Sewell for a loan?"

"Never."

"Oh stubborn pride, good husband."

"Perhaps."

"So what are we to do?"

"Sell the house in town and move to Back Cove. Life will be simpler there. I can cultivate my garden. The sweet peas and day lilies will be in full fettle by July."

"But what of Hephzibah? By retiring there we'll lose what little purchase we have to look after her welfare."

"I'll grant you that's a dilemma. But somehow we'll devise a way. I'm pleased with how she's taken to reading from my library. And there'll still be Sundays, even if we have to drive in from the country. We'll find a way. We'll have to find a way."

* * *

Major Gideon Sewell spent much of the year traveling, first to Boston and later to New York and Philadelphia. In each city he met with other merchants and bankers, and slowly the idea began to take shape in his mind that Portland needed its own commercial bank. As he analyzed the need, the bank would increase the opportunity for wealthy persons, such as himself, to involve themselves in entrepreneurial projects which they would not otherwise undertake in the absence of a guarantee on their investment, while at the same time assisting entrepreneurs who did not have sufficient wealth to fund their own investments.

The challenge for Major Sewell was twofold. First, he had to assemble a pool of shareholders to provide the initial funding for the bank before it could even begin to take deposits. Second, he had to convince the state legislature to charter the bank. The first proved the easier of the two, as he lined up potential backers in each city he visited, as well as among those Portland merchants who had survived the depression and were poised to profit from the anticipated recovery. The second was a greater challenge because it required political skill. For over a month he walked the corridors of the State House in Boston with his proposal in hand and his list of subscribers in his pocket trying to convince the legislators to back his plan. At length he found a champion in a pliable delegate who agreed to sponsor the legislation in exchange for a minority share in the bank. But the political lifting was not easy because many in Boston were uneasy with the idea of establishing a bank just one hundred miles to the north that would compete with their own financial institutions. To them the District of Maine was always, and remained, a backward wilderness to be plundered and given short shrift.

However, his persistence paid off. By the autumn he had lined up the requisite support to move the legislation forward. He returned to Boston for a final appeal and, with lavish meals and freely flowing rum, he convinced the legislators that the bank would redound to their benefit and to that of Massachusetts writ large.

And so was born the Bank of Portland and the career of Major Gideon Sewell as controlling shareholder in the city's first bank as well as merchant and distiller.

34

Duty

1812–1813—Part I

"Gentlemen, our situation is dire," Commodore John Rodgers of the United States Navy announced to the Portland Captains and ship owners assembled in the pews of the First Parish Church. Their mood was boisterous and angry. "Our republic has only three frigates, one of which, the *President*, I command, and nine smaller men-of-war and a handful of revenue cutters. Eighteen vessels in all. Plus one hundred and sixty-five coastal gunboats. The Royal Navy has over one thousand warships, up to and including one hundred and fifty-four massive ships of the line."

"An' whose fault is that?" piped one Captain. "Well, I'll tell you. It all lies at the feet of Mr. Jefferson." The crowd mumbled their assent. "First the embargo of '07 and then the refusal to build a real Navy. Those gunboats with their single swivel gun and shallow draft—the 'mosquito fleet' we call them—can only be used in coastal waters and even then they swamp and are next to useless."

"Here, here," the crowd shouted as they beat the pews with the palms of their hands. Commodore Rodgers stood impassively at the lectern.

"We didn't ask for this war," shouted a ship owner as he stood up and punched the air with his forefinger. "This is all the work of those Southerners and Westerners. Didn't they stop to think that the British so outgun us before they declared war?"

"Gentlemen, gentlemen," Commodore Rodgers reassured them, "I come here not to debate the merits of past policy or the fact of the war but to arrange for our defense. There is much that needs to be done, and with the Navy so small we must work with *you* to do it. Coastal fortifications need to be inspected and upgraded. Letters of marque need to be issued—I understand that the collector of the port, Mr. Isaac Ilsley, is ready to issue them. And private cruisers need to be found or built to protect our coast and fisheries. There is much to be done and not a moment to lose."

The grumbling of the crowd subsided and the assembled Captains and owners became attentive.

"First, you will need to elect a leader to undertake the direction of these endeavors and then empanel a committee to see that they are done. My orders are not to leave this meeting without that leader chosen. So, gentlemen, please proceed."

The Captains and owners began to talk among themselves in hushed tones, and then they broke into huddled groups as they conferred. Adam Hale hung back, judging that at age sixty-three this was better a decision left to the younger members of the community. The groups dissolved and re-formed so that all present had a say within the hearing of each other. After a half hour, Captain Titcomb stepped forward as spokesman.

"Commodore, we have a recommendation for the task—if he will have it."

"Very good, gentlemen, who might that be?"

"Captain Adam Hale, sir."

All eyes in the church pivoted to Adam.

Captain Titcomb continued. "Captain Hale is known and respected by all present. He has sailed these waters since before the Revolution. He knows gunnery and has fought and defeated the British and Barbary pirates. His brig the *Atheling*, though old, is one of Portland's most seaworthy craft and a fast one too. She was fitted out as a privateer and boasts fourteen six-pounders and two bow-chasers. His seamanship is legendary. And he deals fairly."

Adam's face reddened.

"Yes, yes, I well know of Captain Hale," Commodore Rodgers responded. "I believe I see him sitting in the back pew. So, Captain Hale, what say you?"

Adam grew flustered at the attention and groped for words.

"Thank you. Thank you. . . . I . . . don't know what to say. I had not expected this. I'd have to think . . ." He felt ambiguity grip his soul. If only things could be so black and white. There were nuances and shadings to all that was being asked of him and to his role in it.

"Commodore Rodgers, may I speak with you privately?" he stammered.

"Certainly, Captain. Join me in the parson's study."

Once in the adjoining office and with the door closed, Adam unburdened himself.

"I am most flattered by the attentions of my fellow citizens, to be sure, but this war was not of my choosing. I would rather trade with England than fight her."

"I understand, spoken like a good New Englander," the Maryland-born Rodgers said. "But the war has arrived, like it or not, and this is a question of defense of the homeland. With that surely you have no quarrel."

"No, most certainly not. But I have often voyaged to England and there I made my largest market for our timbers. I have friends in that land. And my late son Seth married an English woman and for all intents and purposes became one of them. He died fighting for them."

Commodore Rodgers cast an empathetic gaze at Adam and rocked back and forth on his feet. Adam was struck by his high, intelligent forehead, unruly curly hair, and ruddy Celtic complexion. At length he spoke.

"Captain Hale, you don't know, do you?"

"Know what?"

"About your son Seth."

"I'm sorry, Commodore?" Adam responded shaking his head.

"Well, I shouldn't reveal confidential information, but in this instance I feel it justified. Your son, sir, was an American intelligence officer of the voluntary sort, long reporting to our Minister in London. When he died, he was on a secret mission at the direction of our government. His reporting was invaluable and of many years' duration."

Adam fell back in shock.

"So he never forsake America?"

"No, sir. Never. He was in fact an American patriot."

"Oh, my! Oh, my!" Adam sputtered as he felt his soul warm within him. What a final parting gift from the watery grave of his most beloved son.

At once shamed by Seth's call to action and ashamed at himself for ever doubting him, Adam looked the Commodore in the eye and without hesitation spoke:

"I accept."

* * *

The ensuing six months were a beehive of activity for Adam. Arising before first light, he was pacing the docks and Fore Street by sunrise. He had no trouble empaneling his committee. Together, they conducted an inventory of available ships in Portland and its vicinity. To their chagrin, they found only one beside the *Atheling* fit for duty as a privateer. She was the *Rapid*, of one hundred and ninety tons, a full-rigged brig with standing royals and flying kites. They ordered Mr. Moulton the shipbuilder on Fore Street to convert her into a privateer to carry fifteen guns and one hundred men. She set sail under Captain William Crabtree and made several short cruises with no success. Overburdened by her heavy battery, she was soon overcome by a fast-sailing British frigate and captured. The committee next determined to build a fleet of Portland privateers from scratch. Centering their activities at Clay Cove, which became known as "Gunboat Dock," they laid the keels for a squadron of fast schooners, including the three-master *Dart*, whose masts—upon Adam's insistence—were jointed above deck so that they could be dropped like those of a canal boat in order to hide from an enemy in a cove or at sea.

But that was not all that Adam directed. Working with the Portland Rifle Company, Adam undertook to upgrade the fortifications about the Neck, starting with the battery at Jordan's Point. Adam published a notification that all patriotic citizens were to assemble on an appointed day at Jordan's Point and to bring a pickaxe, crowbar, spade, shovel, or hoe. A week later more than a hundred citizens from Back Cove and inland marched into town to give a day's work on the battery, some of them bringing their teams of oxen. The task assumed a carnival air. On seeing the men marching into town, the town's leading merchants and ministers, led by Captain Adam Hale, shouldered their own entrenching tools and marched through the town gathering recruits as they passed. As the volunteers threw up the ramparts, the carpenters of the town constructed platforms for the cannon.

They also fortified Spring Point, where they erected an eight-gun octagonal blockhouse, sheathed in clapboard, painted white, and surmounted by a carved wooden eagle with spreading wings.

Fearful of an invasion, the ladies of the town were set to work making bandages and wadding for the cannon. Lead ingots were ordered up from Boston, and all citizens with molds set to making bullets.

No detail was overlooked. Adam saw to it that Captain Moody, the keeper of Portland Observatory, mounted a dawn-to-dusk seaward watch with the most powerful telescopes in town. He did the same at Portland Headlight and set up a line of signal fires along the coast to warn of any approaching British fleet, just as he had read the British themselves did to warn of the approaching Spanish Armada.

And then the town held its breath and waited.

Despite the blockade that the Royal Navy had thrown up along the coast of the United States, the big, fast, American forty-four-gun frigates occasionally broke from port and made it to the high seas to seek out, attack, and rain havoc on the enemy. Word began to filter into town of a string of successful single-ship actions. First the *Constitution* capturing the *Guerrière*. Next the *Wasp* capturing the *Frolic*. Then the *United States* capturing the *Macedonian*. And then the *Constitution* taking the *Java*. Against all odds, the nascent United States Navy was taking on the dominant naval force in the world. And as a consequence, spirits in Portland began to lift. Though the *Atheling* remained at cable in the harbor, the town's rapidly built privateers were launched and fitted out and sailed past her like chicks leaving the mother hen.

* * *

Success proved illusory. As the new year unfolded Portland's privateers returned empty-handed. Others failed to return at all. It was soon discovered that the green wood with which they were constructed failed to make seaworthy vessels, and some had literally disintegrated at the first sign of heavy weather.

Beyond Portland, word had come of the humiliating loss of the valuable heavy frigate *Chesapeake* to the *Shannon*. Other American losses followed. Rumors of major naval engagements on the Great Lakes reached the East only sporadically and long after the fact. Adam had heard that Commodore Perry had built up a fleet and was likely battling the British desperately on the lakes. But the outcome was unknown.

Still, Adam and his committee did not rest. The blockading fleet lurked just out of sight offshore and was ready to pounce on any merchant ship that ventured forth. Indeed, with the defeat of Napoleon in Russia, the British now had more resources to devote to the war with America, and they had tightened the blockade. The economy was at a standstill. Trade ceased. The merchants, who had only just begun to recover from the Embargo, were barely able to make ends meet. The town began to turn inward and sullen. As Adam walked the docks and streets, he observed that the often caustic and dry New England sense of humor of his fellow citizens had degenerated into back-biting, recriminations, and finger-pointing. He determined to remedy the decline. He ordered keels for a new draft of privateers laid at Gunship Cove and supervised their construction. He ordered improvements of the earthworks hastily thrown up the prior year and new ones built. He encouraged the commander of the Portland Rifle Company to keep his men in fighting trim. Together, they traveled to Boston to negotiate an extra supply of scarce powder and cannon balls from the state militia. On their return, Adam worked with his former Mate—now Captain in his own right—Spurling to recruit sixteen teams of unemployed sailors, Mainers to a man, to work alongside the militia on practicing gunnery. Every day they assembled at the battery at Jordan's Point and took aim at barrels towed into Casco Bay. Recalling his first experience with gunnery aboard the *Atheling*, Adam took a personal interest.

"Remember, boys, wait 'til the crest of the wave and fire as the ship is going down. Aim at the hull," he instructed the men. "I know there are no waves ashore, but imagine them, think of them, impress them into your brain. Always fire on the downward roll and try to hull 'em. Remember the Brits like to fire their broadsides on the crest of the wave, causing their shots to go high. We can do better and beat 'em at gunnery."

The artillery Captain explained the rest, about loading and ramming and cleaning. With practice, the sailors began to work as efficiently as the artillerymen.

"Speed, men, speed. Now let's get it faster!" Adam exhorted them as he held up his pocket watch, just as he had on the *Atheling* in the year 1784. Time and again they went through the paces.

The artillery Captain also explained developments in gunnery which were new to Adam.

"These long guns we are operating are old-fashioned. They send a small ball a long way. But for purposes of modern naval warfare, the carronade is much to be preferred for the broadside," he advised.

Adam thought of the short, ugly wide mouthed carronade and shuddered as much out of aesthetics as out of stubbornness.

"The carronade, you see," the officer continued, "fires a twenty-four or thirty-two pound ball, so in terms of impact, of pounds of metal thrown, there is no comparing the two for use in the broadside. However, the carronade can only be used at short range, not like your long gun."

"But, Captain, if the British are armed with carronades and we are armed with long guns, will that not make them want to stand off and not approach?"

"Just so, Captain Hale."

"But," Adam continued, "as I think about it, that also means they will only want to engage at close quarters, where they can deploy their carronades to maximum effect, so that places a premium on maneuver for them. And as long as we too stand off, they will not engage. Most fascinating . . ."

Within a week Adam had ordered his fourteen six-pounders and two Venetian bow-chasers hauled from the cellar of his factory house and shipped aboard the *Atheling*. They protruded from her gun ports for all the town to see.

Rumor began to spread: Captain Adam Hale was going to war.

35

Cruising

1812–1813—Part II

"WE'RE BOTTLED UP, JUST LIKE THIS!" COMMODORE RODGERS EXCLAIMED as he jammed a cork into the neck of the bottle of hock that sat before him. The Commodore did not drink, but he wanted to make a point to the assembled Captains and merchants of Portland in Colonel Burnham's tavern. "The blockade is now so tight that our forty-four-gun frigates and other men-of-war cannot leave port. The *President* and the *Argus* are bottled up at Boston. Others cannot leave New York. We sit, our crews idle and ill-supplied. The British lurk offshore and hunt, often in packs of two: a ship of the line which outguns even our frigates, accompanied by its consort, a fast sloop-of-war or frigate for maneuverability. We have to break out. I must carry the new American Minister Mr. Crawford to France. And I intend to carry the war to the enemy. If I can get the *President* from Boston to Portland by hugging the coast I calculate that we stand the best chance of making the break out from here, as the British won't be expecting it. We'll wait for dirty weather and make the breakout then. But I need all the help I can get on this cruise. Captain Hale, will you join the squadron with the *Atheling*?"

"She's armed, and her crew stands ready."

"Good then. We'll rendezvous June 20 in the lee of Richmond Island off Cape Elizabeth. Pray for dirty weather."

* * *

Adam, joined by Captain Spurling in the position of First Mate, eased the *Atheling* out of Portland harbor on the ebb tide in the dark of night and with all lights doused. She drifted southward with only her main staysail and jib set, the better to avoid attracting unwanted attention from any British cruisers that might be loitering in the vicinity. Well before daybreak she was in the lee of Richmond Island and hidden from the open sea. Adam dropped anchor and waited.

Five hours later the American convoy arrived for the rendezvous. But instead of the massive forty-four-gun frigate *President*, Adam saw through his glass a small brig and her two consorts.

As soon as they had dropped anchor in the lee of the island, the slight, fine-featured twenty-eight-year-old commander of the brig, Master Commandant William Henry Allen, wasted no time in calling on Adam. The two seamen sat sharing a glass of madeira in Adam's quarters.

"I am honored you would call on me," Adam offered, cognizant that protocol required him to call first on the Naval officer despite their difference in ages.

The young Master replied with a nasal Rhode Island accent that Adam immediately recognized, "Not at all, Captain Hale. Your work these last months has gained great recognition. 'Tis I who am honored to call on you."

Adam was properly flattered, for, though young, Allen had acquired a sterling reputation under Captain Stephen Decatur when, in the prior year, the *United States* fought and took the *Macedonian*. Indeed, he had been accorded the singular honor of escorting the prize ship home.

"I trust your cargo the Minister is well?" Adam inquired.

"Oh, as well as might be I suppose. Minister Crawford is a politician from Georgia, as you may know. He does not care for the sea and confines himself to his quarters night and day. He has a rather high opinion of himself and regulates his interactions with us in the service. We are, as it were, servants to him, and he treats us as such. Would you care to meet him?"

The two New Englanders eyed one another in the gentle irony of the question and then broke out laughing.

"On to other topics," Adam tacked. "Where are Commodore Rodgers and the *President*? I thought they were supposed to lead the convoy?"

"Ah, well. The Navy Department decided not to risk the *President* in running the blockade," Allen explained. "So it was determined that the *Argus* was to convey Minister Crawford to France. She's a good ship, mind you: fast, only three hundred tons but well armed with eighteen twenty-four-pounder carronades."

"For close engagement," Adam observed.

"Aye, that's the way of it in the Navy now."

"My ship brings long guns. Maybe we can work with that. And what of your consorts?"

"The fourteen eighteen-pounder carronade brig *Pocahontas* and the twelve-gun armed sloop *Rascal*, all small stuff."

"Without the gravitas of the *President* we'll have to make speed."

"Agreed. I'd have you lead. Run in your guns and cover the ports with canvas. With your build as a merchant lumber ship no one will suspect you. You can reconnoiter over the horizon and signal back to us if you spot a hostile sail or are challenged. You will function as our eyes and ears."

"I'll do you one better. I will sail under a British ensign, and as a matter of course I carry two sets of ships' papers, one American and the other Canadian, in case I am challenged. I could divert a boarding party for hours."

"You'll be our decoy then."

"Exactly."

"Our Naval vessels also carry British ensigns should we need them. Oh, I am going to enjoy sailing with you, Captain Hale."

Adam raised his glass.

"To the voyage."

"To the voyage. And to dirty weather these next twenty-four hours."

The weather cooperated. By ten o'clock that night a nor'easter began to blow. By just before dawn it had reached such a crescendo of swells and foaming whitecaps that Allen decided to make a run for it. While still dark, all four ships in the convoy weighed anchor and barged out into the churning North Atlantic. The heavy sea caused the vessels to pitch and roll. As first light broke on the eastern horizon Adam could see the muzzles of the guns on the other ships go under the water on each roll. But they plowed onward with as much canvas as they could prudently spread. Adam reassured himself that the weather tilted the odds in their favor, for no British blockader had search and pursuit on his mind in such a dark and churning sea.

Allen's gamble paid off. By midafternoon they were well clear of the British patrol lanes and headed into the open ocean where their chances of being discovered were small indeed. Moreover, the weather abated as the day wore on so that now they could spread more canvas and gain speed. By sunset, with the *Atheling* in the van, they were headed toward clear skies pointing the way toward France, and the ship's log told Adam they were sailing at a good seven-knot clip. That night Adam slept soundly for the first time in months.

Their passage was swift and uneventful. By the twenty-first day they raised the coast of Brittany, where, by prearranged plan with the French government, they deposited Minister Crawford at the port of L'Oriente and took on fresh water.

It was there, as they contemplated their next steps, that Master Commandant Allen raised a most interesting proposition.

"Captain Hale, what say you we go a-cruising?"

"I'm sorry?" a flummoxed Adam responded. "Cruising where? Haven't you orders to return to America?"

"Indeed so. But my orders are subject to interpretation. They do not specify a route or timetable. I was thinking. Here we are in Brittany. What if we were to cruise the English Channel and head up the east coast of the British Isles on the way home, to follow the route of the Spanish Armada so to speak? Of course we'd keep a sharp eye out for shipping. You have a letter of marque. We could take the war home to England. Now that would have a most salutary effect back home."

"Indeed it would!" Adam effused. His fighting instinct aroused, Adam's blue eyes began to twinkle and the creases on his face broke into a smile as he began to dream. Despite their differing physical miens, the sixty-three-year-old Captain Hale thought he saw a glimmer of his younger self in the youthful commander.

"Well, then?"

Adam thought for a few minutes. The truth was that with all of his losses over the previous years he had little to go back to or, put another way, nothing better to do.

"Why not? I've nothing to lose."

"Good, then. It's settled."

Three days later the small squadron left L'Oriente and headed north, hugging the French coast until it reached the Channel. Then it went on the attack.

The first victim was an Algerine xebec bearing a cargo of Seville oranges. The Americans confiscated the cargo, loaded the precious oranges on the *Atheling*, and burned the xebec. There would be no stopping for prize courts on this flying raid. They set the crew ashore on the coast of Normandy.

Their next encounter was with a coastal British collier. Having no need of the coal, the Americans placed the crew in the ship's jolly boat to sail home and burned the collier and its cargo. This set a pattern of evacuation (as they took care to protect lives), followed by plunder and destruction, that marked their leisurely and wanton cruise up the English Channel. In all, they loitered three weeks and picked their prizes like a shopper in a village market: only the ripest and plumpest were worthy of their attention. Hewing to the middle of the Channel, they passed the naval strongholds of Plymouth and Dartmouth without challenge and then headed up by Poole and Weymouth. There, off the coast of Dorset, they swarmed on a heavily laden brigantine which capitulated immediately. Its cargo of English silver currency and Staffordshire ware bound for Canada was a valuable haul indeed. The Americans divided up the heavy crates between the four ships, with the *Atheling* taking the lion's share.

Both commanders knew that this type of activity could not continue indefinitely without attracting the attention of the British authorities and eliciting a response. Their only close call came when a Royal Navy armed sloop ventured astern the convoy off the Isle of Wight. However, the American ships were all flying British ensigns and so passed covertly through the gauntlet of the Channel, and the sloop took no notice. If she had, the American ships vastly outgunned her and would not have hesitated to sink her. As it was, with rich cargos aboard and the prospect of more to come, the Americans did not wish to risk their mission on a small warship with no value other than her guns.

Nonetheless, the presence of the armed sloop caused the Americans to recalculate their strategy, and they picked up their pace, knowing that it would only be a matter of time before the Royal Navy sent a squadron out to find and destroy them. So they made haste to clear the Channel, and it was with some relief that they counted nineteen vessels seized and destroyed without a single shot fired or a single life lost by the time they rounded the White Cliffs of Dover, which were clearly visible from the ships.

Their joy at rounding the Channel unscathed was abraded, however, by the unmistakable signs of an outbreak of scurvy among the crews of the two consorts: lassitude, irritability, soreness in the legs, splotches on the skin, and bleeding and swollen gums. The Surgeon's Mate from the *Atheling*, a young man from Portland and the son of a Down East Captain who had shipped for the adventure of it, visited both ships and pronounced the diagnosis.

"It's come from their being holed up for months at Boston and being poorly supplied. And then this voyage. Have we no lemons or limes aboard?"

"No," both Adam and Allen replied at once.

"Then what's to do?" asked the doctor.

"We can try the oranges," Adam proffered.

"I'm not certain of their efficacy," the doctor replied, "but in a pinch we'll have to make do."

So Adam ordered five crates of the precious Seville oranges broken up and distributed among the crews of the two ships.

The small convoy then steered into the open ocean on a bearing north-northeast as they headed into the North Sea for the long stretch up the east coast of the British Isles and around Scotland. Most of the ships they encountered were small fishing craft, of no interest to them. However, as they passed opposite Flamborough Head, the scene of John Paul Jones's victory over HMS *Serapis*, the lookout on the *Atheling*, still sailing in the van of the squadron, spotted a slow, lumbering merchant-man sailing on a westward course, no doubt bound for London. She flew a British ensign. The convoy tacked and gave chase for no more than an hour before they had her surrounded and she hove to. On boarding her, the Americans learned she was out of St. Petersburg and Copenhagen. They had stumbled onto a British trade route they had only heard about but never seen: the Baltic trade. The merchantman traveled unarmed because American privateers had never before ventured into these waters and, with Napoleon prostrate after his invasion of Russia, French preda-tors posed little risk. On inspecting beneath deck the American boarding party discovered a cargo of sail cloth and, of more interest, lead and iron ingots for use in the British armaments industry. Then, buried beneath a pile of sail cloth on the bottom-most deck they struck treasure that made their hearts race: three chests filled with Baltic amber and five rundlets brimming with gold rubles, both intended for the London markets. Adam and Allen quickly huddled on how to dispose of her.

"We're too far at sea to get her crew safely back to England in a jolly boat," Adam protested.

"I know. Either we take them with us or we give them back their ship."

"They would be a liability aboard us. We must make haste and round Scotland without distraction."

"I know. So are you agreed then that we don't burn her but take the ingots, amber, and gold and send her on her way?"

"Yes, but there's risk in that, as they will report our position as soon as they land, and the Royal Navy will be on our heels straightway."

"We have no choice. We must take the risk. All the more reason for us to make haste."

"Agreed then?"

"Agreed."

Once again, the *Atheling*'s generous hold was groaning with loot as the American squadron let loose all sails to make speed. They pounded forth into an increasingly choppy North Sea as they bore northward. By the time they reached Scotland a steady drizzle descended on them, but they had yet to spot any hostile warships. The drizzle merged into fog when they reached the passage north of Orkney which would take them over the top of the British Isles and out into the Irish Sea and thence home. Adam led the passage through Orkney with great care, at once glad of the cover afforded by the fog and wary of its risks. The ships slowed to a creeping pace as the leadsman tested the depth every minute with his sounding line. An anxious Adam watched from the quarterdeck: his eyes constantly scanning the fog for the outlines of any obstruction and his body feeling the way the ship sailed, as he read her every mood. After some hours of this difficult passage they cleared Orkney, and the fog began to lift as they entered the waters to the west of the islands. There they turned their course south-southwest and headed for the waters above northern Ireland, making speed as they went, for now the cruise was done and they were homeward bound. Or so Adam thought.

Master Commandant Allen had other ideas. Flush with the hubris of youth and inflamed by his victory over the *Macedonian* and latest string of triumphs, he proposed to Adam a further string of raids.

"Why stop while we are ahead? We shall enter the Irish Sea for one last foray. There's bound to be fat pickings there."

Adam had seen the phenomenon before, including in himself. It was almost like a gambler's fixation. Once the blood was aroused, there was always the temptation to say, "Just one more." But Adam's sixty-three years told him otherwise, and he demurred.

"Haven't we had enough? Why risk it? Far better to hasten home with our rich cargo and bring back the story of our successful venture. Besides, the oranges have not worked a change in the crews of the consorts. Daily they grow worse. They are barely fit for service and are in sore need of recuperation."

Allen thought for a few minutes.

"I understand, Captain Hale. You speak with the wisdom of experience. But I'm confident of my abilities. I could take any British twenty-two-gun sloop-of-war in ten minutes. So you take the *Atheling* back to Boston with the two consorts, and I will tarry here another week or two to cause what mischief I may. I will see you in Boston on my return. Godspeed, Captain Hale."

Adam saw that further attempts at persuasion were useless.

"Good luck and Godspeed, Master Commandant Allen."

And the two men shook hands formally and departed company.

Adam set his sails, hoisted the Stars and Stripes and led his small squadron westward with the *Atheling*'s gun ports still shrouded. Little did he know, although he might reasonably have suspected, that the Admiralty had sent out orders to all available ships to hunt down the *Argus* and its consorts. On entering the Irish Sea, the *Argus* took two more prizes. One of them was a merchantman carrying wine from Porto. The crew looted the cargo, began to drink, and, as with other previous captures, burned the ship. The pillar of smoke from the fire caught the attention of HMS *Pelican*, which had shortly before left Cork in search of the *Argus* and her consorts. The *Argus* was the faster ship but more lightly armed and could have escaped. Instead, Allen's hubris led him to accept battle. In the ensuing fight, the two ships quickly exchanged broadsides. A round shot cut off Allen's right leg in the first four minutes of the battle, but he remained at his station until he fainted from loss of blood. As the battle continued each ship raked the other with broadsides until the *Argus*'s rigging was too lacerated to prevent the *Pelican* from sailing astern and crossing the T. The Americans' gunnery fell short, unlike in most U.S. Navy single ship encounters. The wine may have played a role. At length, after forty-five minutes of fierce gunnery, the two vessels collided, with the *Argus*'s bow against the *Pelican*'s quarter. As British boarding parties assembled, the *Argus* surrendered.

The prize was taken to Plymouth, where Allen died of his wounds two weeks later. He was buried with full military honors in the churchyard of St. Andrew's Church Plymouth. Thus, this twenty-eight-year-old son of Narragansett Bay was to lie forever in the fertile soil of the South Hams of Devon.

Meanwhile, the homeward bound *Atheling*, *Pocahontas*, and *Rascal* enjoyed fair sailing, although the indisposition of the crews of the latter two ships increased daily so that they effectively sailed with only a skeleton complement. The consorts' utility in the event of an encounter with the enemy would be nil. For this reason, and because of her more spacious quarters and presence of a Surgeon's Mate, Adam ordered a transfer to the *Atheling* of the seamen afflicted with the scurvy. At the same time he rehearsed with the two ships' masters a prearranged set of signals to allow the ships to communicate while under way. Adam's mission was to return the convoy safely and as quickly as possible.

And so they continued on a course west-southwest.

* * *

The sail was first visible as a blip on the eastern horizon at dawn: a far-off pyramid caught out and illuminated by the rising sun.

"Sail Ho!" cried the watch atop the *Atheling*'s main mast. "Sail Ho astern!"

Adam, already up and pacing the quarterdeck, adjusted his spyglass sternward. His glass immediately picked out the tip of the jib of the fore-and-aft rigged sloop, a very large sloop indeed if he were to judge from the size of the jib, although the hull of the ship remained hidden below the horizon. Most likely a merchantman, he reassured himself. Perhaps headed for the West Indies.

Throughout the day Adam checked his glass. Each time the sail inched up to reveal more. She was a wicked fast ship Adam told himself. And piling on canvas to get ahead.

As dusk settled over the eastern horizon Adam thought he saw the first outline of her hull. But it was indistinct in the dim light. The matter would only be resolved in the morning. Adam slept fitfully that night, as he could not expunge the mystery of the fast pursuer from his consciousness.

He was up before dawn, and as the first light opened to the east he placed his glass to his eye. With a twist of the eyepiece, the ship loomed into view. She had made good time over night. Adam immediately spotted her to be a large armed sloop built for speed and cutting out expeditions. At her stern Adam distinctly made out a British ensign. So she was a warship. And she was headed straight for the three American ships, no doubt intending to close on them and pound them with her carronades.

Adam instinctively knew that the chase was on.

He ordered all sails deployed on the *Atheling*, and the other two ships followed suit. He ran the calculation in his mind: he was five days out of Boston. If he could maintain or extend his lead over the pursuer, he could elude her and make safe harbor—assuming he could thread the blockade as he approached the coast. The worst option would be for the pursuer to run him into the blockade and then join with one of the big British frigates to pound the three Americans into oblivion. So it was an engagement with two dimensions, both fraught with danger that had to be managed and overcome in sequence. Adam told himself that the next twenty-four hours would tell whether his strategy would work and he could elude the pursuer.

Adam kept his counsel to himself. The watches changed as usual. He shot the noon calculations. He took dinner in his cabin alone, as always. At two bells on the last dog watch he walked the entire deck and checked the straining canvas.

"'Evening, Mr. Payson," he addressed the helmsman at the wheel. "How does she handle?"

"So far so good, Cap'n. Tight and seaworthy and making time. But I fear our pursuer," he replied with a jerk of his head backward over his shoulder. "She's gaining. I don't know how much longer we'll be able to keep our lead. And the *Pocahontas* and *Rascal* are struggling to keep up with us."

"Just keep at it. You're doing a capital job," Adam reassured him. But silently Adam fed the helmsman's comments into his calculations. He decided to sleep on the matter and to make a final observation in the morning. That night he retired early with the *Meditations* of Marcus Aurelius and took encouragement from the world-weary philosopher-emperor.

The following dawn saw the sloop ever closer. Adam made her out to be a large flush-decked three-masted sloop-of-war, easily surpassing the *Atheling* in tonnage. He could now count her nine gun ports to a side, bristling with what appeared to be thirty-two-pounder carronades. Adam quickly did the calculations of throw weight and speed. She would be on him in one more day, and he would be trapped between her and the blockade patrols. He knew he could no longer run. He would have to turn about, steal the weather gauge, and give battle.

At noon Adam stood on the quarterdeck with Captain Spurling at his side to address the assembled crew. Although it was summer, the wind was blustery, and he had wrapped himself in his blue greatcoat with brass buttons. If the British fought in silk stockings, he would fight in the blue of an American Captain.

"Now listen closely, lads!" he bellowed in his now gravelly voice of command. "Tomorrow at eight bells we will turn about and give battle to our pursuer, whoever she may be. The *Pocahontas* and *Rascal* will stand off. The *Atheling* will engage alone. At my signal you will double load the starboard battery with bar shot. At my next signal you will haul the shrouds from the gun ports and run the cannon out. When I give the order to fire you will aim for her rigging, not her hull. Then you will immediately reload with solid shot. On the second broadside, also on my signal, you will aim to hull her. Remember: wait for the crest of the wave and fire only as the ship is going down. After that, fire at will. Any questions?"

None of Adam's well-drilled gun crews raised a hand.

"Good then, lads. Remember the press gangs! Remember your wives and sweethearts! And here's to our American Republic!"

The crew erupted into cheers.

Adam slept fitfully that night and was up before eight bells of the middle watch. Captain Spurling rousted the men out of their hammocks to join him on deck. Each man took his assigned position. Adam stood, wrapped in his blue greatcoat—a solitary and grand figure beside the helmsman at the wheel. Adam anxiously eyed the telltales to check the direction of the wind.

He awaited the sound of the bell in the silent blackness of the early morning. Then it came—clang-clang, clang-clang, clang-clang, clang-clang—weak, tinny, and swallowed in the immensity of the ocean, almost an anticlimax.

Adam turned to the helmsman.

"Ready about, Mr. Payson."

The helmsman shot his Captain a questioning look, for he knew the difficulty of the maneuver the Captain was about to order. The ship could lose headway or, worse, yards or even masts could be cracked or sheared off.

The Captain responded with a curt but reaffirming nod.

"Ready, Cap'n," Payson acknowledged.

"Helm's a-lee. Course nor-nor'east. Pass her on her starboard beam."

"Rise tacks and sheets!" Adam ordered, and the men scurried to comply.

"Haul taut! Mainsail haul!" Adam bellowed.

The *Atheling* shuddered in her course as the rudder turned her and her yards creaked at the strain of the tacking.

"Haul well taut!"

The ship headed off, coming safely all the way around through the tack and then headed up on the opposite tack. Adam eased a sigh of relief.

"Right the helm, Mr. Payson," he commanded with the faintest trace of a smile.

Adam then ordered her stay sails and flying jibs set. Her sails began to fill, and in an instant she was on a course to intercept the pursuer. Adam prayed that with a good hour of darkness remaining she would not be discovered until she was well within range of his long guns. For all the pursuer knew she was just another merchant ship being convoyed by two naval vessels, and the ruse might hold. Then at the right moment Adam would remain just out of range of her carronades and pound her with his long guns, trying to take out first her rigging and top structure, and, that failing, he would hull her with solid shot.

Forty-five minutes into the race, with the two ships heading toward each other, a cannonball landed with a large splash into the water a half mile off the *Atheling's* starboard beam. An instant later the report of the long gun from which it was fired was audible. So they had been discovered, and this was an attempt to put a shot across their bow, only it fell short as the pursuer's long gun was too weak. Adam smiled.

"Starboard battery, load bar!" Adam ordered.

The men immediately did as ordered.

"Stand by for further orders."

The ship slid silently through the velvet blackness, the only sound the rush of the water against her bow.

The two ships rapidly closed on one another and by first light Adam judged her to be well within range of his long guns.

"Lift shrouds and run out all guns," he ordered in a subdued, confident voice.

Within seconds the shrouds were lifted and the muzzles of his long guns protruded from their ports.

"Now, Mr. Payson, wear just here so our boys can get their bearings."

The ship veered portward to expose the full line of her guns to the pursuing warship.

"Starboard battery, fire bar!" he commanded.

A second or two ensued while his gunners waited for the crest of the wave, and then all hell broke loose as the entire broadside erupted from the *Atheling*.

"Reload shot," he immediately ordered.

"Now, Mr. Payson, adjust just so," he said pointing over the helmsman's shoulder to put the ship back on course but keep her out of range of the pursuer's carronades.

Adam glinted through his telescope in the rising smoke to try to assess the damage. He could discern numerous holes through the pursuer's sails, tangled rigging atop, and the top of her main mast clipped off by the bar shot. But she sailed on.

In an instant she replied with a broadside from her carronades. All the shots fell short, sending up a wall of spray between the two ships.

By now the *Atheling* was passing at a distance from the starboard side of the pursuer, which for its part was beginning to maneuver to try to regain the weather gauge and cross the *Atheling*'s T after she had passed.

Adam had expected this maneuver.

"Starboard battery, fire shot," he calmly ordered.

Again, a few breathless seconds ensued while the men got their bearings on the crest of the wave.

A rolling broadside ensued this time as each gun crew let fly fury in succession. The balls from the *Atheling* slammed into the pursuer's hull ripping a string of holes from her bow to amidships.

Still she sailed on until she could outmaneuver the Americans and place her guns within range.

"Reload and fire at will," Adam ordered.

He tapped the helmsman on the shoulder.

"Now, Mr. Payson, just here. Cut just so to starboard and bring her up astern the ship."

As the *Atheling* began to execute the maneuver a ball from one of her long guns smashed into the pursuer's main mast and took it by the board in a great tumble of wood, rigging, and sails. Now demasted, the sloop was helpless.

Adam dared not approach closer, as her carronades still threatened him, but there was no question of her continuing the pursuit. The *Atheling* had neutralized the threat.

Adam thought briefly about what to do with her. To take her as a prize would require him to approach within range of her carronades, and she could still inflict great harm. No, better to let her just sit there, he thought. It would be days before she repaired the damage. And by then he and his consorts would be long gone. Prudence dictated forgoing the prize.

Still, Adam had to know who she was.

Continuing his victory lap around her stern, but sufficiently far off, Adam raised his telescope to read the name emblazoned over her stern transom.

There, highlighted by the rays of the rising sun, he made out the letters:

"*L'Inconnu.*"

The Unknown. Evidently a French corvette captured by the British and pressed into His Majesty's service without so much as a change of name.

"*L'Inconnu.* The Unknown," Adam chuckled to himself.

"*Adieu! L'Inconnu!*" he saluted her as she slid past and behind him.

* * *

The *Atheling*'s voyage and Adam's concerns were not over, however, as he rejoined his consorts and they resumed their course toward Boston. Adam well knew that in the coming days they would have to evade or defeat the British blockade that patrolled the coast. The *Atheling* sailed with her colors flying but with her gun ports shrouded, keeping up the ruse that she was a merchant ship. However, Adam took the precaution of transferring all the pikes and cutlasses from the consorts to the *Atheling*.

Adam set his course straight for Boston. He resolved to avoid the blockaders if he could, but at the same time, buoyed by his recent victory and his confidence in the *Atheling*'s gunners, he found temptation eroding his better judgment. If a chance presented itself, why not roll the dice and go for glory?

The ensuing days passed uneventfully as the three ships made steady progress toward home. The blockade was so effective that they saw no ships, not even a fishing boat, as they neared the American coast.

Less than a day's sailing out of Boston, as Adam sat at dinner, the alarm sounded topside. Adam untucked his napkin, threw it across his plate, grabbed his blue greatcoat and rushed to the deck.

"Frigate off the starboard bow! British frigate!" shouted the watch.

Indeed, there she was sailing off the starboard beam, a sleek, fast, maneuverable heavy frigate, a veritable floating platform of firepower, HMS *Hart*, a glamor ship of the Royal Navy. She was close enough that Adam did not even need his telescope to count her thirty-eight twenty-four-pounder carronades and two six-pounder bow-chasers. Against his fourteen six-pounder long guns and two bow-chasers, it would be no match. And she was already in carronade range, heading straight for the *Pocahontas*. Adam's long-range gunnery advantage had evaporated before the engagement had even started. It was as if she had appeared out of nowhere, so fast she was. Nervously Adam scanned the horizon for her ship-of-the-line partner in the blockade. Seeing none, he stopped for a few seconds to think.

Evidently the frigate mistook the *Atheling* for a merchantman from her lines and from her sailing as she was with her gun ports masked by the canvas shrouds and had not bothered with her. Therein might lie an element of surprise, Adam deduced.

Adam sprang into action shouting orders left and right.

"Captain Spurling, order all port and starboard gunners to stations! Load shot. Await order to lift shrouds and run out guns. Await order to fire and then fire a broadside. Then reload and fire at will! Bosun, arm all the superfluous crew! Pikes, cutlasses, whatever is at hand. I don't care if they have the scurvy, arm 'em and keep 'em below deck until I say otherwise. Sailmaster, brail up the mizzen! Mr. Payson, intercept that frigate!"

Mr. Payson stared for a second, incredulous. A sixteen-gun brig taking on a forty-gun frigate? But he knew Captain Hale and swung into action.

The sky was overcast. A strong breeze blew out of the northeast. As the defenseless *Pocahontas* made haste to flee, the *Atheling* hauled up and stood for its antagonist, while the frigate came rapidly down with the wind nearly aft. Both vessels heeled in the wind. After fifteen minutes of this chase the frigate's drum rolled a beat to quarters. In a few minutes, the frigate broke off her pursuit of the *Pocahontas* and put about and stood for the *Atheling* aiming to take the weather gauge. But Adam also ordered Mr. Payson to tack and stood away, equally intent on maintaining the weather gauge. In another twenty minutes the frigate again tacked and took in her stay-sails to stand for the *Atheling*. Adam ordered the royals furled. Seeing that she would be weathered, the frigate put about again and ran with the wind while the *Atheling* hoisted her flying jib to close and rapidly came up on the frigate's weather quarter. The ships were not two hundred yards apart.

"Haul shrouds! Port and starboard batteries, run out guns!"

The crews flew into action, and the *Atheling* revealed herself for the privateer that she was.

All was silent. The uncertainty of intentions gripped the stand-off. Standing by the helmsman on the quarterdeck Adam stared hard at the frigate which gently rocked in the waves.

One minute turned into two.

And then the British frigate opened the conflict by firing a broadside from its carronades charged with round and grape shot. The blast immediately struck the *Atheling*'s port side before its report reached Adam's ears. Adam and his topside crew instinctively hunched down with the impact. Wood and sharp splinters flew across the deck scouring everything in their path amidships. Pieces of the railing were torn away by the balls, and the grape peppered the rigging. The two long boats on deck sustained a direct hit and were both shorn in half. As usual, the British had fired high.

Adam took in the damage in a glance.

"Port battery, fire!" he ordered.

The *Atheling*'s long guns erupted at once with a heaving blast and billows of smoke. Her balls smashed into the frigate's hull near the water line. Right on target.

The *Atheling* continued under way toward the frigate, and her rapidly reloaded guns began an almost rhythmic rolling broadside as she approached. The frigate responded with deliberation, discharging another full broadside of twenty-four-pound shot into the *Atheling*'s hull. This time the damage was significant as great chunks of her bow were taken out. Still, the *Atheling* sailed on, firing as she went.

The frigate's captain came into Adam's view on her stern deck, and he ordered the crews manning the *Atheling*'s two Venetian bow-chasers to take aim for him, which they did, time and time again. For his part, Adam determined not to present such an inviting target and instead moved constantly about the deck, checking and encouraging his top men and ducking below deck to cheer on his gun crews while Captain Spurling acted as his alter ego transmitting the commands and managing the action. While below deck with his gunners another broadside from the carronades scored a direct hit on the number five port battery gun. The cannon and its carriage flew apart tearing a great hole in the ship's side and sending metal and wood careening through the crowded, hot, and smoke-choked gun deck. Adam was knocked to the deck by the concussion, where he lay stunned and senseless for a good two minutes. But he was untouched by the flying shrapnel, and he haltingly recovered his senses and his feet. Adam assessed the damage: the crew of the number five gun were all killed and the deck ran red with blood and gore. But the remaining crews hardly looked up. They continued loading, ramming, and firing with fury.

"Keep at it, boys," Adam reassured the sweating cordite-smeared faces.

Back on deck topside, Adam found the two ships lying seventy-five yards abreast. The concussion of the ceaseless cannonades had come close to deadening what little way the ships had on. Adam squinted to see through the acrid smoke that stung his eyes as it enveloped the two vessels and the space between them like a mantle. Adam thought he saw the British captain down, prostrate on the deck, and attended by his aides. With more certainty he spotted red-coated Marines beginning to climb the frigate's rigging to take their stations to snipe at the American crew.

"Captain Spurling, see there the Marines!" he shouted over the din at his second-in-command. "Put our sharpshooters on them. They must be taken out."

"Aye, aye, Captain," Spurling acknowledged as he ran forward to deploy the men as the ships slowly approached each other.

The relentless, precisely timed broadsides continued to be unleashed by the British ship into the hull of the *Atheling*, whose own guns barked and jumped as they now fired at point-blank range, but with little more effect than a lapdog yelping at the heels of a mastiff. The crews worked the guns with desperate energy, but the difference in weight was telling on the *Atheling*, whose port side was now riddled with holes from the British shot.

"Cap'n, we're taking on water fast!" reported the breathless, flush-faced master of the orlop deck.

"Well, are the pumps working?"

"Aye, I've got six men working them, knee deep they are. But the water's rising. We can barely keep up. This can't go on much longer. We're losing the battle below decks."

"Carry on. We're depending on you and those Coles and Bentinck pumps."

At that moment the two ships came grinding together with a shuddering groan. Even as the cannonade continued to hammer the hulls of both ships, the grim-faced men thrust and hacked at one another through the open ports with pikes and cutlasses, often occluded by the smoke in a scene that could only be from Hades.

Adam stopped for a fleeting moment to assess the situation. Notwithstanding the probable loss of the British commander and the toll the American sharpshooters were taking on the Marines aloft, Adam realized he was losing the battle. The *Atheling*'s hull could not stand much longer the pounding it was taking. The heavier carronades of the British frigate would prevail in the end. He had to turn the tables of the engagement.

"Captain Spurling, all men on deck to board!"

Adam grabbed a cutlass, and within less than a minute the hatches flew open and Adam's secret army of scurvy-ridden boarders—three times the number a ship of his size might have carried, all shouting, grimacing, and ready for action—poured on deck.

Adam wasted not a second.

"Men, follow me and Captain Spurling!" he shouted as he waved his blade aloft and scrambled up and over the side. As he stood mounting the rail of the frigate a musket ball slammed into his left shoulder and spun him around like a top. He looked down to see blood issuing from the wound which throbbed with a sharp pain. He placed the blade of his cutlass against the wound so that the blade was bathed in blood. Adam was aware that all eyes of his men were upon him. He stiffened himself and raised the bloodied blade high above his head.

"Onward, boys! Follow me!" he shouted. With a resounding hurrah the men swarmed over the hammock nettings and onto the frigate. A minute of intense hand-to-hand combat ensued, as Yankee and Jack Tar blades and pikes swung and lunged in a melee on deck.

Adam fought in the thick of it despite his wound. Then suddenly a searing blow from an unseen enemy cutlass slashed across the back of his neck. It cut to the chine. Adam froze in his tracks and began to swoon, feeling as if the blow had been dealt to the keel of his ship. He could not right himself and realized he would soon collapse on the deck. He reached for a mast to lean against.

But as he did, he saw that the British crew realized they were outnumbered, and they reeled back and began to huddle in a bunch at the stern. A party of two dozen American boarders armed with pistols and cutlasses under Captain Spurling raced below deck, and soon the British carronades fell silent as the gun crews surrendered.

Adam stood propped uncertainly by the main mast out of breath and with his shoulder by now numb and his neck and back drenched in sheets of blood, awaiting the next move. Just as before the engagement the vessel rocked silently in the swell. Only this time, the air was clogged with black smoke and the groans of the wounded and the deck was strewn with fallen spars, rigging, and downed sails.

At length a small taut voice issued forth from the stern.

"Captain Baring lies dead. I am Lieutenant Hallock, the next in command. With regret, HMS *Hart* informs you that she strikes her colours."

Adam heaved a sigh of relief as he slumped back against the main mast and the pent-up tension drained from his body.

A half hour later, while the Surgeon's Mate worked to staunch Adam's loss of blood, clean and bind his neck wound, and remove the ball from his shoulder, all without sedation, Adam queried the doctor and gave orders to Captain Spurling, both of whom attended him.

"Doctor, pray, what are the losses?"

"We suffered twenty-one killed and thirty wounded. 'Twas better on the *Hart*. She suffered sixteen killed and eighteen wounded."

"Truly, they were winning the battle until the last minutes. Captain Spurling, come close. I have instructions for you. Divide up the British crew between the *Pocahontas* and *Rascal*. Place a prize crew on the *Hart* from the *Atheling*. Thirty men should suffice. Then lash the *Hart* to the *Pocahontas* to have her towed into Boston. I don't know if the *Atheling* will make it, she's so shot through. She's cut to pieces. Are the pumps still working?"

"Aye, they are Captain. We'll get her into port."

That evening, as dusk fell, the bedraggled convoy slipped into Boston harbor. As soon as they had docked along Gray's Wharf and set foot on land, a great excitement gripped the port as news of the captured British frigate *Hart* spread like summer lightning. It was there in the harbor for all to see, pummeled, pierced through the hull, and flying the Stars and Stripes. A large mob—men, women, and children—carrying torches assembled on the quay and marveled at the spoils of war, some reaching out to touch the frigate's hull. Rumors also began to spread of the captured wealth in the ships' holds: gold, silver, amber, pottery, and lead and iron ingots. While Adam sought additional treatment for his wounds at the new Massachusetts General Hospital, Captain Spurling posted a reinforced guard on the wharf until the cargo could be offloaded.

The next day the newspaper headlines shouted of the "Miraculous Capture!" and informed the citizenry of the "Encounter Worthy of David and Goliath!" A buoyant Commodore Rodgers called on Adam that morning in the hospital. After inquiring as to his health and being reassured that the wounds were clean and healing and he would be back on his feet within a week or two, the Commodore confided that the *President*, under his command, would seize the opportunity of the breach in the blockade forthwith and sail out to take the battle to the enemy on the high seas, for which Adam offered his heartiest congratulations and best wishes.

At the end of the week, as Adam was preparing to leave the hospital, Captain Spurling called on him.

"I'm afraid I bring bad news about the *Atheling*," he slowly advised Adam, his voice almost quivering with trepidation. "She's a total loss. I've had three appraisers look at her, and they've all concluded she is beyond repair. Her only value is in scrap."

Adam simply stared.

"But that cannot be," he finally mumbled. "She's old I know, but, but . . . and I have no insurance on her. The insurers canceled the coverage when she was issued the letter of marque."

"But look on the bright side, Captain. You have the prize of the *Hart* and of all the captured cargo. It'll just be a matter of time before the prize court makes you whole."

A dejected Captain Hale returned to the vessel that had been his life. He resumed residence in his cabin while he attended to the many duties occasioned by her return. He bargained with the scrap dealers for her ultimate disposition. At the end of the day, he sold her for pennies on the dollar. So too with her long guns. Though not in high demand, the Navy could make use of them and agreed to purchase them for the Charlestown Naval Yard. Adam could not bear to depart with his two Venetian bow-chasers, however, and he ordered them sent Down East by wagon to Portland.

Adam next turned to filing the paperwork with the prize court for his shares in the captured frigate and cargoes. The Boston lawyer whom he had engaged to assist in the process brought vexing news after two weeks: the matter was a complex one and might not be resolved for some time. Apparently there was a legal question as to his entitlement to any share in the *Hart* because she was a warship and not a merchantman and had been captured while he was merely accompanying two United States Navy vessels on an official mission. And had not the crews from those warships effected the capture themselves when they boarded the *Hart*? As for the cargoes seized in the English Channel and North Sea, why they were the work of the *Argus* and not the *Atheling*. No, the lawyer advised, there was no point in waiting in Boston until this proceeding sorted out the facts. Adam's interests were well represented, and he was in good hands. He should return to Portland. He would be contacted as soon as the court ruled.

Adam visited the *Atheling* one last time at Gray's Wharf. He strolled her quarterdeck, he visited the wreckage that was her gun deck and he paid homage to her orlop deck and pumps below. He grasped her taffrail and closed his eyes. He said good-bye to the *Freckled Whelp* turned *Atheling*, his home, his ambitions, indeed his other wife. He then departed Boston.

However, when he reached Portland, he noticed that things were different. On walking along Middle Street he passed one of the local Captains, a man he had known for at least twenty years.

"Mornin' Commodore," the Captain said. "Welcome home."

Adam thought little of it. But then later that day as he strolled Union Wharf, he ran into a knot of Portland Captains, all old acquaintances.

"Commodore, glad to see you back. Portland is proud of your service."

"Aye, Commodore, you're the toast of the town," another chimed in.

And so Captain Hale became Commodore Hale, or more simply "The Commodore," in the estimation of his peers. The name stuck and never left him.

36

Not Glory But Remembrance

1812–1813—Part III

THE BRITISH BLOCKADE DREW EVER TIGHTER. THE UNITED STATES
Navy ordered the brig *Enterprise*, with fourteen eighteen-pounder
carronades and two long nine-pounder guns under the command of
Lieutenant William Burrows, northward to Portland to protect coastal
shipping. Like others in her class, she was a converted schooner and over-
armed. With a crew of one hundred and two, she also was overmanned
for her size. Because of the blockade she scudded Down East, clinging
to the coastline lest she be intercepted by a superior British force. She
arrived at Portland in August and lay at anchor within the protection of
the well-concealed harbor.

On the morning of Saturday, September 4, a fisherman arrived
in Portland harbor and reported to Lieutenant Burrows the presence
offshore of the Royal Navy brig *Boxer*, under the command of Captain
Samuel Blyth. Of comparable but inferior armament than the *Enterprise*,
she was patrolling near the mouth of the Kennebec just forty miles north
and east of Portland. The *Enterprise* counted a number of young men
from Portland among her crew, and excitement grew for a chase. Lieutenant Burrows wasted no time. He decided to strike. The wind was light
and southerly and the tide was running in, so the *Enterprise* was unable
to sail directly out. Instead, she ran down to Spring Point and attempted
to head seaward, but the tide proved too strong. At that, Lieutenant

Burrows ordered the ship's boats lowered. Full of sailors singing at full throat and arrayed in a line before the brig, they pulled the oars and rowed the ship against the tide and clear of the coast. She then bore away for the Kennebec.

The next day, Sunday, there was great anxiety in the town about the outcome of the engagement. Early Sunday morning Adam Hale and other citizens of the town gathered at the base of the Observatory. Its keeper, Captain Moody, was as anxious as anyone to discover the news. The Observatory could accommodate only a handful of people, however. Captain Moody admitted Adam, along with other proprietors of the tower, and they ascended the staircase to the observation deck. The light house on Seguin Island near the mouth of the Kennebec was visible by telescope on the clear day, and Captain Moody kept his practiced and watchful eye trained on it. Shortly before noon he shouted:

"Smoke! I see the smoke of the *Boxer*'s challenge gun! And now I see the smoke of the *Enterprise*'s gun accepting it!"

Adam and the other guests crowded for a look, each taking his turn at the telescope. Far, far off and dissipating, the smoke was indeed just visible to Adam's eye. Captain Moody shouted the news to the crowd gathered below, who gave up a roaring cheer.

For the next several hours the two ships maneuvered for position, and there was no further smoke to report. Thinking the battle was over, the crowd below began to disburse.

Then, in midafternoon Captain Moody announced that he saw the smoke of more guns. The fight had begun, but he could see neither ship.

And so Sunday ended.

The following day Captain Moody atop the Observatory spotted the *Enterprise* signaling as she approached Casco Bay. She was sailing under the American flag and so was the brig she had in tow. Captain Moody immediately dispatched runners to Fore Street with the news. Adam heard the runners crying, and he straightway joined the growing throng in the street.

The two ships soon entered the harbor and dropped anchor just off Union Wharf below Adam's gutted and burnt-out storehouse. All who wished to were allowed to board. Adam was one of the first. The British

Boxer was greatly cut up in the hull and about her rigging. She was hulled so many times by the *Enterprise* that each hole was barely more than an arm's length apart from the next one. The *Enterprise* had also been hulled, and an eighteen-pound ball had gone through her foremast and another through her main mast.

The commander of each ship lay dead on the deck of his vessel, one covered by an American flag and the other by a British ensign. The flag of the *Boxer* was defiantly nailed to her main mast, at her Captain's orders, so it could never be lowered. Nor had it been. Soon the accounts of the engagement began to pour out from the survivors: of how both commanders had fought with utmost bravery, of how Captain Blyth was killed early in the action by an eighteen-pound shot, of how Lieutenant Burrows was felled by a canister shot to his thigh but lingered in agony on deck refusing to be taken below until he learned that the victory was his. In the ensuing days both captains were buried with great fanfare side by side atop Munjoy Hill.

* * *

Earlier in the year, at the suggestion of the Navy, Adam had filed a request for compensation for the loss of the *Atheling*. The Navy forwarded the request to the President, who forwarded it to the Congress. Adam heard nothing. He began to resign himself to the suspicion that his request had gone the way of his spoliation claims and, so it increasingly seemed, his prize money.

Six months later, in late December, Adam received a package that arrived via the Boston post mail coach. It was small but weighty. He sat at his desk at home in Back Cove as he opened it. Inside was a sheet of printed parchment paper. It started off with the ruffles and flourishes of a string of "Whereas" clauses: "Whereas the Congress of the United States of America . . .," "Whereas, Captain Adam Hale . . . services above and beyond . . .," "Whereas, Captain Adam Hale . . . exhibited exemplary valor . . .," It finally got to the point: "Now therefore, in grateful recognition of the aforesaid services, the Congress of the United States of America has ordered struck a Commemorative Medal . . .," "Done this Third

Day of August in the Year of Our Lord 1813 and of the Independence of the United States of America the Twenty-seventh."

Accompanying the drum roll of the parchment was a dark blue jeweler's box. Adam pressed the button and opened it. Inside rested a shiny brass medal, maybe three inches in diameter—not gold, not silver, not bronze, but brass. Adam took it out and held it up to the window. The Great Seal of the United States straddled its obverse side. Adam turned it over. The reverse bore a representation, allegorical Adam surmised, of what appeared to be Penobscot Bay or some approximation thereof, complete with tall pine trees, a ship in the distance, and two Indians with tomahawks and peace pipes. Running along the top perimeter were the raised letters of Adam's name. At the bottom perimeter, also in raised lettering, was the motto *"Non Gloria Sed Memoria."* Not Glory But Remembrance.

Adam puzzled what it meant. Not Glory But Remembrance.

He turned the heavy medal over several times and ran his index finger over the raised relief. It was pretty, no doubt. He was at once honored and touched to be so singled out for recognition. Or was this merely the consolation prize for a compensation claim quietly shelved? Adam preferred to think not.

"Non Gloria Sed Memoria." Not Glory But Remembrance. Whatever could that mean?

Adam allowed himself to admire the medal one more time. Then he placed it in the drawer of his desk, confident that he could withdraw it at any time, run his finger across its lovely shiny surface, and gain whatever strength it signified and imparted.

37

The Black Razee

1814

THE AMERICAN VICTORIES OF 1813 DID LITTLE TO ALLAY THE RELENT-less British advance. The blockade only tightened. At year end 1813 the reelected President Madison signed an even more restrictive embargo than those approved by Jefferson. This time coastal trade between American ports was outlawed, as was fishing outside harbors. Commerce ground to a complete and utter standstill. Even more ominously, by September of 1814 the war had turned against the Americans in some very particular ways.

Thus, it was no surprise that the Portland Captains, merchants, and Selectmen, deprived of work, passed their long days in Colonel Burnham's Tavern.

"It's outrageous!" thundered one of the town's Captains, as he put down his newspaper and pointed with his eyeglasses at the article he had just read. "The British impressed six of our sailors from Harpswell, and when they tried to escape they hung 'em as deserters. Right from the yardarm, they did, of a great black frigate flying an Admiral's flag. And then they paraded 'em up and down our coast, dangling from the yardarms like sacks of potatoes in plain view of our towns and farms!"

"What? Just to mock us?" asked another Captain.

"That, to be sure," Adam Hale observed. "But also as a warning to impressed men not to try to escape."

"It's all the work of a new Admiral, I hear," added a merchant. "He was sent out from London to take command. They want to break us."

"Portland's next. I know it," predicted one Captain.

"Aye," responded another. "The British have already occupied Eastport, Machias, Blue Hill, Castine, and Belfast. They've looted Hampden and Bangor and set a Biddeford shipyard afire. All of Maine east of the Penobscot has been seized and incorporated back into the British empire. It's only a matter of time until they strike at Portland."

"Up to now I haven't thought they'd take on Portland," Adam observed. "We've hardened our defenses, and our militia is all called out and entrenched. But there is only so much we can do."

"But Commodore, do you think militia scare British regulars?"

"They're all we've got."

"Aye. And Massachusetts will do nothing to aid us," added a Selectman. "It's been short shrift from Boston for almost two hundred years. They never did like us Mainers. The smug Boston Roundheads have always thought us to be a passel of outlanders and rubes."

All the Captains grumbled in agreement.

"And the federal government, that's even worse. They're run by Southerners and Westerners, who foisted this cursed war on us. Not only is the government bankrupt, it's losing the war."

"I hear talk they might institute a draft. The President has asked Congress for a conscription bill."

"Tyranny!" shouted another as he slammed his fist on the table. "When will we stand up as free men and do what is necessary?"

"That's the kind of talk that has Little Jimmy Madison worried. He sits there in the President's Mansion—well, no, he lost that too when the British burned Washington last month—well, wherever he crouches and hides, he knows secession is in the air and he could lose all of New England. Why, I've heard a rumor, just a rumor mind you, that he's moved federal troops from the border with Canada to Albany, all the better positioned to attack and occupy us, his own countrymen, should New England make a move to secede."

"He wouldn't dare."

"Wouldn't he now? The whole country has come unraveled."

"This British invasion is God's punishment for being wicked," opined another Captain as he sought a theological explanation for Maine's misfortune.

Adam was taken aback.

"I can't see how the Almighty has a thing to do with it. We haven't been wicked. The venality lies at the feet of those who run roughshod over our interests, those who run America to suit their own constituencies. That's in the political realm, not the spiritual."

"Well, what about those who profit from the invasion—are they not wicked?"

Adam dropped silent. He knew the reference was to Gideon Sewell, although none would raise it so pointedly out of respect for the Commodore. He well knew that his son-in-law quickly sized up the invasion as an opportunity to make money and had set up shop for the time being in Castine, where he manipulated the massive black-market trade between Halifax and Boston.

"God's punishment or not, we must do something," resumed the gadfly Captain. "Gentlemen, do ye not agree?"

All heads nodded.

"But what?" Adam posed. "We are in the weakest of positions."

* * *

Ten days later a bright and breezy Saturday morning in September followed the passage of a fast-moving shower that swept through Portland and cleaned the streets at dawn. At eight o'clock the sound of distant cannonading rattled Portland. Adam dressed quickly and raced to the Observatory, where he found a handful of his fellow Captains, merchants, and Selectmen already ascending the staircase to the observation platform. Captain Moody had the telescope trained toward the blockhouse at Spring Point, the channel, and, in the distance, Portland Head Light.

"They're coming!" he warned the gathering. Taking the scope again, he talked excitedly as he watched. "I count five, no, six men-o-war—sloops, a bomb ketch, and in the van a great heavy frigate. She's a razee, a ship of the line with her upper deck removed, huge and terrible in her armament, I'd say. I count sixty-four guns, all carronades. And she's all black. I've never seen her like before. And—what's this?—she is flying the blue flag of a Vice-Admiral of the Royal Navy at her mizzenmast. The firing is all ours, from one of our sloops standing off. The squadron is not bothering to respond. They are all under full sail and heading toward the channel right smartly. Here, have a look."

Adam and each Captain, merchant, and Selectman in turn took the scope. It was exactly as Captain Moody had described. The immense black frigate, with her guns run out but her gun ports not delineated by the usual band of white, followed by her consorts, was headed past Cape Elizabeth and toward the channel leading to Portland. The cannonading from the American sloop was little more effective than mosquito bites. The British squadron would soon enter the channel. From there, going at speed, they would brush past the weakly manned blockhouse at Spring Point and have the harbor and city at their mercy.

"What do you suppose they want?" asked one Captain as he pulled away from the telescope.

"That's easy," replied another. "It is Mowat all over again. They've come to reduce Portland to rubble!"

"Aye! Aye!" all grumbled in agreement. "We can't allow that to happen."

"Danger, never far away, has come to our way of life in Portland," added a Selectman. "We cannot allow the civilization for which we have worked so hard be destroyed."

"We must go out to meet them," Adam counseled. "To ascertain their intent, to seek terms if we must, but armed and resolute in our dignity and bearing."

All present agreed. Abandoned by both Massachusetts and the federal government, Portland would capitulate rather than suffer a second destruction.

"So be quick about it," Adam ordered. "Go home and grab your coats and swords and whatever arms you have, and we will meet at Union Wharf in twenty minutes. Captain Deering, your sloop is the fastest in the harbor. May we enlist her services in our embassy?"

Captain Deering nodded.

Minutes later the citizens clambered aboard Captain Deering's boat and set sail in the blustery wind. Adam wore his blue greatcoat cinched about the waist by a sword belt from which suspended the cutlass that he wielded aboard the *Atheling* in its capture of the frigate. They raced toward the channel as Captain Moody, now joined by a throng of other citizens, kept an anxious watch from atop the Observatory.

No sooner had the Americans cleared the harbor than the British squadron hove into view. But instead of heading for the town it veered nor'east and dropped anchor off Peaks Island in the bay. The black frigate lowered a cutter, which rowed ashore at the island, as if to claim possession.

"Good," Adam advised his comrades. "We will head straight for Peaks and treat with them there."

The American sloop made short work of the waters of Casco Bay as it passed where Adam had started out to vainly implore God for answers following Seth's death. The marine amphitheater of the Bay was as beautiful as ever, diminishing the tribulations of the humankind who had invaded it.

The Americans berthed their boat by the rickety dock that extended from the western side of the island facing the town of Portland and disembarked. Not a hundred yards inland, they found the British landing party in a pleasant meadow overlooking Portland. A rock ledge bordered the meadow at its far end, and outcroppings of boulders and glacial rubble dotted the field. The grass in the meadow was still slick and wet from the morning rain. Mud bespattered the polished black boots of the dozen British officers, who, together with their attendants, comprised the landing party. They bore maps and telescopes by which they were studying the town and its fortifications opposite.

Adam spoke first.

"Gentlemen, I am Commodore Adam Hale of Portland, and these are my fellow citizens," he explained as he gestured toward his compatriots. "We have come to ascertain your intentions. We wish you no ill, but, if forced to fight, we shall. Our preference, however, is to talk as between cousins."

An awkward silence ensued among the scrum of British officers. At length one edged forward from deep within their ranks.

"Captain, and I mean Captain, Hale! If I do live and breathe!" he announced as he came forward.

"Spicer!" Adam blurted.

"That is Vice-Admiral Spicer to you."

Adam's heart sank to see the warted nose and equine face, grown much puffier and red with age and dissolution, beneath a black wig: unmistakably Sir Ponsonby Spicer, Baronet. Only this time he boasted the impressive epaulettes of a Vice-Admiral of the Royal Navy. An épée still extended from beneath his coattails.

"You are armed," Spicer observed.

"So I am," Adam replied.

"When we last met you said the honor's mine."

"So I did."

"I have waited a long time for this day to meet you on the field of honor."

"What is honor?"

"You would know nothing of honor, I suppose," Spicer deflected the question as he turned accuser. "A rude and righteous American is all you are, full of ignorance and yet so sure of yourself."

"Fie on you! Why do you come at me like a barking dog ready to devour? You have turned into quite the accuser! Is that how you—who do not even know me—perceive me? If so, I fear you misperceive."

"And what do you perceive?"

"I perceive a tyrant who has invaded my land, threatens my home, and accuses me."

"It is you who misperceive. I only do my duty."

"More than that: you stole my son's freedom with your press gang and his life with your levy in Iberia."

"I never met your son. I did not know your son."

"No. You may have never met him, and for that I thank God. But you knew him."

Adam thought for a moment about whether he failed in his recognition of his own self as badly as Spicer had failed in his own recognition.

Yes, he was righteous, not only in his citizenship and in his war-making but also in all his dealings. All his life he had elevated that attribute of righteousness as essential to his integrity. And he realized for the first time that perhaps that was what most bothered Spicer. Their chance encounter over thirty years before triggered Spicer's obsession, which, fueled as it was by absence, had no grounding in a course of dealing between the two men, which after all would have been to ground it in reality. Rather, the Baronet's vaunting, preening pride and sense of "honor" nourished and fed his hatred over the years.

Adam continued:

"You fight me not to gain from me but to declare who or what you are by eliminating who or what I am: that righteous person, as you say. You do this out of insecurity. I suspect, Admiral, that you have the unending urge to buttress your image of yourself. But your image of self is flawed. You misrecognize who and what you in truth are. This failure renders you . . . tragic."

Spicer did not deign to respond.

"Shall we?" he asked.

"I did not seek this fight, but nor shall I turn from it."

Both men removed their coats in order to fight in shirtsleeves. Adam noticed for the first time the spindly, short legs of the coatless Baronet.

Spicer lifted off his black wig and handed it to one of his Ensigns. His head was shaven but covered in gray stubble like iron filings. He looked older, plainer, more mediocre when thus laid bare. Neither combatant was in his prime. Each was in his sixties, though Adam was the older by perhaps five years. Against Spicer's undoubted expertise with the sword Adam counted on his own fighting trim, larger frame, and hard-gained life experience to try to balance the scales. Still, he did not know the practiced moves of fencing, and he feared he would lose.

Moreover, Adam regretted his choice of weapon. Though a useful tool that could do brute damage in the hands of an experienced seaman, the heavy broad cutlass was meant more for slashing than stabbing. In contrast, the light, thin épée delivered a crease from a thin point, but in its length and precision, guided by wrist, thumb, and forefinger, it was the more effective weapon. He knew that with such mismatched weapons he was at a disadvantage.

Adam also knew that bouts were usually over quickly, often in a matter of a few minutes at most, but he was resigned to wherever fate would take him.

Spicer took a step forward and assumed the fighting position. He held his épée in a French grip, with his thumb on top and his index finger underneath, tucked up against the guard. He offered only his right profile, with his épée and body aligned, his knees slightly bent and his left arm elevated in limp balance. It was a curiously elegant stance but one that at the same time wavered with tension and energy about to explode. His jaw was set, and his cunning gray-green eyes looked not at his blade but directly into Adam's. They bespoke at once calculation and the confidence in his superior ability that would allow him to outmatch his opponent with surgical precision.

"*En garde!*" Spicer announced as he laid down his challenge.

Shaken from his musings, Adam raised his cutlass and adjusted his stance to match as best he could that of his opponent and to await the attack.

He did not wait long.

Spicer stepped forward and with alacrity thrust his blade toward Adam's chest. The initiative having thus been established, Adam knew he would be fighting a defensive battle. He stepped back and parried the thrust in tierce with the forte or lower half of his cutlass, over which he exercised the strongest control, striking the foible of Spicer's épée. Still, the blow had come too close for comfort, and Adam was at a loss for a riposte.

Spicer advanced and closed on him with another lunge. Again Adam retreated and parried the attempt. Adam realized that by ceding ground with each movement he would eventually be backed against the rock ledge and unable to defend himself. Spicer would have him where he wanted him, pinned like a butterfly in a shadow box, the latest in his no doubt large collection. He had to break the momentum of the attack.

Onward Spicer came, impeccably inline, frowning, and with discipline, not letting up. He executed a half lunge or feint. Adam took the bait and lunged to parry, only to see the flash of the épée, suddenly gone, reappear in seconde lower down. He twisted his flank out of the line of attack with only a fraction of a second to spare.

Still unable to mount a riposte, Adam parried furiously as Spicer executed a relentless redoublement of attacks which Adam parried in tierce and then in quarte and returned to garde. The broad flat blade of the cutlass clashed almost nonstop with the sleek cold steel of the épée. However, Adam refused to cede further ground. By now he had begun to grow winded at wielding the heavier blade, and he broke into perspiration.

Seeing his attack momentarily stalled, Spicer detached and caught his breath for several seconds. However, his épée quickly rose again in fighting position. This time, Adam plunged forward, on the offensive for the first time, trying to lay down a slashing blow to his opponent's head. However, Spicer easily parried it in quinte with a deft flick of the wrist, and as Adam withdrew he felt a searing pain crimp the left side of his abdomen. He dared not look down, but Spicer's eyes and faint smile told him he had scored a hit. Adam began to feel the moist warmth of his blood as it started to soak his shirt and run down his pants leg like urine.

Adam forced himself to ignore his wound because he realized that to stop would be fatal. No sooner had he composed his stance than Spicer came at him again with a thrust, which he deflected with a parry in quarte, stopping the intended high-line cut to his chest and sending the blade of the épée capering off at an angle. A deft maneuver, Adam congratulated himself. Still, Adam saw no opening for a counterattack.

Spicer backed off, paused, and then executed an appel, striking the ground with his leading foot to distract and unsettle his opponent. Adam did not flinch, and Spicer immediately resumed his offensive by lunging forth with a rapid, violent attack that barely afforded Adam time to parry and return to garde. Spicer pressed his redoubling with furious speed, grunting with each thrust and his face a mask of utter concentration. Adam's responding parries were immediate, reactive, and unable to gain any purchase; he could go no further than to *chasser les mouches*, to swat at flies. Adam's inline stance began to waver, and he stepped back a few paces, ceding ground. In truth, Adam by now was exhausted by repeating his defensive measures over and over again, and the loss of blood from his wound began to make him feel light-headed. He did not know how much longer he could sustain a defense.

Sensing that Adam's defenses were beginning to unravel, Spicer gambled with a short lunge in quarte. Adam lowered his body and extended a stop-thrust to try to break the attack. The effort fell short, but, fleetingly distracted by the unexpected maneuver, Spicer failed to notice a rock outcropping hidden by rain-slickened grass in his path of attack. His foot tripped on the rocks, and his ankle turned momentarily on the wet grass that lay over the outcropping. In the half-second before Spicer could regain his footing, Adam saw that Spicer's épée was oncoming but just off course and that Spicer was undefended. Desperate, Adam seized the opportunity provided by the only opening he had seen in the seamless attacks of his opponent. Adam ducked to evade the oncoming blade. He instinctively dropped his left hand to the ground and lowered his body under Spicer's oncoming épée. At the same time that he ducked, Adam extended and braced his left leg for strength. In a burst of dexterous agility he then planted his right leg squarely forward, bent at the knee and rigid, while straightening his sword arm upward. The result was a powerful diagonal lunge from below anchored by his extended rear leg. Spicer recognized the maneuver as a *passata-sotto*. For a fraction of a second he wondered if Adam even knew of the term. However, Spicer's speculation was inapposite, for he was too late in regaining his balance to defend against it. His eyes widened in shock as Adam summoned all his remaining strength and the brute killing power of the cutlass to find his mark high on Spicer's torso. Adam drove the blade horizontally deep into Spicer's right breast, where, unknown to Adam, its razor-sharp point delivered a fatal blow by severing the subclavian artery.

Spicer's forward momentum halted. Adam jerked his blade free and moved back in order to parry the expected counterattack. Spicer stood reeling but still armed. His face was a rictus of shock. He raised his blade as if to attack once more. Adam looked into Spicer's gray-green eyes. Gone were the calculation and confidence which would have signaled an attack. Out of instinct, experience, or righteousness, he was not sure which, Adam raised his cutlass and delivered a violent slashing coup across Spicer's exposed and vulnerable neck. The blow severed Spicer's jugular vein. Spicer dropped his épée and collapsed to the ground. He lay in a heap in a gathering pool of blood staining the green grass of the meadow as his life rapidly drained from him.

"Is he dead?" asked one of the American Captains.

"Yes, or he soon will be," Adam responded. "But don't worry, this one will rise again. He always does." The American Captains did not understand, but Adam understood all too well.

The British officers who had been watching the duel from a respectful distance began to move their hands to the pommels of their weapons. Spotting this, the American Captains unsheathed their own swords and, gathering an exhausted Adam in a protective half-moon formation, slowly backed off down the meadow toward their waiting sloop. Their arms remained raised and their eyes never left the British invaders until they reached the boat.

Captain Moody from atop the Observatory spied through the telescope as the Americans embarked and shoved off with their sails full of wind. He also watched the confusion and consternation that spread through the British landing party and how, almost an hour later, they gathered up the body of the Admiral in a tarpaulin sling and bore it to their cutter, how they rowed with it back to the black frigate and hauled it onboard, how the frigate had raised signal flags to its consorts, and finally how the squadron headed back Down East from whence it had come.

Adam's wound proved to be superficial as no vital organs were touched, though he had lost considerable blood. Dueling was of course illegal under the law of the District of Maine. An inquest was held shortly afterward. No charges were filed.

* * *

Three months later Adam found himself seated in a Concord coach with lawyer Stephen Longfellow, Junior and his eight-year-old son Henry Wadsworth Longfellow as they made the liver-jarring, bone-rattling trip to Hartford to attend a hastily called conference of the New England states. Adam stared out the window at the passing frozen December landscape, all a dismal and dreary essay in gray. He had been asked by the

Portland Captains to accompany Mr. Longfellow, who was the delegate from Maine. Adam's role was that of an "observer," an ill-defined status but one which apparently was intended to ensure that the Captains' views were made known. Mr. Longfellow occupied himself in the coach by reading law books and various treatises on constitutional law, while his son, a precocious little chap, scribbled incessantly in a notebook. In short, they were polite, quiet traveling companions.

Once at Hartford, Adam learned that only the official delegates were to be allowed into the deliberations at the State House and that the proceedings were to be secret. Therefore he passed his days at a nearby inn idling away the time by reading the newspapers, discussing rumors of secession with other "observers," and taking long walks. He was useless. He might better have never come. Each morning he took breakfast with Mr. Longfellow in the inn and pried him for information about the convention. But Mr. Longfellow was a circumspect lawyer who gave away nothing.

After two weeks of increasing frustration and as the convention's deliberations grew later into the night with each passing day, Adam sat down with Mr. Longfellow to celebrate the New Year over dinner on a bright and cold day. Mr. Longfellow, whether from exhaustion or the several glasses of madeira they had each consumed, was in a more loquacious mood than was his norm in their early morning breakfasts. At length he turned to the convention.

"Commodore, what would you say were the convention to go the way of secession? Not that it will, you understand, but let's put it as a hypothetical."

Adam responded with his right eyebrow arched. He well knew that the hypothetical masked likely reality.

"How do you think that would be received by our neighbors in Portland?" Mr. Longfellow pushed him.

Adam rocked back in his chair and thought before responding. At length he spoke.

"Well, Mr. Longfellow, we've been sorely abused by the government in Washington, and there's sentiment aplenty in New England for going out of the Union to make our separate peace with London and restore navigation and commerce. But I have to think that with all we've been through, starting with those who bled and died in our War of Independence, it would be shameful to admit defeat and toss our great experiment to the dogs. There are ideas for which we fought and indeed must continue to fight. Among these are the preservation inviolate of those exalted rights and liberties of human nature for which our countrymen fought and died. Likewise, there must be a determination to promote between the respective States that union and national honor so necessary to their happiness and to the future dignity of the American Empire. No, sir, I cannot speak for others, but for me I await a better day, which surely shall come, and I remain a Union man."

Mr. Longfellow said nothing.

Four days later the convention concluded with a report and a series of resolutions signed by all the delegates, thus signaling unanimity. Mr. Longfellow handed the documents to Adam as soon as they were public. Standing by the fireplace in the inn, Adam read the results with growing satisfaction. The report stated that New England had a "duty" to assert its authority over unconstitutional infringements of its sovereignty. The convention also proposed amendments to the Constitution prohibiting any trade embargo lasting over sixty days, requiring a two-thirds Congressional vote to declare offensive war or restrict foreign commerce, and limiting future Presidents to one term. Nowhere was secession mentioned.

As the convention broke up and Mr. Longfellow and other delegates traveled to Washington to present its report and negotiate for the terms that had been agreed, Adam took coach again for the long, jarring return journey to Portland alone. As he sat bouncing from side to side, he had many hours to reflect: on the havoc wreaked on New England's economy by narrow partisans, on the British seizure of half of Maine, on the failure of either the national government or Massachusetts to protect his homeland, and, underlying it all, the ever-widening gap between the high ideal of America's Revolution and the reality of politics as practiced in the new democracy. And yet he remained loyal to the ideal and longed for the day when it could be restored. However, he knew he was too old to fight political, as well as naval, battles. No, Cincinnatus would return to his farm for good. Back Cove beckoned.

Word had not yet reached American shores that the Treaty of Ghent, signed in Europe just days before, had ended the war and that the British would relinquish their occupied territory in Maine. America was, for the moment, whole again.

38

Stepmother Dear Redux

1816

"ELBOWS OFF THE TABLE!" BATHSHEBA SHOUTED AS SHE SCOWLED AT Hephzibah, who sat at the far end of the dining room table while the family enjoyed a dinner of rack of lamb with English peas and roasted potatoes. At fifteen Hephzibah had begun to lose her weight and was turning into a comely young woman. She bore a sharp blue-eyed, sandy-haired resemblance to her grandfather Adam. Her emergence into womanhood rankled Bathsheba all the more.

"I'm sorry, Stepmother Dear," Hephzibah murmured as she absently shifted her arms away from the table.

"Honestly, you have no manners. You don't belong at our table," Bathsheba spat, as she grew visibly more irritated. "In fact, from now on, you will dine where you belong—with the servant girls in the kitchen, eating the same fare as they do—fish stew, cold porridge, and bread. You will eat from wooden bowls rather than dine on fine china. We'll see how you like that, missy."

"I'm sorry."

"I'm sorry, *Stepmother Dear*. Now off with you to the kitchen."

Henry, a precocious dark-haired little boy aged seven, busied himself with his lamb chops while she walked out in silence, with each step of her shoes striking against the hard wooden floor to punctuate her estrangement from the family.

"Don't you think you were a little harsh on her?" Gideon asked his wife once Hephzibah had left the room.

Bathsheba rose from her seat and put her hands around her husband's shoulders. She leaned down smiling and whispered in his ear.

"She's so malleable in my hands. She's unformed and cries out for direction. We'll form her into a proper lady. Trust me."

Gideon smiled back and let the matter drop.

Henry did not.

Each evening at supper he tucked away a little of the meat or a sweet from the dessert plate into his napkin and delivered it surreptitiously to Hephzibah in the kitchen after the meal.

* * *

"I know I have been remiss," Adam conceded to Nabby. "But what with the voyage to South America and the troubles of the late war, I have had little time to attend to the issue of Hephzibah's well-being."

"We must act," Nabby prodded him. "The situation has gone from bad to worse."

"But what can we practically do? We live out here in Back Cove. Winter is coming on, and the roads will soon be impassable except by sleigh. And I have little money, while Gideon Sewell is one of the wealthiest men in Portland. What leverage do we have?"

"I don't think that Gideon is an evil man. It's just that he is so . . . preoccupied and singularly attuned to his business interests. No, the problem lies with Bathsheba. She is evil. We must confront her and try to take custody of Hephzibah. If she hates her so, perhaps she won't resist. Let me think on it as a woman."

"Fine, but not for long. I agree that we must act and do so by early in the new year."

"So we shall, dear husband."

39

Theophany

1817

ADAM HELD THE REINS OF THE SLEIGH AS IT GLIDED THROUGH THE
new snow, dry and powdery, on a Sunday morning in January. He and
Nabby rode bundled in the heavy buffalo lap robe on their way from Back
Cove to pick up Hephzibah for church in town. They drove in silence.
It was a quiet, pristine, frigid day with a bright blue sky. The branches of
the dark green fir trees in the dense forests that lined the road drooped
with the prior night's snow. Vapor poured from the horse's nostrils, and
with each step of the trotting horse the sleigh bells tinkled jauntily as the
leather straps slapped the beast's haunches. Adam's mind as he drove was
a winter's mind: blank and at one with the cold and blanketing whiteness.

After church Nabby intended to have her well-planned discussion
with Bathsheba. She did not look forward to it, and for the preceding
week she had grown increasingly tense and strained. More than once she
had cut Adam off with, "Please don't interrupt me. I am thinking."

"Adam, stop the sleigh," Nabby requested in a tight voice. "I feel ill."

Adam shot his wife a glance and saw instantly that her visage had
grown ashen and that her eyes showed pain.

"Whoa!" he ordered as he drew up on the reins. "What is it, my love?"

Nabby held her kid-gloved hand to her chest.

"I think it's my heart. I feel so . . . constricted. It's crushing . . ."

Adam dropped the reins and enveloped her in his arms.

He saw in her eyes for the first time ever a hint of panic as she looked into his own eyes searching for an answer, for reassurance.

Adam sought out her hand and tightened his grip.

"I love you, Nabby."

He kissed her cold pale cheek. He felt a barely perceptible shudder. And as he held her in his arms she died.

Adam sat in silence, dwarfed by his loss and by the immense and overarching beauty of the Maine woods that surrounded him. He cocked his ear to hear the sound of Down East. All was still and silent. The only sound was that of the patient horse shifting from foot to foot.

Adam realized that he was at once a nonentity and at one with the landscape, as surely as if he had been buried in the snow. His love was gone, the battles were all gone, the sea was all gone. And he beheld himself in the vacuity that enveloped him.

For the first time ever in his life he speculated whether the Divine Being with which he had such a personal relationship was in fact Satan or, to be more exact, whether Satan had entered and stolen the relationship by assuming the guise of the Godhead. Surely Satan's powers were so great that he could pose as God and play havoc with one poor mortal.

Or perhaps he had no relationship with the Divine and had been only talking to himself for years. Dressed as he was in his Sunday suit, wrapped in a shawl, and bundled in a buffalo robe, he had none of the intimacy that the simple and naked Adam and Eve shared with God before the Fall.

And yet, once again, Adam cried out in his mind for an answer as he held Nabby's hand in his in a silent vigil, the protector of his beloved in death as in life.

"God, why me? Why has this happened to me?"

The muffled mantle of new-fallen snow did not respond.

"God! Do you not hear me? Why don't you answer me?" Adam pleaded with an edge to his voice.

Then casting aside his last shred of Stoic principle which would have inured him to accept suffering, he demanded vindication.

"If I have wronged, put me on trial, place me in the dock and let me make my defense, for I have my side to tell!"

Still nothing but a deafening, almost symphonic silence. Adam wondered if the silence was meant to be instructive.

Oh, to be Moses on Mount Sinai or Saul on the road to Damascus, Adam thought, how blessed it would be to encounter the Divine face to face, to see and to touch, to have a revelation. But, no, five times cursed, and Adam was to be denied this balm!

Driven from silent entreaty to audible pleading, Adam railed against the heavens.

"Why treat me so? I have led a blameless life. This is not fair! Does this happen to me because you have not yet subdued the forces of chaos or because you have improperly ordered the universe?"

Only silence answered.

Adam gripped the side of the sleigh with his left hand while with his right he held up Nabby's dead hand heavenward and shouted in full cry.

"Do not turn your face from me, Oh Lord! I am in trouble! I need you to answer me speedily!" he commanded.

And then the whiteness and silence spoke. Not in a whirlwind or a pillar of fire but in the tough voice of a demanding Captain that entered into Adam's brain from he knew not where. Perhaps it was born of snow blindness or perhaps it was only his own mind thundering at the nothingness that surrounded him. Or perhaps he had read what the voice said before, and his mind was only playing tricks on him. Or perhaps not. Its source did not matter.

"Gird up your loins like a man, for I will demand of you, and you will answer me. Where were you when I laid the foundations of the earth? Where are the foundations fastened and who laid the cornerstone when the morning stars sang together and shouted for joy? Speak if you know. Who enclosed the sea with lands and stayed the proud waves when they issued forth? Who made of clouds the garment of the earth and of the darkness of night a swaddling band for it? Have you entered into the springs of the sea or walked in search of the depth? Can you bind the sweet influences of the Pleiades or loosen the bands of Orion? Shall a fault finder contend with the Almighty? Anyone who argues with God must respond."

Adam sank back in stunned silence. He did not answer the rhetorical questions because he knew that God did not seek wisdom but was imparting wisdom with his questions, while at the same time not answering Adam but shifting the subject. The unspoken answer to the questions was that God, and not Adam or any mere mortal, creates and orders the cosmos. Adam had no answer to the realization of his own insignificance in the face of the Almighty. He could not possibly comprehend what God was doing. However, he did understand that the universe is not a threatening primordial sea or the desolate wilderness of *Pilgrim's Progress* but, rather, rational, elegant, and productive of good. Indeed, Adam was the person he was because he was shaped by and a part of it. Indeed the Abbé was right: God did not create evil.

By asking God at each turn why a tragedy had befallen him he had trivialized and personalized the sweep of God's grandeur. Made in the image of God, he had the hubris to question God when he could not possibly have known the grand scheme of the universe. He had in effect been asking the wrong questions, just as the Abbé had said as they sat in his darkened room in Paris. What Adam needed to do was to recast his questions to ask about the order of Creation, of which he was only a small part. Although he had more knowledge of the Creation than the average man from his years of sailing the world, he realized his knowledge was limited. This knowledge of the limits of his knowledge humbled him. All he could do was guess at the overarching structure, realizing that he knew only a small part of the truth and that not well. Perhaps, just perhaps, evil was a waste product of the Creation, which was of such force that it must have left detritus in its wake. It was a slag heap, left churning, from that act of unbounded and breathtaking grace.

But how to deal with it?

Suffering was perhaps not disproof of God but revelatory about the basis of the universe. The point was neither that his suffering was to be solved or explained by God or that it was insignificant in the face of Creation but that Adam, as a mere mortal, could never know how it fit into the grand scheme of things. What mattered was not asking "Why me?" but "How should I respond to tragedy?" Like the blind man at Siloam, perhaps he had not been afflicted at random or because he had sinned but so that the works of God might be displayed in him. And Adam realized that the conundrum was at once ancient and profound, for across the ages mankind had devised no intellectual progress to explain suffering as it had devised to explain the workings of the stars and the planets or the ordering of plants and animals.

For this Adam sank back into the sleigh in the wisdom of profound silence, not forced there by God but realizing that he was in no position to argue with God. Instead, he just sat with Nabby and was at one with her and with the universe.

And then after perhaps a half hour, or maybe it was an hour—he could not tell—he stood and raised his arms heavenward. In praise of his God and in defiance of the Devil or whatever other forces buffeted him he forced himself to shout a reaffirmation of his faith.

"Alleluia! Alleluia! Alleluia!" he cried. "The Lord gave. The Lord has taken away. Blessed be the name of the Lord."

A high branch in a nearby fir tree shifted in salute and dropped its burden of snow to the ground with a cushioned thud.

And Adam took up the reins and drove his beloved home.

40

Passing the Torch
1818–1821

MAJOR GIDEON SEWELL ATTACKED FINANCE WITH HIS CUSTOMARY thoroughness. He applied his analytical skills to ask what made it tick and how could it be done differently in ways that others had not thought of and that could profit him, just as he had with the merchant, distilling, and banking businesses. The process was not an overnight one. He read, he talked with other merchants and bankers as he traveled up and down the East Coast, he entertained visiting foreigners. But most of all he applied his imagination to ask: how could this be done better, what unmet need might it serve and how?

One morning, while walking along Middle Street, the realization hit him: the abolition of the slave trade in 1807 was driving up the price of slaves, making them more difficult to procure and costlier to buy. Consequently, Southern planters, especially in the newer states, would need more capital in order to operate. And the way to get them more capital would be to mortgage the value of those slaves and convert the mortgages into bonds for sale on the secondary market. In the Bank of Portland he had just the vehicle to accomplish this.

Major Sewell called a special meeting of the bank's Board and explained the plan. Although some were skeptical at first, he convinced them that it would work. The sole lawyer who sat on the Board asked if it would be legal. Major Sewell replied, "That's what you're paid to advise us." The lawyer and all others at the meeting looked at each other. Not one could come up with a reason why the scheme would not be perfectly legal. It was pure and efficient capitalism applied within an existing legal framework.

Thus Major Sewell engineered the "slave bond." The bank operated through its network of correspondent institutions throughout the South to have planters compile lists of their slaves for use as collateral with attendant valuations attested by third-party appraisers. The planters then mortgaged the slaves to the bank, which lent to the planters. To provide capital for the loans, the bank packaged the mortgages and sold them as bonds to investors from all over the United States and even abroad in London, Amsterdam, and Paris. The bond holders, many of whom lived in free states or even in countries where slavery was illegal, did not own slaves, only bonds backed by the value of slaves.

The system spread, all parties other than the slaves profited, and the price of slaves went up. One unintended effect of the rising prices was that they helped to fuel continuation of the illicit slave trade which operated *sub rosa*.

Major Sewell prospered even more. If he had ever stopped to ask himself if the practice were immoral, which he never did, he might have responded that it was amoral. Or at least that is how Adam Hale judged it when he learned of it.

* * *

The case of Adam Hale was growing more problematic with the passing years. Now well into his late sixties, he had repaired full time to Back Cove, coming into town only once a week to see Hephzibah. The loss of Nabby had proven to be the final breaking point. His books and his gardens were his solace.

His heart grieved at his losses and because he was unable to change the life of his sole heir, his granddaughter Hephzibah. In the years of his retirement at Back Cove he had tried. There was his attempt early on to pick up where Nabby left off at her death. He knew he could not reason with Bathsheba, but perhaps Gideon would prove more tractable. He therefore called on him at his office.

"It's a good thing you retired from the mast trade, Commodore," Gideon informed him on meeting.

"How's that, Major?" The use of formal titles somehow facilitated the discussion.

"The timber lands are being all bought up by the paper companies, and they have other uses for the wood. Why, right now my bank is financing the purchase of thirty thousand acres up the Kennebec by a paper conglomerate out of Fitchburg, Massachusetts, and if all goes well they'll buy even more, on the Penobscot as well. Nope, the mast trade is a thing of the past. In five years it will be as dead as the dodo."

Irked by the insult to the source of his livelihood and reputation, Adam did not know how to respond. He was suddenly aware that he sat before Gideon awkwardly, his great frame barely held by the chair, at odd angles and with his hat crumpled in his lap like a humble supplicant before the smooth-cheeked younger man. He straightened his body and cleared his throat.

"I've come to see you about Hephzibah," he stated.

"Oh, she's as happy as a clam and thriving too," Gideon cheerily responded.

"That is good news, but I—"

"She is growing into a fine young woman under Bathsheba's tutelage, you know. We are so fortunate that Bathsheba has taken the time and interest to instruct her."

"But I—"

"But of course you visit her most Sundays, and that shall continue."

Suddenly aware that Gideon had conjured up an alternative reality, Adam felt as if he were sailing into a fogbank that hugged the horizon.

"So what did you want to raise?" Gideon asked.

"Nothing," Adam replied. And there he let the matter stand, resigned but not becalmed.

In the ensuing years there were still the Sunday outings to church, but with no town home to which to take her, no home cooked meals, no gentle woman's touch from Nabby. To be sure, he brought her books from his library, which she enthusiastically read and discussed with him, but until she obtained her majority he was helpless to free her from her stepmother's household. And yet he felt she was so much a part of him, not only in her physical resemblance but in her mind and spirit as well.

In his gathering years Adam occasionally harked back to his conversation with Lord Hormsby in the Vauxhall Pleasure Garden decades earlier. Lord Hormsby, who by now surely must be dead, had instructed him on Cicero's vision of old age. Adam was now approaching Lord Hormsby's age at that time. In retrospect, Lord Hormsby now reminded Adam more of Seneca than of Cicero. Seneca once told a correspondent that he was discussing "troubles which concern us both, and sharing the remedy with you, just as if we were lying ill in the same hospital." At the time, Lord Hormsby's balanced and reassuring assessments of old age provided comfort and hope. But now, faced with the reality of old age in fact, Adam's struggle to make sense of his life had assumed a frenetic and eclectic air as he rummaged through the attic of his own life's experiences, the Bible, and the classics.

First, and easiest, was the matter of money. Adam had made and lost it. He respected it as a useful tool but as nothing more. In this, he felt his life better spent than that of Major Sewell. The Bible told him that the wealth of the earth, all the sapphires and all the silver and all the gold— indeed all the great timbers marked with the King's Broad Arrow—did not constitute wisdom. He knew the price of wisdom to be above rubies. He knew that wisdom is to be found only in the fear of the Lord and that to depart from evil is just the beginning of understanding.

Or so Adam had told himself. He had long ago departed from evil, and fear of the Lord was his daily companion, even now as he sat in figurative ashes and sackcloth. But where was the redemption from this loving God? For this was the promise that he found in the Bible. It had not come, even though he lived a just and reverent life and avoided all evil. Was the Resurrection also a lie?

Or so he asked himself, for in later years he had begun to stray as he sought answers among the pagan Stoics. They used the term *logos* differently than the Bible did, even though some of them nudged deceptively close to a concept of one God. For them, as interpreted by Adam, understanding the power of choice was crucial. The invincible person was one who can be disconcerted by nothing that lies outside the sphere of choice. One must cede control of what the world has already removed from one's control anyway and keep ever present in mind the very worst that can happen. In this he was guided most particularly by the emperor-philosopher Marcus Aurelius, whose *Meditations* had become his bedside companion. Paramount was a recognition of reality and in that recognition lay the kernel of how to cope. This *logos* helped Adam to pass his days, sailing both into the wind and away from it, tacking incessantly to adapt to fate's vexing vicissitudes. But, in other respects, the philosophy of the Stoics was at best an anesthetic applied to numb the pain. It did not solve the problem. It lacked the promise of hope. At the end of the day Adam acknowledged that he should not be taken captive by philosophy.

So too had matters of state and citizenship let him down. Adam's reading of history instructed him that Rome's success rested on three pillars: its constant celebration of courage and self-sacrifice, the discipline and organization of its military which made its legions invincible, and, most importantly, the Roman constitution which provided the stability and balance that allowed Rome to surmount cycles of history. Where had America gone wrong? The Revolution and even the War of 1812 provided examples of the first pillar, but the second was at best an imperfect affair. The Constitution provided the promise of the third pillar—a nation of laws to provide stability and balance—but it was being constantly manipulated for partisan ends. Though there was much to be treasured in the great American experiment and notwithstanding his view of the Hartford Convention, sadly Adam foresaw a future when those ideals would be little more than words and in which legions of self-serving politicians and the ignorance of the populace whom they manipulated would betray the best hope of mankind. Already a lesser, silent generation, so different from his own generation of Founding Fathers, had come of age. Many of Adam's contemporaries complained about this generation of their children. But therein the hurt was even deeper, for Adam had lost all his children and lacked even the luxury of complaint.

That brought Adam's thoughts to his family, the fundamental unit of social organization. Family members counted for all. They were the accompaniment with which he walked in this life, the pleasure of their company measured in only a few precious decades. But for Adam, the passage of time had been little more than a process of loss. He often turned over in his mind the forms of evil which led to the losses of those he loved most. His role, if there were one, in their demises was not evil but well intended. In purchasing the maps, in moving to Portland, in sending two of his sons to sea he had acted only from the best of motives, even if such pure intentions had caused lethal damage. No, there was more at work here. In the cases of Thankful and Juvenal, it was natural evil, pure and simple: disease and a storm at sea. In the case of Jezreel it was the evil of man exercising his free will, borne equally by Jezreel and Major Gaskill. The cases of Seth and Nabby were more nuanced. At first blush they could be called instances of natural evil, but there were also elements of free will involved: Seth, though ordered into the theater by Spicer, had exercised his free will to volunteer to the American Minister, and Bathsheba had exercised her free will for moral evil by causing Nabby's distress and death, thereby bearing equal weight with the natural causes as the true assassin of Nabby.

Or, in fact, Adam asked himself, were all five deaths the handiwork of the third form of evil: Satan active in the world? A lifetime later, he had no clearer answer than he did when he sat in the Abbé's *hôtel* in Paris while the French Revolution's opening coda played around him.

As then, he reminded himself that the causes did not matter. The end result was the same whatever the cause. Only the damage mattered, unchangeable, ineradicable damage.

But, as Adam had slowly learned, the pertinent question was not "Why me?" It was "How do I fit into a universe I only dimly comprehend other than to live justly and sing praises to the almighty Creator of this universe?"

Adam did this, as he turned back to the Bible for the best answer. But the classics also got in a final word as well, as he concluded that at his age he had merely become the rotting matter that inevitably dies off and becomes the fuel for new ideas and commitments of the succeeding generation. Nothing is born without another's death, he reminded himself. Decomposition is essential for any new flowering. Was he succumbing to the hard-earned wisdom of Lucretius, underlined in pencil in another volume he kept by his bed, that "the sum of things is perpetually renewed. . . . The generations of living things pass in swift succession and like runners hand on the torch of life?"

41

The Veiled Coquette

1822

EVERY MORNING ADAM INSPECTED HIS FACE IN THE LOOKING GLASS AS he shaved at the wash basin in his rented room on Smith Street. He had moved two years before, when he had to sell Back Cove to meet his living expenses. The house was on a cobblestoned lane that clung to the backside slope of Munjoy Hill. In Adam's heyday sailors and small artisans lived on the incline. By now it was a street of pushcarts, rooms that rented by the week—or, in some cases, by the hour—and the occasional wafting of the scent of three-day-old mackerel dropped by the seagulls that wheeled and screed overhead.

Although well into his seventy-third year of life, the Commodore still counted himself a vigorous man. To be sure, he grumbled at the occasional complaint, such as encroaching deafness and stiffness in the joints—a touch of the arthritic discomfort that is the curse of Anglo-Saxons. But his face was still not creased by wrinkles, save for the crows' feet that had crept about his eyes for most of his adult life, and his sandy hair still hung full and long, albeit traced generously with steel gray. His considerable frame perhaps stooped a little more and was a touch smaller than when he was in his prime, but that mattered little, for his nose and blue eyes still commanded attention. Occasionally, as he shaved, he inspected his face in the looking glass and allowed himself a smile at the corner of his lips in the knowledge that he was still a man in full at a time when many of his contemporaries were dead.

The Commodore now led a simple life. Such was the rhythm imposed by penury. Mrs. Grogan, an Irish woman, came in to cook for him twice a week and to clean. He ate like a fo' c'stle hand—cod chowder, hardtack, and the occasional Indian pudding. His possessions had dwindled to what could be stored in the old sea chest at the foot of his bed and in the single dresser beneath the window. Save for a dozen books, he had sold his library to the Portland Atheneum for a pittance but with the immeasurable compensation of a lifelong privilege of borrowing from that institution whatever he wished to read. He had long ago parted with his prize possession, the Venetian bow-chasers, to meet living expenses. However, he kept the brass medal struck by a grateful Congress. Each morning when he arose he placed it in his palm and fingered it, keeping its shine new. How much in his life had been tawdry and as tarnishable as brass, Adam often observed as he held the medal in his hand. "*Non Gloria Sed Memoria*." Not Glory But Remembrance. Now, at long last, Adam understood the import of the cryptic and puzzling inscription: he had no glory, only memories. It elicited a hollow laugh from him whenever he read it.

In good weather Adam spent the mornings on the promenade looking eastward over Casco Bay, Nabby's walk, reading and watching the sun rise from the Atlantic and warm the islands spread out before him. Every day, foul or fair, he walked to Fore Street, near his old business house, where a bench on the street or a seat in the Exchange became his quarterdeck. Those old Captains who remained knew him and traded the gossip of the town with the Commodore, as he was universally known. Indeed, Adam made a point of these forays as much to spite his son-in-law as for the companionship. All the old salts knew the story of Adam Hale and Gideon Sewell, and, without a word or allusion or ever a question, attested their loyalty by their companionship. Adam found some justification in the small but wise court over which he presided.

Not that there was any question of their helping the Commodore in his straitened circumstances. With the tonnage shipped from Portland still not recovered from the disaster of the Embargo of 1807, they were hardly in a position to lend a hand. But even if they had been, that was not the way in either the new State of Maine or, for that matter, the old District of Maine. Adam Hale's business was his private affair, and his problems were his alone. One did not interfere.

Of course there were long, lonely hours between his forays out, particularly in the late afternoons when the sun set so early in the winter months or as he lay falling asleep at night. With Nabby gone for some years, Adam had begun a courtship with another siren. She came not as a barreling coach as in his earlier years but as a veiled coquette, at once beautiful and comforting. Adam and the coquette flirted. They danced. Adam longed to place his head on her soft bosom and have her enfold him. She was lovely and each time more enticing. Old age, Adam observed, had its kindnesses. Or, once again, was the veiled coquette merely Satan in one of his many guises, like the Greek gods of old who took human or animal form, male or female, at will? After all, Genesis and the Book of Wisdom told him that death was the Devil's creation, not God's. Or was she perhaps a mermaid, both loved and feared by superstitious sailors around the world? In the sharp light of the morning Adam knew she was a phantasm and rejected her. But she would always come again, and each time the flirtation grew deeper and more profound and even sensual. Adam suspected that someday he would succumb and blend his body into hers.

But that was not yet to be.

Every Sunday without fail Adam stirred himself from his room and walked the half mile down the hill to the First Parish meetinghouse for services. He had been forced to sell his purchased family pew years earlier, so now he took his place in the pew reserved for visiting strangers, far back of the row occupied by Gideon Sewell and Bathsheba. At least the ploy avoided inconvenient conversation. Having attended the meetinghouse for almost forty years he knew where each family, each person, sat, much as God in the Gospel knew each hair on our heads and each thought of our minds.

On a cold and bright Sunday in late March he took his customary place and immediately noticed that something was out of the ordinary in a pew nor'nor'east of him by four rows. The sanctuary of the church was graced by what he instantly recognized as the most beautiful woman he had ever seen in his life. Who she was or where she came from he had no idea. But there she was: an exquisite profile with an aristocratic nose and deep blue eyes, her face elegant in proportion and flawless beauty, her blonde hair worn in curls in the style of a Roman matron like Dolley Madison's and surmounted at her forehead by a blue silk band on which were emblazoned the stars and the moon. Her fashionable blue-striped silk dress draped her statuesque figure and rising breasts as if it were the merest accompaniment to the underlying beauty of her body. And the most remarkable thing of all: she turned and smiled. Her flawless beauty exploded into an array of warmth and feeling that enveloped and washed over Adam like a wave. It was an immediate and unsought intrusion into Adam's world, unmistakable in its implications. Adam could not remove his eyes from her, swept away as he was with her raw and electric beauty.

Adam tried to guess her age. At her side sat a small girl, well dressed and with a head of hair the color of tow. She might plausibly have been in her early thirties, perhaps more, perhaps less. Less than half Adam's age, he stated self-consciously to himself. But somehow that was an irrelevancy. Throughout the readings and the prayers and the interminable sermon Adam caught himself sneaking a look at her from the corners of his eyes whenever decency allowed. She occasionally turned to look back at the congregation, perhaps with a touch of the nervousness of the newcomer, and each time Adam feared she caught him out in his returned stare and he quickly averted his eyes. Adam perceived that she bore a special bond with her daughter, to judge from the attention and interaction between the two of them, and that they inhabited almost a microcosmic world that excluded all others. She delighted in the girl and in her motherhood, and each time her gaze alighted on another small child in the congregation that special smile, so warm, so greeting, so enveloping, burst forth and shared its beauteous rays all about her. Adam was smitten and transfixed.

The ensuing Sunday and each Sunday thereafter Adam attended church not to worship God but to worship her. He found his intervening week a dull, low spell enlightened only by his thoughts of her, which he rationed out to brighten his weekdays. He looked forward to each

Sunday morning as the high point of his week, and he basked in the afterglow of her presence each Sunday afternoon. He bathed in each wave of emotion at the sight of her, an accumulation of waves which relentlessly and inexorably eroded the mortar of the brick wall that he had so stoutly built about his life. There was no mistaking the thralldom now in which he was held. However, Adam could not think of a way to make contact with her without having it, well, misunderstood. After four Sundays he still did not know her name or whether she was married, widowed, or otherwise. A certain quickness or even nervousness surrounded her motions. No sooner had the service concluded than she and the girl disappeared, gone until the next Sunday.

As March wore on into a delayed spring Adam retrieved from the bottom of his sea chest his old blue captain's greatcoat. Adam inspected it for moth holes and, satisfied that there were none, tried it on. The coat still fit and even cloaked his aging frame in the aura of youth and vigor. He spent a long dark Saturday evening polishing the brass buttons by candlelight so that they gleamed as they did when he commanded the *Atheling*. The next morning, Adam wore the coat to church. The desired effect, the full and august captain as he strode into the church with a gust of cold air from off the bay and took his seat, drew a quick and appraising glance from the blue-eyed beauty which Adam did not fail to notice. He had stolen the weather gauge.

Throughout the Reverend Doctor Nichols's sermon Adam turned over thoughts in his mind like a well-worn coin. How natural, how normal it would be simply to introduce himself to her under the guise of welcoming her to the congregation. Of course, he, and presumably she, knew that there was a subtext to the overture. Thus, it was false and therefore unworthy. Maybe a better tact was to cut her out and fire a broadside, tell her the truth: that she was the most beautiful woman he had ever met. But he had not, strictly speaking, *met* her. Moreover, that was a risky ploy that tipped his hand and courted embarrassment. What if she did not reciprocate his affections? No, that would never serve! So, yet another Sunday slipped by, the victim of Adam's indecision.

One Sunday, when winter was belatedly giving up its grip to the short Maine spring, Adam overheard a fellow congregant after the service refer to "Emma Coatesworth—Mrs. Coatesworth—who is new to the parish with her young daughter." Adam did not know the man well, but he wanted to interrupt him and ask, "Who is this 'Mrs. Coatesworth?' Was she married? From where had she come? What was she as a person (for all his joy in her presence, Adam admitted his ecstasy had not been born of her heart or her mind)?" Adam turned to inject himself into the conversation but immediately realized how jarring such an intrusion would be. The stranger would surely note his interest and wonder why he asked such questions. Rumors would spread. Better, like his hero the late General Washington, to control his impulses and master his urges. Adam sank back.

Still, Mrs. Coatesworth continued to exert her inexorable influence over Adam. So captivated had Adam become that he sensed a crumbling of the other pillars of his life. When he stopped to analyze it, which he did often, he suspected that his obsession with Mrs. Coatesworth, as one-sided as it was, was not like looking through a pane of glass into the soul of the person on the other side but more like looking into a mirror, as shallow as a pane of glass coated with mercury: was he only seeing himself in return? Worse still, his fixation on Mrs. Coatesworth had moved in, made itself at home and displaced his interest in religion. True, he still went through the motions of participating in the service, but he realized that as he did so his mind was elsewhere, fixated on the lovely creature before him. This, Adam acknowledged to himself, was separation from God and therefore sin. Was Mrs. Coatesworth, like the other woman in his life, the veiled coquette, just the Devil in another guise sent to him to lure him from the one true God? Adam did not know but found the possibility unsettling. Perhaps he should confess his fixation, and his sin, to the Reverend Nichols and seek his learned guidance. Adam weighed this course heavily but in the end concluded that he should not bother the minister with his petty follies. No, this was a lonely vigil, as solitary as picket duty or a graveyard watch on the South China Sea.

On other occasions Adam thought his interest in Mrs. Coatesworth more normal, more appropriate. Were not the winds of romanticism sweeping Europe and even America in art and music? Perhaps he was just being current with the times—surely an appropriate awareness. After all, Adam was widowed and free to court and remarry at any time, as so many of his contemporaries had after losing their wives to childbirth or disease. There was no scandal or shame in that. With this in mind, Adam resolved to bring the matter to a head.

Sunday July 28 was one of those rare bright mornings of the foisson of summer when sunlight dappled the leaves of the trees along Congress Street and just a hint of an afternoon scorcher rose with the sun from across Casco Bay. As Adam took his customary borrowed seat in the visitors' pew, he noticed that the windows on both sides of the length of the nave had been thrown open, admitting the outside in so that the sacred space and nature joined and mingled in a cacophony of sensations of bustling silks, powdered summer muslins, throat clearing, sunlight, and street noise.

Mrs. Coatesworth and her daughter entered and took their places. As they waited for the service to begin, Mrs. Coatesworth turned to look back at the congregation. Or was it at Adam? The deep blue eyes flashed and the warming smile exploded in his presence and bared her soul and, in so doing, his as if they both were as naked as Adam and Eve.

Adam thought of the women in his life, each so different and yet so enticing: the unimpeachable Nabby, the veiled coquette, and—oh how delightfully fate had knocked him up—Mrs. Coatesworth.

The Reverend Nichols read the Lesson. Adam cocked his head.

"The voice of my beloved! Behold, he cometh leaping upon the mountains, skipping upon the hills. My beloved is like a roe or a young hart: behold, he standeth behind our wall, he looketh forth at the window, shewing himself through the lattice. My beloved spake, and said unto me, Rise up, my love, my fair one, and come away. For lo, the winter is past, the rain is over and gone; the flowers appear on the earth; the time of the singing of birds is come, and the voice of the turtle dove is heard in our land; the fig tree putteth forth her green figs, and the vines with the tender grape give a good smell. Arise, my love, my fair one, and come away."

Adam instantly recognized the Song of Solomon. So it would be: a course sou'sou'west, to seas he had never sailed. Today Adam would tell Mrs. Coatesworth the truth of his affections.

A Psalm followed and then a hymn, but the Song of Solomon still sang in his ears and in his heart.

The Reverend Nichols announced the Gospel, and Adam at once detected a rude shift in the breeze, as jarring as any that Nature or Christianity delivers:

"And he said, That which cometh out of the man, that defileth the man. For from within, out of the heart of men, proceed evil thoughts, adulteries, fornications, murders, thefts, covetousness, wickedness, deceit, lasciviousness, an evil eye, blasphemy, pride, foolishness: All these evil things come from within, and defile the man."

There followed one of those great silences at which the Meeting House excelled, as if to let the words sink in and each communicant to ponder which transgression applied to him. Adam fondled four words that had just been spoken: adulteries, fornications, covetousness, lasciviousness. And, oh yes, maybe foolishness.

The sonorous bronze bell in the tower of the church, no brass imitation, broke the contemplative silence with its measured toll. Adam shivered as each paced stroke of the clapper, not to be hurried, sounded at its own inexorable tempo. As he did, the outside intruded in through an open window as Adam spied the ropes and wooden swing that hung from the strong low branch of the oak tree in the churchyard swaying back and forth, its occupant departed moments earlier to join parents in the worship service. For an exquisite moment that stretched into eternity, the arc of the child's swing matched the pace of the bell as it swung tolling to and fro.

And Adam was reminded of the other woman in his life: the child, his granddaughter Hephzibah, whom he had so often swung on that swing.

The child was Adam's last vision. As he held her before his mind a sudden sweat broke his brow as a viselike seizure gripped his side. Adam ceased to see, and time hung suspended. It might have been a minute, a day, a week, Adam knew not. In some perverse unraveling of what was knitted in the womb, he could hear but he could not see or speak. From somewhere came a preacher's voice:

"The wolf also shall dwell with the lamb, and the leopard shall lie down with the kid."

Adam thought he understood. In his pain and blackness he realized that he was being sent a message.

"And the calf and the young lion and the fatling together; and a little child shall lead them. And the cow and the bear shall feed; their young ones shall lie down together: and the lion shall eat straw like the ox. And the suckling child shall play on the hole of the asp, and the weaned child shall put his hand on the cockatrice's den. They shall not hurt nor destroy in my holy mountain; for the earth shall be full of the knowledge of the Lord, as the waters cover the sea."

They shall not hurt nor destroy. My holy mountain. The knowledge of the Lord, oh, most precious of all knowledge.

As the waters cover the sea.

Adam ceased to reason, and he passed over into that realm where the knowledge of the Lord rewards faith. His covenant was fulfilled.

* * *

The following Tuesday was a blustery humid day with thunderstorms scudding in, even in the morning, from across the westward mountains. The burial in the Hale plot beneath a simple white marble ledger stone at Eastern Cemetery was perforce a hurried affair. Gideon Sewell had made the arrangements and presided over the ceremony with assistance from the Reverend Nichols. Sewell was the only member of the family present. Bathsheba had forbidden Hephzibah to come. Mrs. Coatesworth, it turned out, was otherwise engaged. A handful of aged Captains, contemporaries of the Commodore, attended.

As they approached the grave site, Gideon Sewell hurried the mourners along.

"Look, gentlemen," he said as he pointed with pride to a newly erected purple stone monument in the latest fashion of a table which stood not twenty yards away. "Here is the Sewell family tomb. This will stand for the ages."

The old Captains went along politely, but not one was later to say that he was impressed.

When the Captains arrived at the grave, the attendants all too quickly lowered the plain wooden coffin into the tomb on straps. Once it had settled, the Reverend Nichols tossed a handful of dirt on top and mumbled solemn words about "dust to dust" and said a final prayer from the 77th Psalm:

"Your way was in the sea, and your paths in the great waters, yet your footsteps were not seen."

And the burial service was over. The Captains stood about, not quite ready to take their leave.

"At least it was quick. He didn't suffer," mumbled a tall and bent old-timer dressed in his brass-buttoned blue greatcoat out of respect for his friend and colleague.

"Aye," replied another, identically attired but stout and balding with a fringe of wispy hair that blew in the wind. "Dr. Noyes says it was a stroke or seizure. You saw it in the church, didn't you? He stopped breathing and slumped over. It was as if his heart stopped or his brain just ceased to function. He passed right there, sitting in the pew."

"Would that we all might be so fortunate—"

"Aye. The Commodore was a blessed man. And not just in his departing. He was blessed in his living too. Always treated people fairly. Made and lost a fortune. Raised a fine family, though he suffered grievously in losing them. Taught himself and never stopped learning. Had an inquiring and discerning heart and mind. Sailed the open seas and carried the American flag to the courts of Europe. He was a Captain of the old school, when to sail forth and do commerce was to make our Republic great. He was a citizen of virtue, a true Cincinnatus."

Another wrinkled, even older Captain with blue eyes surmounted by brows like whisk brooms, who had long served as a Deacon at Old Jerusalem, spoke up.

"The Commodore was all that and more too. He had the courage to will and to persevere. He wrestled not just against the flesh and blood of men but against powers, against the rulers of the darkness of this world, against spiritual wickedness that inhabits high places. But he never gave in or lost his faith. If he had, he would have lost all he had, for that was all he had in the end. As it was, he remained whole and never fell into the abyss. He had the spirit to know and to love God."

The other Captains all round nodded in assent.

"But was there joy and wonder in that knowledge?" the balding Captain asked.

The wizened old Captain cast a hard, doubting glance Down East in the direction from which all wealth and tribulations came before knotting his eyebrows and reverting his apprising blue eyes—as lucid as a New England September morn—to the tarrying Captains.

"Joy? What has joy to do with it?" he said as he curled down the corners of his mouth with Puritan disdain. "But wonder, most certainly and in the glory of all its facets. To have fought nature and man and to have won every time he ventured out in a ship is a matter of wonder. And there's the wonder of whether evil is a force—when you know full well that energy must be summoned to resist it. If wonder means awe, then do you not wonder at our helplessness and incomprehension before the Divine? And do you not wonder why the rational mind of mortals—try as it might—cannot master the reason for evil in God's creation?"

Silence reigned, as always.

"Is not evil the arena in which we are condemned to define ourselves as moral human beings?"

Author's Note

HEPHZIBAH DID NOT TARRY LONG AFTER OBTAINING HER TWENty-first birthday to depart the house on Elm Street and her stepmother. By then she had grown into a tall and handsome young lady who bore an uncanny resemblance to her late grandfather the Commodore. All the town knew who she was and her heritage when she was out and about. She also was a well-read and intelligent young lady, thanks to her grandmother's tutelage and her grandfather's books. These interests had led to her employment as an assistant librarian at the Atheneum. In short, she was attractive, intelligent, independent—and impecunious. The last point affected her prospects of obtaining a husband.

Henry Sewell grew up and went to sea, becoming a Captain and ship owner in his own right at an early age. He made a fast fortune in trade with Cuba and New Orleans. He died in New Orleans of yellow fever while still in his twenties. He left his not inconsiderable estate to his half-sister Hephzibah out of pity for her mistreatment. Within one year of the death of Henry Sewell, Hephzibah Sewell married a successful Portland banker. They had two sons. The family survived.

In the 1970s, vandals smashed the ledgers stones and destroyed the tombs of both the Hale and Sewell families in Eastern Cemetery on Munjoy Hill. Today the families lie in unmarked graves. Captain Adam Hale's storehouse on Fore Street no longer stands. It is now the site of a driveway check-in for a Hyatt hotel. Major Gideon Sewell's house is long gone, replaced by the Portland Public Library. The Portland Observatory still stands. It did not prove to be a Tower of Babel. And Major Sewell's ballroom chairs still adorn a living room.

In writing the scene on Captain Adam Hale's argument with God following the death of his wife, the author consulted the Book of Job in his great-great-grandmother's Bible dating from the early nineteenth century. The Bible had rested for over one hundred and fifty years on a high shelf. Opening the Bible, he found clovers pressed in the very pages in the Book of Job that he sought. They were almost certainly placed there by the real "Hephzibah" on some sunny summer's day in Maine in the middle of the nineteenth century. Now brown and friable, they were a message across the centuries from the hand of the real "Hephzibah" to her closest living descendant. It was a moment of supreme grace.

Glossary

ADMIRAL OF THE BLUE—A FLAG-RANK NAVAL OFFICER. THE RANK OF Admiral consisted of three tiers under the command of the Admiral of the Fleet: Admiral, Vice-Admiral, and Rear-Admiral in descending order. The structure for Admirals was further divided into three squadrons—red, white, and blue in descending order, each with a van, middle, and rear division commanded by an Admiral, Vice-Admiral, and Rear-Admiral respectively. Thus, a Rear-Admiral of the Blue was the lowest-ranking flag officer.

Admiral of the White—The next stage up on the ladder of promotion above Admiral of the Blue. Thus, a Vice-Admiral of the White outranked both a Vice-Admiral of the Blue and a Rear-Admiral of the Blue.

Appel—In fencing, to beat the ground with the ball of the foot as a maneuver to unsettle an opponent.

Baulk—To haul mast timbers to the nearest waterway for transportation.

Belay—To secure a running rope, often used in handling sails, to a cleat or belaying pin. The latter, usually made of wood and stored in holes along the fife rail, was often used as a cudgel or weapon.

Berline—A large heavy enclosed carriage drawn by four or six horses.

Bilbo—An iron bar with sliding shackles attached to the deck used to secure the ankles of prisoners.

Binnacle—A wooden box that houses the compass of a ship, usually located near the ship's wheel.

Bosun—Short for Boatswain, a petty officer, normally one of the ablest seamen, who exercised a variety of tasks aboard ship, including supervising sails and rigging and calling men to duty.

Bow-chaser—A small bore long gun mounted in the bow of the ship and used for long forward shots in pursuits.

Bower anchor—One of the two largest anchors located at the bow of the ship. The "best bower" is the bower located on the starboard side.

Brig—A two-masted square-rigged ship whose rear or main mast also carries a lower fore-and-aft rigged sail with a gaff and boom. The brig was a common ship design in late eighteenth- and early nineteenth-century America and was widely used for merchant ships.

Broad reach—"Reaching" is when the wind is coming from the side of the ship. A "beam reach" is when the wind is at a right angle to the boat. A "close reach" is a course closer to the wind than a beam reach but below close-hauled. A "broad reach" is a course further away from the wind than a beam reach but above a run. In a broad reach, the wind is coming from behind the boat at an angle. This represents a range of wind angles between beam reach and running downwind.

Bumbo—A concoction of rum, sugar, water, and nutmeg whose popularity with Caribbean pirates endowed it with a certain cachet among the seafaring set.

Capstan—A revolving wooden cylindrical mechanism used to weigh or lift an anchor or other items. It is operated by sailors who push capstan bars inserted into sockets in the capstan.

Carronade—A squat, short-barreled cannon that fires a heavy shot over a shorter distance than a long gun. Carronades were introduced in the late eighteenth century and became commonplace by the time of the Napoleonic Wars.

Chains—Wooden mounting attached to the exterior of a ship's hull used to secure the lower shrouds of a mast to the hull.

Chasser les mouches—A old French fencing phrase that pejoratively refers to frantic parrying resembling the swatting of flies.

Close-hauled—Sailing with sails pulled in as tightly as possible in order for the ship to sail close to the wind, thereby allowing the ship to travel diagonally to the wind direction or "upwind."

Coaming—Elevated border around hatches on deck designed to prevent water from running below.

Commodore—A Captain in command of a squadron or station. Sometimes used as an honorific title.

Consol—A British government-issued investment security, short for Consolidated Annuities.

Cross the T—An offensive maneuver in which a warship evades the broadside fire of its opponent and passes to the stern of its opponent, allowing it to fire with its own broadside on the most vulnerable part of the ship.

Cuirassier—A cavalry soldier wearing a cuirass or breast and back plate armor. More specifically, an armored French heavy cavalryman wearing a cuirass.

Cutlass—A short, heavy naval saber.

Cutter—A short, broad boat belonging to a warship capable of being either rowed or sailed and used to carry passengers.

Cutting out—The capture of a ship in port.

Dead rise—The line rising upward horizontally from the keel rabbet (the point where the top of the keel connects to the hull) to the chine (or sideboards). It rises on each side of the keel in a straight line, or "dead rise," creating the flat V shape of the bottom of the hull.

Dhow—An Arab vessel, usually with a single mast and lateen sail.

District of Maine—The legal status of Maine when owned by Massachusetts prior to its obtaining statehood in 1820.

Drogger—A small coasting vessel used in Jamaica and the West Indies.

Épée—A narrow, sharp dueling sword, triangular in crosssection and used for thrusting.

Fid—A conical wooden pin used to separate strands of rope when splicing.

Fife rail—The uppermost rail on the elevated wooden sides of the stern of a ship extending above the deck. Also a railing surrounding the main mast used for storage of belaying pins.

Foible—In fencing, the front blade of a sword, from mid-blade to point, used in the attack.

Forecastle—The upper deck forward of the foremast; also the quarters of the crew which are beneath this portion of the deck. Also known as the "fo'c'sle."

Foretopman—A seaman stationed at the top of the foremast, usually an experienced and skilled sailor.

Forte—In fencing, the rear and stronger part of the blade, from hilt to midpoint.

French grip—In fencing, a generic term used to describe any of a variety of semistraight sword grips, most often with the thumb on top and index finger underneath tucked against the guard or quillions.

Gaff—A spar used to secure the head of a fore-and-aft sail.

Guano—The excrement of seabirds, found principally on islands off the coasts of Chile and Peru, and used for fertilizer.

Gunwale—The top edge of a vessel's side.

Halliard—A rope or tackle used to raise sails, spars, etc. Also spelled "halyard."

Harrison chronometer—An instrument first conceived in 1736 and perfected over the next thirty years by the English watchmaker John Harrison for accurately determining longitude, thereby revolutionizing navigation.

Hawse—The portion of the bow of a ship containing the hawse-holes which allow passage of the anchor cable.

Hawse-hole—One of two cylindrical holes in the bow of a ship through which the anchor cable runs. To rise "through the hawse-hold" means to come up from the lowest ranks.

Hermaphrodite brig—A brig which has the foremast of a brig and a main mast of a fore-and-aft rigged schooner.

Holystone—A sandstone block used to clean and scour the deck of a ship.

In tierce—The third of eight parrying positions in fencing, used to defend the upper sword arm portion of the body and the most important parrying position in saber parrying in that it covers the whole side. Other parrying positions, ranging from low to high, include in seconde, in quarte, and in quinte (the last being a head defense).

Jackass brig—A brig which has a square topsail and topgallant sail instead of a gaff topsail.

Jib—On a brig, a triangular sail that extends from the bowsprit to the foremast.

Jolly boat—A ship's small boat used for multiple tasks, often hoisted on davits at the stern of the ship.

Keel—The main foundational timber of the ship upon which the rest of the ship is constructed, in effect the backbone of the ship.

Keelson—A lengthwise timber that runs along the bottom of a ship parallel with and bolted to the keel in order to fasten the keel and floor timbers together.

King's Broad Arrow—A mark blazed on living trees or etched on cannons and other naval stores consisting of three strokes in the shape of an arrow /|\, denoting British naval property.

Leeches—The nonsecured edges of a sail, such as the vertical edges of a square sail.

Leeward—Any side that is in the lee of the wind, that is, sheltered from the wind.

Letter of marque—Legal authority from a government or monarch to outfit a vessel and use it to attack and seize merchant shipping in what would otherwise be an act of piracy; more fully known as a "letter of marque and reprisal."

Linstock—A pole holding a lit match used to fire a cannon.

Lobscouse—A sailor's stew comprised of salt meat, vegetables, and crumbled sea biscuit.

Lunge—In fencing, to make a forward thrust with the blade simultaneously with a large step or stomp forward.

Master—The Captain of a merchant vessel, more of a generic term denoting command rather than a rank.

Mate—The rank of officer of a merchant ship next below the Master.

Orlop—The lowest deck of a ship.

Parry—In fencing, to block or turn aside an opponent's blade, a defensive maneuver.

Passata-sotto—In fencing, an evasive action initiated by dropping a hand to the floor or ground and lowering the body under an opponent's oncoming blade, often accompanied by straightening the sword arm to attempt a hit on the opponent. Also known as the "Night Thrust," presumably because it is such a risky move that it should be performed only in the dark.

Pawls—Short bars hinged in one direction on a capstan to prevent slippage or backward motion caused by the weight of the item being lifted, such as an anchor being weighed.

Phaeton—A light open carriage, often fast and unstable; the sports car of its day.

Pink—A small square-rigged ship used primarily for coastal trade and fishing.

Port—Facing toward the bow, the left-hand side of a ship.

Post-Captain—A Captain in the Royal Navy who is the commanding officer of a post ship, meaning a rated ship having no fewer than twenty guns.

Quarterdeck—An elevated deck at the stern of a ship from which the Captain supervises the operation of the vessel, often used as a promenade and regarded as the private preserve of the Captain.

Quintal—A measure of weight equal to one hundred pounds; used to weigh cod and other dried fish.

Quoin—A wooden wedge with a handle used to adjust the elevation of a cannon.

Rabelo—A long, narrow lateen-rigged, high-prowed river craft, probably of ancient Phoenician origin, used to transport port wine down the Douro River in Portugal.

Ratline—A small, tarred rope attached horizontally to a shroud to form a step by which sailors ascend and descend the rigging.

Razee—A large ship of the line with its upper deck or decks removed, rendering it a heavy frigate.

Redoublement—In fencing, the act of attacking again and again. Also called "redoubling."

Reef—To reduce the area of exposed sail by rolling the sail up and securing it, to take in sail.

Scarphed—The joining of the notched ends of two pieces of timber to make a longer one, as in a keel.

Schooner—A fore-and-aft rigged vessel of two or more masts, often built for speed and used in the coastal and West Indies trade and occasionally as a naval vessel.

Sennit—Cordage used to make halliards.

Sheet—A rope used to manipulate a sail.

Shroud—A major element of the standing rigging of a ship used to support a mast. Parallel ropes or ratlines ran through the shroud to provide a ladder giving seamen access to the mast.

Sky sail—A high light sail above the royal sail used in a favorable light wind.

Sloop—A small, single-masted, fore-and-aft rigged vessel with a mainsail and jib. Also a small warship carrying guns only on the main deck.

Smack—A single-masted, fore-and-aft rigged vessel used in the coastal trade or fishing.

Smoke—To understand, to discern.

Snow—A two-masted, square-rigged merchant ship similar to a brig, but also having a small trysail mast behind the main mast.

Sounding lead—A device made of lead used for determining the depth and nature of the ocean floor. The lead was attached to a long line and was heaved into the water by a leadsman, who observed and called out the depth as denoted by marks on the line. The tip of the lead was charged with wax which could pick up sand or gravel confirming that it had touched bottom and indicating the nature of the ocean floor.

Spanker—A fore-and-aft sail set with a gaff and boom on the main mast of a brig.

Starboard—Looking toward the bow, the right-hand side of a ship.

Staysail—A triangular, fore-and-aft sail extended on a stay (part of the standing rigging that supports a mast).

Stop-thrust—In fencing, a thrust delivered to the opponent at the moment the opponent advances to attack.

Studdingsail—A supplemental sail set on a small yard and boom beyond the leech of a square sail, used in light winds. Also spelled "stunsail."

Tack—To change a ship's course by turning the bow to and across the wind in order to place the wind on the opposite side of the ship.

Taffrail—The uppermost stern railing, on larger warships often bearing elaborate carving.

Tampion—A wooden disk used as a wad in a breech-loaded cannon.

Theodicy—The vindication of God or divine providence in relation to the existence of evil in the world.

Topgallant sail—The third sail above the deck.

Wale—A thick timber forming the outer side of a ship.

Warp—To move a ship by pulling on a warp, that is, a rope attached to a kedge anchor; used to move a ship about a harbor or road, especially in the absence of a breeze.

Wear—To come around on another tack by turning the ship's head away from the wind, thereby bringing the bow around on a new course.

Weather gauge—A position in which a ship is windward of another vessel and in line of attack against that vessel.

Acknowledgments

I DETERMINED TO WRITE THIS BOOK WHEN, AS A TEN-YEAR-OLD, I vis-ited the grave of my great-great-great grandmother on Munjoy Hill in Portland, Maine. She died at age thirty and was the real-life model for Thankful Hale Sewell. The outlines of the story were passed down to me by my great aunts, who in the nineteenth-century portion of their lives were closer in time to these events and knew some of the people depicted in this story. A major impetus for writing it came when St. Antony's College, Oxford University, offered me a fellowship in 1991 specifically to write the prototype of this book, a novel of historical fiction exploring the differing concepts of citizenship in the United States and Great Britain. I was unable to accept the fellowship because of family obligations at the time, but I nonetheless started to write the book. The process took over twenty-five years, mostly working during summer vacations overlooking Somes Sound on Mount Desert Island, Maine.

Many people influenced this book, either wittingly or unwittingly. Among those many, I would like to acknowledge the late Ralf Dahren-dorf, Baron Dahrendorf (1929–2009), Warden of St. Antony's College, Oxford, who was the first to believe in it; Drs. Frank Wade, Barry Seltser, Ron Conner (1945–2011), and Rowan Williams (all for their contribu-tions to my understanding of theodicy); Captain Taylor Keith, U.S.N. (Ret.) (for matters naval); classmate and Down Easter Peter Blachly (for helping me navigate the Kennebec and for his many helpful comments on the manuscript); Andrew Stifel, former member of the Cornell Uni-versity Fencing Team (for matters of swordsmanship); and Guiseppe di Lampedusa (for inspiring me with his saga about another type of prince).

Finally, I wish to thank my agent Roger Williams for taking a chance with fiction and believing in this story, and my publishers George Jepson and Jed Lyons for bringing it to fruition.